Praise for Brian Herbert and Kevin J. Anderson

"*Hellhole* is a military SF story of galactic proportions. . . . Brilliant strategist, lover of Old Earth history, and cast-off of a now-defunct noble line, Adolphus is a Robin Hood for the galaxy to unite behind. The characters are easy for the reader to believe in, brought to life through not only their own emotions but also the responses and thoughts of the individuals around them."

—*Booklist* (starred review)

"Combines the best of space opera with galactic intrigue and a cast of memorable characters. Fans of David Weber's Honor Harrington series and the Star Wars novels should enjoy a new entry into this popular category." —*Library Journal* on *Hellhole*

"If you like science fiction on an epic scale, you have to read *Hellhole* . . . really!" —*BookThing*

"Drawing on Frank Herbert's massive body of notes, the coauthors of the new Dune series continue their expansion and illumination of the unexplored pieces of one of the genre's most significant and powerful stories. Highly recommended."

—*Library Journal* (stared review)
on *Paul of Dune*

"Unquestionably, Herbert and Anderson can spin a great yarn while producing a vivid, mystifying universe, filled with characters that are both endearing and loathsome."

—*BookSpotCentral* on *The Winds of Dune*

HELLHOLE
INFERNO

BOOK THREE
in the
HELLHOLE TRILOGY

BRIAN HERBERT
and **KEVIN J. ANDERSON**

A Tom Doherty Associates Book • New York

This is a work of fiction. All of the characters, organizations, and events portrayed in this novel are either products of the authors' imaginations or are used fictitiously.

HELLHOLE INFERNO

Copyright © 2014 by DreamStar, Inc., and WordFire, Inc.

All rights reserved.

A Tor Book
Published by Tom Doherty Associates, LLC
175 Fifth Avenue
New York, NY 10010

www.tor-forge.com

Tor® is a registered trademark of Tom Doherty Associates, LLC.

ISBN 978-0-7653-6260-5

Tor books may be purchased for educational, business, or promotional use. For information on bulk purchases, please contact the Macmillan Corporate and Premium Sales Department at 1-800-221-7945, extension 5442, or write to specialmarkets@macmillan.com.

First Edition: August 2014
First Mass Market Edition: June 2015

Printed in the United States of America

0 9 8 7 6 5 4 3 2 1

Jan, this is yet another book that I dedicate lovingly to you. In the years of our marriage you have blossomed in so many ways artistically, demonstrating a creative range that includes painting, sculpture, interior design, photography, and even great story ideas.

—*Brian Herbert*

To Louis and Louise Moesta, who supported their quirky son-in-law's work unfailingly for more than twenty years, told their friends, and showed their pride in so many ways.

—*Kevin J. Anderson*

Acknowledgments

Special appreciation from both of us to our agent, John Silbersack; Bess Cozby and Tom Doherty at Tor; editor Pat Lobrutto; narrator Scott Brick; Mary Thomson for transcribing all of Kevin's audio files; and especially Rebecca Moesta.

HELLHOLE
INFERNO

1

Three Constellation warships descended through a sky that was spider-webbed with vapor trails. Pilots guided the bristling vessels to the staging field at the Aeroc military complex, where they joined the numerous other warships already landed in formation. By now, Commodore Percival Hallholme had lost count of the new arrivals, each one with new armor and reinforced shielding, loaded with all the armaments the Diadem's government could muster.

As he assessed the massive preparations, Percival nodded to himself and muttered, "Putting everything on the line this time."

After stinging defeats at the hands of rebellious Deep Zone planets, led by his nemesis General Tiber Adolphus, the Constellation was expanding the war. No hesitation, no reservations, no mercy.

And not much of a plan, Percival thought, but he didn't express such reservations out loud. It would not be appropriate for the ostensible commander of the operation.

This influx of additional warships—all rounded up by Lord Selik Riomini—increased the confidence among the Diadem's fighters, although Percival knew that the sheer quantity of ships would not guarantee a victory. He had faced General Adolphus before, numerous times, and in their last encounter at Hallholme—a planet named after the Commodore and not-so-affectionately nicknamed "Hellhole" by the colonists—Percival had suffered an embarrassing defeat, forced to retreat.

Now it was time for a rematch.

The Aeroc military yards were bustling. The upbeat victory tempo of "Strike Fast, Strike Hard!" rang out from widely distributed loudspeakers. The Commodore watched attack ships loaded with fresh, untrained recruits who had rushed to sign up after Diadem Michella saturated them with propaganda and fear. She painted Adolphus as a monster and a threat to human civilization itself, and worse, the rebel General had allied himself with a mysterious alien race that had the power to possess innocent victims, filling their minds with bizarre memory-lives.

The crisis was enough to inflame the population—at least those who believed the Diadem's words and concurred with her fears. Many people were not so easily swayed. And Percival knew full well that the old woman's portrayal was not precisely accurate. Nevertheless, he was bound by his duty.

As he crossed the parade ground to the towering military headquarters building, he wore a crisp new uniform from the Army of the Constellation. It was more modern and stylish than the old uniform he'd worn during the General's first, failed rebellion fifteen years ago—back when Commodore Hallholme made his name as a hero. In historical images from those old battles, Percival had looked bright-eyed, optimistic . . . and gullible.

Although he still sported the same distinctive mutton-chop sideburns and steel-gray hair, he looked older and thinner now, carrying the weight of years and regrets. His degenerative limp was much more pronounced.

He had retired at the end of the last rebellion and intended to stay out of the limelight, wanting nothing more than to tend his grapevines, play with his grandsons, and let his son Escobar be the next renowned military hero.

But as the new rebellion went sour, Percival had been dragged out of retirement and pressed back into service at the Diadem's command. His fresh uniform was adorned with colorful, even gaudy, medals—some of them earned, some merely for show.

Forcing himself not to show weakness or hesitation despite his chronic limp, he strode at a brisk pace that exuded authority. With briefing documents tucked under one arm, he walked past fountains and military memorials, obelisks engraved with thousands of names of the fallen, but his thoughts were preoccupied. Diadem Michella and Lord Riomini had requested a special briefing, and Percival knew he would have to tell them what they wanted to hear.

Five sleek fighters streaked across Aeroc's sky, performing aerial maneuvers, which impressed those who were impressed by that sort of thing. A man like Commodore Hallholme knew that combat would require more than tricks this time.

He mounted the marble steps of the pillared headquarters building and glanced at the engraved quotes from past heroic commanders. One of his own pithy sayings was included somewhere, but he had never bothered to find it. Pennants of noble families hung outside the arched entrance, arranged according to their financial sacrifice. Inside the hall, red banners carried the names of lesser families who had lost sons and daughters during the bloody battles of the General's first rebellion.

Percival lifted his chin and made his way down the

oddly empty hall to the giant simulation chamber. With a glance at his chronometer, Commodore Hallholme saw that he was precisely on time, and he entered.

The curved ceiling of the simulation chamber was embedded with high-res holographic projectors. During wartime the chamber had been used for combat scenarios and tactical planning, but in the decade of calm after Adolphus's exile to Hellhole, it was primarily used for wealthy noble officers to experience immersive simulations of the Battle of Sonjeera or other famous engagements—particularly the ones in which Commodore Hallholme had defeated the rebel General. That way the participants could imagine being heroes themselves.

The Diadem and the Black Lord sat in VIP participation chairs in the prime viewing area. They did not rise as Percival presented himself to them.

Diadem Michella Duchenet was so ancient that she might have been a poorly preserved museum piece. Thin and wrinkled, she was not frail, but remained intimidating in her old age, with bird-bright eyes and quick movements. Defying her own mortality, Michella remained lean and healthy, keeping herself fanatically fit, as if she intended to rule for yet another century. Over her long reign, the old woman had survived many battles, and Percival knew not to underestimate her. Generally, Michella liked to present a sweet, maternal demeanor, convinced that her people loved and adored her, but she was as comforting as a bed of glass shards.

Beside her, Lord Riomini sat dressed entirely in black, as usual. The Black Lord was two decades younger than Michella, his body soft, eyes hard. Though he was primarily a politician and businessman, he did not fear command and had seen battle firsthand. But unlike a commander who simply had a war to win,

Riomini had something to prove: He wanted to be the next Diadem.

Percival held out his briefing papers. "I have the report you requested, Eminence."

Upon his return to Sonjeera in defeat, the Commodore had offered his resignation, but Diadem Michella refused to accept it. Since then, he felt as if he were more of a military trophy than a useful participant.

Now, instead of taking the report, Michella lifted a hand that was overburdened with jeweled rings. "We are not here to discuss inventory, Commodore, but to talk about your upcoming conquest of the Deep Zone. Fifty-four valuable worlds have broken away from the Constellation. We need them back."

Riomini added, "The lost wealth is incalculable. The political embarrassment is even more devastating."

Arguments and replies boiled up within him, but Percival kept silent. Better to say nothing than to point out that this current clash was an unnecessary crisis of the Diadem's own making.

"Present your overview, Commodore." Riomini operated controls linked to his seat, and the vault filled with stars, showing the settled systems of the Constellation, the twenty central Crown Jewel planets and the fifty-four outlying Deep Zone worlds.

Percival nudged the controls of the galactic model himself, calling up a standard template. Bright blue lines radiated outward from the center of the star map to each one of those worlds. Twenty established lines connected the Crown Jewels, and an additional fifty-four extended into the less-populated Deep Zone, connecting the dots. "With Sonjeera as the hub for all stringline travel, Eminence, you control all of the stringline paths, and thus all commerce throughout the original Crown Jewels as well as the new DZ worlds."

Another nudge of the controls, and a secondary web-work of red lines radiated from one of the distant un-obtrusive points—planet Hellhole—in a network that linked every one of the Deep Zone planets. He was sure Michella understood the credible threat that Adolphus could wield—and had already wielded.

"The General's independent stringline network gives him a strategic advantage that we cannot overcome. Now that he has secretly laid down those alternate iperion paths, the DZ no longer needs the Constellation. And because his rebels are fanatically independent, they are willing to sever every one of the old lines binding them to Sonjeera if they feel threatened. We know the General will do it, cutting the entire Deep Zone loose from the Constellation. He's already cut his own direct stringline to Hellhole."

That was how Adolphus had stranded the first Con-stellation retaliatory fleet—commanded by Percival's son Escobar. The General had left the fleet adrift in empty space, and then he had seized all those ships, tak-ing thousands of soldiers prisoner—including Escobar. "It's an ancient tactic, an army blowing bridges to deny the enemy vital access across rivers or canyons. For General Adolphus, those canyons are many light-years wide. If we attack him directly, he will do it without hesitation, and then we'll never be able to get him."

Both Riomini and the Diadem listened, but they appeared bored. "That is old news, Commodore," the Black Lord said with a quirk of a smug smile. "You're not aware of what has changed. That is why we sum-moned you."

Michella couldn't contain her excitement. "We have a route into the Deep Zone—one the General will not suspect."

Riomini reached out to touch the hovering image of

an insignificant Deep Zone speck at the edge of the frontier network. It glowed when he selected it. "This is how you will achieve victory. Tehila."

Percival was familiar with the names of all Deep Zone worlds, but knew little about this one.

Michella explained. "When the General declared independence for all the frontier worlds, by fiat, he did so without the knowledge, cooperation—or *desire*—of many Deep Zone worlds. When he embroiled them in this unnecessary war, not every planet was pleased to be part of it. In fact, most of them were shocked."

Riomini's mouth twisted in a cruel grin. "Theser was certainly shocked when I demonstrated the consequences of their unwise choice." The Black Lord had led a punitive assault that turned Theser into a smoldering, uninhabited rock.

Percival still didn't understand. "How does Tehila factor into this? What is its significance?"

The Diadem said, "Tehila's planetary administrator, Karlo Reming, never had any desire to leave the Constellation, and now he wishes to come back into our protective embrace. He and his people want our forgiveness."

Percival raised his eyebrows, was unconvinced. "All of his people want that?"

"Enough of them," said Riomini. "Administrator Reming is about to stage a purge to get rid of any Adolphus loyalists. Then he will seize and secure the stringlines, both the path to Sonjeera as well as their connection into the Deep Zone network. Through him, we will have a back door right to the General's doorstep."

Michella's papery lips formed a terse smile. "The way will be wide open for you, Commodore. Your fleet is almost ready. Take those ships to Tehila, secure the planet, and establish a beachhead from which to swoop down on the General. Crush planet Hallholme just like the asteroid that struck centuries ago."

Upon hearing the new option, Percival felt an unfamiliar hope. "That will give me a chance to rescue my son, along with the other prisoners the General is holding." He suddenly remembered. "And your daughter, too, Eminence. I will do everything in my power to see that Keana is returned safely to you."

Michella gave an unconcerned wave. "Defeating General Adolphus and restoring order throughout the Deep Zone is your primary goal, Commodore. Naturally, I love my daughter, but she is an adult and she went to that awful planet of her own free will. Now she's been possessed by one of those hideous aliens." The old woman shuddered visibly. "I doubt there is a cure for it, so I have to consider her already lost. They are casualties of war—my daughter, your son. A price we have to pay."

Riomini spoke up, as if wanting to make certain he was included. He shook his head. "And my poor grand-niece with her two boys, left fatherless when we lost Escobar."

"Escobar is still alive," Percival said pointedly, "as far as I know."

"Yes, let us hope he is," Michella added without any apparent sincerity. "For now, begin planning your military operation. Move your ships from Aeroc and stage them at the Sonjeera hub. Be ready to move as soon as Administrator Reming has taken over Tehila and opened the door for us."

2

In the empty conference room, General Tiber Adolphus paced in front of a reinforced window, gazing out at the rugged landscape. His dark eyes were perpetually serious, his black hair neatly trimmed out of military fastidiousness. The square-jawed man had accepted a new uniform, deep-blue with golden general's stars on the collar—a garment copied from the one he'd worn during the first rebellion. His beloved Sophie Vence had tracked down the original jacket from a collector, but that one was a historical artifact. This facsimile fit him well and suited his purposes, reinforcing his role.

After the previous night's smoke storm, fragments of trees and alien shrubs lay strewn around the grounds of his headquarters estate, which he had fondly—and ironically—named Elba, after ancient Napoleon's home in exile. Even with the political turmoil across the Deep Zone, the smoke storm reminded him that local crises could still cause significant damage, and this planet was neither a kind nor a gentle place.

Two men in coveralls worked hard to restore the area around the General's mansion, loading debris into a motorized garbage bin. The sky remained a greenish yellow, still unsettled from the storm. After more than a decade on Hellhole, Adolphus had learned to recognize the various sky colors and conditions. Though his extensive network of weather satellites monitored the storm fronts, he could often tell on his own when and how the capricious weather would change. The General never took anything for granted. He was always learning, always alert.

Behind him, Adolphus heard a familiar stirring,

shuffling noise, and he turned as two of the planet's original inhabitants—Encix and Lodo—entered the conference room. They remained beside the long table, since none of his chairs could accommodate the aliens' bulky sluglike abdomens, though they had humanoid upper bodies.

Though the Xayans were ostensibly his allies here on Hellhole, he remained tight-lipped, suppressing his anger toward the two Originals. They had kept tremendous, dangerous secrets from him—involving a threat that could obliterate this entire planet. The scope of what they had hidden held extraordinary repercussions for him and for the entire Deep Zone.

Encix and Lodo remained silent while the General continued to look out the window, pondering how he should confront them and demand answers. He was certain the aliens still had more to reveal.

A groundcar rumbled up outside and discharged its passenger, a tall, shapely woman with shoulder-length auburn hair: Keana Duchenet, arriving for the scheduled meeting. The Diadem's daughter looked outwardly unchanged, but she shared her consciousness with a resurrected alien personality, Uroa, whom she had awakened from the slickwater pools. Keana was only one of many hundreds of converts who had taken on alien lives and memories. Together, Keana-Uroa was one of the most powerful of the "shadow-Xayans," possessing high telemancy skills.

Though he was frustrated with the aliens and their unknown agenda, General Adolphus needed every possible ally in order to face enemies from all sides. But he also needed to trust these strange creatures if they were to fight side by side to protect this planet.

Ever since the Deep Zone had broken away from the corrupt Constellation, General Adolphus had commanded a motley army of cast-off humans. They manned patched-together warships from the old rebellion, as well as hundreds of newer vessels seized during the Constellation's failed attacks. In addition to his traditional tactics, Adolphus made use of Xayan telemancy, which had enabled him to defeat Commodore Percival Hallholme.

Yet he had hardly been able to celebrate after the Commodore fled back to Sonjeera in disgrace. Despite their help, he now knew the aliens did not share the same goal as he, and Adolphus realized he had never really *commanded* them at all. For the Xayans, this was no more than a coalition of convenience, a means by which they could achieve their evolutionary and spiritual "ascension," their racial destiny called *ala'ru*.

Summoning his force of will, though he did not know how effective it would be against the implacable Xayans, the General turned from the window to face the two unusual visitors. "You failed to tell me that you had another terrible enemy of your own. You kept that information from me, even though you've known for some time that the Ro-Xayans are out there, and that they still want to destroy you. You could have warned me, warned Candela. We could have saved many of those people before the asteroid impact."

Encix said in a flat voice that masked any recognizable emotion, "If we had achieved *ala'ru* before they found us, it would not have mattered."

"After the Ro-Xayans destroyed Candela, you told me they also bombarded this planet with an asteroid centuries ago." He felt his skin grow hot. "You didn't consider that information relevant?"

Lodo sounded just slightly contrite. "We have revealed everything to you now, General Tiber Adolphus. We are certain the Ro-Xayans are aware that we survived their first attempt to exterminate us, and they will surely come back to finish annihilating our species."

Encix added with greater urgency, "Our only hope is to achieve *ala'ru* before it is too late! All the more reason for us to convert more of your people, awaken more Xayan lives from the slickwater pools, and increase the collective power of our telemancy."

Adolphus clenched his jaw. "I am no longer certain I can trust you."

The hidden enemy, the Ro-Xayans, were a splinter faction of the alien race that swore to prevent the wondrous evolutionary ascension toward which most Xayans strove. The rogue faction had wrecked their home planet and nearly wiped out their own race rather than let their rivals win. Such a betrayal angered Adolphus—especially now that his human colonists were caught in the middle of an ancient feud he could neither prevent nor understand—but he also resented that Encix and Lodo had not been forthright.

Keana-Uroa was ushered into the conference room by a member of the General's staff. The Diadem's daughter stood straight-backed, a far cry from the naïve and giddy noblewoman who had first come here to Hellhole without a clue about how to take care of herself. Now, she wasted no time with pleasantries, showing the power of her human personality as well as the alien who jointly inhabited her mind. "We must seize every possible defense, General. This planet will be caught in a vise between the Army of the Constellation and the Ro-Xayans, two enemies who wish to see our complete destruction."

He turned to her, keeping the hard edge in his voice. "My defensive planning is hamstrung when my allies withhold vital information from me. The Xayan presence in your mind understands about the Ro-Xayans—

I know it. Tell me what you know. *All* of it. Otherwise I have no way of properly preparing."

He wished Sophie could be here to advise him, because she gave such wise counsel, and he enjoyed her company—but she was at Slickwater Springs, tending to the only other surviving Original alien, Tryn, who had been seriously injured in the backlash of a telemancy attack before the destruction of Candela.

More aloof than angry, Encix said, "We are not required to share all information with you."

"*I* require it." He could not penetrate the alien's large, black eyes, nor could he crack her unreadable expression. "When you asked, I agreed to help support your race's goal to achieve *ala'ru*. I allowed willing human volunteers to immerse themselves in slickwater to reawaken your race. You should be helping me protect this planet, but instead you exposed us all to an even greater threat."

The two Originals remained inscrutable, and the frustrated General turned to the Diadem's daughter. Keana nodded, said, "I anticipated why you wanted me here. Yes, I have spoken with Uroa in my mind, debated him, and finally convinced him. Even I didn't know the broad strokes until now, but I forced my companion to reveal some of what he knows." She glanced at the two Original aliens; Encix seemed angry with her, but Keana apparently didn't care about that. She focused on Adolphus. "Weeks ago, when Cristoph de Carre and I were in the museum vault, Lodo abruptly destroyed an artifact stored there, a telemancy enhancer. At the time, he refused to explain why he did that, but now I know he wanted to make sure the object wouldn't attract the Ro-Xayans."

"That effort failed," Lodo said. "The shadow-Xayans had already used too much telemancy, and it could not be hidden. When Tryn and her seed colony unleashed their burst of telemancy to destroy the Constellation stringline hub, she attracted the Ro-Xayans directly to Candela. It was a shout they could not ignore."

"And you see what happened!" Encix said, sounding oddly shrill. "Two asteroids smashed into Candela, destroying everything there." Her voice became more urgent. "Therefore, we *must* achieve *ala'ru* before the same thing happens to this planet."

Adolphus scowled. "My people live here. I would rather prevent it from happening at all."

Keana closed her eyes and heaved a long, deep sigh before she journeyed into her inner realms. "I will learn what I can, General."

—⁓—

A bubble of stillness formed around Keana as she blocked off distractions inside the Elba conference room. She sensed reluctance from her internal companion Uroa, but she was persistent and forceful, and he finally surrendered to her pressure, clearing a mental pathway so she could see facets of his life and thoughts that had previously been unavailable to her.

Centuries ago, before the asteroid impact eradicated the Xayan race here on Hellhole (except for those who used extreme measures to preserve themselves), Uroa had been a powerful representative, working with Zairic, Encix, and many others in their all-consuming drive to reach *ala'ru*. Now, however, Uroa was also part of *her*. Keana had resurrected him from the slickwater pools, and he wanted to survive, just as she did. And they needed each other to do so.

She went deeper into her own mind, into his preserved memories, as if soaring into the farthest reaches of space. Far ahead, she saw a pinpoint of light, growing brighter. The alien's telemancy was guiding her into his original life. As Uroa now lived in her body, Keana saw herself as an invisible observer in his. Through inhuman eyes, she looked skyward, part of Uroa, resigned to his fate, the fate of the Xayan race, and everything he knew. In the image she saw, Uroa was surrounded by thousands of other Xayans, their large, soft bodies crowded together, their antennae twitching as they shared an all-consuming fear in their last moments. Every one of them knew what was coming—a gigantic asteroid like a cosmic sledgehammer hurled by the telemancy of vengeful Ro-Xayans.

Seeking their own route to survival, Encix and a group of six Originals had sealed themselves in preservation chambers buried kilometers beneath the surface, hoping to be awakened someday. The rest of the Xayan race, though, gambled their future on unproven slickwater, pools of psychic energy that would store their personalities, their memories, and possibly their souls.

But with time so short, only the most prominent Xayans were allowed to store their lives in the pools, individuals chosen by the great visionary Zairic. Not all could be saved—only the best and the brightest of the race, so that one day they might reawaken and continue their racial mission. The selection process had involved judgment calls and politics, and Uroa had not agreed with all of the decisions. Still, when it came to the moment of crisis, he, like the others, seized his only chance.

A bright spear of light, the deadly asteroid ripped through Xaya's atmosphere, guided by their own prodigal cousins. At the last possible moment, Uroa and the last Xayans on the shore plunged into the quivering pool of silvery liquid, which was already a teeming reservoir of lives. They dissolved away their bodies and sentience, hoping that the slickwater might survive the impact.

After the strike mortally wounded the planet, the Ro-Xayans had departed, leaving their world for dead. Centuries passed, the human colonists arrived, and an unsuspecting explorer stumbled upon the pools. . . .

Though Uroa's memories survived, that last horrific moment was still very much of a death, and the Xayan civilization would never again be what it once was. But the resurrected lives did not want to rebuild the past; rather, they were focused on reaching *ala'ru*. And with the hybrid vigor made possible by their symbiosis with human partners, their evolutionary leap seemed more achievable than ever.

And still the Ro-Xayans would do anything to stop them.

Emerging from her vision, Keana opened her eyes. General Adolphus was staring hard at her with his arms folded across his chest, waiting. Only a moment had passed. When she spoke, her voice was rough and grainy, controlled by Uroa. "We understand your need to defend this world against human enemies from the Constellation, but we are so close to our sacred destiny. *Ala'ru* would eliminate the Ro-Xayan concerns, and your enemies as well."

In a rush, Encix added, "Yes. Now you understand, General Tiber Adolphus. We must bring more converts, create more shadow-Xayans, awaken more of our stored lives from the slickwater. We have one last chance to achieve *ala'ru* in time."

"The Army of the Constellation will attack us soon," Adolphus said. "I am sure of it."

"My mother will not wait," Keana-Uroa agreed, this time in her own voice, then the voice changed back to Uroa's. "But the Ro-Xayans may get here first."

3

When the wondrous pools were discovered on Hellhole, Sophie Vence had seen a business opportunity. Filled with alien lives, marvelous experiences, and almost magical powers, the slickwater attracted the desperate and the curious.

At the time she was already one of the most powerful women in Michella Town, managing supplies for the settlers who arrived on stringline haulers from Sonjeera. But the slickwater pools offered something much different, enticing pilgrims to saturate themselves with alien lives and memories.

Sophie was never tempted to do so herself, and neither was Tiber Adolphus, but he had made an agreement with the surviving Originals to allow the resurrection of their race in exchange for their help in protecting the planet against the Diadem. Sophie had established a settlement at the nearest three pools, first a rough camp and then a rustic resort she had named Slickwater Springs. As the numbers of shadow-Xayan converts grew, Sophie had constructed outlying bungalows and a larger lodge building to accommodate them all.

At the resort she neither encouraged nor discouraged the volunteers; immersion had to be their own decision. When acquiring an alien partner personality, they would gain wondrous insights, abilities, and memories, but they also surrendered part of their humanity. The converts spread the word, proselytizing about the wonders they had experienced, the abilities they acquired.

With the threat of the Constellation military and the even greater danger of the Ro-Xayans, however, increasing the number of converts had become more important than ever.

Even so, she had no intention of joining them. Sophie had already lost her son Devon to the mysterious waters, and she did not want to lose herself or her close relationship with Tiber Adolphus. . . .

In the brightening morning, Sophie climbed a steep trail on the shady side of the ridge that bounded the valley containing the slickwater pools, to where she could reach a sunny vantage. She wanted some private time, quiet time, away from the people at the bustling lodge complex. It was worth the exertion.

Catching her breath, she reached the top of the ridge and gazed down at the three mirrorlike ponds that were surrounded by boardwalks, fences, tents, bungalows, and the main lodge building. From here, the slickwater looked so placid, so tempting, but Sophie knew how many changes those alien pools had brought to the already struggling planet.

Events seemed frustratingly beyond her control. Soon she would head back to Elba to be with Adolphus again, but for now she had her private suite inside the main lodge. She couldn't be everywhere, no matter how much she might want to be. Back in Michella Town, she had other people to manage her warehouses and distribution operations, and many assistants helped run Slickwater Springs.

From the top of the ridge, still feeling the burn of exertion in her legs, she saw people milling about below. From a distance they all looked human, although many of them had the eerie alien eyes, a spiraling unnatural shimmer that indicated they shared their minds with a resurrected Xayan.

The converts had used telemancy to build an ever-growing settlement nearby, a separate colony that featured bizarre alien architecture, surrounded by a burgeoning forest of alien red weed. But many of the shadow-Xayans remained behind at the slickwater pools to help shepherd the new converts. Their odd behavior made her uneasy, though she had been forced to swallow her doubts when Devon became one of them.

Even now that her son was gone, Sophie allowed shadow-Xayans to remain in the camp, so long as they assisted with running the facility. The numbers of converts grew as urgency and anxiety swept through the DZ. The people were afraid of bloodthirsty Constellation reprisals, such as the Black Lord's massacre on Theser and the Ro-Xayans' planet-destroying vendetta that had wiped out Candela. Sophie and the General knew that the alien telemancy might prove to be their only salvation.

But undergoing that change wasn't for her.

From the top of the ridge, she looked across to the adjacent valley, which held a strikingly different settlement—and this one concerned her in an entirely different way. The rapidly constructed, fenced-in camp held thousands of Constellation military prisoners taken from the Diadem's retaliation force led by Escobar Hallholme. All those starving soldiers had surrendered after months of being stranded in space, and the General didn't know what to do with them.

Sophie had to ensure their safety, and provide them with food and shelter until the conflict was resolved— even though they were responsible for the deaths of Devon and Antonia. The camp was supposed to be just a temporary situation, but even so, she found it emotionally difficult to be fair to the prisoners. This made her try harder to do the right thing, the legal and moral thing, to treat them as respected prisoners of war.

She didn't want those responsibilities, didn't like the

corner she'd been backed into, but Adolphus had asked her. She had given him her word, and he was counting on her. . . .

Her moment of solitude was brief. Sophie saw a man climbing the trail toward her, recognized him by his long blond hair as the veteran Peter Herald, who helped her run Slickwater Springs. Though he was now a shadow-Xayan, combined with an alien presence named Arnex, he had proved to be invaluable at the lodge and camp. He moved up the steep, difficult trail at a brisk and easy trot.

An officer in Adolphus's first rebellion, Herald had been injured, his lungs scarred—and he had been one of the first humans to enter the slickwater, hoping to be healed. The effect on him had been dramatic, erasing all signs of his debilitating injury. Ever since becoming a shadow-Xayan, Peter Herald had moved with new vigor and grace, although no number of years could erase his ingrained military bearing.

Reaching the top of the ridge, Herald greeted her in a strong voice that was much different from his former raspy, pain-racked whisper. A faint, otherworldly shimmer spun in his eyes, and he was barely even panting. "I watched you struggle up the slope, Sophie Vence. You're overburdened with responsibilities. I promise you will have far more energy to complete your duties if you immerse yourself in the slickwater. You'll be amazed at how good you feel . . . if you allow yourself."

She turned away, wishing he would stop pressuring her. "No thank you, as I've told you many times before. You, and all shadow-Xayans, promised you would not coerce me."

Herald seemed more disappointed for her sake than for himself. "I will continue to use gentle persuasion.

The benefits are obvious, and I am hoping to make you reconsider."

Emotions welled up inside of her, and she lashed out at him. "The slickwater already took my only son from me! I don't want to be like you, or like any of the shadow-Xayans." She started to say something more, then stopped herself. Many people shared the blame for the loss of Devon and his girlfriend Antonia Anqui . . . not just the slickwater.

Herald appeared startled by her vehemence. "I am aware of your pain, but a Xayan presence would comfort and strengthen you."

In a clipped voice, she cut him off. "I'm a stubborn woman. It's my own choice. Encix promised that no one would be forced." She frowned. "With Slickwater Springs, I've gone to great effort to recruit converts for you. That should be more than enough."

"And it is. You will not be forced." Herald bowed, then slipped back down the trail, leaving her alone again as he called over his shoulder: "But I can still hope."

—m—

By the time Sophie made her way back to the resort complex, the sky was darkening with angry clouds; there had been no rain for weeks, just meteorological bluster, but even with satellite reports Hellhole's weather was unpredictable and dangerous. The dry air crackled in her nostrils.

Walking through the camp, she strode along a boardwalk that skirted the pools. She heard the excited chatter of new converts regaling others with stories about the alien lives they adopted; she saw fresh arrivals who hesitated before taking the plunge. With more and more people immersing themselves, there had been occasional accidents, as optimistic or desperate volunteers slipped into a coma instead of emerging revitalized with vivid memories and exotic powers. These new volunteers had to make up their own minds.

She very much wanted this whole crisis to be over. If the Xayans were correct, their awakening race was very close to the psychic critical mass they needed, and then they would ascend to some higher plane of existence, leaving Hellhole to the colonists. She doubted that would solve all problems, but she was confident Tiber Adolphus could handle the rest. She smiled at the thought of him.

She loved Adolphus, but in the flurry of events surrounding the war, there had been little time for them. He and Sophie had already struggled together to tame a planet—wasn't that enough? She felt deeply weary, both physically and emotionally.

A group of shadow-Xayans gathered at the edge of the largest pool, crowded together. Among them, Sophie saw the large, misshapen form of the Original alien Tryn. With her caterpillar body and human torso, Tryn already looked strange, but now the female Xayan was physically distorted and twisted, damaged in a disruptive surge of telemancy that had ricocheted along the stringline to Candela. Tryn had survived—barely—along with one human convert, Tel Clovis, although both were gravely injured. The other converts on the Candela seed colony had been wiped out in the backlash.

With laborious movements, Tryn worked her lower body to the edge of a sloping ramp that led from the boardwalk down into the shimmering slickwater. The gathered shadow-Xayans watched, offering silent encouragement but no active assistance. Alongside Tryn, the injured Tel Clovis limped and shuffled. Both were in pain, their flesh fused and half-melted. Clovis was so deformed he barely looked human anymore.

Reaching the ramp, Tryn placed one of her soft arms around Clovis's shoulder. The pair hesitated, as if gathering courage, and then together they slid down the ramp and into the oily liquid. They sank under with barely a ripple, and a few moments later they emerged, rising above the surface. Tryn floated in the slickwater as if it were alien amniotic fluid, her large body buoyed by the reservoir of racial lives. With her bent arms, she cradled Tel Clovis against her torso, and both of them drifted together, communing in silent telepathy.

Tryn said aloud, "Thank you," and turned to the gathered shadow-Xayans who observed the strange ritual. Her smooth alien face was unreadable.

"What is happening?" Sophie whispered, but the converts continued to stare.

As if releasing something inside of herself, Tryn relaxed, collapsed, and *dissolved* into the slickwater. Her skin, her cells, her entire body dissipated as if surrendering to the liquid. Clovis tried to hold on to her, but her alien body softened and flowed, slipping through his fingers and vanishing.

Now, though, the distorted man gained a new strength and vigor. He seemed to draw upon the energy and life that Tryn had surrendered. The convert's twisted back and arms straightened, realigned, and he began to swim, striking out freely in the slickwater. He laughed, and his eyes shone with an even more intense strangeness, as if he had just been reborn.

The shadow-Xayans happily welcomed him back.

When Clovis made his way back to shore and climbed the ramp, dripping viscid fluid from his body, he wore a beatific expression. "I already had a Xayan companion, but now I am more. I am three . . . and I am many." His peculiar voice thrummed, as if he carried layers of alienness within him. The intensity in his shimmering eyes spiraled, frightening Sophie when his gaze fell on her. But he didn't seem to be focused on her at all.

"Now I am also Tryn, who is merged into my mind in a manner that has never before occurred. I have absorbed the essence of a fully alive Original Xayan, a unique synthesis . . . because that is what Tryn knew had to happen. Now I am more than any of the other shadow-Xayans. I can see more and do more, accomplish more, experience more. I *know* more. The possibilities expand like kaleidoscope views."

Clovis reached the boardwalk before turning back to gaze out on the pool from which he had just emerged, breathless with excitement.

Shadow-Xayans gathered closer, while some of the curious potential converts also listened. Still feeling trepidation, Sophie stepped up to him, sounding pragmatic. "I hope that whatever you learned can help save us from the Ro-Xayans. *If* they're coming."

The shimmer in Clovis's eyes sharpened, and he smiled at her with just a hint of his old personality. Sophie had known this man for many years, back to when he and his husband ran the secret construction project of the Ankor spaceport. "We must go to Sonjeera—that is where we will retrieve Cippiq and Zairic. Their remnants are in a quarantined hangar, sealed there after Diadem Michella destroyed their bodies, but important traces are still there, and we need them. I know it. Zairic will give us the key to reaching *ala'ru* immediately—and then we can defeat the Ro-Xayans."

Sophie put her hands on her hips, knowing that the

shadow-Xayans didn't recognize sarcasm. "Well, it's simple then. Just go and ask the old Diadem nicely." Michella Duchenet was already desperately afraid of what she called "alien contamination," enough so that she had placed an impenetrable quarantine zone around a spaceport hangar. No one would be able to break through all the security systems.

"There will be a way," Clovis said with such power and confidence that he nearly drove away all of Sophie's doubts. Unable to argue, she could only watch in awe and unease as Clovis turned away from her and walked with restored health and vigor down the boardwalk toward the heart of the resort complex. Other shadow-Xayans fell into formation behind him.

Seeing his transformation, two of the hesitant humans made up their minds, and entered the slickwater before they could reconsider. . . .

4

Ishop Heer had noble blood. He could feel it running warm and hot through his veins. He had proved his pedigree to the lords and to Diadem Michella herself, and he was entitled to regain his family birthright after seven centuries of ignominy. It was his due.

He had spilled a lot of noble blood to obtain it.

And since the ambitious noblewoman Enva Tazaar had been disgraced and stripped of her holdings on Orsini, Ishop Heer had asked to rule her former planet. A small enough reward for all the years of dark service he had given the Diadem.

He had planned carefully for this, worked hard to attain it, step by bloody step. *It was his due!*

He had presented his irrefutable case in the Council chamber. He had looked at the gathered nobles, expecting to watch them accept him as one of them. He had the proof. Yet they had either scoffed or ignored him, brushing aside his assertion. Even Diadem Michella dismissed his claim with an amused chuckle and told the Council to get back to important work. Knowing he was one of them, the nobles still regarded him with scorn! Despite his lineage, they saw him as a person who did not realize his place in society, a mere servant who should never hope to sit at the master's table.

Oh, Michella appreciated his service, and she made use of his skills whenever she needed something done. She offered him rewards—villas, money, women if he so desired. But what he desired was his birthright. The Diadem refused to understand that.

In a gracious gesture, Michella had recently transferred the title on a large central-city apartment to him, even though she had already given him a different house not long before. This was a furnished unit on an upper floor with a partial view of Heart Square and the government buildings, including Council Hall. She expected that these perks, and perhaps a pat on the head, were all that was necessary to ensure his loyalty.

Even though she knew exactly what Ishop was capable of, Michella did not seem to realize that she had made a dangerous enemy. He had already attempted to kill her once, but that was just practice. Ishop vowed to keep trying until he succeeded.

Fuming, he used an ID transmitter to unlock the door to the new apartment. Like throwing a dog a bone! Despite his large frame, Ishop moved smoothly and gracefully, remaining wary, always vigilant against anyone trying to harm him. His pale-green eyes spotted no threat. He wiped a sheen of sweat from his shaved scalp.

He had been to this apartment only once before and knew it would never feel like the home he deserved. He should have been the lord of a nobleman's palace, ruler of a planet. Now as Ishop stepped into the foyer, he smelled fresh paint. He saw his red-haired assistant Laderna Nell arranging paintings and sculptures in the parlor, government-commissioned works by various local artists. He saw the expensive masterpieces as nothing more than trappings. Consolation prizes.

Laderna came out and greeted him with a kiss. His assistant was thin, even gangly, with brown, almond-shaped eyes and a steady, intelligent gaze. She was his confidante as well as his lover, and they celebrated with sex whenever they accomplished some part of their overall schemes. Ishop knew she fancied more of a close personal relationship than the physical one they already had, but even so, she recognized the requirement that he take a *noble* wife, since he was of noble blood himself— regardless of whether the Diadem recognized his claim. Laderna wanted him to succeed, and she would bask in his glory.

Yes, she truly was a perfect partner, with shared goals and the desire to help him achieve the glory he deserved. They both agreed that it was essential for Ishop to advance as far as possible in the hierarchy of the Constellation, and Laderna would let no one stand in his way—not even herself. At times, it bothered him that by not accepting her as a person equal to his station, he was in effect treating Laderna just as Michella had treated him. But at least he recognized Laderna's value; he would never forget that, and he often told her how much he appreciated her.

It was the rest of the Constellation that frustrated him so.

In the parlor of his cold, uncomfortable new apartment, Ishop studied a glass sculpture, a hodgepodge that included a cornucopia, a flower, and some impossible sea creature. "I don't like this one." With a wave to emphasize his artistic judgment, he knocked the piece over, shattering it on the hard tile floor.

Scowling, taking out his deep-seated anger at how he had been treated by his supposed peers, he wandered around the apartment, breaking other pieces, even slashing a painting with a knife.

Laderna did not scold him as he released his frustrations. "We can say that vandals ransacked the place before we arrived, and that we want a new security system."

"They'll just replace these pieces with artwork that's just as bad," he replied, then smiled. "And if necessary, we'll keep getting our security system redone."

They shared a gourmet meal and wine in the dining chamber, delivered by an in-house catering service that the landlord provided for the tenants. It was a convenience, but not the same as having a personal serving staff.

As she finished her rare filet with butter-drenched mushroom caps, Laderna said, "At least we know that Enva Tazaar won't be eating a meal like this. Where she's gone, she may have to settle for a warmed noodle dish in a company cafeteria."

Ishop smiled. "Do they have cafeterias on Tehila? I thought on a backwater planet like that, she might have to hunt her own food with a rock and a stick." After the noblewoman's disgrace and death sentence, Ishop and Laderna had secretly arranged for her escape out to the Deep Zone planet of Tehila—strictly because they knew it would embarrass Diadem Michella. In fact, Enva did not know the identity of her mysterious benefactor. He suspected, though, that even in her exile Enva was no wilting flower of a noblewoman; she was tough, ambitious, and resourceful.

A pity that the woman's plans to overthrow Michella had failed. She would have made a worthy Diadem, or a valuable noble wife for Ishop. Enva was exiled now, but someday she might reclaim her house and wealth. Further changes were in store—he and Laderna would make sure of that.

Laderna saw his preoccupied expression. "What are you thinking about?"

He told her only a half-truth. "How I wish I could get even with Michella. I have noble blood, just as she does."

She smiled. "And you and I have a lot of that blood on our hands, from each of the houses that wronged your family so many centuries ago." She gave a wistful smile. "I have so enjoyed helping you go through the list. If only we could have finished it—"

Ishop cut her off. "It's finished."

"No, we still have a Duchenet name on the list. Simply tricking Michella's daughter into a dangerous war zone isn't good enough—and we know Keana Duchenet is still very much alive."

Ishop grimaced, not wanting the reminder. "I'll eliminate the Diadem herself, sooner or later. That'll take care of the Duchenet name."

"That may be too difficult, at least for now. She is well-guarded, and lucky." Laderna raised her eyebrows, and he could tell she was holding a secret. "But I have found another."

He was surprised. "Another Duchenet? Some distant cousin?"

Laderna took her time with a bite of the mushrooms. "No, someone very close. Remember, Michella has a sister. Haveeda."

"*Had* a sister. Haveeda disappeared decades ago. No one has seen her in—"

"Thirty-two years. But it doesn't matter. She is still alive—I found her."

Ishop raised his eyebrows, always admiring her skills. "How?"

She sniffed. "After all I've accomplished so far, you need to ask? I tracked down all the old records of noble families from when your ancestors were banished. I compiled the evidence that you have noble blood. I found all the tiniest clues, no matter how cleverly they were hidden. Do you think tracking down Michella's sister was really all that difficult? The Diadem thinks she covered all the tracks, swept Haveeda under the rug. But I just needed to look a little harder. I have my methods, just as you have yours."

Now Ishop was intrigued. "Where is she?"

"Michella has been hiding her for years, keeping her quiet because Haveeda witnessed something in their childhood. It was never proved, but I am convinced Michella murdered their own brother. Haveeda probably saw it. Right now she is being hidden on Sandusky, no doubt under extremely high security—I am still tracking down her exact location."

Ishop stopped eating, no longer interested in the food or wine. "Sandusky? An unpleasant place—full of laboratories and isolated research centers, isn't it? If she's been trapped there, poor Haveeda must be quite distraught. It would be a humanitarian service to take the woman out of her misery."

"And finally check the last name off our list." Laderna nodded. "I am ready to leave in the morning. I'll finish the job."

"Then Haveeda is as good as dead. Your track record is impeccable, dear Laderna—in fact, we might as well celebrate our success tonight."

She smiled back at him and began to unbutton her blouse.

5

Exiled. Fallen from grace. But at least she was still alive. Enva Tazaar tried to comfort herself with that, but didn't quite manage to convince herself. The injustice of how far she had sunk simmered within her, but she was helpless—for now. She had been cheated, sentenced to death, and forced to flee from the Crown Jewels to save her life. Diadem Michella had made a spectacle of her, stripping Enva of her noble titles and holdings, her family prestige and wealth.

The Tazaars had built a grand empire on Orsini for centuries; her father had been a great lord whose power and personality had been a match for even Selik Riomini—until Lord Tazaar was murdered by an unknown assassin, leaving Enva with the wealth and power.

But she'd lost it all and now found herself on this worthless frontier planet of Tehila. Everything had been torn from her, like an infant stolen from its mother's arms. If only Enva had moved more swiftly and consolidated her noble alliances, she could have been Diadem herself by now, replacing the vile old leader. She had arranged a cooperative pact with General Adolphus on condition that he help her remove the spiteful crone from power. Enva was sure the General had not betrayed her—no, it was someone else.

By now, if Michella had her way, Enva would have been executed—painfully and slowly, before a large audience. But she had frustrated the old bitch's plans in that, at least. Enva could cling to this as a small victory. She had been locked in a high-security Sonjeera prison without any real reason to hope, but someone—she had no idea who—had given her a chance to escape, smuggling her away on a secret transport aboard a stringline hauler heading off into the Deep Zone, as far away as conceivable.

Now she was safe enough, although forgotten and powerless. But she was still Enva Tazaar. She had the skills and ambition to change her situation. One step at a time.

Ready to go to work, she clipped on her ID badge before entering the Tehila administrator's mansion. The badge identified her as "Enva Lien" and the picture showed a woman who was still unfamiliar to her. Beautiful—nothing could hide that—but her blonde hair was now close-cropped and dyed a muddy brown. She wore no makeup on her pale face—giving her the appearance of a clerk, a civil servant, someone beneath notice. Enva felt a knot of resentment whenever she looked at herself, but it had to be this way . . . for now.

Having run the government on Orsini, Enva had a talent for details; she understood the minutiae as well as the broad strokes and implications. When she'd arrived on Tehila, her mysterious benefactor had left her a small stipend with which to establish herself. She had a tiny apartment and was forced to rely on the kindness of Deep Zone strangers. Enva Tazaar was unfamiliar with the concept of charity. She had been a hard-edged planetary ruler, with little patience for those who could not take care of themselves. The people of Tehila, pioneers accustomed to helping one another for the survival of the colony, gave Enva what she needed, once she demonstrated her willingness to work.

With her skill set, she pursued and easily obtained employment with the Tehila government offices. The job was dull, but easy for her, and she worked her way up quickly, although she was careful not to draw attention to herself. Until old Michella was deposed, or simply died from old age or too much spite, Enva was in danger. Her death sentence remained in place.

Someday, she would make her way to General Adolphus on Hellhole, reveal her identity, and help him overthrow the Constellation. For now, "Enva Lien" was just a minor functionary, a nondescript bureaucrat.

She walked up the wooden steps of the administrator's headquarters. Each day when she reported for work, Enva found it amusing that the Tehila colonists called this a "mansion." On the remote world, they had nothing else to compare it to.

Tehila's primary city had been established around the spaceport where regular shuttles took off for the stringline terminus ring in orbit. Previously, trade had flowed along the stringline to the Sonjeera hub, but General Adolphus had astonished them all by laying down a new Deep Zone stringline network that connected the frontier planets before he unilaterally declared a war of independence against Diadem Michella Duchenet.

Inside the Tehila offices, minor functionaries milled about, taking care of clerical emergencies, filling out forms, filing documents, performing rote jobs. Her office mate was bent over her desk in consternation. Maruni Li was easily flustered and just as easily manipulated. Middle-aged with salt-and-pepper hair, she had already met or exceeded her life's minimal ambitions. Many bland workers just like Maruni had served Enva on Orsini: a government couldn't function without them.

A man paced the office, presenting a new report full of images. Enva had worked with him before, but she wasn't quite clear on his name or responsibilities. He was flustered about some problem at the Tehila spaceport.

Maruni's face melted with relief when she saw Enva. "Good, you can help us with this. We don't want to overreact, but no one seems to know the best solution."

"I'll try to help, but first I need to know what the problem is."

"It's the walumps," said the man who had brought in the new documents. "Last night they erected six more mud huts right on the edge of the spaceport."

Enva frowned. "You'd think the noise of landings and takeoffs would bother them."

"I doubt anything bothers them," Maruni said.

The innocuous and oblivious herd creatures were nicknamed "walumps"—short for "walking lumps," which was an apt description, Enva thought. Each of the creatures had spindly legs and arms, rounded bodies like misshapen boulders, and a head that tucked down into its main body like a turtle's. Walumps lived together in herds, or colonies, or hives—no one could quite tell. The passive creatures were completely indifferent to the human colonists.

Attempts to communicate with the walumps had failed to evoke any kind of response—not anger, nor fear, nor defensiveness. They built their mud huts wherever they liked. They spoke with one another in low murmurs, but showed no reaction whenever a human addressed them. Because they cooperated with one another, built structures, and obviously communicated, they were classed as intelligent, but they were also an enigma.

Enva scanned the reports, saw that a group of the creatures had erected numerous rounded huts, as if they had decided the edge of a spaceport was just the perfect place for a new settlement. "Leave them alone, so long as they don't get in the way of space traffic. But if they build huts that encroach on our operations, then use dozers to knock them down."

"That's what I was going to suggest," said Maruni Li. Beside her, the man with the report muttered and agreed, seemingly glad to have someone offer the suggestion, which would let them point fingers back at Enva should anything go wrong. She could hold her own regardless.

Much of her clerical work involved claims filed by refugees from the ruined planet of Candela. After asteroids destroyed Candela, hundreds of thousands of refugees had spread out to any other Deezee world that would take them. Because Tehila had so much unclaimed land, many refugees had come here.

The original Tehila colonists did not like the intrusion, however, nor did they much care for the tyrannical way that General Adolphus commanded that their planet accept so many extra refugees. Tehila had no choice in the matter, even though they were already strapped for resources.

From the grumbles, Enva had come to understand that many people here had never wanted to be part of the General's rebellion in the first place. Tehila was so isolated that the Constellation paid little attention to it; the inhabitants had not felt as repressed by the Diadem as other Deezee colonists did, so independence wasn't such an urgent matter for them.

Enva could understand the General's thinking about

the refugees, how the Deep Zone worlds had to pool resources and support those who needed help. With her experience, she could see the broader picture. Other Deezees, though, including even an important man like Administrator Reming himself, had no such wide-ranging understanding and could not think beyond their own parochial concerns. They needed a better leader, a deeper thinker.

If Enva's plans worked out right, she would soon rise to a position to take over as Tehila's planetary administrator. And that would be just a start.

Now, looking at grievances from the Candela refugees, she compiled a summary of domicile requests, homestead applications, filings for food packages and relief, zoning alterations to allow the construction of multiple-unit dwelling complexes, colony kits removed from storage. The sheer number of people who needed interim shelter was staggering. The new crowded dwelling complexes reminded her of refugee camps; the comparison was problematic but unavoidable. Their situation would improve—like her own. In the meantime, everyone had to endure.

She finished her report quickly, but killed time for an extra hour because Administrator Reming was not accustomed to sheer efficiency. When Enva saw her opportunity, she went to his office to deliver the final document. The door was ajar, and she pushed it open.

Reming's personal offices were more cramped and less well-appointed than those of a simple bureau deputy back on Orsini. But Karlo Reming seemed to consider them—and himself—extremely important. Enva saw that he was in deep discussion with three other men and one stern-looking woman.

"I've rearranged the station shifts," that woman said.

"I personally chose all personnel aboard the terminus ring from the Hellhole line. That's important."

One of the men said, "We need to secure the Sonjeera line as well. If anything happens to that, this plan falls apart."

"When do we send our ultimatum to the General?" asked Reming just before he looked up, and showed surprise when he saw Enva poking in through the door.

She averted her eyes. "Excuse me, Governor. I didn't mean to interrupt."

"This is a private meeting," snapped the third man; he was pale and angry.

"This is one of my best employees," said Reming. "Sometimes she's too efficient for her own good. I wish I had more like her." To Enva, his chuckle sounded like a nervous affectation.

"I didn't mean to intrude, Administrator." It was hard for her to maintain a meek and subservient demeanor, but she was growing more practiced at it. "I brought the resettlement reports you requested." Her pulse increased from hearing the snippet of conversation. What was Reming up to? "I'd like to offer my services, too. You mentioned that someone needs to go to Hellhole to deliver a report to the General?" Her thoughts were racing. She had been looking for an opportunity to leave all this behind and present herself to the man who should have been her ally, to reclaim her position of power.

"We said nothing about going to Hellhole," said the stern woman.

"Yes, you did," Enva said.

Administrator Reming waved his hand. His hair was more gray than blond. His eyes looked sad, with heavy bags under them. He tried to dismiss Enva's comment. "Nothing you need to worry about."

Enva said, "I just want to put in my name as a volunteer. I've always wanted to see Hellhole."

Reming blinked. "You *want* to see Hellhole?"

Enva just shrugged.

"I'll keep you in mind if an opportunity arises." The administrator took the resettlement reports from her, glancing at the lists of Candela refugee requests: lodging, food, homesteads. He made an angry sound. "Parasites. Why did they all have to come here?"

"I believe it was because their planet was destroyed, sir," Enva pointed out. The others just scowled at her.

Reming shooed her away. "That will be all for now, Enva. I'm very busy." He set the reports aside, and she knew he didn't care about solving the Candela refugee problem, simply wished it would go away.

But she had watched and listened, and wheels had begun turning in her mind. She decided to find out what was going on.

6

Candela hung mortally wounded in space, the corpse of a once-beautiful world.

Even before the stringline scout ship arrived above the damaged planet, Tanja Hu felt acid tears burning her eyes as dismay and hatred boiled up along with a bitter helplessness about how she had been unable to prevent the disaster.

Piloting the ship as they raced along the iperion path from Hellhole, Ian Walfor fell silent, considerate of her grief. He didn't need to utter any comforting platitudes, did not gently squeeze Tanja's hand, although she would have appreciated that.

He decelerated toward the stringline terminus ring that had once been a symbol of hope, a new transportation network that connected all the DZ planets like a safety net. It should have been the start of a commercial golden age for her planet, for Theser, for new consortiums of trading partners.

When Candela appeared before them now with all its devastating scars, though, Tanja couldn't help but gasp. Even the normally loquacious Walfor had no words. Tanja's throat constricted, and the tears blurring her vision could not dull the horrific image of the devastated planet. She felt as if they were attending the wake for a dead world. "I knew what to expect, Ian, but I had to come back anyway. I had to see it for myself." She shook her head. "I had to know for certain what was left."

Tears trickled down Walfor's face as well. His voice was hoarse. "The Constellation has inflicted plenty of harm on us, but we can't blame them for this."

No, for the Candela tragedy she couldn't blame Diadem Michella. The Ro-Xayans were entirely responsible for this.

No one had even known about the militant faction of the alien race until they struck a deathblow against Tanja's world. How could anyone fight such a powerful foe? And if Encix's fears were correct, the Ro-Xayans would come back to finish their work on Hellhole with an even more appalling asteroid bombardment. . . .

Tanja had been Candela's hard and efficient planetary administrator, helping her planet thrive in spite of the Constellation, which was always there to demand tribute, but absent and unhelpful whenever aid was needed. She'd been an early rebel, along with General Adolphus, but in all of her plans and efforts, no one had thought to watch out for planet-killing aliens from the past.

"I remember how much it hurt when my uncle Quinn and his village were buried in a mudslide—too much mining and too little safety, just so they could meet the Diadem's production quota," Tanja said bitterly. "I'd never been so heartbroken, never imagined the pain could be greater, but now . . . my entire planet has been murdered."

Walfor reached over, stroked Tanja's long black hair. She closed her eyes and let him, then opened them again. She felt obligated to stare at the ruins of Candela; she owed that to herself. Her world had been a proud independent colony before the Diadem annexed the entire Deep Zone into the Constellation. The jungles were lush and fertile; the city of Saporo, floating on the gem of a harbor, had been magnificent. An old funicular on a rail had once taken sightseers to the top of a hill so they could look across the verdant landscape.

Now, though, Candela had been beaten bloody. A pair of gigantic asteroids had fallen like anvils from the sky on a malicious coordinated course. Remaining there in orbit until the last moment, Tanja had watched the inevitable and appalling cosmic strikes. Centuries ago, the planet Hellhole had suffered from a similar titanic impact that wiped out most indigenous life-forms there, including the Xayan civilization. That impact had cracked Hellhole's crust, ignited volcanism, and churned the climate so badly that the planet still writhed in pain, even hundreds of year later.

But what Candela had suffered was far worse. Huge craters still simmered with lava oozing up from the mantle. Impact rings were like ripples of rock extending for hundreds of kilometers. The jungles had been leveled and incinerated. The atmosphere was clogged with smoke as forest fires continued to surge across the landscape. Scarlet cracks showed shatter lines across the expanse of the continents. It would be centuries before even the most daring pioneers could set foot here again.

It was a cosmic irony, Tanja thought, that even with so much devastation, the stringline terminus ring remained intact in orbit, allowing swift travel from Hellhole . . . although there was no reason for anyone to go back to Candela.

Finally, Walfor spoke. "At least you saved two hundred thousand people, Tanja. *You* led the evacuation. They didn't all die. We had some warning."

"I didn't do enough," she said.

His brow furrowed, his gaze hardened. "You did what you could. No one could have saved more."

Her expression softened. "Yes, at least we did that—thanks to you." If Walfor hadn't accidentally discovered the inbound asteroids, aimed and accelerated by the merciless Ro-Xayans, Candela would have had no warning at all.

Walfor deployed sensor packages to take detailed readings to chronicle the devastation down there. "I want a full record, including deep geological scans."

"Maybe with armored shelters a camp could survive down there, for a while at least." Tanja couldn't take her eyes from the awful devastation. "But why would anyone want to go there? There's nothing left."

Walfor kept his voice low, as if in apology. "To see if the iperion can still be mined, of course."

She didn't resent him saying it, knew that past the doorway of her grief she had pragmatic concerns to deal with. She was a planetary administrator without a planet. Candela had been the Deep Zone's only known source of the vital molecular tag that allowed superfast stringline travel. The only other source was the planet Vielinger in the Crown Jewels, and those mines were nearly played out.

"No one will ever be able to find iperion in that mess down there," she said. "With all that upheaval? The whole landscape has been reshaped."

"Yes, but we know it's there." Walfor's expression held forced hopefulness. "If not here, we need to hope our prospectors find iperion on other worlds. They've increased their efforts throughout the DZ. With all those planets, someone is sure to find another deposit."

Tanja wasn't so hopeful. "We know how incredibly rare iperion is. Just because we found a strike on Candela doesn't mean it exists on any other planet, particularly not one of the habitable ones."

He smiled at her. "Ah, that's where you're wrong, my dear. We found iperion on Candela *and* on Vielinger. Finding the substance on one planet makes it an anomaly. Finding it on *two*, and especially two that are widely separated, means that it's not unique. There's no reason we can't hope to discover it on three, or four, or many more planets. We just have to keep looking."

"I hope you're right." She tried to turn her thoughts elsewhere, to other important matters. Hundreds of thousands of Candela refugees needed to be relocated, settled. Most had gone to Tehila, which was where she and Walfor planned to live for the time being. Ian Walfor had also lost his home after Commodore Percival Hallholme attacked his icy planetoid of Buktu, capturing all the inhabitants—all of Walfor's friends and family—and destroying everything in his wake.

Apparently sensing what Tanja was thinking, he frowned. "I hope you and I find another home soon. The DZ has already lost two planets."

"*Three* planets, counting Theser. Sia Frankov and all her people slaughtered . . . leaving another lifeless world like this one."

"Theser was devastated, but not like this. I visited

there. Yes, its main city was leveled, the people killed, but we can colonize the place again—and right now. When the Ro-Xayans destroyed Candela, though, they meant for that place to be lifeless for a very, very long time."

A chill went down Tanja's spine, as she thought of the warnings Encix had made. "And they're not finished yet." She turned away from the scarred planet, gazed out into the emptiness of surrounding space. "Widen your sensor net, Ian. Let's make sure there's nothing around here spying on us."

They searched the planetary emptiness with scanners and circled the world, still checking—but detected nothing out of the ordinary. Nevertheless, Tanja continued to watch, wary. The ominous feeling wouldn't go away. She couldn't shake the sensation that something was watching them. And it wasn't friendly.

7

Lord Selik Riomini rather liked the appellation people used for him—the Black Lord—but it hardly said everything about him. True, he traditionally dressed in black, and his house flag was predominantly black, and he kept a number of obsidian sculptures in his villas and manor houses. Yet, black did not describe his moods, because he was often quite pleased with the ever-widening reach of his power.

The color black did, however, nicely suggest the danger he presented to anyone who dared to oppose him.

Queasy from the spicy lunch he'd eaten, Riomini rode in an armored staff car that made its way from his Vielinger manor house, passing through an ornate gate at the western entrance of the estate. Black paramilitary vehicles led and trailed his staff car, bristling with weapons; his ubiquitous female guards rode alongside his car on high-speed cycles. Black flags fluttered on all of the fenders.

Lord Riomini took a formidable force whenever he traveled from Aeroc. As part of his aggressive persona, he liked to let his enemies know that he could strike with great ferocity at any time. That was how he'd wrested Vielinger, the Crown Jewels' only known source of iperion, away from the inept de Carre family.

Riomini's staff car passed through a military guard station and entered a fortified industrial complex, then came to a stop in front of the largest building. He had an appointment to meet with Commodore Hallholme, who was delivering prisoners he'd captured from the rebel world of Buktu out in the Deep Zone. Riomini intended to put those enemy captives to work in the iperion mines, but first he had an inspection to complete.

Surrounded by his entourage, the Black Lord strode into the building, where he inspected an assembly line of spacecraft engines, where robotic arms fitted parts and performed quality-control tests. At Riomini's side, the stocky facility manager rattled off details, while Anson Tebias, the Black Lord's most trusted adviser, accompanied them, waiting for an opportunity to talk. In his mid-thirties, Tebias was tall and painfully thin; he made Riomini think of a stretched-out noodle, but Tebias was a very intelligent man, and he gave good advice.

The facility manager said, "As you know, my Lord, these spacecraft engines are destined for the Constellation fleet, so we must make certain each one is perfect. It is generous of you to fund this operation for the benefit of all."

With a smile, Riomini said, "I'm only doing my duty for the Constellation, as any person of means should do."

But Selik Riomini harbored deep resentment toward Diadem Michella, who did not adequately appreciate his contributions. He should already be the next Diadem, but the old woman kept stringing him along, never fully endorsing him, toying with him and other candidates. At one time his main competition had been Enva Tazaar, but even after the ambitious noblewoman's fall from grace, Michella had not embraced him. And she refused to retire . . . or die.

"Excellent work," he told the facility manager with a knowing glance at Anson Tebias. "Keep constructing the new warships. There's no telling how soon we may need them."

Regardless of how Diadem Michella snubbed him, he would make assurances of his own.

—◆—

Leaving the industrial complex, Riomini's convoy was delayed on the main Vielinger highway by an accident between a cargo hauler and a transport bus. There were several injuries, and wrecked vehicles blocked the road. Showing no patience, Riomini commanded one of his armored military vehicles to push the wrecks and emergency vehicles off the road. He needed to be on his way.

By the time he reached the iperion mines, Commodore Hallholme was already there, resplendent in his gold-and-black Constellation uniform as he paced outside one of five landed transport copters. Riomini had wanted to make a grand entrance to impress the old soldier; instead, delayed, he had to mumble excuses as he stepped out of his staff car.

Though he was the old veteran's superior, Riomini always felt intimidated in Hallholme's presence. The Commodore's legendary status and judgmental demeanor had a way of unnerving him.

With only a cursory salute to the Black Lord, Hallholme signaled for his men to begin unloading Buktu prisoners from the burly copters. They had been held in custody since the Commodore's return in defeat from his last engagement with General Adolphus, but Riomini had pulled strings to get them transferred here to Vielinger. Several hundred expendable laborers would come in handy in the dangerous mines. He would save on expenses by trimming safety margins. Better to put DZ rebels at risk than loyal citizens.

As the teams of guarded prisoners were led into the main mine entrance, the Commodore approached Riomini. "The Buktu captives are now in your care, my Lord. I gave them my word that they would be treated humanely. Is there anything else you need of me today, sir?"

The words sounded good, but the Black Lord found the old Commodore's tone irritating, an edge that did not sound adequately deferential. Riomini waved a hand. "Go, and await my further commands."

Hallholme nodded stiffly, gave another salute, and hobbled back to his aircraft. The copter had already taken off in an efficient-seeming rush by the time Riomini reached the mine entrance. A tall Nordic man identified as the leader of the prisoners, Erik Anderlos, listened as the mine supervisor issued gruff instructions to the new captive work crew. Anderlos did not look pleased, although he grudgingly joined the other prisoners.

The iperion mine supervisor, Lanny Oberon, wore dusty gray coveralls. He greeted Lord Riomini with a slight bow.

Riomini said, "Work these prisoners hard, and deal severely with troublemakers. Feed them just enough to keep them working."

Oberon also looked displeased to hear the rough instructions. He'd been known to speak his mind and had kept his position only due to his expertise in extracting iperion from difficult veins. "The de Carres would never have used slave labor—they ensured the safety and well-being of the miners. But you are not giving me the budget or authorization to do that, my Lord."

Riomini said, "Our priority here is to ensure the efficient operation of the mine and to produce the maximum amount of iperion. We have to extract whatever is left in the veins. You seem to be forgetting that these prisoners are enemy combatants, traitors to the Constellation. By rights, they should have been summarily executed, but this way they can perform a useful duty to make up for their crimes." Then he added, as a concession, "Any funds we save by using these prisoners will go toward improving the structural integrity and operating efficiency of the mines." He looked around. "Where's the maintenance foreman? That's his responsibility."

"Jando Knight is on duty underground, sir, going about his rounds. Do you also wish to speak with him? I am in charge of orienting the new workers."

"No. He knows what I expect of him." Riomini narrowed his gaze. "As do you, Oberon."

The supervisor was not intimidated. "I will perform my job faithfully, my Lord. No one is better at my job, and I've always been loyal to my employer, but I must also protect the welfare of my workers."

"Don't forget, these are *enemy* prisoners—if they get a chance, they'll cut your throat."

"Yes, my Lord." Oberon bowed again, and trudged toward the main iperion mine shaft.

8

The large prison encampment near Slickwater Springs was surrounded by two high fences thrown together with construction wire and livestock mesh barricades taken from Sophie Vence's warehouses in Michella Town. The holding area had been built quickly after General Adolphus accepted the surrender of the Constellation soldiers. Tents and prefab colony huts offered shelter but few comforts.

Adolphus's camp guards patrolled the perimeter in vehicles and on foot. Despite the guards and the fences, Bolton Crais knew that the rugged, hostile landscape of Hellhole was the primary deterrent to escape.

In theory, it was only a temporary settlement, but Bolton knew the resolution of the conflict was far from over. He and his fellow prisoners of war had been here for many weeks already. It seemed like an eternity.

Around him, the camp was a buzz of activity as he climbed the steps of a wooden frame building at the center of the complex. Though the structure was not quite completed, it was being used as a makeshift entertainment hall, as if the prisoners had resigned themselves to staying here for some time. They had access to movie and game loops as diversions from the tension and boredom. When finished, the building would be a meeting hall, where Redcom Escobar Hallholme would address his captive officers, and where Sophie Vence, as the camp administrator, would meet with Bolton or other camp representatives to listen to their complaints and respond to them. Two evenings ago, after a growler storm had skirted the valley and injured more than a dozen prisoners with static discharges, the officers had gathered outside the building, voicing concerns that the temporary shelter of the camp was insufficient to protect them from threats.

Sophie made no secret that she resented the POWs and what they represented. She merely replied, "If our hospitality bothers you, maybe you shouldn't have come to our lovely planet in the first place. I believe you intended to raze all of our colony settlements to the ground?" She was particularly brittle around Redcom Hallholme—with good reason, since his treachery had resulted in the death of her son and his girlfriend. "You haven't even experienced the razor rain yet, or the spawning of cannibal beetles."

In times of tension, Bolton was the one who could speak in a reasonable tone, trying to make the best of the situation. "Nevertheless," he pointed out, "we did surrender under promises from General Adolphus that we would be taken care of. Leaving us vulnerable to known meteorological hazards is not keeping us safe."

"You of all people, Major Crais, shouldn't quibble about promises made or kept." Sophie drew a breath, calmed herself with a visible effort, and responded in a lawyerly tone. "When the Army of the Constellation went to war against us, all your soldiers assumed the risk of unknown dangers. When we accepted your surrender, we admittedly assumed certain responsibilities for your welfare. We are doing our best to accommodate you in a humane manner, but don't be so foolish as to ask that we build a fully secure prison complex to accommodate thousands. General Adolphus can't be expected to provide more protection for enemy troops than he does for his own people, or for himself. Welcome to Hellhole—welcome to reality."

Her remarks had elicited a murmur of discontent

from the officers, but the more Bolton thought about it, the more he felt she was right. Under the circumstances, the captors seemed to be doing what they could.

With a sigh, Sophie added, "Your men and women have all the incentive they should need to do the work. When this large building is finished, it will serve as a solid emergency structure in the event of a storm. You'll have to crowd inside during any crisis, but you should be safe enough."

Under a hurry-up construction schedule, only some of the windows had armored glass in them; the others were boarded up or covered with plastic film while the glass was manufactured. The communal building was sturdy, but Bolton was worried that the more permanence the camp had, the less likely it would be that the prisoners were freed anytime soon..

Hellhole was cut off from the Crown Jewels, and though Bolton knew that the Diadem, Lord Riomini, and Commodore Hallholme would be searching for a new avenue of attack, he did not hold out hope for imminent rescue. And Keana Duchenet—who was still his wife, but no longer entirely human—had not offered a solution either. Bolton had joined this mission hoping to rescue her, wanting to protect her. That had not turned out as planned. . . .

Now, as Bolton stood outside the communal building, he heard machine sounds. Through the open doorway he saw a POW construction crew at work inside the central hall, erecting and reinforcing a stage from which Redcom Hallholme could address large crowds. The Redcom had quietly summoned Bolton and several top officers to a secret meeting that would be held amid the construction noise, where their words would not be overheard.

Bolton sat outside in the shade of an overhang while he waited for the others. A future garden had been staked out on his left, but the terrestrial vegetables and even a clump of ornamental flowers were not thriving. An unusual type of native blue ground cover had been planted around the communal tents, and at least it was doing well. Leaning down, he plucked one of the tiny succulent leaves and squeezed moisture out of it.

With a wistful sigh, he remembered that back on Sonjeera, his wife had dabbled with gardening, manipulating indoor plants in their mansion like an orchestra conductor directing a performance—while their servants did the actual dirty work, as well as discreetly replacing any flowers that died, so that Keana believed in the prowess of her green thumb.

Back then, Keana had been bored and oblivious, married to him due to an alliance of noble families rather than romance, although Bolton had cared deeply for her, and still felt that way. In those days, she never would have soiled her hands. But Keana had changed a great deal since then, and so had Bolton. So had the entire Constellation.

Naïve and ill-prepared, Keana had rushed out here to rescue Cristoph de Carre, the son of her disgraced lover, but she had not known what she was doing. Hellhole had swallowed her up and changed her, joining her with an alien personality. Bolton had lost her long before that, but he had always hoped to get her back. Now, there seemed little chance of that.

Diadem Michella, who seemed irrationally paranoid about alien contamination, had written off her own daughter, but Bolton would never give up on Keana. He still loved her, and had promised to protect her. When she went missing, he had insisted on joining Redcom Hallholme's strike force for the express purpose of trying to rescue her. Instead, he and all the Constellation soldiers were trapped in this fenced compound.

He hadn't seen Keana in days. He wished she would visit him here in the camp more often. She had come twice since his capture, and he knew she still had feelings for him, but Keana was changed and overwhelmed with other concerns . . . undoubtedly alien concerns. He wished his life could go back to normal, but that would never happen now.

As if summoned by Bolton's thoughts, one of the strange Xayans entered the camp, accompanied by three human figures who glided forward, as if in a trance. Bolton looked up, saw the other human prisoners shy away from the alien creature's long pale body, the strange flat face, the quivering feelers that extended from the smooth forehead. Bolton identified the creature as the one called Encix. The few alien survivors seemed intently interested in the pool of prisoners inside the camp. Encix had repeatedly tried to convince them to immerse themselves in the slickwater pools as an offer of freedom—an offer that no one had accepted. Yet.

But he was much more intrigued to see the accompanying humans—converts who had immersed themselves in slickwater, acquiring alien lives. They were changed, different, intimidating. And one of them standing next to Encix was Keana.

His heart leaped and he stepped forward even while other prisoners shied away. "Keana!" She looked at him as the alien moved forward on a long caterpillar body. Her eyes were distant, but he could still see his wife there, still knew she could interact as herself even though her mind was in a kind of symbiosis with an alien presence.

A faint smile crossed her face. "Bolton, we are hoping to convince you—and all these other prisoners—

to join us. To achieve your freedom. If you come to the slickwater, there would no longer be any need for you to stay in this camp."

His chest went cold. "I . . . can't do that."

Emerging from the main command tent several rows away, Redcom Escobar Hallholme marched in front of two other junior officers, Lt. Seyn Vingh and BluCap Agok Yimidi. The Redcom flinched noticeably when he saw the Xayan, clearly wishing he could avoid contact, but Bolton realized that Encix was coming toward the central building with a purpose.

The Redcom looked angry. "You are not welcome here, and none of my men and women will let themselves be possessed by aliens. You're wasting your time."

Encix said, "That is because you don't understand the wondrous opportunities . . . and you don't understand the urgency."

Escobar and the two other officers joined Bolton outside the meeting hall, facing the alien and the shadow-Xayans accompanying her. Anxious Constellation soldiers turned their attention to Encix as she proceeded along the dusty thoroughfare and stopped in front of the officers. Keana stood beside the alien, like an equal, but she let Encix speak. "Who will leave this camp and become one of us?"

"General Adolphus made reassurances," Escobar said. "We will not be harmed. We will not be forced."

"Of course not," Keana said. "No one is to be coerced. We hoped you would at least consider?"

Bolton's heart ached, wanting to be with her, but he couldn't leave his comrades, nor did he want to lose himself . . . certainly not like this.

"You can go now," Escobar said. "You have no place here."

They regarded one another in silence, and then the

alien's voice thrummed through a facial membrane. "You are the leaders of this group of humans. You are the ones I must convince, so that your faction assists us. This planet is threatened. You must see reason."

Keana added, "Encix is telling the truth. Your people have the opportunity to save this planet and save the Xayan race."

Encix said, "If your faction would accept the slickwater and reawaken more of us, we would have sufficient numbers to reach *ala'ru*."

"Why should we care about your strange race?" Escobar said. "You are allied with our enemy, so you are our enemy."

"The Ro-Xayans are the only significant enemy," the alien said. "The squabbles of your factions will be irrelevant if the Ro-Xayans destroy this world."

"You have already made the offer. No one is interested. No one will *ever be* interested," Bolton said. "I'm sorry, Keana."

Escobar was adamant, though Bolton could sense his uneasiness. "You can't force us. We are prisoners of war."

Encix seemed baffled, and the shadow-Xayans looked at the prisoners pityingly. "But you could become enlightened, you would receive remarkable powers of telemancy, and you would understand far more than you do now. Merge with us in a unique synchronicity of races." The Xayan's antennae quivered. "Why do you resist?"

"Because we are *human*," Escobar insisted. "And we have no interest in giving that up."

The alien turned to Bolton, as if she knew exactly who he was. "Keana-Uroa is quite satisfied with her own transition. Perhaps she can convince you."

Keana faced Bolton and said, "I can't."

Encix raised her voice, so that all the bystanders could hear as well. "Any prisoner who becomes a shadow-Xayan will be freed. You will join us. You will have abilities and memories that you can only begin to imagine. You have all witnessed the power of our telemancy, how we defeated and drove away your powerful attack fleet."

Escobar lifted his chin. "My father will be back to avenge that defeat."

"If your offer is so great," Bolton added, "why hasn't General Adolphus become a shadow-Xayan? Or Sophie Vence?"

"That is their choice for now. Eventually, they will reconsider."

Glowering, Escobar took a step closer to the alien, as if it required all his courage to approach her. "There is nothing you could say to make us join you. None of my soldiers want any part of you. Leave us in peace."

Encix remained silent, quivering and unreadable. Finally, she added, "You may reconsider when the Ro-Xayans come. By then, I hope it is not too late. We must achieve *ala'ru* at all costs."

The officer prisoners stood together, firm; the other POWs continued to whisper among themselves. Bolton said to Keana, "You should go now. You have made your case. If we change our minds, we'll let you know." He drew a breath, added, "Sorry."

The alien made a sound of displeasure and retreated from the camp. As she glided down the path, the prisoners moved aside, giving her free passage toward the fenced gate. Keana and the other converts went with her. When Keana looked over her shoulder at him he saw a glimpse of the deep sadness and disappointment she carried. Then they left through the guarded gates.

Even after the entourage was gone, with Keana out

of sight, Bolton still felt his pulse racing. Escobar was sweating, and the other two officers looked as if their knees might buckle. "That alien will not give up so easily," Vingh said. "I don't think she'll take no for an answer."

"She will be back and try harder to coerce us," said Yimidi.

The Redcom narrowed his gaze and said in a hard, low voice, "That only confirms what I was already thinking. We can't just cower here and wait for my father. We need to break out of this camp—it is a prisoner's duty to escape."

"But where would we go?" asked Vingh.

He whispered with greater urgency, "Away from here, away from the alien pools. We could make our way overland to Michella Town, steal a ship at the spaceport, get out to one of the other DZ worlds."

Bolton was uneasy. "We're getting ahead of ourselves. We don't have supplies, don't have charts or shelter, don't have weapons or tools—"

Yimidi picked up on the idea. "This camp isn't secure. It wouldn't be hard to steal some supplies and get a small group through the fences. Once we're out in the open, we could make good time. Most of this planet is an uninhabited wasteland."

Excitedly, Escobar said, "If even a few of us can find a way back to the Crown Jewels, we'll let them know what's going on here. My father can't prepare his attack without information. It's our duty. We have to do our part."

Trying to be more realistic, Bolton said, "You're forgetting how dangerous the landscape is around here. This is Hellhole! We don't know the terrain, or the hazards that we will face."

Escobar silenced him with a glare. "We are trained soldiers in the Army of the Constellation. How about you two? This is not an order. It is a time for volunteers."

Bolton didn't think it was a wise plan, but he could see the Redcom wouldn't change his mind. The idea had obviously taken hold with Yimidi and Vingh. He sighed in resignation. "If you choose to make this attempt, I will go with you." Bolton felt obligated to stay with his commanding officer. "But the fewer of us, the better. A small group has less chance of being seen, and we can be more nimble."

9

Though Sophie maintained separate living quarters of her own, she stayed with Tiber Adolphus at Elba whenever she had the chance. They were lovers and partners, though the ongoing crisis did not permit them to see each other as much as they would like.

When Sophie arrived at the headquarters mansion, Adolphus greeted her with a warm smile and a weary but lingering embrace. He wore a blue-and-gold striped robe, and his black hair was slicked back, as if he had just stepped out of the shower. She noticed a bit of dark beard shadow on one side of his chin, which apparently he had overlooked when he shaved—a sign of how preoccupied he must be.

"I brought some very important news." She stepped aside to let her companion join her at the door. "Tel Clovis is the one with the message."

The rejuvenated man was barely recognizeable, no

longer twisted and damaged from the stringline back-lash on Candela; after his second slickwater immersion and his fusion with Tryn, Clovis now stood straight, healthy, vibrant. The man had been so insistent on delivering his message personally to the General that he had wanted to use his increased telemancy to levitate and fly himself and Sophie across the open air, but she declined. With a standard craft, she had gotten them here in an hour.

Adolphus stared in surprise at the other visitor. He had known Tel Clovis well when he served as the manager of the Ankor spaceport construction. "You look like your old self—except your eyes seem stranger, brighter."

"I'm stronger, General," Clovis said. "I now have Tryn within me as well as Balcus, my first companion."

Sophie nodded. "Tryn could not be healed, and so she surrendered to the slickwater in order to join Tel."

"That means only two Originals remain," Adolphus said. "Do Lodo and Encix know?"

"I am still here," the man said in an otherworldly voice. "I am now Tryn-Clovis." The eyes spiraled and the voice thrummed. "And I have a message, a new possibility that will let us reach *ala'ru* faster than we expect."

Adolphus glanced at Sophie. She said, "You're not going to like it, Tiber, but hear him out."

They joined the General in his well-appointed study, where he had once kept transparent display cases of alien artifacts found by prospectors, long before anyone knew about the Xayans. He took a seat at his desk, firm and businesslike, despite his casual robe. "And what is it you propose?"

Tryn-Clovis said, "Someone must recover the remains of Cippiq and Zairic from Sonjeera. Zairic was the original visionary who fostered our march toward *ala'ru*, and he was the one who saved us by creating the slick-water. A vital part of him remains in the residue in the quarantine hangar . . . and that would be very useful to us."

Adolphus drew his dark brows together. "Their remains are completely inaccessible, according to what my spies have reported from Sonjeera—sealed in resin and under heavy guard. Michella is terrified of any contact with the Xayans. How do you expect to get in?"

Tryn-Clovis was unconcerned. "We must find a way. Bringing the memories and energy of Zairic back into our shared pool of telemancy will be an invaluable catalyst. I—and a group of companions—will require transport to Sonjeera."

Sophie let irony creep into her tone. "He's quite convinced, but not very practical."

Tryn-Clovis continued, "When I was in the pools, I experienced a powerful vision through telemancy. We are all in agreement that we need to rescue Zairic. Even from such a great distance, we are all connected, and I could sense the power still there in the Xayan residue trapped in that hangar. I know that if I can absorb what remains of Zairic and incorporate the afterimage of his presence, I will be able to accelerate *ala'ru*."

"And how do you expect to get there?" Adolphus asked. "The direct stringline from Hellhole to Sonjeera is cut. You'd have to go via one of the other Deep Zone nodes."

"Then that is what I will do. Once I reach Sonjeera, I will find a way to enter the quarantined hangar and retrieve the remains. That will give me what we need to save the Xayan race and alter the fate of this planet. It is a chance we have to take. The memories of Tryn inside me know the true powers that Zairic can awaken, if we liberate his memories, his telemancy, and all of his companions."

The General exchanged glances with Sophie. He said to Tel Clovis, "Keana Duchenet may have information to help you, since she spent her life around Sonjeera and she had access to isolated areas that no one else knows about. As a shadow-Xayan, she'll want to help you."

Sophie said, "First, you have to get to the quarantined hangar. And that means you have to get past all the Crown Jewels security around the spaceport and the main stringline hub."

Adolphus smiled. "We have people who've done that before. Don't underestimate the risks, but if you succeed, it seems that we have a great deal to gain."

Clovis stood straight, as if nothing would move him. "I'll have far more shadow-Xayan volunteers than I need, General. Just give us a chance to get to Sonjeera."

Adolphus nodded. "I already have a couple of good operatives in mind."

—◦◦◦—

According to flight records, two of his most trusted pilots, Turlo and Sunitha Urvancik, were due to arrive at the Ankor spaceport. Former Constellation linerunners, the husband-and-wife team had infiltrated the Crown Jewels numerous times since the General declared Deep Zone independence.

The Urvanciks had just returned from a run to the DZ planet Hossetea, and Adolphus met them in the Ankor admin building as soon as they disembarked. He sat across from Turlo and Sunitha in a private conference chamber, where a filtered window provided a view of the landing field. Shuttles departed and arrived, accompanied by a flurry of landing downboxes.

Turlo had wide shoulders and a broad face, with pleasant features but not strikingly handsome. He was of medium height, with brown hair and dark eyes, and a natural tan. His pretty, olive-skinned wife, Sunitha, had an exotic look to her, with thick black hair and almond eyes.

Both of them had a sense of determination that made them completely reliable. Their only son, Kerris, had been killed during the General's first rebellion, serving in the Army of the Constellation, but the Urvanciks had turned against the Diadem when they learned that the reported cause of his death was a lie. Once they defected, they were utterly loyal to General Adolphus.

Now, Turlo carried two packs, slinging them onto the floor while Sunitha took a seat. Both of them looked troubled. Without any preamble, Sunitha said, "We're glad to find you here in person, sir. There's a lot to report, and something you need to know."

"Unrest brewing on Hossetea," said Turlo, without his characteristic good cheer. "Demonstrations against the planetary administrator, Sylvan Greer—and even more anger directed toward you, sir. They burned you in effigy in the largest city, along with a crude image of a Xayan."

"He doesn't need to know those details," Sunitha interrupted.

"Yes, I do." Adolphus was surprised and dismayed by the report. "I have heard no grievances. What is causing the trouble?"

"We kept our distance, sir," Turlo said. "But we picked up enough. The people are saying that Hossetea never wanted a war against the Constellation, that you forced this whole problem on them."

Sunitha added, "And they don't want to be allied with aliens against their own people."

Furrowing his brow, Adolphus said, "I'd better send in a larger surveillance team, along with more security personnel. You'd think Hossetea would be glad not to pay a backbreaking tribute to the Diadem. Don't they want to be free?"

"I think they don't want to do the work it takes to be free, sir," said Turlo.

"Should we turn around and head back there with a message, General?" Sunitha asked.

Adolphus shook his head. "No, I have a different mission for you, a difficult one. How would you like to sneak into Sonjeera?"

Turlo smiled. "That's always fun."

"It won't be fun," Adolphus said, "but the Xayans insist it's important."

Knowing that Tanja Hu and Ian Walfor were due to arrive in an hour with their firsthand observations of devastated Candela, Adolphus kept the conference room as a temporary office. He sent for a plate of curry and garlic fish fillets on fry-pasta from one of the concessionaires in the terminal building, and ate while reviewing the disturbing information about Hossetea. He was just finishing his meal when the two travelers entered.

With his weathered skin and ruddy good looks, Ian Walfor carried himself with confidence. Though he was the planetary administrator of the remote DZ world of Buktu—now empty and abandoned—he was also the best space pilot Adolphus had ever seen. Close behind him, Tanja Hu was a tall woman with high cheekbones, large eyes, and inky black hair.

Adolphus pushed his meal aside while Tanja swung

herself into a seat. "We have thousands of images of Candela, General, but the conclusion is simple. No one is going to settle there for a long, long time. The damage is many times worse than what happened to Hellhole centuries ago." She shook her head. "We'll never be able to mine iperion from the wasteland."

"Then we need to find another source," Adolphus said. "I've increased search parties and prospectors across the Deep Zone, but no one's found any new evidence yet."

Tanja's voice was husky. "I'll devote my efforts to making sure my refugee population gets settled and integrated into Tehila society, and the same on the other planets where my people have been dispersed."

Walfor stood by one of the large windows, gazing out at the landing field. He seemed angry. "We could go back to my Buktu, rebuild there. It's empty . . . all my people gone, taken prisoner by Commodore Hallholme." He looked up. "Has there been any word from the Crown Jewels? Any ransom demands? Could we consider trading some of our military prisoners so I can get Erik Anderlos and my people back?"

Adolphus had considered that already, but there were no lines of communication. "I can make overtures. The Commodore took them all prisoner, and we know he uses hostages for leverage in desperate situations."

"We don't even know if they're still alive," Tanja said.

A dark expression crossed Walfor's face. "And he portrays himself as a man of great honor! He keeps reaching new lows."

Adolphus said, "I suspect they are still alive. Commodore Hallholme will view the Buktu population as prisoners of war, which places certain obligations on him. He will expect the same treatment from us with his son Escobar and our POWs." He felt he had the measure of Percival Hallholme, although he was less sure about Diadem Michella and Lord Selik Riomini.

Walfor turned away from the filter-glass window and slumped into a seat at the table. "What about Theser instead? Lord Riomini's warships leveled the main city, but the planet is still habitable. We could resettle there."

Adolphus glanced over at Tanja. Her friend Sia Frankov had been the planetary administrator of Theser, murdered along with all her population in the Black Lord's attack. "It would be fitting to populate that world with Candela refugees. Sia would like that, wouldn't she?"

Tanja's eyes flashed behind a sheen of bitter tears. "Rebuilding there would be a way to show the Constellation that their attack didn't defeat us. It's worth considering."

He remembered all the traumas and tragedies that Tanja had endured. "And what about the boy under your care—the son of your assistant, who was also murdered by Constellation treachery? Did he go with the Candela refugees to Tehila?"

Tanja said, "Jacque saw his mother killed in front of him, and he was at my side when we watched Candela die." Her voice hitched. "I didn't want to leave him in a crowded refugee camp on Tehila. He's been through so much already. I sent him to a school and a very welcoming family on Nielad. He'll be fine—and far from the turmoil here."

Walfor gave her a wan smile. "Tanja wants to be sure the boy is protected, and this way, she can still travel with me."

Adolphus rose to his feet. "Resettling Theser will take time and considerable effort. Right now, I want you to go to Tehila to make sure the needs of the refugees are being met."

Before departing, Tanja and Walfor each shook the General's hand. These were more than wartime comrades; they were friends, and he could count on them, just as they could count on him. It was one of the unexpected benefits of warfare and strife—learning who deserved such feelings, and who did not.

10

Under the supervision of Keana-Uroa and Encix, the shadow-Xayans trained with their telemancy, performing more and more spectacular exercises. And because the demonstrations took place just outside of the prisoner camp, and in clear view of the Constellation soldiers, the displays served the additional purpose of showing all those potential converts what they would gain if they immersed themselves in slickwater.

The shadow-Xayans were gathered on a promontory that provided a clear view of the rocky valley that spread out beyond the camp and off to the line of rough hills and wilderness beyond. A thrum of telemancy hung in the air, and Keana could feel Uroa's psychic energy increase inside of her. The newer converts practiced simpler tests that helped them ignite and control their telemancy, while Keana observed and offered her advice.

Keana and Uroa had an uneasy arrangement to share the awareness and impulse functions of their body—an understanding that was put to the test during the daily telemancy exercises of the shadow-Xayans. As one of the stronger and more resilient of the converts, Keana-Uroa helped to hone the cooperative mental skills of the growing crowds of shadow-Xayans. Someday, Keana knew, their adeptness in telemancy might save this planet, and might save the alien race.

They had developed a game to test and challenge the burgeoning telemancy abilities. From this promontory, she could look out upon the course, seeing the tall pylon on the valley floor that served as a marker. Students had to levitate large objects around the pylon and then return the objects to the shadow-Xayan settlement in the extreme distance. Keana could see curved free-form alien structures poking above a forest of dense, ethereal red weeds. The manipulated objects were not mere stones, but entire buildings.

Raised by the converts' telemancy, five buildings hung in the air now, cruising slowly toward her. One yellow structure with black ornamentation was a considerable distance ahead of the others, a neatly uprooted shop building. It spun in the air—a waste of energy, she thought, although it was a showy demonstration of skill.

Many of the prisoners inside the camp were watching, some fascinated and some fearful. So far, though, very few had agreed to become converts. Not even Bolton. Keana refused to coerce him, although she knew she could make him change his mind.

Encix looked at all those soldiers from the Constellation as if they were resources to exploit. Though the alien's features were unreadable, Keana felt uneasy about the Original's edgy intensity.

"We will reach *ala'ru* soon, but we need those other humans to join us." It was a constant refrain. "Our numbers and strength are growing. Those prisoners can see all the wonders we can achieve." She raised her soft, pale arms. "We will be like gods once we finally ascend."

Keana had spent far too much time with the powerful delusions of her own mother, and the grandiose comment from Encix disturbed her. But before she could protest, Uroa's presence surged inside her mind, taking control and thrusting Keana into the background. His vehemence surprised her. "Do not speak of us as gods! We are not destined to become *gods*. *Ala'ru* is about our evolution, about reaching our potential—not aggrandizement or glory!"

Keana could do no more than listen, shunted to the back of her own mind as Encix and Uroa sparred verbally in an exchange of unintelligible telepathic transmissions. Keana could sense the growing dislike Uroa felt for the domineering Encix.

Now, the yellow-and-black building rounded the pylon, edging gracefully close, and headed back toward the shadow-Xayan settlement in the alien forest, away from the fenced prisoner compound. The other four buildings were minutes behind the leader, but as they all completed their turns around the pylon, the front-runner began to lose altitude. As the student lost control of the telemancy, the structure dropped to the uneven rocky ground, tumbled, and broke apart.

From the prisoner camp came a burst of loud cheers and catcalls. Encix turned to regard the debacle, exuding disappointment.

In a matter of moments, the broken parts of the crashed building darted back into the air and began to reassemble themselves—controlled by the embarrassed student—but by the time the components were rejoined, the other objects had flown past and were well ahead in the race.

"Our focus is on too many things," Encix said. "We must have the same goal."

"We all want to save this planet," Keana said. "Even if we go about it in different ways."

The alien just regarded her with an unreadable expression, then turned away as if in further disappointment.

Concentrating on the shadow-Xayan race, Keana reached out with her mind, enhancing distant details with telemancy. While the former leader tried to catch up, the other trainees reached the distant valley and the lush forest of waving red weeds. The students were required to land the structures in their original places on the ground, with no sign that they had been disturbed, not so much as a bent leaf on an alien plant.

Other telemancy exercises resembled something she had once seen in a carnival sideshow, with the shadow-Xayans raising the same object into the air, one at a time, to see who could lift it the highest. Not long after her conversion, Keana had placed second in that competition, behind young Devon Vence. . . .

After the unusual air race passed them, Keana-Uroa, Encix, and several other observers levitated themselves into the air, and in a group they flew toward the shadow-Xayan settlement. Encix drifted ahead, leading them as if to show that her telemancy was the strongest.

At the settlement, additional competitions were designed to strengthen individual and collective telemancy powers, with the goal of unifying the shadow-Xayans so they could protect the planet against outside attacks, as well as to help them reach their evolutionary ascension.

But to become like *gods*? Keana remained troubled by Encix's blithe statement. She hated the thought, as did Uroa. Encix regarded the activities with a harsh judgmentalism.

Once the group arrived at the growing settlement, they all landed gracefully. Keana saw more and more new converts coming from Slickwater Springs, still wonderstruck after having immersed themselves in the alien pools. The site had gotten more and more crowded, but it was not designed to be a permanent colony, merely a temporary place for the converts until they reached *ala'ru* . . . however long that might take.

As the threat of Ro-Xayan retaliation loomed over them, Encix kept urging the humans to plunge themselves into the slickwater. Their combined telemancy was growing demonstrably stronger—as was Keana herself. She wondered if they might be strong enough to thwart an incoming asteroid, like the one that had originally destroyed Hellhole. Encix continued to push, but it was doubtful that today's demonstrations would have convinced large numbers of the Constellation prisoners to join them.

Yes, the existing converts were growing stronger, thanks to Keana's constant training. But she had no idea whether it would be enough.

11

After managing the iperion mines on Vielinger for years while his father dallied, and then suffering the ruin of his family and his subsequent exile to Hellhole, Cristoph de Carre had felt far too many burdens of responsibility for a young man who was not yet thirty. In fact, his prior life didn't even seem real to him now. His father, Louis, had brought about the de Carre family's downfall due to his alarmingly indiscreet affair with Keana Duchenet, and while in a pampered Sonjeera prison after the scandal, Louis had killed himself because he couldn't handle the shame.

Cristoph was a different sort of man, though. After coming out to the Deep Zone, he had worked hard to convince General Adolphus of his worth. And he had certainly done so.

After being put in charge of excavating the wondrous museum vault of Xayan treasures deep in the core of a mountain, he was now helping the Original alien Lodo catalog the stored remnants, hoping to find some exotic weapons or defensive tools. By this time, most of the valuable relics had been extracted from the vault for further study, and the surviving Original aliens were obsessed with *ala'ru* to the exclusion of all else. But as the unofficial curator of the vault, Cristoph felt sure that the numerous intriguing artifacts had some value. Lodo occasionally joined him in the vault, and the good-natured alien seemed to have a certain fondness for Cristoph.

The dim illumination in the subterranean chamber revealed thick, interlocking blocks around the walls, covered with bas-relief strips, friezes, and indecipherable writing. Niches and sealed containers held mysterious treasures, and the young man didn't pretend to understand most of them. Whenever he touched the exotic items, he did so with great care.

While Cristoph slept in the vault on occasion, he preferred to arrive early and spend a day there before returning to his apartment in Michella Town in the evening. Sometimes he went to a local tavern, where he met other people worried about the imminent threats to their planet. Sometimes he even found a female companion, but his work was too intense and the dangers facing Hellhole too all-consuming for him to let himself fall into a serious relationship. He remembered his father's indiscretions too much to be tempted like that. . . .

Though the vault was deep underground and there was no natural light, Cristoph's chronometer told him it was midday. Lodo's large body glided from niche to niche past the relics of his own race. "Once we reach *ala'ru*, none of these objects will be of concern to us, no matter how precious and valuable they seem now. Be sure you enjoy and appreciate them for the rest of us who are too busy to do so."

Cristoph thought he detected a hint of a joke. "Of all the Originals, I think I like you the best, Lodo."

The alien thrummed, making a sound of amusement. "That is not a particular triumph, as Encix is the only other one who remains."

"But I would have said the same when Cippiq and Tryn were still among us."

Lodo thrummed laughter. "Yes, the best among four is somewhat more impressive."

Now the Xayan turned to the displays of preserved artifacts, pushing his sluglike lower body along the stone floor with soft brushing noises. Faint shapes wavered and crackled in the air over his head, eerie squiggles of illumination that accompanied him as he squirmed up a stone ramp to a higher level. He seemed reticent today, strangely quiet.

Cristoph always felt a sense of wonder and mystery in the vault. He had cataloged what he knew about the relics and sent regular lists of his findings back to General Adolphus. On some days when he arrived at the deep chamber, he found that an object had been moved, or had vanished, or that a new object had appeared. He suspected that Lodo or Encix were responsible, though he didn't understand why they would be mysterious about their own relics.

As Lodo puttered about on the upper level, Cristoph examined a small box made of a slippery lightweight material. He especially liked the embedded jewel that glowed crimson whenever he opened the lid. As he stared at the jewel, he sensed Lodo approaching from behind him.

"Ah, I recall that treasure from long ago," the alien said. "Once, this jewel sat on a pedestal at the center of a chamber where the leaders of our civilization would meet. Zairic, Uroa, Encix, and others. In our last meeting there, we discussed how we might survive the approaching asteroid, how we could preserve our civilization. I was entrusted with bringing the jewel down here for safekeeping, along with many of our finest relics . . . just in case."

Cristoph closed the lid and returned the box to a high natural shelf of stone, but Lodo reached out to grasp it. "I will take this with me now, as a special reminder of what we once were. Everything else, though, will remain here in the vault. It is done now. We are all done here."

Cristoph was puzzled. "What do you mean?"

Lodo's facial membrane vibrated, but did not form comprehensible words. Then his smooth-faced countenance grew dark. "Encix and I have decided to seal this chamber and leave it. These items only serve to anchor our minds to a physical past. There is no longer any use in studying what remains here."

"You're just abandoning all this? Our own scientists still have a great deal to learn here. I haven't finished cataloging it all, and we'll still be here after you ascend . . . or whatever."

"You must leave, and I must leave. This vault will be sealed. Our entire focus is now to attain *ala'ru*. With the Ro-Xayans coming, that is our only chance. Nothing else matters."

Lodo pressed close, edging Cristoph out of the museum vault and toward the powered vehicle that would take them up the tunnel to the surface. "If your telemancy is growing stronger with more converts, can't you protect us from the enemy?"

"Our entire race wasn't sufficient to deflect *one* asteroid from the Ro-Xayans, long ago. Thanks to human vigor, we grow stronger than ever, closer than ever . . . but our rival faction will not be content to send a single projectile this time, as they proved at Candela. All this"—he raised his arms—"is just a distraction. Right now, we cannot afford distractions. Time is too short."

"But you promised to help us defend Hellhole against the Constellation, too."

"We might still do that, if we can. After *ala'ru*, there will be no more threats to this planet." The Xayan turned back to the cave opening. "Come outside with me. I'm going to seal the entrance."

The energy of telemancy crackled loudly over Lodo's head, making snapping sounds. Cristoph hurried to exit the museum vault, although he felt a heavy disappointment. On his way out, as he passed a small display alcove, he noticed it was empty—and he was certain that earlier in the day a relic had been there, a silvery domed object. He wondered what else Lodo had secreted away before turning from all of the "distractions."

12

Answering the Diadem's urgent summons—something was always urgent, it seemed—Ishop Heer was escorted toward the private terrace by a tall, angular butler with a neatly trimmed mustache. Even as he walked through the spacious main rooms of her lavish apartment, Ishop could hear old Michella shouting outside. The butler studiously pretended to be deaf, but slowed his pace so the Diadem could expend her vehemence before he stepped out onto the terrace and interrupted her with the guest.

Ishop pretended to be the dutiful lapdog as always, the useful expediter, the man who could be counted on to do any dirty job for the throne . . . but apparently a man who could never be considered an equal. Maybe today he would find an opportunity to nudge her off the high terrace. Accidentally.

The butler paused at a discreet distance and turned to Ishop. "My apologies, sir. It'll be just a moment."

On the terrace, Michella hurled a plate of food into the face of a servant, bloodying the man's nose and causing him to cringe back as she roared, "I told you yesterday that my food has too much salt—you were instructed to have the amount reduced by half! How dare you bring me a plate full of brine like this? Perhaps I should have *you* cut in half. Are you trying to kill me?"

The old woman sat in a loose-fitting exercise outfit at a small terrace table, shaded by a large umbrella. She had just finished her daily vigorous workout, impressive for her advanced age. Ishop knew that her shouting had raised her blood pressure far higher than any amount of salt would have. Her volatility alarmed him. Although ruthless and vindictive, she had not been so mercurial, even childish, until recently. The outrageous crippling actions taken by General Adolphus, the grumbles of the powerful noble families, the betrayal and loss of her own daughter, and the horror of spreading, alien possession—all had made her borderline irrational.

Scattered on the tile terrace lay the mangled remnants of an omelet with spicy peppers and rich marubi sauce.

It was normally one of the Diadem's favorite dishes, but she had discarded it in dramatic fashion. The servant stooped to clean up the mess, holding a napkin to his bloody nose as he stammered an apology. "I gave the chef your explicit instructions, Eminence. He seems to have forgotten."

In response, she hurled a ceramic teapot at him, striking him on the forehead and leaving a gash. The teapot exploded on the tiles, spraying its hot contents like a bloodstain. The blow stunned the man, causing him to drop the food he had been cleaning up. He looked at the old woman in imploring surrender, desperate to please her but having no idea how to do so. He seemed unable to gather his thoughts or organize his movements. Blood dripped unattended from his forehead and nose.

"Get out, before I order your execution."

The man fled.

Ishop stepped calmly onto the terrace. "Such a pity. Was that our pot of tea?"

Michella fumed, but his presence always seemed to calm her. "Not everyone is as reliable as you, dear Ishop. I wish I had ten of you."

"You will have to make do with only me, Eminence." *If there were ten of me, all of them would be plotting your demise . . . and one of them would have succeeded by now.* He turned to command the hesitant butler at the terrace doorway. "Send someone to clean up this mess, and have a pot of afternoon tea brought to us, along with little sandwiches and cookies. We have business to discuss."

"Yes, sir," the butler said, then turned to the Diadem. "Shall I instruct the chef to prepare another meal, Eminence?"

"I'm too upset to eat now, but notify him of my extreme displeasure and of the consequences should he ignore my instructions again."

The butler hurried away, leaving the two of them alone.

Ishop took a seat across from Michella. He could have picked up one of the sharp fragments of the shattered ceramic teapot and sawed through her leathery neck. But he dismissed the idea. Too gory, and too slow.

Leafy potted ferns and planter boxes full of bright flowers stood around the perimeter of the terrace, and from this height the diners had a pleasant view of the palace gardens. Maybe he could lure her close to the edge and give her a little nudge.

Interrupting his fanciful thoughts, another manservant appeared like a nervous rabbit, hopping from mess to mess, cleaning up the debris in efficient silence. The tea and hors d'oeuvres arrived just as the servant was finishing.

When they finally had privacy again, Michella looked at Ishop. "I need you to search for information. Commodore Hallholme is planning our military operation, but Lord Riomini has been quite remiss about keeping me in the loop. Has there been word from Administrator Reming on Tehila yet? When is he planning his purge so our ships can have unimpeded access to the Deep Zone? I am anxious for this to be over."

For his own purposes, Ishop had already been spying on communications, using the Diadem's authority when necessary. "I have monitored stringline traffic and saw no record of any message drones or small ships coming from the Tehila route. The silence is disturbing. What is Reming waiting for?"

Michella sipped her tea. "Before we send our Constellation forces out there, we need to make certain

General Adolphus hasn't spread his filthy alien contamination around the Deep Zone. I would hate to learn that Tehila is infested. Then we'd have to sterilize the whole planet before we could move onward!" She made a disgusted sound. "Another waste."

"Don't forget how those powerful aliens nearly wrecked the Commodore's fleet with their mysterious powers. We don't know yet if the new warship shielding will be effective against that kind of attack."

Michella frowned. "I am assured by some of our best military minds that the new precautions will work, because they *must* work." She seemed confident, or perhaps she just wanted to believe that her forces would finally succeed, despite past failures. She had refused to give the Black Lord any opportunity to study the only physical specimens they had of the aliens, which might have given the weapons engineers additional information; she absolutely insisted that the multiple layers of quarantine never be disturbed.

"Those hideous aliens already damaged our stringline hub, Ishop. We can't just sit here and wait for them to overwhelm the Crown Jewels. We have to go on the offensive, don't we? We have to keep probing, trying to find their weaknesses."

"Yes," he said with a hard smile. "We already know there are cracks in the General's supposedly unified rebellion. Tehila is the prime example, but we know of unrest on Hossetea as well. And there may be other hot spots."

"Hossetea? Where is that? Who ever heard of Hossetea?"

"You used to rule it, Eminence. It is one of the fifty-four Deep Zone worlds."

"And I will rule it again, when we put an end to this nonsense." Despite her insistence that she wasn't hungry,

Michella ate several of the small sandwiches. Ishop just sipped strong black tea on the terrace, and when he didn't answer, she pressed, "Don't you agree?"

"Of course, Eminence."

She grew more cordial, as if she'd already forgotten the debacle with the servants. "Are you comfortable in your new apartment? Is there enough room for you and your pretty little assistant?" She seemed to be teasing him.

"My assistant is currently away on business, and I have been too busy to go back to the apartment." He smiled stiffly. Laderna had already departed on her secret mission to Sandusky, to find and kill the Diadem's hidden sister. "You know as well as I do, she isn't all that pretty."

"As long as you appreciate the gesture I made. It is my reward to you for your fine service."

Ishop hated that apartment, loathed this withered scab of a woman. He felt like squeezing his fingers around the Diadem's neck until she stopped breathing. Thanks to Laderna, Haveeda Duchenet would soon be dead. That would not give him the same joy as murdering the vile Michella . . . but it was a step in the right direction.

"You could even be in line for larger rewards, if things go well for you." The Diadem's tone was either tempting or taunting. "You mentioned wanting a planet of your own?"

Surprised, he looked across the table at her. "You've changed your mind, Eminence? As I mentioned before, Enva Tazaar's former planet would be perfect, and I promise not to disappoint you—"

When Michella laughed, the cruel sound cut through him. "Don't be silly! Orsini is too important, but planet

Hallholme is a possibility, if anything's left after we're through with it. Once General Adolphus is crushed, I might find a way to give that world to you as a reward, so you can impose my will."

"Hellhole?" He heard an edge of anger in his own voice, tried to calm himself. "Eminence, I appreciate your generosity, but I am more suited to living in the Crown Jewels than in the Deep Zone." A slow death for her . . . yes, it would be more satisfying.

She sipped her tea and smiled, not seeming to realize how much he detested the very sight of her. "That's all right, dear Ishop. I'd rather have you here with me anyway."

13

In performing services for her boss and lover, La- derna had traveled extensively, though few people ever noticed her movements. She was unobtrusive, intention- ally so, and curious. She had gone to various Crown Jewel planets where particular nobles lived. No one saw her arrive or leave . . . but when she was done, the tar- get was no longer alive.

The "List," as she and Ishop called it, had originally contained the names of twelve noble families—powerful families who had disgraced and destroyed the respected Osheer house centuries ago, then left them to wallow in obscurity afterward. When Laderna discovered the truth about his heritage, how his descendants had hid- den or forgotten their past, Ishop had insisted on an ap- propriate form of revenge. Together, they had selected a representative from each family to die. Just to be fair.

Of course, the descendants had nothing personally to do with the ancient crime against Ishop's family, but the punishment was still easy to rationalize because the modern representatives of those twelve families had benefited from the ignoble acts of their predecessors. It was only appropriate for them to pay a price.

Together, Ishop and Laderna had chosen the ones most deserving to die, or easiest to kill—and the two of them had made a game of going methodically through the names, taking turns or working together. Only the name of Duchenet remained.

Now, as she stood at a window in a business hotel on Sandusky, Laderna smiled with anticipation. The streets of the capital city of Zensan bustled with efficient activity, commerce, research, secrecy; though it had a small population, Sandusky was still one of the core Crown Jewel worlds, run well by the Zenns, a noble family that made a great deal of money selling biological products developed in their advanced laboratories.

Having checked into the hotel several days ago under an assumed name and cleverly forged documents, Laderna had observed activities in Zensan and the surrounding countryside, particularly noting the isolated research complexes. She inquired, ostensibly on behalf of her "fiancé," about working at one of the Zenn laboratories.

In preparation, digging deeper, she had learned details about Michella Duchenet. Her brother Jamos had been found dead (the matter muddied and covered up), and Haveeda had suffered psychological problems before disappearing decades ago. Laderna had her own suspicions about Michella's murderous personality, even at an early age, and that her sister had been pressed into silence. Extreme silence. She'd vanished without a trace.

But Laderna would find her. And kill her . . . a pathetic representative of the last family name on the list. It was the victory she needed, and she wasn't convinced Michella would even be disappointed about it.

As she performed her quiet investigations on Sandusky, Laderna did not risk bringing up the name of Haveeda or Duchenet. She baited a man in a highbrow cocktail bar by asking him if any famous people lived around there. He'd rattled off the names of eminent biological researchers, as well as nobles. Then, while nursing a drink, he'd added, "Of course, some say the Diadem's sister lives on Sandusky as well."

Laderna controlled her excitement. "I suppose she's in one of those mansions on Fairhaven Hill, with panoramic views of the city and the mountains."

"No one's seen her in years." He snorted. "I hear she's in a sanitarium just outside of town."

In ensuing days, Laderna had tracked down four sanitariums on Sandusky. One of them, the Cove Institute, specialized in the discreet institutionalization of members from the wealthiest families, keeping them out of the public eye so they could cause no further embarrassment. The managers of the sanitarium ran the facility like a high-security bank, refusing to reveal who their clients were. Laderna made a visit of her own, by now with a fully developed story.

The Cove Institute was an elegant old structure built of rare green marble that reminded Laderna of the facets of an unusual jewel. The building was six stories tall and expansive, with four wings extending from a central core. The entrance featured immense white columns and the statues of famous Sanduskan scientists in heroic poses.

In the echoing entrance hall, Laderna gave her false name and offered the story that she and her fiancé were considering a move to Sandusky. Then she lowered her voice and added that his wealthy family was concerned about the well-being of a troublesome, mentally ill uncle. At the mention of wealth, the clerk sent for what she called an "adviser" to consult with Laderna.

Minutes later, a pink-cheeked man in a spotless white lab coat identified himself as Johan Zenn. Assuming he was a member of the planet's ruling family, she was taken aback. Yes, perhaps she had found the place hiding Haveeda.

She reached out to shake his hand. "Very nice to meet you."

His grip was limp, his blue eyes dull. "I'll show you some of our facility. I could recommend the best form of commitment for a troubled family member."

"My fiancé's uncle has been increasingly unstable, blaming his family for all of his failures in life. He's unable to work and has made many disturbing and irrational comments. We are all quite worried about him." She looked around. "Perhaps he would feel at home in a place like this. Cost is no object."

He nodded. "I understand completely. Let me show you around."

"I assume you have different levels of security for the various patients," Laderna said. "For someone of his stature, we want the greatest discretion and confidence."

The facility was as clean and spotless as Zenn's lab coat. The sanitarium, down every corridor in every wing, was of an old classic design, but the materials looked surprisingly new, with no patina of age. Several of the sections had viewing glass, so she could look inside and see patients in communal surroundings, or lab workers doing biological research on the leading causes of mental illness.

In the east wing, they passed a section devoid of viewing windows, and Laderna saw a very young woman in a lab coat enter through a metal door after pressing her hand against a scanner plate. The door closed before Laderna could see inside.

"I find your facility most interesting, Mr. Zenn," she said.

— ◆◆◆ —

Three nights later, after following one of the maintenance women home, she presented the woman with an enormous bribe—more than she was likely to see in the rest of her working life. Laderna found it extremely ironic that the funds she was using to corrupt this employee came directly from Diadem Michella's largesse to Ishop.

From her tour and other surreptitious investigations, Laderna had the general layout of the Cove Institute, as well as a sense of their security measures. Fortunately, the sanitarium's security was primarily designed to control the patients and prevent them from breaking *out*. Slipping *in* should be much less of a challenge.

The maintenance woman was adept, hardworking, and reliable. When Laderna met her in the small, rented hotel room, the woman was furtive and nervous. She brought images of the full floor plan of the institute, blueprints of ventilation systems, electrical grids, even a time chart of security personnel. "I brought you everything I could get hold of. It took a great deal of searching. Not easy," the woman said, as if hinting at something—more pay, no doubt—which Laderna studiously ignored. She saw a list of patient designations, but without names. She could crunch the information, though, and extract specifics. Since she already suspected where Haveeda Duchenet was being held, she could approach the answer from multiple directions.

"And how do I get inside in the first place?" Laderna asked.

The maintenance woman was sweating. "That'll be harder. Every employee is coded into the security system, allowed inside only during designated shifts. A palm-print scanner verifies my identity before I can get through the door, and I won't be allowed to slip a second person into the facility. There are weight sensors to verify it."

Laderna assessed the maintenance woman, confirmed that they were nearly the same size; the woman's brown uniform would fit her well enough. "I have a way around that," she said.

After Laderna had killed the woman, donned her clothing, and gathered up her severed hand, she was ready to go.

After midnight, Laderna used the woman's cold palm print to pass through the identity scanner at the Cove Institute's rear entrance. Once she launched her operation, speed would be vital. She had no interest in covering her tracks or being subtle—she *wanted* Michella Duchenet to know that her sister had been a very specific target. She needed to work her way through the facility with all possible speed, dispatch Haveeda, and then disappear. For Ishop.

Wearing the facility's uniform, Laderna arrived at the central guard station, where she stunned the guard and disabled the surveillance system. She had memorized the floor plan, the blueprints of the systems, and had crunched through the patient IDs; she was convinced she knew where the Diadem's sister had been held all these years. It was probably a tiny, pampered apartment in the facility, someplace where Haveeda could cause no trouble. Laderna planned to put an end to her as quickly as possible. She moved on to her target.

In her plan, she had timed every movement, and had very little room for error or delay. She would depend on speed, brashness, and accuracy; she would do it alone.

This time, she used the guard's severed hand to get through heavier security, sliding aside a thick metal door to a windowless section. Yes, Haveeda must be in here. Laderna needed to hurry, finish her task, and be away. Afterward, she already knew how she would disappear.

Inside the high-security section, she found herself in a small entrance foyer, with cubicles containing lab equipment, cleansuits, and protective magnifying goggles. At this late hour, no one was around—the maintenance woman's schedules had been accurate. Inside, she expected to find one or more confinement cells for patients of the sanitarium, luxurious rooms for the highest-priority, wealthy but disturbed guests. One of them was the Diadem's sister.

She passed through a second doorway and heard a strange silence, an electronic barrier that dissolved when she touched an identity scanner. Inside, additional doors each had a control panel. Her pulse quickened as she went to the first one. The data image on the screen provided the patient's name and brief personal history, but this was not the name she wanted. She kept moving from door to door until she found Haveeda Duchenet.

This door had a simple manual mechanism that locked from the outside. Laderna had expected something more complex and secure; if Haveeda became violent she could probably have broken through the simple lock. Considering all the other precautions, Laderna found it a curious lapse.

She pulled the door open to feel a blast of cold vapor, as if Haveeda's room was highly refrigerated. Inside, she saw no distraught patient, no sleeping woman on a hospital bed, no well-appointed apartment . . . merely a sealed tank in the center of the room. Fascinated, she stepped over to it.

With growing confusion, Laderna wiped sparkling frost from a curved observation panel, and to her surprise she saw a woman lying inside, preserved and frozen. Her eyes were open, staring straight up. It was the Diadem's sister.

She had expected to find Haveeda held as a prisoner, but not *this!* It was shocking, but nevertheless she had a job to do, an important accomplishment to impress Ishop. The problem was, how could she kill a person in suspended animation? Cutting off the medical monitors and life-preservation systems . . . not as dramatic an end as she had hoped for, but the result was what really mattered.

She noticed a small access port on the side of the tank, as well as a pair of insulated gloves. She reached for the gloves, sure she could accomplish enough damage if she wrecked the life-support and monitoring systems. This was not a mission for subtlety; in order to make Ishop's necessary point, others needed to *know* what had happened to Haveeda.

Just as she reached inside the cryo-tank, she heard a noise behind her. Three guards burst into the room and tackled Laderna, slamming her to the floor.

14

While the walumps intrigued Enva Tazaar, anthropologists had apparently grown bored with them. The native creatures were enigmas, but at the end of the day, not all that interesting. Enva found it amusing that the creatures were so preoccupied with themselves, unaware of and uninterested in the tumultuous events out in the galaxy. It made them seem either enlightened or oblivious.

On a day off from her clerical job, she took her easel and watercolor paint supplies she had purchased in town. A tribe of twenty walumps had built mud huts on the edge of the paved landing zone. Three nights previous, they had erected huts right in the middle of the pavement, but the administrator's office—on Enva's recommendation—dispatched dozers to knock them down and clear the area. Some dozer drivers yelled at the walumps, who paid no attention as their huts were destroyed. They simply rebuilt them the next night in the same place, and they were plowed down again the following day. . . .

Enva dabbled with her watercolors to capture the walumps. The creatures shuffled in slow circles near their huts, but she couldn't discern any particular interactions. Enva painted them, capturing their noble innocence, their primitivism. It was a good day.

Enva had always fancied herself an artist. As the daughter of Lord Azio Tazaar, she'd had everything she could want, creating exotic aerogel sculptures. She liked the design and the curves, and played coy when critics asked her what the sculptures meant. Because of the power of her noble family, her aerogel sculptures had sold for high prices, and many lesser nobles showed their support for Lord Orsini by purchasing his daughter's art.

When Enva Tazaar took over the family fortunes and expanded Orsini wealth and influence, she'd donated one of the aerogel sculptures to the Sonjeera palace, part of her campaign of trying to convince old Michella that she, Enva, would be a better successor than the evil Black Lord.

She had lost that gamble, though. Lost everything. And the fact that Enva now felt content to relax and paint, with no political purpose in mind, worried her. She didn't want to disappear into obscurity. If she wasn't careful, she might put her ambitions aside, make excuses for one delay or another.

She needed to move further in her career in the administrator's office, making herself not just excellent, but indispensable. For days, Karlo Reming had been agitated and intense, and she'd not seen him like this since she started to work as a meek functionary. The administrator had been conducting many private meetings and had asked her and Maruni Li to keep a tally of the space traffic to Tehila with a paranoid attention to detail. He took a particular interest in scheduling the normally lackluster crews that manned the two stringline terminus rings in orbit—one connected to the iperion route to the Hellhole hub, and the second, embargoed one, that went back to Sonjeera.

Enva's instincts told her something was afoot. Working in the administrator's office, she interacted with dozens of bureaucrats, some wearing business attire, others in paramilitary uniforms that weren't quite the same as those of the General's Deep Zone Defense Forces.

The Candela refugees were crowded into communal prefab dwellings, but they caused little trouble despite cramped living conditions. She thought those people were still in shock from their ordeal. They had few amenities, but other habitation complexes were under construction, so they knew their circumstances would improve. Original Tehila colonists, though, seemed unhappy about having to provide for all these unexpected new settlers.

In studying the space traffic patterns as she was instructed, Enva had noted an interesting new arrival. A trade ship flying in from the Hellhole hub carrying supplies and colonization equipment earmarked for the Candela refugees—and the pilot and copilot were listed as Ian Walfor and Tanja Hu. They asked for no special treatment, but Enva recognized their names. She assumed Reming would want to know that two former planetary administrators had come to Tehila, where they could be of great help organizing and caring for the refugees. But for some reason the pair had chosen to arrive without fanfare. Very odd. Maybe Hu and Walfor wanted to keep a low profile. Perhaps it had something to do with Administrator Reming's plans, whatever they were.

As a woman who had created many schemes herself, Enva could see telltale signs of what Reming was doing, though she didn't understand his goal. She decided that some information was best kept to herself. She had no particular loyalty to the Tehila administrator. In fact, in her overall scheme, she intended to supplant him as soon as possible. And Hu and Walfor might provide a good opening for her to present herself to General Adolphus on Hellhole. That could be her first step in emerging from exile.

She finished her watercolor painting and signed it "Enva," then paused to weigh the risks, wondering if she dared put her actual surname there. But it wasn't time for that yet. Instead, she left her last name off. For now.

All afternoon as she painted the walumps, she had watched shuttles rising up to orbit. At first, she hadn't paid much attention to how many were loaded with uniformed men. She was familiar with the spaceport schedule, and now realized that at least three times as many outbound ships had departed as usual—and no returning craft had landed. She saw no downboxes arriving from inbound commercial ships. What was going on up there in orbit?

She packed up her watercolors, sealed them in her case, folded the easel, and covered her painting of the walumps and their strange huts. It was good work, but not her best.

Abruptly, she realized something was happening, though the creatures didn't react. Enva looked around, her brow furrowed. She saw vehicles racing across the paved landing fields. They were loaded with armed men and women, and they swarmed toward the barracks where the General's DZ Defense Force soldiers were typically quartered. Several privately owned ships were on the ground. More trucks rolled around the perimeter, securing the spaceport.

Enva stood with her painting gear, watching. Just a bystander. The uniformed men and women looked at her as they drove by, as if assessing whether she was a threat.

Then she received an urgent summons from the administrator's office on her private comm. All employees, without exception, were to come to the mansion immediately. "No one is excused."

Enva stashed her art supplies before making her way over there. As she raced up the mansion steps, she saw wide eyes and frightened expressions among her coworkers. They were confused and frantic. Men and women in security uniforms locked offices and stood guard. Others took custody of a yelling and indignant man.

"What's going on?" Enva asked.

A female office worker rushed by, too harried to pause to give an answer. But Enva reminded herself of who she really was and used a crisp commanding tone to demand a reply. The woman stopped and turned. "There's been a purge! Administrator Reming has taken over, severing ties with the General's loyalists!"

In disbelief, Enva pressed for more information, but the woman said impatiently, "All employees are required to check in at the administrator's office and have their IDs verified. You'll get your answers there." She ran off.

Enva hurried to Reming's primary office. She tried to imagine what kind of coup had occurred, what the man could be thinking. She heard snippets of conversation, but none of it made sense. A guard scanned her ID, checked her name off a list, and frowned at her. "Administrator Reming has been waiting for you. There's much work to do—he needs competent people to help." He ushered her inside the main office.

Reming looked up when Enva entered. His face was florid, the bags under his eyes seemed lifted now. He was excited. "Ms. Lien! There's so much chaos right now. I need your help organizing things." He grinned. "I have good news for all of Tehila."

Maybe not everyone would consider it good news, she thought. "I heard something about a purge, but I don't understand."

"After today, we return to the good graces of the Constellation. We're no longer at war or under threat. I've torn Tehila free from the General's rebellion. We never wanted any part of it, and now we're safe from retaliation. We don't have to live in fear anymore."

In the office, Enva recognized the people with whom Reming had engaged in his surreptitious scheming. One reported, "All DZDF soldiers have been confined to barracks. We've rounded up the known Adolphus supporters and locked them up."

Another said, "The Sonjeera stringline terminus is ours and secure, Administrator."

A transmitted report blared over the speaker in the office. "Hellhole stringline is also secure. One casualty, an Adolphus supporter who tried to blow the terminus and kill us all. We stopped her."

Enva's mind raced as she tried to grasp what had happened. "You took over both stringlines—the one connecting us with Sonjeera, and the one to Hellhole. For what purpose?"

"I had to assure complete control," Reming said, "before any fool engaged a demolition charge and cut the lines, stranding us."

Now it made sense. Reming had stacked the crews with his own loyal personnel. Now he could open the floodgates, controlling the line back to Sonjeera, which the General's rebels had held hostage. She also knew that the vast majority of Tehila's population, and especially the refugees from Candela, would not approve of the change; even with the hardships and the turmoil, very few wanted to go back to the Constellation. Reming was going to have very little time to consolidate his takeover.

A grinning officer in the new militia uniform presented himself at the administrator's door. "The spaceport is secure, sir. All ships are impounded. No space traffic in or out. The next scheduled shipment from Hellhole is tomorrow, but we can seize that ship when it arrives.

That will delay any word getting back to General Adolphus. We'll have time to consolidate our hold."

Reming smiled at Enva. "As you can see, there's much work to do. We have to dispatch a stringline drone immediately to inform the Diadem that Tehila belongs to the Constellation once again. Commodore Percival Hallholme can bring in his fleet now, and once he gets here we won't have to worry about the restless populace. Tehila will be his new base for the reconquest of the Deep Zone."

———※———

Upon learning that Ian Walfor's ship had been suddenly impounded and the entire spaceport nationalized, she couldn't believe that she and Ian had blundered into such a mess. They had filed the proper documentation, claiming to be unremarkable Candela refugees with a load of supplies for the Tehila settlement. Having heard complaints, she wanted to see how Administrator Reming was treating her people.

And now, this astonishing purge. A minority had used surprise and ruthlessness to seize power, and hamstring the Adolphus supporters—but it could not possibly last for long. Tanja didn't understand what Administrator Reming could be thinking.

When she and Walfor rushed back toward their ship, hoping to get away before the situation grew worse, they found the armed militia guarding access and taking full control of the spaceport. The two of them spotted Walfor's ship among the other landed vessels, ships that had arrived from the Hellhole hub bringing cargo, passengers, and refugees.

A guard prevented Walfor from entering the holding area. "All space travel has been shut down, sir. All access to ships is cut off. No one is allowed off planet. The stringline terminus rings are under planetary control."

Incensed, Walfor said, "You have no right to impound my ship. There's been enough turmoil in the Deep Zone. General Adolphus is trying to keep us safe from Constellation attacks."

The guard stiffened. "General Adolphus and his illegal rebellion are no longer relevant. When Commodore Hallholme brings the Constellation military here, it will put an end to all unrest."

"But you're the one causing the unrest," Walfor pointed out.

Tanja felt bitter anger boiling up in her, and she feared that her companion was about to shout, reveal his identity, and demand to be taken to Administrator Reming. She squeezed his arm. "We'd better go, Ian. We don't want to be part of this. Let's wait for calm." She practically had to drag him away, and he kept staring back at his impounded spacecraft on the landing field.

Loud announcements were broadcast from Reming, who fancied himself a powerful planetary leader, though as far as Tanja could recall, he had never done much in the planning meetings after the Deep Zone declared independence. Reming had taken no part in the initial plans to break free of the oppression either, because the General did not consider him trustworthy, unlike George Komun, Sia Frankov, Dom Cellan Tier, and the rest of the original conspirators.

Over the public transmission, Reming announced, "Today, Tehila is liberated. We are no longer forced to be part of a rebellion against the Constellation. After intense negotiations, I reached an agreement with the Diadem, one which forgives Tehila for any indiscretions and makes us exempt from any punitive actions she orders against the rebellious DZ worlds. Within a few days,

Commodore Percival Hallholme will arrive with the Army of the Constellation, and he intends to use Tehila as his base of operations. Our nightmare is nearly over, my friends. The Constellation is coming to rescue us!"

Tanja doubted many people would rejoice to hear the news, certainly none of the Candela refugees. Most of the Tehila colonists had previously resented being beholden to the Diadem and her tribute, and they had fought hard for their independence—now they were betrayed. Once Commodore Hallholme's fleet arrived, however, they wouldn't have any chance. The Constellation would take and hold this planet.

Walfor looked dismayed. "We're stuck here, Tanja. We can't leave."

"True enough, but maybe it's an opportunity." She raised her eyebrows. "No one knows we're here. You and I are in a perfect position to do something . . . unorthodox."

15

Fifteen DZ Defense Force peacekeeper ships returned unexpectedly to the Hellhole stringline hub, captained by Lewis Naridar, a competent veteran who had joined the General and his defeated troops in exile on Hellhole.

As part of his duties, Naridar had been assigned to patrol and protect Hossetea, one of the many frontier worlds the General had never visited. Ever since breaking away from the Constellation, Adolphus had made a point of sending military patrols so that all of the Deep Zone knew they were part of a larger community.

He had been concerned when the Urvanciks reported

unrest on Hossetea, but now that he saw the peacekeeper force returning, he feared the situation had grown remarkably worse. It made no sense that a good man like Captain Naridar would abandon his post and race away, but before he could respond Adolphus needed to know what was going on. He immediately placed all of the Hellhole guardian ships on alert.

As the Hossetea peacekeeper ships arrived at the stringline hub, the General opened the comm from his Elba command center. On-screen, the veteran captain saluted and spoke respectfully. "Hossetea is cut off from the Constellation, General. Drastic measures, but necessary."

Adolphus felt cold. "We don't have the iperion supplies to reestablish that route. Cutting the stringline should be our absolute last recourse."

Naridar didn't flinch. "I realize that, sir, but isolation was the only way I could contain the situation. There's been a . . . a mutiny, a rebellion. I don't know what to call it. The Hossetea planetary administrator tried to break away from us and contact Constellation forces to request, uh, *rescue*. He would have opened the floodgates for an enemy force."

Confusion and anger roared within Adolphus. "Some people insist on strangling their own freedom! Take a shuttle down here, Captain, so you can give me your full report."

—⁓—

Many considered General Tiber Adolphus a strategic and tactical genius. Through his careful planning, several large-scale operations—such as the original rebellion and his surprise creation of a new DZ stringline network—had come off with a high level of precision.

His plan to unify the Deep Zone and break away from the Constellation had been designed to achieve victory with minimal bloodshed, but he'd never expected independence to be simple.

Diadem Michella was a vengeful, bitter old woman who lashed out at any perceived slight. She had sent an enormous punitive fleet to reassert *her* rule of the Deep Zone, but Adolphus had anticipated that tactic, trapped Escobar Hallholme's entire fleet, seized the ships and thousands of Constellation soldiers. Next, he had defeated his old nemesis Commodore Hallholme's fleet with the help of Xayan telemancy.

That should have been an inconstestable enough victory, but Adolphus did not consider the DZ safe. Not yet. The initial declaration of independence was one thing, but now he had to hold his fragile coalition of frontier planets together, even when some of the worlds were actively trying to tear it apart. . . .

Lewis Naridar arrived, looking impressive in his old rebellion uniform. Some of the veterans kept their clothing to commemorate the days when they had almost defeated the Constellation. They found no shame in being exiled out here to the Deep Zone, and now saw it as a matter of pride. Naridar was in his early fifties, with short gray-brown hair and a calm demeanor. He had always been decisive, an excellent officer in the heat of battle. Now he removed his cap and presented himself to the General. "First things first, sir. Hossetea poses no further threat to the independence of the Deep Zone. That much is taken care of, at least."

"I'm pleased to hear that, Captain, but I wasn't aware that Hossetea's grumbling had reached the point of becoming a viable threat. What happened?"

"They're restless, sir. A group of influential Hossetea colonists had strong ties and family members back on

Sonjeera, primarily the family of Territorial Governor Ophir. Now the relatives are cut off—and not happy about it."

Adolphus remembered Ophir, a pampered man who liked his fancy clothing more than his governing duties . . . not the sort of person who belonged in the Deep Zone at all. He had received his position through family connections and, likely, bribes. Though responsible for administering twelve Deep Zone worlds, Ophir had missed the entire rebellion because he happened to be on Sonjeera when Adolphus announced DZ independence.

"With trade cut off from the Crown Jewels, many of Governor Ophir's family members resented the loss of luxuries and culture. Hossetea's planetary administrator, Sylvan Greer, is his nephew," Naridar explained. "Greer insists that his people never wanted any part of your war of independence and tried to run back and hide under the skirts of the Constellation. Fortunately, I learned what they were up to before they could cause further damage. I put a stop to it."

Frowning, Adolphus leaned across his desk. He had imagined that kind of trouble and had briefed his patrols. Naridar would have known what to do. He had stationed fifteen DZDF peacekeeper ships at Hossetea against a possible surprise Constellation attack, but also as a show of force. "Continue."

"Administrator Greer meant to seize my vessels, hold the stringline, and escape to Sonjeera, where he expected to be welcomed with open arms." Now Naridar cracked a smile. "I didn't let him do that, and I made a command decision—extreme, perhaps, but now he can't possibly run back to the Diadem. Nobody from Hossetea can go there. I thought of what you would have done, General."

Adolphus had a dark feeling. "So you blew their stringline to Sonjeera."

"I cut off Hossetea from the Crown Jewels entirely, then took my peacekeeper ships and departed, leaving them high and dry. I realize my action cannot be undone, but the Hossetea problem is neutralized and contained for now, until we can get our own people there and secure the government. At least there will be no attack from the Constellation."

Adolphus nodded slowly. Yes, he would have made the same decision. "You did what you had to do, Captain, and you also demonstrated to the Diadem—and everyone else—that we are willing to cut off the DZ if necessary." He felt his cheeks burn in anger. "I need people like Greer removed from positions of responsibility all across the Deep Zone. We have to hold the DZ together until we can grow stronger, more self-sufficient and independent." Time—he just needed time.

While Naridar remained at attention in front of the desk, the General got up and paced his office, listening. Adolphus's mind spun with all the crises that had to be dealt with. "I can defend against the Army of the Constellation—I know how to do that. But if the Ro-Xayans come to bombard this planet, as Encix insists, I'll have a whole new problem to solve. How can I fight incoming asteroids, like the ones that destroyed Candela?" He shook his head. "I wish I had more men like you, Captain Naridar. It would make my job easier."

The veteran stood before him, straight-backed, expressionless. "There are plenty like me, sir, and we're all loyal to you. You have more of us than you realize."

16

The Urvanciks' last run to Hossetea had been unpleasant, thanks to the simmering and angry population, but Turlo and Sunitha were much more tense now as they sneaked a team of shadow-Xayans into the Crown Jewels.

"I told you a linerunner's life would be exciting, my dear," Turlo said to his wife.

"I believe you said the exact opposite," she replied, "but this is the way it turned out." The couple huddled together, sharing warmth inside the dim confines of a modified downbox, a sealed cargo container that also held the rest of their infiltrators.

"We can always use our telemancy if it is necessary," Tryn-Clovis said. "Don't underestimate our abilities, but we do not wish to draw attention to ourselves."

Though they couldn't see anything outside, the downbox shuddered as it dropped away from the holding clamp on the hauler framework, and Turlo felt the walls shift as he readjusted his perception of "down." Two of the shadow-Xayans muttered in surprise, but the rest sat quietly, waiting.

"Don't worry. Exactly as expected," Turlo said. "We're in the hands of gravity now."

As they dropped into lower orbit and rapid insertion into Sonjeera's atmosphere, they were falling blind, but Turlo knew what was happening. He had the schedule, and he had made his contacts. He would have to trust the General's loyalists who still remained on the capital world, keeping a low profile but maintaining secret lines of communication.

"Stuck in a falling box with you," Sunitha said to her

husband with a forced smile. "I suppose there are worse places."

He didn't ask her to name one.

—⁓—

After accepting the covert mission from General Adolphus, Turlo and Sunitha had discussed the plan with Tryn-Clovis, as well as Keana Duchenet. Keana had given them insights into the underground network beneath the Sonjeera spaceport, but Adolphus's loyalists working in and around the spaceport would also be able to provide more up-to-date information as soon as the team managed to get to the surface.

Tryn-Clovis had already selected fifteen of his fellow converts to join him on the mission to retrieve the residue of Zairic and Cippiq. The powerful shadow-Xayan held a flood of memories and revelations from the two alien lives inside him, and Turlo had slipped secretly into Sonjeera many times. He and Sunitha knew how to get to the spaceport, and the shadow-Xayans' unexpected telemancy powers should give them a tactical advantage. Even so, the Urvanciks did not underestimate how difficult it would be to infiltrate the quarantined spaceport hangar.

"Just getting to the capital will be a challenge," Turlo had explained to the silent, confident group at the Ankor complex on Hellhole, "but my wife and I have done that before. Once we get you to Sonjeera, it'll be up to your team to do what's necessary at the quarantined hangar."

Tryn-Clovis did not have a shred of doubt in his voice. "We'll do it."

Their linerunner ship, the *Kerris*, had flown from the

Hellhole hub out to the quiet DZ world of Nielad, where occasional ships still went back and forth into the Crown Jewels, trading black-market products and engaging in a few humanitarian missions. At Nielad, the strange passengers transferred to a specially equipped downbox marked as nondescript cargo, which was then loaded aboard one of the illicit stringline haulers. The hauler had switched to the old Constellation network and headed off toward the bustling confusion of the Sonjeera hub.

With the Urvanciks' secret connections in the giant stringline hub and commercial nexus, it took little effort for the right person to change a few records, alter a schedule, and add one particular unmarked downbox for a scheduled drop down to the main Sonjeera spaceport. . . .

Now the Urvanciks and the shadow-Xayan team huddled inside the insulated shipping container. They fell toward the surface, listening to the outside rumble of atmosphere during their controlled fall.

"It'll be a short flight," Turlo said.

Sunitha squeezed his hand. "The log marks this as an empty box waiting to be filled with outbound cargo," she explained to the team, although they had already gone over the details. "We've found an insider down there with up-to-date information on the setup. Someone should meet it on the ground to let us out and guide us to where we need to be."

"If the right person is on the dock schedule," Turlo said.

"We will manage," said Tryn-Clovis.

The downbox had an interior coated with a special organic film that exuded breathable oxygen from dense cells, an experimental design that would have allowed the shipment of live items under normal commercial circumstances. The advantage of the film was that it did not produce the energy signature of traditional life-support systems, so it would attract no attention.

Sunitha sniffed the sour air, made a face. "I'll be glad to be out of here." The downbox rumbled and vibrated as it was buffeted in the atmosphere.

"We've been in confined places before," Turlo said, then leaned over to kiss her on the lips.

"Our danger will come after we land and the downbox is opened," said Nico-S'blek, one of the shadow-Xayans.

Tryn-Clovis emerged from his own thoughts. "And then I can fulfill my revelation. The residue of our great leaders will be a catalyst to push us to *ala'ru* much sooner than expected."

"First we have to get into the hangar," Turlo cautioned. He already had plans in motion, contacts to make, and Sunitha would acquire secret details of the spaceport. He began to think they might have a chance.

Finally, decelerators kicked in, and all the hidden passengers held on as the container slowed on approach to the paved landing zone. The container came to a rest, and the background noises of atmosphere fell silent, eventually replaced by the sounds of a lifter that grabbed the downbox and placed it on a conveyor. The container lurched and swayed as it was moved.

"We're being taken across the landing field," Sunitha said. "We'll know soon where we are . . . and if we're in big trouble."

When the conveyor stopped, they felt the downbox shift as it was off-loaded. Turlo heard muffled voices outside, then the dwindling sound of an engine as the conveyor departed.

"I hope we see a friendly face when the downbox opens," muttered one of the shadow-Xayans.

Turlo and Sunitha both sat anxiously, breathing heavily, holding hands. Tryn-Clovis had his eyes closed, meditating, apparently reaching out with his telemancy. "I think we have succeeded . . . at least, in this part of the plan."

Yet more than an hour passed, which only increased their tension. Turlo didn't know how long they needed to wait. The downbox should have been greeted immediately by one of the General's operatives. Since there were no windows, he couldn't see a thing outside, didn't even know what the local time was, whether it was night or day. If they had to make their escape, slip out into the city and lie low while they reformulated their plans, Turlo didn't know if he had the proper contacts.

Tryn-Clovis continued to stare into an indeterminate distance, as if frozen in time and space.

Finally, the sound of a latch mechanism echoed through the container walls, and a small personnel door opened. Turlo took a deep, agitated breath, held Sunitha close, and stared into the bright light and at the single silhouetted figure there.

To his relief, he recognized Epson Jacobi, a classmate from pilot school. Jacobi had been living on Sonjeera as a deep-cover operative, one of the General's loyalists. He spoke in a low, urgent voice. "This way—hurry!"

Outside, dusk had fallen, and a forest of garish lights illuminated the spaceport complex. Ducking low, the group scurried out of the downbox, stretching stiff legs, taking cover in shadows wherever they could. Jacobi guided them in a serpentine course around heavy machinery.

Across the field, troops and vehicles were being loaded onto military shuttles. When Turlo paused to stare at the big operation, Jacobi explained, "Commodore Hallholme is massing yet another fleet for a new assault on the Deep Zone. He's got some secret plan."

The news alarmed Turlo and Sunitha, but Tryn-Clovis remained focused. "We cannot concern ourselves with that now. We must complete our own mission in time to make a difference."

They hurried a short distance into a small, dark admin building, and then Jacobi took them down a stairway to a hidden chamber. A hatch above them closed, and Jacobi flipped on a screen that showed multiple images of the broad spaceport, including the large military force being loaded and launched into orbit. Another screen showed images from orbit, which displayed nearly full military stringline haulers up near the stringline hub.

Tryn-Clovis said, "Since the quarantined hangar was once a busy spaceport building, there must have been numerous means of access. They can't all have been sealed."

"I wouldn't recommend it, but that's not my business," Jacobi said. "I've done my part by getting you here and digging up all the detailed information you could possibly need. Now, I need to slip away to maintain my cover. The rest is up to you."

"That's all we need," Turlo said. "Thank you."

"I still think you're crazy, but if the General says it's important, I won't question his judgment."

"It is vital," said Tryn-Clovis. "Our race's destiny depends on it."

After giving the shadow-Xayans an odd look, Jacobi left them with files and a blueprint that depicted the locations of spaceport buildings, as well as a network of passageways that ran beneath the complex. A detailed list of security measures and checks had also been included, so the team could make their precise plans. Everything within the vicinity of the contaminated hangar had been sealed off, but Tryn-Clovis did not seem concerned. He reassured Turlo and Sunitha, "With our telemancy, our team will do what the Diadem considers impossible and undo the damage she has caused."

"Yes, the old bitch caused a lot of damage," Sunitha said.

Turlo gave a suspicious glance toward the images of the busy attack fleet being assembled in orbit. "One other good thing—with Diadem Michella so preoccupied with that new military operation, she'll never expect us right underneath her nose."

17

Two thirds of Percival's invasion force was loaded and ready to go, but the ships remained in orbit above Aeroc, where the General's spies were not likely to see the preparations for the massive launch. When Percival was prepared to launch, his entire fleet would rush to the Sonjeera hub, transfer to the Tehila line, and race out into the Deep Zone before anyone could figure out where the Commodore was going. He didn't dare give his enemy a chance to prepare for the surprise attack through a vulnerable back door.

His flagship's systems had been overhauled or replaced, ready for the next military engagement. All of the ships he had brought home after his previous embarrassing defeat at Hellhole were ready for combat, even against the General's mysterious and powerful alien allies.

Constellation weapons scientists studied the battle damage inflicted by the Hellhole aliens and did their best to concoct defenses against them. The burst of mental powers had melted and fused every weapon system, similar to the blast that had struck the Sonjeera stringline hub.

The damaged scanning systems in the Commodore's surviving ships, as well as records from the aftermath of the hub disaster, had revealed trace data about the alien energy pulses—a sort of electronic DNA that was left behind. Percival did not understand it, nor did he need to. The engineers worked frantically in postmortem analysis to protect the vital, vulnerable components. The new firing systems synchronized the protective shielding with microsecond gaps that would allow the captains to fire their offensive weapons.

But the shields had not yet been tested in battle against the real exotic enemy. Optimism was not proof.

Sitting in his headquarters office at the military yards on Aeroc, Percival perked up when Duff Adkins arrived to issue his report. He was always glad to see his adjutant and friend. They had served together for years, retired to Qiorfu, and settled into comfortable lives; neither man had ever dreamed of being called back into service, but when the Diadem coerced the Commodore into carrying the battle standard again, Duff did not hesitate before joining him. Many assumed the Commodore merely wanted to recapture lost glory, but he had never been at peace with how he'd won that first war against Adolphus, years ago.

Percival skimmed the data summary Duff handed him, but knew that if his adjutant had given a stamp of approval, he had nothing to worry about. On orders from Lord Riomini, many reserve military ships had been withdrawn from the Crown Jewels and reassembled at the Sonjeera hub "for added defense," and they now waited for the rest of the fleet to arrive, as soon as they received the green light from the Tehila administrator. If all went according to plan, the entire outbound fleet would tarry at the stringline hub for no more than an hour. No spy would have a chance to send a warning to Adolphus in time.

For now, they just waited and stewed until word came that the Tehila purge had been successful and that both stringline terminus rings were secure. "We need to be ready to launch on a moment's notice."

"We are, Commodore." Adkins stepped closer to Percival's desk. "Do you believe Administrator Reming can succeed, sir? If his coup fails, we could lose everything."

"If we lose that chance, we look for another one. There'll be other weak spots in the DZ." He let out a heavy sigh. "I don't have to tell you that I am weary of this. If Escobar weren't being held prisoner, I'd simply let the Diadem and Lord Riomini fight their own battles against General Adolphus."

Adkins raised his eyebrows. "I've never known you to give up on a fight."

"It's not a fight I would have provoked in the first place. This mess was unnecessary. Though he's my enemy, General Adolphus has a particular sense of honor, and I can respect that. As for the Diadem and the Black Lord . . ." He shook his head. "They don't operate on the same principles as you and I do." Percival wasn't normally so incautious; perhaps he didn't care anymore.

He remembered how he had looked forward to facing Adolphus at the outset of the first rebellion. Incensed that the man wanted to destroy the Constellation's natural order, Percival had seen the General as a worthy opponent, but one to be defeated. During the war he had treasured each well-deserved medal as he received it . . . but not the last one. That medal held different significance.

The Diadem had forced Percival to shatter his own sense of honor, commanding him to use reprehensible tactics to defeat the rebels at all costs. And Percival had achieved that victory, but it was a Pyrrhic one. He had defeated himself at the same time.

Worse, the Diadem congratulated him, put him on a pedestal, named him a great war hero without ever acknowledging the moral price he had paid. In fact, judging by her attitude, Michella had lost no sleep over it.

And after exiling the defeated General, the Diadem broke her word again, sabotaging shipments, contaminating food supplies, damaging equipment that Adolphus and his colonists desperately needed to survive. Percival had tried to make up for that by secretly sending cargo containers with the things the General needed most. If Michella ever found out what her own Commodore had done, she would no doubt execute him in a petulant rage. . . .

Adkins touched his earadio and scanned down to new information on his data screen. "Six more battle-ready warships just arrived by stringline, sir. Four from planet Sandusky, two from Ogg."

Shaken out of his reverie, Percival said, "Have them loaded aboard the stringline hauler." He glanced at the chronometer. "I'm returning to my barracks quarters for the time being. I need to prepare my uniform."

—◆◆◆—

Commodore Hallholme could have had a palatial officer's residence, but he'd requested standard quarters, nothing spacious or fancy, because he didn't want to feel at home. He had to promise himself this assignment was only temporary.

When he'd transferred to Aeroc, he had brought his old uniform, despite its wear and tear. It was a proud reminder of his glory days, and when he donned it again now, the garment made him think of possibilities, but also of failures.

When Lord Riomini led his punitive operation to Theser, he'd been so proud to show off the destruction he'd caused, obliterating an entire rebel colony world just to make a point—and it was more than just a warning to the rest of the Deep Zone rebels. Unrest was growing in the Crown Jewels as well, and Riomini's ruthless attack on Theser served as a subtle warning to the Crown Jewel citizens, should they consider expressing their discontent.

And Percival was supposed to support such people? He sighed. He was honor-bound to defeat General Adolphus and reassert control, free the thousands of prisoners he held, and save his son. He knew Escobar had gotten in over his head, so Percival had to do everything he possibly could to bring the younger man home. *That* was his real incentive for defeating General Adolphus.

Percival pulled on his old uniform jacket, straightened it, and regarded himself in the mirror. The Constellation outfit didn't look as good as it once had, but he would wear it anyway.

18

Lord Riomini rode as a passenger in a military whirler piloted by one of his black-uniformed female guards. He heard the soft purr of the craft as it hovered over a private landing field behind the old Adolphus manor house. It wasn't the real reason he had come to this planet, but it certainly made an acceptable excuse. He was the strong and supportive uncle standing by his poor grieving grandniece whose husband had been captured by the enemy. Elaine believed his sincere words, the comforting promises. Riomini was good at that.

He'd come to Qiorfu to attend to business at the nearby Lubis Plain industrial zone, but first he would make a show of visiting Elaine, the wife—not yet widow, alas—of Redcom Escobar Hallholme, who had so badly messed up the retaliatory strike on planet Hellhole. It was a social obligation, but an important one. He had to console her about her fool husband, who remained one of General Adolphus's prisoners of war. No one would imagine the real, secret plans the Black Lord was developing on Qiorfu.

His grandniece and her two sons would not want to hear about Escobar's utter failure, but would instead keep viewing him as a hero. Riomini would protect them from the truth. When planet Hallholme was recaptured, he doubted the Redcom would survive the engagement.

Elaine met Riomini on the flagstone patio of the old mansion, part of which dated back more than two thousand years. Until the end of the last rebellion, Qiorfu had been the homeworld of the Adolphus family, but the planet had been awarded to Commodore Hallholme after the victory.

Tall and elegant, Elaine crossed the patio and greeted her granduncle. She had secured her black hair with a golden clasp shaped like the Hallholme family shield. She had been sitting underneath an umbrella, watching her two sons play a game with luminous balls rolled across an obstacle course on the groundcover. Behind her, a female servant stood by a hedge, watching the boys.

He noticed that Elaine's eyes were red. She appeared to have been crying as she sat alone, so he would have to console her. That was to be expected. "Now, my dear, you must hold out hope. We haven't yet been able to rescue your husband, but we have every reason to believe Escobar is still alive."

She rubbed her eyes. "As a prisoner of war! He'll probably be used as a hostage, too." She looked up at the boys scampering across the lawn after the glowing spheres. "I haven't told Emil or Coram the awful truth yet. They still expect their father to come back triumphant at the head of the fleet any day now."

"That may still happen," Riomini lied. "General Adolphus is holding thousands of our soldiers prisoner, but the Commodore insists that he can get them back."

"If anybody can do it, my father-in-law can. I have faith in him."

"We all do," Riomini said.

He stared beyond an olive grove to an expanse of flat land in the distance. The Lubis Plain shipyards had once held a mothballed military fleet from the first rebellion, but recently Riomini had expanded the industrial facilities. Now he was using them for something very different.

Noticing him, the boys discarded the spheres and came running over. "Uncle Selik!" cried eleven-year-old Emil.

His brother, two years younger, was just as tall. "Did

you bring our Daddy home with you?" Coram looked around, disappointed not to see Escobar.

Selik and Elaine exchanged glances. He said, "Your father is still far away, at war. But don't worry, we'll bring him home safely."

"He'll win." Coram sounded certain.

Emil flushed. "That General Adolphus is a monster."

Riomini couldn't stop himself from smiling. "Yes, he is. Your father has been captured, but he'll be taken care of until we can rescue him."

Elaine glared at him for telling the boys even that much.

The Black Lord wasn't worried about what she thought, or about her husband's welfare. He was far more concerned about Escobar letting all those Constellation warships fall into enemy hands than about the loss of one blundering officer. He was also angry that his special operative, Gail Carrington, had not completed *her* mission of eliminating Redcom Hallholme if he should fail. Riomini had never known Carrington to let him down.

He smiled at the boys, belying his inner thoughts. "I want you both to be brave and help take care of your mother until we can bring your father home. Will you do that for me?"

Emil nodded, but Coram looked confused and lost. Riomini decided he had stayed just long enough to convince his grandniece that he was concerned for her well-being, then he made his excuses to go.

His pilot was waiting for him in the whirler, and they rose into the air, spiraling away from the manor house, heading toward the Lubis Plain industrial zone.

The landing fields there were entirely under his control, and they now served as part of a huge secret operation he ran concurrently with the official expansion

of the Army of the Constellation. Years ago, the Riomini family had funded the creation of the military
force, and as soon as he succeeded Michella Duchenet
as the next Diadem—a foregone conclusion, he knew—
all the military operations in the Constellation would
be his to use as he saw fit. In the meantime, Riomini
had made his own plans, as insurance.

When the whirler set down on one of the secure
paved fields in the industrial complex, Riomini stepped
out to meet ten of his black-garbed guards, all female
and all deadly. A short, lean woman saluted. "My Lord,
the facilities are ready for your inspection." With a narrow face and auburn hair tied back in a tight bun, Rota
Vindahl was only in her mid-twenties, but her loyalty
and fighting skills were so significant that he'd made her
the guard commander.

Riomini followed the group toward the squat, windowless factory buildings and the handful of military
and commercial aircraft parked on the landing field. As
far as an outsider could see, this was a maintenance
facility for spacefaring ships, but the Lubis Plain operations had a far greater purpose than that. Over the past
year, Riomini had covertly bankrolled the construction
of many more warships in vast underground hangars,
where they were hidden from Michella's nosy inspectors. The clandestine fleet was *his* to control.

A wide platform lowered the entire group down
into the ground. The lift took him past level after level
of stored military vessels in subterranean hangars.
Uniformed Riomini workers bustled about on every level,
servicing ships, testing engines, installing weapon
charges. There were small fighter craft, armed security
ships, patrol vessels, shuttles, stringline drones, and
remote-operated launchers. High bays held transports,
destroyers, cruisers, frigates, and sweepers; even deeper

underground were heavily armored cargo ships, weapons platforms, and battleships. This clandestine fleet was his private military force, far more powerful than anything he needed to defend his holdings.

He spent hours now absorbing the immensity of his military force, walking past ship after ship. Finally he instructed his escort to take him to see the fast-attack fighter ships closer up, even asking to be an observer in a test flight, so that he could fly in one during a practice run. Pleased and satisfied with the progress he was seeing so far, Riomini couldn't stop smiling.

But he still felt a deep resentment for being forced to create this fleet in the first place. Diadem Michella should have retired years ago, should have allowed him to take the Star Throne while she faded into graceful obscurity. But the old crone refused to admit her own mortality and would not name him her heir apparent, and that had fostered dangerous, widespread doubts about succession. If he was forced to reveal this powerful fleet, though, then all doubts would be erased.

Michella had slapped him down, showing her cruelty by forcing him to watch as she immolated an earlier team of his female commandos. He had defied her orders by trying to break into the quarantined hangar so his experts could study the preserved alien corpses. It was a vital step in developing defenses against further exotic attacks, but Michella had been too terrified to take the risk. She was irrational. She was no longer fit to lead the Constellation.

Lord Riomini could not allow that woman to keep making such serious mistakes. He had to take decisive action of his own, for the good of the Constellation—and now he had the fleet to accomplish anything he wanted.

19

It was a huge celebration in Council City, though arranged so hastily that all the customary banners and gala decorations looked haphazard. Michella had called for the sudden festival, a wild and patriotic commemoration, and the people accepted her whims. The old Diadem loved her shows, Ishop knew, but this one seemed more capricious than usual—an extravagant, even outlandish celebration of an old obscure victory by Commodore Hallholme at planet Indos. The engagement had been a relatively minor one in the old rebellion, and the people were somewhat baffled by the need for an unexpected commemoration. Still, no one would argue when Michella Duchenet commanded a new worldwide holiday and an outpouring of patriotism.

To Ishop, it seemed a poor excuse. Michella had to have her pomp, but at least she was careful not to reveal the true reason for the spectacle. General Adolphus and his hidden supporters here on Sonjeera could not be allowed to suspect this was a de facto sendoff for the Commodore's latest attack.

Just ten hours ago, in the middle of the night, a secret courier drone had arrived bearing the announcement that the purge of Tehila was successful. The Deep Zone planetary administrator had secured both terminus rings and now controlled both stringlines—the one from Sonjeera, and the other that ran to Hellhole. An immediate announcement had also been sent to Aeroc, where the Commodore's fleet was gathered, just waiting for their instructions.

Percival Hallholme would already be on his way. At the Sonjeera hub, he would load up all the other military vessels assembled there under the excuse of "added security," then without delay his fleet would launch out to Tehila, where he would set up a forward base of military operations.

The Diadem could not restrain her excitement, but at least she restrained herself from making an ill-advised public announcement about Tehila. Even so, Michella would not deny her people a morale-boosting (and distracting, Ishop thought) celebration, even if the public didn't know the real reason for it. All around him, the mood was joyous, patriotic. Bands played the exuberant "Strike Fast, Strike Hard!" march incessantly. Ishop didn't think he could stand to hear any more of it.

In contrast to the high spirits around him, Ishop remained in a dark, edgy mood. He had no patience for the gaiety, preoccupied because he hadn't received any word from Laderna. Ishop would much rather be celebrating the death of the Diadem's sister! But Laderna had been on Sandusky for days, sending him no message whatsoever. She was normally more efficient than that, and she had never previously failed any assignment he'd given her.

Now, in the midst of the loud, garish, and colorful parade, Ishop was forced to ride beside the old Diadem. They sat together in an ornate carriage as they passed through the cheering throngs. At another time, he would have considered it an honor that Michella chose him to accompany her, for all to see, but now he saw it as a burden. Any honors she bestowed on him were mere crumbs compared to the lavish rewards that he truly deserved.

With misplaced, and unappreciated, generosity, Michella had given him a white-and-blue uniform decorated with phony military medals. "I am officially appointing you my Aide-in-Chief, Ishop. It is a well-respected position. Congratulations."

He had scrutinized the uniform. "Is this a position reserved for a nobleman?" He had been serving as her top aide for years, although he'd never been given a formal designation for what he did.

"It is a new position," she said with a sniff. "The details are still being defined."

In a way, this foppish uniform and meaningless bric-a-brac served the opposite purpose of what she intended; Ishop feared it would only subject him to ridicule from his fellow nobles.

Why was she giving him another apartment, an absurdly ostentatious uniform, and a new title? Were those signs that she felt a twinge of guilt at how she'd been treating him? And if so, did those meaningless rewards make up for denying him his noble heritage? Of course not.

She patted him with her gnarled hands, which reminded him of reptiles. "My way of keeping you satisfied, dear Ishop . . . and keeping you close." She watched him closely, and he schooled his expression, keeping it blank. But what did she mean by that?

With cheering crowds lining the way, the state carriage left Heart Square and made its way along a circuitous route. Michella waved, while Ishop tried to melt back into the seat. He had once saved this woman from an assassin's bomb during a similar carriage ride. She had thanked him then, too, patting him on the head, granting him a few baubles to show her appreciation. Like a puppy that had done a trick.

If Michella had an inkling of his deep hatred, how much he wished he could kill her, her heart might simply shrivel up and stop beating. She glanced at him now, saw the hard smile on his face, and undoubtedly took it as a good sign before turning to wave at the crowds who didn't even know exactly what they were celebrating.

Soon, Ishop knew that he and Laderna would hold their own celebration, finishing their list at last. He knew the resourceful girl would figure out a spectacular death for Haveeda Duchenet, and he couldn't wait to hear the details. He wished he could have been there at her side, but that would have caused·far too many logistical problems, and Ishop had to keep himself studiously separate. Even so, he managed a small smile to himself.

No, Ishop had not acquired the expected noble title and properties that were his due, but at least he had the satisfaction of revenge against all those who had harmed his family long ago. And in the process, he'd grown quite close to Laderna. Yes, she was a most worthy assistant, a good partner, a team member in his most exclusive team. When she returned from her last mission, he decided he had to find some way to show Laderna how much he valued her . . . unlike the way Michella treated him.

When the formal procession reached the Sonjeera spaceport for departure to the stringline hub, Ishop saw even more people crowded in cordoned-off areas. He knew the old hag intended to go up and board the Commodore's flagship so she could give the fleet an appropriate sendoff. Ishop also thought she would insist that he accompany her up to orbit. She probably thought he would appreciate basking in her reflected glory.

But Michella seemed . . . off, as if she expected something from him. Furtive glances, flickers of anger, a questioning lift of an eyebrow. What scheme did she have up her sleeve now?

Thanks to massive round-the-clock work, the giant stringline hub had been repaired after the alien attack that had resounded along the iperion line from Candela. Seventy percent of the facilities were back online now, and the gathered "additional defense" ships filled most of the available spots.

Michella stepped down from the ornate carriage and called, "Come, Ishop. People are watching. Stay in line." As he followed her toward the waiting shuttle, he knew the audience was looking at him, and he felt embarrassed and angry in his gaudy uniform. In his work, he preferred to remain unnoticed. He didn't like people paying attention to him.

When they finally boarded the shuttle and Diadem Michella ordered the access sealed behind them, a protected silence settled down on them. Ishop finally began to relax. He sat across the aisle from Michella and had to keep pretending that this was important to him, that he felt honored to be with her. She would want to chat with him during the flight up to orbit. He drew a deep breath, summoned his energy, and played his role.

Michella reached over to pat his arm with a clawlike hand. "You are a fine aide, Ishop. I doubt there has ever been another so loyal or so competent. I know you would never betray me."

He suppressed a shudder. "Thank you, Eminence. I always do my very best for you."

Her vulturelike eyes flashed. "A pity that you can't have a similarly reliable assistant. But that's too much to be expected." Suspicions and alarms immediately surfaced in his mind, but before he could ask what she meant, Michella handed him a film note. "I received this at breakfast. It's quite disturbing, but nothing for you to worry about. I'm certain you had nothing to do with it. The matter has already been taken care of."

Struggling to mask his reaction, forming a carefully sculpted look of surprise, he took the note from her. "My assistant, Eminence? I'm sure I don't know what you mean. She has taken some personal leave and I haven't seen her in several days."

Michella gave him a look that seemed to show that she didn't believe him for a moment. She kept chattering without letting him read the note. "Ishop, I don't hold it against you, but really you must choose your help more wisely in the future. You yourself saw how I dealt with Lord Riomini's guards who defied my absolute quarantine on the sealed spaceport hangar—I had to incinerate them alive, poor things. But a necessary lesson. The Black Lord knows the painful consequences of defying me."

"But . . . what does that have to do with Laderna Nell?" He felt a cold stone in his chest.

She *tsk*ed. "Your assistant was caught trespassing in a very sensitive area on Sandusky, carrying forged identity documents. If she told you she was taking personal time, it's a good thing we caught her. Apparently, you were duped. I never imagined you to be so easily fooled, Ishop."

Ishop stared down at the film note. Michella knew damned well she was no patsy. "I . . . had no idea, Eminence." His mind spun. Did Michella know?

"Of course you didn't."

And what about Haveeda? He had to protect himself. What kind of cat-and-mouse game was the old woman playing? "I will get to the bottom of this matter. Where is my assistant now? I wish to speak with her. I'll get the answers out of her—you know I will." Because it was expected, he forced himself to add, "I take full responsibility for her actions."

In a matter-of-fact tone, Michella said, "Oh, no need for you to do anything, Ishop. The woman has already been interrogated by Sandusky authorities."

As the shuttle lifted off with a roar, making them lurch in their seats, thoughts screamed inside his head. What should he say? What should he do? Had Laderna revealed anything? Looking at Michella, he thought he saw the cruel edge to her demeanor again, as if she knew full well how Ishop had been involved, and what Laderna had attempted to do to Haveeda. She was pushing him, testing him . . . torturing him.

He maintained perfect, precise control over his expression, but he could not keep his body from perspiring. He hoped she didn't notice.

Michella continued in a dismissive tone, "Alas, we'll never know. The foolish girl died during questioning. The Sandusky researchers used some very harsh biological agents in an attempt to pry information from her, and they weakened her so much that she had to be placed in quarantine, awaiting further interrogation. Before that could take place, she was exposed to a flesh-eating virus. Accidentally, of course. I'm afraid there isn't much left of her body, but I signed it over for their research purposes, so that she can be of some use."

She watched him, her eyes like scalpels. He felt a prickle of sweat on his brow. "I suppose that's for the best," he said. He was screaming inside.

"Yes, I suppose so. I'm certainly glad I didn't have to take measures against you. What happened to Lord Riomini's guards should be a lesson to you, too." Michella leaned back in her seat and closed her eyes, humming to herself. "Before you hire a new assistant, I will have my chief of staff make suggestions."

Ishop sat frozen in panic. For the first time in years, he felt utterly helpless. And alone.

Michella settled into her own seat. "We'll worry about that after the Commodore launches his fleet to Tehila. It'll be glorious."

20

For his entire adult life, Bolton Crais had been an officer in the Army of the Constellation, and by virtue of his noble birth he had always felt imbued with a sense of honor, a duty to be moral and trustworthy. Unfortunately, not all nobles held themselves to such a high standard.

After the initial defeat of General Adolphus, the Army of the Constellation had been nothing more than a place for gala military parades and routine patrols. Promotions were purchased with bribes or awarded on the basis of bloodlines. As a mere logistics officer, Bolton had never expected to shoulder the onerous responsibility of making life-or-death combat decisions.

Now, in the Hellhole prisoner-of-war camp, Bolton felt duty-bound to protect his fellow soldiers, including Redcom Escobar Hallholme. On several occasions during their abortive retaliatory mission, Bolton had seen the Redcom make unwise decisions. He'd given his advice, but if the Redcom chose to ignore the suggestions, he had to accept the will of his commanding officer.

For two days, Bolton had tried to convince the Redcom and the two other junior officers not to go through with their impulsive escape scheme, insisting that they had insufficient information to plan properly, no sense of the local geography or natural hazards, no equipment or weapons. But they would not be convinced, so he was forced to accept the idea. Since Redcom Hallholme intended to go, his logistics officer volunteered to do whatever he could to help. By observation and careful accounting, Bolton had quietly saved the man before.

Vingh and Yimidi were excited as they implemented

their plan with Redcom Hallholme, although Bolton doubted they could ever make their way across the unforgiving landscape to distant Michella Town, then seize a ship at the spaceport, and make their way via a roundabout stringline path back to Sonjeera. Bolton did not want to destroy their hope; instead, he needed to do everything possible to make the attempt succeed.

He only wished he could see Keana one more time. Maybe he could even talk her into helping him.

After breaking out of the camp and slipping past the sparse guards—the first obstacle they had to overcome— the four escapees planned to head overland, seeking a patch of wilderness where they hoped no one would follow. The other POWs had agreed to hide the absence of the escapees for as long as possible to give them a chance. Assuming that Hellhole itself provided a sufficient deterrent against foolish escape attempts, the General's guards did not take roll call but simply let the prisoners live in the camp until such time as they could either be returned home or assimilated into the Hellhole colony.

Escobar assumed they could make good time and be far from the camp before their absence was noted. The escapees would journey overland, keeping away from any established travel paths. Along the way, they might find a mining settlement or some other industrial oasis. As a man who liked to plan down to the last detail, Bolton felt uneasy about such a seat-of-the-pants scheme, especially on a hostile world, but Escobar's insistence replaced all other answers.

As they pooled their plans and assessed their skills, BluCap Agok Yimidi reminded everyone that he was an experienced technology officer. Previously, he had worked with Bolton to install the self-destruct virus in the captured retaliation fleet, which had destroyed many impounded Constellation vessels rather than let them fall into enemy hands. Yimidi had a special interest in stealth technology, and he managed to improvise some makeshift camouflage generators from available materials in the camp. Although Bolton was skeptical, Yimidi insisted that he could cobble together a crude stealth shield that would temporarily veil a Trakmaster, one of the colony's common overland vehicles. That would hide them from most searches unless trackers stumbled right on top of the stolen vehicle. Escobar convinced them that they had to take the chance.

It had been well past midnight when the four got under way. Slipping through the perimeter fencing proved relatively easy, after other prisoners kept the patrolling guards busy with a diversion. As the group sneaked off into the night, Escobar mocked the gullibility of the General's security; Bolton worried that the laxness signaled that the guards believed escaping into the wilderness was so obviously dangerous as to be completely absurd. He had a bad feeling about this venture.

The four men kept low to the ground, carrying supplies toward a parking compound where Trakmaster vehicles for Slickwater Springs were kept. The vehicles operated on reactive fuel pellets, and each one was already loaded with a month's supply, certainly enough to get them to Michella Town. Slipping through the shadows and selecting a vehicle at random, the four men loaded the stolen supplies, climbed aboard, and waited while Yimidi set up his makeshift camouflage system.

"It's not perfect, but the best I can do," Yimidi whispered to Bolton, as he connected a compact apparatus to the cab ceiling of the Trakmaster. "This should keep us from being detected by long-range scans."

"It might give us the advantage we need," Bolton said. He swung into the driver's seat, and Escobar climbed in beside him, activating the navigation system. Yimidi and Vingh scrambled into the back compartment. A devout man, Lt. Seyn Vingh took a few minutes to pray each day but joked that as a military officer in wartime, he was often forced to do it with one eye open. As Bolton started up the humming engine, he heard Vingh murmuring one of his prayers. Bolton prayed, too, that they could get far enough away from the camp before anyone came to investigate. He suspected someone would notice the missing Trakmaster sooner than any missing prisoners.

The heavy vehicle rolled forward slowly, crossed the boundary of the parking compound, and headed onto a paved road that connected the camp with Slickwater Springs. But Bolton swung off the well-traveled path and rolled out onto the open landscape, away from customary traffic patterns.

Inside the cab, Escobar called up options on the nav-screen and gave Bolton a heading, taking them farther from the road and the low lights of the camp and the much larger Slickwater Springs compound. Though the burly vehicle was designed for rugged terrain, the four passengers were jostled about as the Trakmaster crawled up a grade.

Ahead, through the light-enhancing night-goggles he'd found in the driver's compartment—since he didn't dare use bright running lights—Bolton studied the bleak and sterile landscape. The terrain was formed of ash and mud that piled up after the asteroid strike, and eroded into strange shapes by centuries of wind and rain.

The Trakmaster's database had a library of previously cataloged terrain images, which helped them chart their route. According to the data on the screen, Michella Town's spaceport was a long, hard distance away.

The vehicle rolled over knobby shrubs and wound down into a wide arroyo, where they would be hidden. The channel of the wash led them toward a sheer wall of exposed rock, but Escobar insisted that the nav-system showed a way through.

As Bolton drove into the darkness, his companions began to believe that they had gotten away after all. Bolton was sure, however, that the difficult part was just beginning.

Much of the terrain looked confusingly similar, but Escobar guided him into a side channel that widened and sent them toward the imposing escarpment. Before long, they reached the base of the wall of rock, with a cliff towering high overhead. Escobar studied the nav-system, then pointed to the right. "We can get through over there."

With his goggles, Bolton discerned a dark vertical line in the cliff, and headed toward it. The Trakmaster bumped over a pile of boulders and down the other side, reaching a half-hidden vertical defile.

"Is it safe to go through?" Vingh asked from the back compartment, though he could see little in the darkened vehicle.

By now, they had gone many kilometers from the fenced camp, and Bolton risked turning on the Trak-master's powerful headlights for the first time. Spears of light shone into the opening, revealing boulders on the ground and high, rough rock walls on either side. But the narrow slot looked passable.

"We have to go this way," Escobar insisted.

Bolton took a deep breath and rolled forward, hoping that the walls didn't close in farther down the de-file. In the back, Vingh and Yimidi slid open their side windows so they could look up at the sheer rock faces on either side.

Yimidi shone a spotlight up the cliff on his side. "Is that algae growing on the rock? Patches of yellow and black stuff, twitching and flowing. Look at it move! I think it's keeping pace with us."

"I don't like the sound of that," Bolton said.

"Increase our speed," Escobar said. "Don't stop until we're out of here."

"Close the windows," Bolton said. "Remember where we are."

The windows snicked shut, and the Trakmaster rumbled on while the escapees sat together in silence, the air thick with their shared trepidation. Yimidi shone a handlight through the window but could no longer see the flowing algae.

The heavy vehicle slid and shifted sideways as the tracks struggled to gain traction on uneven surfaces. Looking at the headlights in front of them, Bolton was astonished to see that the vehicle was rolling over a thick carpet of moving algae that gathered around them. Yimidi yelped, said that green ooze was seeping through the floorboard. He stomped on the algae, forcing it to retreat as if it could feel pain. "We need more speed!"

More of the strange growth seeped through the rear of the vehicle. Vingh and Escobar struggled to squash the algae wherever it oozed inside. Trying to accelerate, Bolton spotted a tongue of something slick and yellow crawl over the top of one of his boots in the cab; he shook it loose and stomped down with his free foot. The Trakmaster rocked and shook as he drove it through the defile, dodging the largest rocks. The boulders around them were all yellow and black with the slithering vegetation.

Algae began to cover the side windows, and some even seeped across the cab controls. He used the wiper blades to smear the growth from the windshield, but his visibility rapidly waned.

Escobar switched on an interior light and jabbed a knife blade into a small twitching growth, making it retreat through one of the cracks. In the rear, the other two men kept driving back the infestation. "Damn it!" Yimidi spat and squirmed. "Some of it sprayed in my mouth!"

Bolton shuddered, but kept driving through the defile as fast as he dared. The windshield became more and more opaque, until he could see through only a narrow opening, and he didn't dare open a side window to stick his head out and peer ahead. Tumbled boulders made the path even more of an obstacle course, and he tried to steer around them as best he could.

Even with no visibility, he had no choice but to keep going or the algae would engulf them as they rolled forward. Clinging to his nav-screen, Escobar helped by calling out compass directions, trying to keep them going. Bolton was afraid to slow down.

While Yimidi continued to wipe his mouth in disgust, Vingh asked, "Does this rig have a collision-avoidance system?"

As he asked, the vehicle slammed into a hard obstacle, but the thick algae offered some cushioning. Desperate, Bolton backed up and then sped around another boulder. Escobar flipped switches on the dashboard, until the nav-screen switched to a ghostly gray-green view, showing objects in front of them. "There! Follow the screen image."

Bolton did not argue. He increased speed, and in the nearly obscured glow of the headlights, he could make out the end of the long, narrow pass. Although he didn't know what lay on the other side—perhaps a cliff or a crevasse—he kept going. They had to get away from the algae. Reaching the end of the narrow defile, he slowed, then committed himself and accelerated.

To his great relief, the terrain opened up, letting him roll the Trakmaster downhill at a high speed. The vehicle finally exited the canyon, reaching a hard, rocky surface that was bumpy and uncomfortable, but better than the infested, claustrophobic defile. Thick algae began to slough off the vehicle, dropping away as if in surrender.

"We're not going back that way again," Vingh said. "We couldn't return to the camp if we wanted to."

"We don't want to," Escobar insisted.

Everyone concurred, but Bolton heard anxiety in their voices, as they all wondered what lay in store for them on their way to Michella Town and freedom.

21

In utter silence, bound by telemancy, the group of shadow-Xayans slid smoothly through the tunnels beneath the quarantined section of the Sonjeera spaceport. They followed Turlo and Sunitha, who carried their digital charts and navigated the commando team through the complex and deadly labyrinth.

All dressed in dark clothing, they wore face masks to protect against any poison booby traps the Diadem had likely left around the sealed hangar. Light enhancers gave Turlo a greenish view of the catacombs. The air down here was cold and clammy, saturated with a death-like stillness, and a musty, unpleasant odor. He didn't like this at all, but he and Sunitha couldn't go home until they had helped Tryn-Clovis accomplish his mission.

The shadow-Xayan team had well-coordinated

movements, and they followed Turlo's guidance without complaint. As they worked their way farther along under the spaceport, they grew more excited and intense. By now, they were approaching the resin-sealed hangar that had entombed the remains of Zairic and Cippiq and several long-dead converts.

With all the time they had spent on Hellhole with the Xayans, neither Turlo nor Sunitha were worried about "alien contamination." Rather, Turlo was far more concerned about the Diadem's traps and defensive measures. He knew Michella was desperate and prone to irrational, extreme reactions.

Sunitha followed close behind him, carrying an electronic blueprint provided by Keana Duchenet and annotated by the General's loyalist, although both of them had memorized this complex network of passageways. Moving ahead, the shadow-Xayans were giddy in their belief that the mission would be a success.

He could tell Sunitha was beginning to question what they were doing. Turlo knew that the Xayans—even in their human-hybrid forms—were so different that he could never fully understand them, or *trust* them. What if the shadow-Xayans had their own purposes? What if the goal of saving Hellhole was not at all their highest priority?

Turlo paused beneath the green illumination of a tunnel emergency light and gestured for the others to remain there while he crept around a corner. He felt a chill run down his spine, but saw nothing down the adjacent tunnel. Sunitha pressed close, gave him a quick nod, and the team moved forward again into an immense subterranean chamber. After Sunitha checked the electronic blueprint, Turlo shone a light upward to illuminate a large mark on the ceiling, a hardened plug that covered a hole.

"According to the records," he said to the shadow-Xayans, "the sealed hangar you're looking for is five stories above us, encased in resin, completely sealed. Lord Riomini's own team originally broke into this access tunnel, so the way is clear—at least for now."

Upon reading the summary, Turlo had been surprised that the Black Lord would send people in here against the Diadem's express orders, but he had been anxious to get tissue samples from the Xayans so his scientists could study them. Apparently, the Diadem's forces had captured Riomini's team here in the tunnels and then, irrationally terrified of alien contamination, she had incinerated the team—alive.

"We've all been around the shadow-Xayans and the slickwater. The whole idea of contamination is nonsense," Sunitha said.

"Not to Michella," said Turlo. He carefully studied the vital information Jacobi had provided, seeing that Michella had installed even more defensive fail-safes, poison booby traps, and possible explosives in the time since. Now he looked around uneasily, knowing the incredible risk they were all taking.

"We will take care of any traps with telemancy," Tryn-Clovis said.

Turlo sniffed and picked up the odor of something dead again. Maybe it was a premonition. . . .

Knowing how close they were to the entombed passenger pod, the shadow-Xayans were impatient to proceed. Tryn-Clovis stared upward with his spiraling eyes. "Step back out of the way." Phantom flares of illumination flitted around the convert's head, then a long blue blade of energy shot toward the sealed hole. He cut through the resin with his directed telemancy, and the solid plug fell to the floor and rolled against a wall. Tryn-Clovis nodded. "Now we have access."

Without speaking, the shadow-Xayan commandos raised themselves with telemancy, lifting their bodies up through the opening. Squiggles of energy snapped and burst in the air around them. Turlo felt a jerk on his body, and he and his wife were hauled upward, following the group.

They all gathered in a chamber on the next level up. Several shadow-Xayan commandos brought forth silvery metal balls, which hovered in the air. Tryn-Clovis gestured. "Send them in."

As if fired from a gun, the telemancy-propelled balls shot into the shaft overhead, whistling through the air. Ahead, Turlo heard sharp pops, followed by hissing sounds, and he protectively pushed Sunitha away. "I think they triggered the poison gas." Though he and his wife wore protective facemasks, he instinctively held his breath as white, filmy smoke exuded from the access tunnel and curled around the commando team. But the shadow-Xayans used their telemancy to push the gas away into the catacombs, where it dissipated harmlessly.

More metal balls sped into the tunnel, sweeping for additional booby traps, and spun in circles to slice through the resin plugs that filled the shafts. "Soon we will have full access," Tryn-Clovis announced. His energy was rising, but his tone gave no hint of impatience.

Before long, the access tunnel was entirely silent. The shadow-Xayans waited, looking to their leader.

To be sure, Turlo sent in a small robotic camera from his pack, which transmitted multiple screen images of the entire tunnel ahead. "It's clear." He realized he was breathing harder.

Using telemancy to propel himself, Tryn-Clovis floated into the access tunnel, followed by the rest of the shadow-Xayan team, while the two humans were drawn behind them. With powerful blasts of telemancy, the converts had shattered and cleared the blockades of resin that crowded the area.

Turlo and Sunitha emerged at last onto the floor of the quarantined hangar. There, he saw the silent and dark passenger pod.

Tryn-Clovis had already formed another blue blade of telemancy, which cut through additional layers of resin so they could enter the sealed passenger pod that held the bodies of the fallen Xayans. The debris fell away to reveal the interior of the pod.

Entering with silent awe, the team found the residue of the Original alien Cippiq, along with what remained of Fernando-Zairic and three other dead converts, as well as the lone human victim, Vincent Jeñet. Dissolving in death, Cippiq had oozed all over the deck of the pod, leaving only an imprint of his body and those of his companions.

Crouching, Tryn-Clovis dipped his hands into the still-moist alien residue, causing the shimmering ooze to glow. As if it had become alive, activated, the viscous liquid ran up his arms and quickly blanketed his body like an organic film. The shapes on the floor vanished as the residue quested outward like pseudopods until it became a thick, translucent layer over Clovis's entire body. The fluid seeped into his mouth, and when he spoke, his wavering voice sounded as if he were underwater.

"I have retrieved all that remains of Zairic and Cippiq, the preserved power they left trapped here. It is exactly as I envisioned—with the presence of these powerful telemancers, we have what we need to accelerate *ala'ru*!" His oddly alien voice was tinged with amazement. He lifted his arms, and the translucent ooze sloughed in different directions before clinging tighter to his body.

Turlo's skin crawled. Next to him, he saw Sunitha swallow hard.

"Zairic was always the strongest among us, the genius who first proposed our ascension, who created slickwater to preserve our race. He still knows how to draw together the racial memories and activate *all* the slickwater on Xaya, summon so many stored souls and make them rise up and *demand* to be resurrected. They will join with human hosts to increase our power in one final surge, and that will unleash the latent telemancy inside! There is no longer time to wait for full cooperation among the humans."

Turlo looked at Sunitha, feeling his concern grow. "This isn't what we expected."

As Tryn-Clovis spoke, part of his original personality manifested, and tears began to stream down his cheeks, visible beneath the strange membrane. "It is unfortunate that we have to do it this way, but from now on, humans will be *forced* to do what we need. All the latent minds will be awakened from the slickwater. For *ala'ru*!"

The alien eyes focused on Sunitha Urvancik in an eerie, spiraling gaze. The look frightened Turlo, but his wife suddenly had a beatific, mesmerized expression on her face.

Turlo also felt pulled toward Tryn-Clovis's spiraling eyes, but he found the strength to step in front of Sunitha, pushing her away. All the shadow-Xayan commandos stood together in rapt silence, drinking in the power that shimmered from their leader.

The preserved ooze glowed, as if awakening from a deep sleep—and suddenly it surged across the deck of the passenger pod in all directions, sweeping over the

Urvanciks and all the shadow-Xayans before they could move. Now engulfed, they continued to stand, but none of them had any voluntary impetus or thoughts.

Turlo was unable to move, no matter how much he struggled. Inside his mind, he saw the intense presence of Zairic manifesting in his imposing original Xayan body—and Cippiq as well, along with images of countless other Xayans, like a hall-of-mirrors, with the aliens interacting in their magnificent, long-lost civilization.

Next, he saw the faces of humans—Vincent Jenet, Fernando Neron, and his beloved wife, Sunitha, all gliding by slowly, gazing beatifically into the distance. He knew they felt the exciting, amazing potential of *ala'ru*. But it wasn't right.

He didn't like this at all! Struggling, Turlo tried to reach out for his wife, to touch her face, but she did not look at him. Then his wife and all of the other images faded away. Turlo was left feeling the deepest sadness imaginable.

The cacophony of alien lives grew louder around him, rising higher and higher. Fighting against the intrusion of raw sound, Turlo seized control of his thoughts and realized something very important—that there was a very dark side to *ala'ru*. It was not the glorious racial ascension that the Xayans had represented after all. Now he saw a hellish vision of what they'd been hiding, the huge-scale devastation they would blithely cause. *Ala'ru* was not anything magnificent at all. It had to be stopped!

But he couldn't fight it. The countless alien minds and lives condensed within the slickwater, stored and waiting, were finally unleashed. In a sudden and violent rush, the noises and voices swelled up until they overwhelmed his thoughts, engulfing him completely.

22

In orbit above glittering Sonjeera, Diadem Michella sat in the royal viewing area of the enormous stringline hub, where all her iperion lines intersected, and watched Commodore Hallholme's ships arrive from Aeroc. Two enormous military stringline haulers came in carrying the gigantic fleet, which the Commodore would use to seize Tehila.

The unscheduled arrival caused quite a stir, for such an overwhelming force took over much of the hub facilities. Employees, merchants, and visitors were even more astonished when the supposed defensive ships around Sonjeera immediately began to load themselves into the frameworks. With military precision, they aligned themselves to designated docking clamps. It was a perfectly coordinated operation—exactly as Michella had expected from Commodore Hallholme.

She felt energized, eager for the military stringline haulers to crush General Adolphus once and for all, so that she could return the recalcitrant Deep Zone worlds to her network. She intended to go aboard the flagship to give the Commodore her blessing, knowing he would appreciate it.

Waiting for the military hauler to finish its docking activities, Michella stood in the transfer terminal where she could see the orbital traffic. Ishop Heer paced before the large window plate as the giant haulers aligned themselves on the outbound iperion line. Ishop seemed to be avoiding her, as if he were agitated about something. She suspected he might have been up to something by sending his assistant to Sandusky, perhaps to gather some kind of blackmail information about Haveeda. Ishop would have been the mastermind behind the plan, of course, and the foolish girl was just his scape-goat.

Michella could not decide what Laderna Nell had been doing on Sandusky, how she had tracked down Haveeda, or why she had broken into the sealed chamber. The captive assistant had revealed absolutely nothing during even the harshest interrogation. Incredible loyalty.

Nevertheless, Michella thought she knew what Ishop had been up to. Somehow, he had learned of Haveeda's whereabouts, given his assistant instructions to spy so that he could use the knowledge of the Diadem's cryogenically frozen sister as a bargaining chip. For blackmail? Ishop was Michella's pet, and she had thrown him so many bones, but he was a natural schemer. He must have been trying to gain leverage to pry even more rewards from her. His abilities and resourcefulness made him invaluable to her, but now she would have to watch him more closely, keep him on a tighter leash.

Michella had known him for a long time, knew his schemes and his personality. He was not a man who allowed events to affect him, but the news of his assistant's unfortunate—and deserved—demise had obviously been a severe blow. Excellent. He needed a harsh lesson, as Selik Riomini had. Ishop would know better now.

It amused her to have thwarted him in this attempt to get more perks, but when people always wanted something from her, she found them irritating, such as Lord Riomini in his too-persistent quest to become the next Diadem. She sighed. Michella faced so many challenges as a ruler.

Instead of rejoicing in the launch of the Constellation fleet, Ishop seemed too upset to sit still. He didn't like to fail. She hadn't shown him the disturbing images of

Laderna—writhing, consumed by a flesh-eating virus while the Sandusky researchers watched and recorded her bodily degeneration—but she would. Then Ishop would learn his lesson, as Riomini had learned his. Neither of them would step out of line again.

Now, on to more important matters.

She could see only the front edge of the second military hauler, which was also ready for departure, all crew and supplies loaded aboard. When the docking bridge was secure, she strutted toward the access passage. "Come, Ishop. We will go aboard the flagship and bid the Commodore farewell. It will be a fine morale boost for his crew."

Refrains of "Strike Fast, Strike Hard!" played over the stationwide intercom—appropriate for the occasion, she supposed, but she was beginning to find the music tedious. Walking forward, she muttered, "Strike *successfully*—that's what matters most! I hope Commodore Hallholme doesn't let us down again. I want an end to this conflict—we must stop the General before he lets the aliens loose in the Crown Jewels! We barely averted disaster when they came here the first time." When her aide made only a noncommittal noise, she snapped, "Oh, Ishop, stop sulking."

"Yes, Eminence."

When she was escorted to the flagship's bridge, she allowed the Commodore to greet her. Ishop lingered behind her, but he knew his place and she wasn't concerned with him. "Commodore Hallholme, I have placed my hopes and my faith in you and all your brave crew. Now is the time to crush the evil rebel General and bring peace back to the Constellation."

The old Commodore bowed. "Yes, Eminence. I believe this operation has a high chance for success. The last defense ships are being loaded aboard the hauler and securing themselves to their docking clamps—fifteen minutes ahead of schedule."

"You are very efficient, Commodore." She gave him a sweet smile. "General Adolphus won't know what hit him."

Hallholme bowed again. "We can hope so, Eminence."

Through the large bridge screen she could see the curve of Sonjeera below with its mosaic of urban grids and sapphire oceans. The view changed as the stringline hauler positioned itself for departure out into the Deep Zone.

She was startled to receive a priority override signal on her private comm, the coded, high-security device she always kept with her. The signal was set to be triggered under only the most extreme circumstances, and now a holo display popped up in front of her eyes. Michella recoiled when she realized what the automated alarms signified.

The quarantine has been broken!

In horror, she watched the images from her implanted tunnel cameras that sent automated transmissions. Alarms indicated the resin had been shattered, the seals breached. Intruders had already gotten inside the quarantined hangar that held the alien bodies!

"Ishop!" she cried. At first she thought Lord Riomini had sent another commando team inside. He had already tried that once before, and she had burned his team alive, just to teach him a lesson. He wouldn't be so foolish as to try the same thing. Would he?

Then she saw the figures moving there, no one she recognized, a motley group of men and women with no consistent uniforms, no specialized equipment . . . and they used obvious mental powers! Levitating themselves, shattering barricades with telemancy. Michella gasped. They were possessed humans!

She felt sick and dizzy. She had deemed the deadly creatures and their possessed human companions too dangerous to be touched, too volatile to be moved. She had locked it all away, commanded that no one approach. And now a group of alien-possessed humans had broken inside. Despite all of her stringent precautions, Council City might already be contaminated!

Ishop came closer, sensing her panic. "What is it, Eminence?"

Commodore Hallholme immediately went on alert, appearing ready to act as soon as he understood the emergency.

She cursed, feeling panicked and helpless. "The quarantine—the alien contamination has been set loose!" What if it was already too late? The imagers picked up a stealthy party trying to infiltrate. They'd already broken into the resin-sealed hangar and were now inside the alien-infested passenger pod! She couldn't stop herself from gasping when she thought of the contamination getting loose, already oozing into the air, creeping out into the spaceport. Spreading across the city! All those millions of people! Yet, there might be no way to stop it now.

Reacting to the urgency in her voice, Ishop emerged from his petulant mood and understood what was happening. He had been beside her when the infected emissaries arrived at the Sonjeera spaceport, the ones who were intent on possessing *her* and all the people of the Crown Jewels. He knew the horrific dangers they posed just as well as she did. In fact, Ishop was the one who had reported Lord Riomini's previous attempt to break through the quarantine, so he definitely understood Michella's feelings.

"The silent alarm is coded directly to *me*," she said, realizing that many of the Commodore's bridge personnel were waiting for an explanation. "I installed additional security, as well as an extreme fail-safe system. I should have been warned sooner, but a series of outer alarms didn't go off. Our enemies must have sabotaged them somehow." She shook her head. "I see no recourse but to use the fail-safe system now. Contamination is already leaking out. There is no time to lose."

Ishop studied the flow of incoming images and swallowed hard. The intruders had broken into the sealed pod where the festering bodies had been entombed. His voice cracked with alarm. "We don't dare take any chances, Eminence! They've released what's trapped inside, and there's no telling how far or how fast it'll spread."

Her voice was hard and angry. All her blockades, her guards, the booby traps, the poisons . . . everything had failed. The intruders were actually *inside* the pod! "I will not let them contaminate Sonjeera. My security troops are responding, but they can't possibly be fast enough, or thorough enough. They'll be contaminated the moment they enter the zone."

Commodore Hallholme interrupted, "Eminence, does this emergency delay my mission? Is there something my forces should do?"

"No, prepare to depart immediately, Commodore. The danger may be even greater than I fear."

She knew the intruders could not be allowed to leave. She had no idea who they were or what they intended to do—but if they were already infected, *possessed*, they could destroy Sonjeera, the Crown Jewels, perhaps even the human race. Michella's mind raced. "We have to stop the wildfire from spreading—at all costs."

Commodore Hallholme strode across the bridge toward her, but she had to do this for herself. With a control link coded only to her, Michella called up the embedded flashpoint devices she had installed underground. She could not take half measures. She had to be a leader and make the proper decisions. No uncertainties, no chances taken.

The vaporization bombs would leave no doubt, and she didn't hesitate.

Before anyone could ask her to reconsider, Michella triggered the blast, and multiple warheads buried beneath the hangar ignited in a shock front as intense as a star core. The searing energy vaporized the hangar, most of the busy spaceport, and every speck of life for a kilometer around, including an industrial complex and a low-rent housing section of the capital city. Once the energy dissipated, nothing more than puddles of sterile glass would remain down there.

Even from orbit, she could see the bright flash. She gave Ishop a hard smile. "It's the only way to be sure."

The crew on the flagship's bridge gasped to see the blinding explosion from the spaceport, and magnifiers showed the expanding sphere of light like a sun going supernova. Alarms rang through the stringline hub; all space traffic was placed on emergency hold.

"You certainly took care of the problem," Ishop said. His tone was dismissive, even carrying a hint of sarcasm.

Hallholme was aghast. "Eminence, what have you done?"

Michella lifted her chin, aloof. "We couldn't afford the risk, Commodore. Those casualties are necessary sacrifices to protect us all. I won't underestimate how insidious those aliens are, and they were about to get loose."

Sonjeeran security sent an urgent message, demanding to speak to the Diadem, trying to affirm that Michella was safe. A blustering voice came from the bridge comm screen. "Commodore, we need to find the Diadem! There's been a huge explosion at the main Sonjeera spaceport. Possibly the work of terrorists, likely Deep Zone sympathizers. We are locking down the string-line hub."

Michella caught her breath. Yes, maybe she could blame it on terrorists. . . . No, that would dilute the importance of what she had done, how she had saved them all. The population would be stunned to learn the truth, but it was unavoidable. They had to know that they were saved, that *she* had saved them.

"No need for that," she said. "I am fully aware of what happened, and why." She turned to Hallholme. "Commodore, please allow me to address the stringline hub and all of Sonjeera. I have an important announcement."

Looking flustered and appalled, Hallholme snapped commands to his communications officer, who arranged for Michella to stand in the transmission field. The other bridge personnel looked confused and nervous, staring at the image of the still-expanding vaporization plume that was consuming the spaceport and part of the capital city.

Michella let herself show no anxiety, even though she had not yet decided what she would say. Her heart was beating hard as she realized just how close they had come to total disaster down there. If she had not acted in time . . .

When the comm officer nodded to her, Michella addressed all stations on the ground and in the hub complex for broadcast across the planet. She would also make sure that copies were carried throughout her worlds.

"As your Diadem I have ensured the safety of the Crown Jewels," she transmitted. "It was a terribly hard decision on my part, requiring the sacrifices of many who were unfortunately in the blast zone. But a group of unknown intruders breached the quarantined hangar down at the spaceport, and they were beginning to release the contamination we so carefully tried to contain. I had to be sure."

As she explained her actions, blithely assuming everyone would accept her claims, the bridge crew and the Commodore himself observed her with shock and disbelief, rather than the relief and admiration she expected. Michella ended her transmission with haughty confidence. "I only hope I acted swiftly enough. I command all Sonjeeran citizens to be especially vigilant to spot any strange behavior that might be a sign of alien contamination."

After she finished, she was perspiring, and her stomach was knotted. What if the aliens had already begun to possess the city? How long had they been loose down there? Ignoring all the people on the bridge staring at her, she turned to Ishop. "Perhaps it's best if I don't go back down to Sonjeera . . . at least not immediately. We don't know how insidious this could be. We'd better be sure."

She did not want to cause widespread panic. The vaporization of half the spaceport and a large section of the city was going to cause enough pandemonium. She chose what seemed to be the wisest course of action. "Commodore, we must not delay. If nothing else, the turmoil will be an additional diversion so that Adolphus loyalists won't have any idea where your fleet is going." She lifted her chin in what she considered a brave and determined gesture. "Our time has come. We must depart immediately—and I intend to accompany you to Tehila. I will be there in person to observe the operations for your historic conquest." In truth she didn't dare set foot back there until she was convinced the contamination had been sterilized in time.

The Commodore froze. "You're leaving Sonjeera in such a time of crisis?"

"It is a matter of priority. I can't be everywhere, and I choose to be present at the liberation of the Deep Zone. In the long run, that is far more important."

Hallholme muttered, "I doubt the populace will see it that way, Eminence."

"They will see it the way I tell them to see it." She gestured toward the helmsman. "Go on, send a signal to the hauler pilot. Let us be on our way—we have a planet to conquer!"

23

Pleased with the progress of his secret fleet, Lord Selik Riomini had awakened in a fine mood in the spacious guest quarters at the Lubis Plain industrial complex. His weapons system designers had been upbeat in their reports, the assembly supervisors announced that all was on schedule, and his stealth accountants had successfully hidden the giant drain of funding.

Yes, a perfect plan, a well-oiled machine . . . just as the Constellation would be when he ruled it. The Black Lord demanded excellence, and he received it.

Considering the insulting treatment Diadem Michella regularly poured on him, Riomini was not often in a cheerful mood, so he relished it now. He emerged from the guest residence smiling and went down the front stairs, still tasting the delicious seafood frittata on his lips. The primary ingredient had been bluecraw, a long-necked marine animal found in Qiorfu's remote lakes.

When his political and military affairs settled down, Riomini intended to make a fishing trip for bluecraw. He'd done that once before—a political operation, not a vacation; Riomini and one of his ambitious generals had spent a day spearing the creatures, and in the process he had cemented an important alliance.

On the grassy central commons, the compact Rota Vindahl greeted him with cool efficiency. The commander of his personal guard force stood next to Harlowe Konn, a beautiful and intelligent blonde, whom Vindahl had named number two. Riomini had taken Harlowe as a lover for a time, and she had been adequate, enough that he would consider it again. Each of these women was the combat equal of Gail Carrington, Riomini's former commander, who had been lost on Escobar Hallholme's disastrous mission. . . .

After both women saluted, Vindahl reported, "The lancer pilot is ready for you, sir. The aircraft has been checked and prepped for your test flight, as you ordered."

Still smiling, he accompanied the two women across the industrial site to a black boomerang-shaped aircraft with high-powered armaments on its undercarriage. When the test engines were humming, Riomini boarded through a lower hatch and climbed into the large hemispherical cockpit on top. Riomini slipped into a seat behind the pilot, a dark-skinned man in a uniform and cap. As the safety harnesses snapped into place, he told the pilot to take off.

"Yes, my Lord." The pilot nudged the engine controls, and the plane took off in a steep ascent, then circled sharply over the manufacturing and storage buildings of the complex. "Several of the older warehouses on the north end of Lubis Plain have been emptied for this demonstration, sir."

"I look forward to it." Riomini took pleasure in recalling that the structures had been built by the Adolphus family when they ruled Qiorfu. They would make good targets.

Per his instructions, the pilot swooped low over the buildings and launched a missile at one of them. The old warehouse exploded in flames, and the pilot didn't flinch as he swooped the aircraft to the right and destroyed a second building. Then, suddenly, he flipped the lancer upside down and streaked through the smoke and flames, before ascending at an extreme angle. At a high altitude, the flying wing flipped over and hurtled back toward the surface.

Pressed back into his seat, Riomini yelped in protest, but the restraints prevented him from moving. He hadn't been told about this!

Moments before the craft could crash, however, the pilot recovered smoothly and skimmed over the surface. His voice was calm. "Nothing to worry about, my Lord. Just demonstrating this aircraft's capabilities."

"Land this damn thing!" Riomini shouted. He had seen enough.

"Sir, I was instructed to show you the full range of this warcraft's capabilities. I'm the best test pilot in the force."

"*Test* pilot? I was told the lancer is a proven fighter craft, fully vetted and tested."

"No, my Lord—this is a *missile* lancer, not one of the smaller fighter lancers. I was given to understand you wanted to participate in a true test flight?"

Riomini did not want to look like a coward in front of the underling, nor would he allow himself to appear rattled. He forced his breathing into a calm rhythm. "Thank you, but this flight is over. I've got business to attend to."

"Yes, my Lord. I have to maintain speed." He swooped upward, circled, and dove back at a steep descent angle. Silently cursing, Riomini closed his eyes and held his breath. He hoped he wouldn't throw up.

The lancer touched the ground, and Riomini was about to breathe an agitated sigh of relief when he heard a loud scraping sound beneath the undercarriage. "Hold on, my Lord!" The pilot's voice held genuine alarm.

Riomini had no idea what he was supposed to hold on to, but the restraints folded even more tightly around him. He smelled something acrid burning, with fumes creeping into the hemispherical cockpit.

The lancer scraped across the landing field, and even through closed eyes Riomini saw bright flares of sparks that flew up as the craft skidded. Then a wave of flame washed over the cockpit, and smoke poured into the chamber. When Riomini dared to open his eyes, he saw the pilot slumped forward over the controls, not moving.

The aircraft finally screeched to a stop, and Riomini struggled to release his safety harness. As his eyes burned, he fought to remain conscious, and managed to crawl away from the flames and smoke. He made his way headfirst down the short interior stairway to the lower hatch. He pressed against the door, triggered the emergency release and pounded—but it wouldn't open.

Someone pushed him away with a firm grip and hammered a weapon against the controls, deactivating the interlocks. He couldn't see through the smoke, but he thought it must be the pilot. Flames were roiling all around. The hatch finally opened, and the other figure shoved him out into the open air. They tumbled together onto the pavement, and he realized it was Harlowe Konn. Somehow his deputy guard captain had gotten inside the cockpit. She grabbed Riomini and dragged him away from under the burning plane just before her uniform burst into flames.

A fire-response vehicle rolled up, and emergency workers in jumpsuits spilled out, directing a white foam onto Konn, who had fallen to the ground as the flames took hold of her uniform. She thrashed about while behind them, the lancer was fully engulfed in flames. Through the transparent cockpit bubble, Riomini could see the pilot still slumped over the controls. In seconds he was gone, consumed in fire.

Vindahl and a contingent of black-uniformed guards swarmed around Riomini and whisked him to safety. He cast a glance back at Harlowe Konn, who lay thrashing on the ground, but Vindahl kept him moving. "That was close, sir. Are you all right?"

He drew a deep breath. "I think so. I never asked for an experimental aircraft. Was that an attempt on my life? Was the craft sabotaged?"

"We will find out, my Lord."

Riomini managed a tight smile, considering how the other Lubis Plain personnel could be encouraged to spread stories among themselves about this episode, emphasizing his own bravery. He could use this tragedy to his advantage; it would strengthen group unity. It was a pity about the pilot, although the man was obviously incompetent despite his claims. If Konn survived her burns, she would never be the beauty she'd once been, but perhaps she could still be useful as a fighter.

Straight and formal, Vindahl issued a crisp report. "More urgent news, my Lord—another disaster on Sonjeera. One of your spies just arrived after commandeering a stringline ship. As soon as he reached the Qiorfu terminus ring, he transmitted an emergency report on high-security tightbeam."

Riomini brushed himself off, feeling his heart turn cold despite the minor burns on his hands. "Another disaster? What now?"

Showing no expression, Vindahl said, "Seven hours ago a terrible explosion obliterated most of the main Sonjeera spaceport and part of Council City. It was centered on the quarantine hangar containing the alien bodies."

Riomini was alarmed, and he could imagine a wave of sabotage and attacks across the Crown Jewels. Was General Adolphus moving against them? "What caused the explosion?"

Now Vindahl looked awkward. "Diadem Michella claimed responsibility for triggering the blast. Personally. She said it was to prevent the release of alien contamination."

Riomini blinked in surprise. He had not imagined the woman's paranoia would extend so far. "The people will tear her apart for that!"

"Perhaps she knows that, my Lord. The Diadem has fled Sonjeera, accompanying Commodore Hallholme on his flagship. She just . . . left with the fleet."

Riomini tried to absorb all that he had just heard, and then the implications dawned on him. This was not a disaster at all—it might prove to be the biggest opportunity in his life! He could not let this stand. For the good of the Constellation, he had to seize his chance.

He squared his shoulders. "Obviously, the Constellation needs a new leader, a competent one for a change."

It was time to make use of his clandestine fleet.

24

Hellhole's second spaceport was on the other side of the continent from Michella Town in a region rich in copper, iron, and tin. As his transport flyer circled for a landing over Ankor's main field, General Adolphus saw the tall stacks of metals-processing factories in the distance. Smoke from the foundries drifted into the pale, greenish sky. As the leader of this planet, he took a moment to recall all the work it had taken to build this gigantic complex, in secret, in order to achieve his grand plan to connect the entire Deep Zone.

He had accomplished the seemingly impossible, a grand vision that few people would even have attempted. But the details and the second- and third-order consequences threatened to crush him.

Keana-Uroa, four other shadow-Xayans, and the Original alien, Lodo, joined him aboard the craft. Two seats needed to be removed in the passenger compartment in order to accommodate the alien's caterpillarlike undercarriage.

With the converts' continued concern about the possibility of a sudden and unexpected asteroid bombardment from the Ro-Xayans, the General had increased interplanetary surveillance to the extent of his technological capability. While traditional observation satellites scanned the vicinity, and DZDF scout ships patrolled the system, the Xayans claimed they could provide even better tools. Adolphus would take every advantage he could get.

Lodo had developed new extremely high-resolution sensor packages by cobbling together components taken from artifacts in the deep museum vault. The technology had been developed long ago, when the doomed Xayans had watched the first asteroid smash into the planet.

As the flyer landed outside the main spaceport operations, the alien peered out the side window. "Even from here, I can sense the deep slickwater reservoir that runs beneath the surface. It resonates with power and lives."

Adolphus shook his head at the bad memory. "Upwelling slickwater has caused significant problems here already. The Ro-Xayan scout ships seemed particularly interested in this area when they flew overhead. I thought they were spying on our spaceport, but was slickwater the reason?"

Lodo spoke in his low, thrumming voice. "No, the other faction did not know about the existence of slickwater, but they remember this region from our golden age. Some of our most magnificent cities once stood here . . . and the Ro-Xayans destroyed them all. When I come back here, I feel only sadness to see that nothing remains of our glorious past . . . nothing but memories of long ago."

Adolphus saw the tall launching structures of the spaceport, the expansive landing areas, the nearby mines and smelting operations. Although not nearly as glorious as an exotic alien city, they served his purpose— and under other circumstances they would have been his crowning achievement. But freedom was not easy, and the fight was far from over. As the General, he could use his military skills to fight against the Constellation, but how could anyone fend off an asteroid impact . . . or more than one? He had to find a way.

At the spaceport, cargo upboxes and passenger shuttles ascended to the main stringline hub in orbit, where they would be dispatched to other Deep Zone worlds. Several years ago, when he had built the stringline hub, he'd hidden it from the Diadem's inspectors. But now that the Constellation knew of its existence, the hub was a dangerous, but unavoidable, point of vulnerability. He kept the orbiting facility well guarded, but the recent unrest on Hossetea had made him disperse his limited number of DZDF peacekeeping ships, hoping that would quiet any grumbles from other dissatisfied planets.

Which left the Hellhole hub less defended than he would have liked. It was like a delicate game of juggling sharp objects.

After they disembarked at Ankor, Adolphus led the group toward the main building, where Rendo Theris waited to greet him. The jittery, overwhelmed spaceport administrator looked more nervous than usual. "As you requested, sir, we've cancelled all shuttle and upbox launches so that you can position the new Xayan satellites. Other ships are docked at the stringline hub, waiting for us to clear the operations, and the last downbox landed half an hour ago." He shuffled his feet. "How long is this going to take? There's already a backlog in the schedule."

"An hour should be more than enough time for us to complete the launch," said Keana-Uroa.

Adolphus used a firm voice, reminding the man of the big picture. "You won't mind the delay, Mr. Theris, if these alien satellites spot an incoming asteroid."

The administrator groaned. "Yes, I suppose a planetary evacuation *would* cause a lot more scheduling problems." He looked around, glanced up at the sky. "Any sign of those mysterious ships? Are the Ro-Xayans still spying on us?"

Not long ago, the enemy aliens had sent swift ships that—they now knew—had seeded wilderness areas of the devastated planet with native but extinct life-forms.

The General couldn't understand why the alien faction would restore all those life-forms if they simply intended to destroy Hellhole again. He didn't intend to let them do that.

"As we approach *ala'ru*, our enemy will no longer content themselves with mere observation," Lodo said. "But with our satellites, we will be able to watch for *them*."

He glided over to the flyer's cargo hatch, accompanied by the shadow-Xayans. They removed a large parcel, using telemancy to help them lift the package. They unwrapped the protective layers to reveal a smooth, silvery polyhedron.

A young man emerged from the headquarters building to join them, Cristoph de Carre, dressed in a work uniform. He smiled at Lodo. "So you decided to put some of the relics into service after all."

Lodo's oversized eyes glistened. "I am pleased to find a use for them."

Cristoph shook the General's hand, then looked awkwardly at Keana, clearly reminded of how—in her previous life—she had been responsible for the downfall of his family. But both he and Keana had changed greatly, and by nature the young man was inclined to be forgiving. He turned to the shadow-Xayans who busied themselves in silence. "Can I help?"

Lodo gazed up at the sky. "We have all the help we need." The converts looked toward orbit, their humanoid eyes spiraling. The large parcel lifted from the ground to hover in the air by them, waiting.

"We can launch from right here," Lodo said. "We do not need other equipment."

The package opened by itself, and ten round white objects emerged to float in the air, while the shell dropped in pieces to the pavement. The white spheres spun to show the intricate tracery on the curved surfaces, like dense, folded snowflakes.

"With these, we can observe from all directions," Lodo said. "Other shadow-Xayans can view through them simultaneously and keep watch."

"They'll detect any threat from the Army of the Constellation as well?" Adolphus asked. "We have more enemies than just the Ro-Xayans."

Keana-Uroa nodded. "Yes, General, but even my mother will be the least of our concerns if the Ro-Xayans come against us."

Cristoph studied the glistening spheres. "They look too fragile to survive the stresses of a standard launch."

Lodo sounded amused. "This is not a standard launch."

The alien lifted his soft-fingered hands skyward, as did the shadow-Xayans. In smooth silence, with only the rushing sound of displaced air, the satellites streaked up through Hellhole's atmosphere, spreading out in different directions. Without engine exhaust or any chemical means of propulsion, they left no plumes trailing across the sky.

When the group of satellites had vanished high out of sight, the converts lowered their hands. From the flyer's open cargo hold, Lodo levitated a silver hemisphere, which sparkled and hung in front of his large alien eyes. Cristoph recognized it. "That's another item you removed from the vault."

"It was necessary. I did not want to abandon items that might help us, no matter what Encix requested. That device will help them operate properly." He peered into the curved surface. "Yes. All of our sensor probes have safely reached orbit."

Rendo Theris still looked harried. "So . . . now can

we get back to regular launches and landings? We've got commercial ships backed up at the stringline hub." He seemed more flustered than was warranted, as he usually did.

Lodo gave a slow nod. "Yes. Everything is clear now." They all headed toward the headquarters building, where they discussed how many shadow-Xayans would need to remain at Ankor to monitor the orbiting sensor probes. The General noticed that Lodo conversed often with Keana-Uroa, who was becoming the de facto leader of the converts.

Adolphus was interrupted by a priority communication from Sophie. She had sent the message directly to the spaceport, and she knew not to interrupt his mission unless it was extremely important. He immediately felt alert, ready to respond to whatever she needed. When he took the transmission, Sophie looked beautiful but grave on the screen. "Four prisoners escaped from the camp, Tiber. They're missing."

He was alarmed, angry, and concerned. "Where the hell do they expect to go? How long have they been gone?"

"It happened two nights ago, but we just discovered it. They stole a Trakmaster and supplies, then drove off into the uncharted landscape." She hesitated. "It was Escobar Hallholme, Bolton Crais, and two others."

Feeling disturbed, Adolphus focused on the problem—Hallholme and Crais were the most valuable POW bargaining chips. "They can't hope to survive without preparations out there. I thought they were smarter than that."

Her gray eyes flashed. "Redcom Hallholme does not seem to be a man who thinks about consequences. I knew he would cause more trouble." Sophie had little respect for the man after he had broken his word during the surrender ceremony, which resulted in so many deaths. "We should have executed him for all the bloodshed he caused."

He fought down his anger, knowing he had to deal with this crisis, which might have serious repercussions if he ever faced the Constellation military again. "I gave my word those soldiers would be kept safe, and unlike a Hallholme, I keep my word. It's the only way I will lead."

Sophie looked disappointed in herself for the suggestion. Then she said, "Fools don't survive long on Hellhole."

Keana interrupted, "Bolton is not a fool. He's acting out of honor." Her pretty face was filled with concern. Despite their marital separation, it was obvious that she still cared about him.

Adolphus shook his head. "We have to track them down. If the Commodore's son dies—even from his own stupidity—the blame will still fall on me. I will not let that happen."

"I sent out search teams," Sophie said, "but these four don't want to be found. And it seems like a lot of trouble for a group of murderous fools."

"We have to get them back before this planet kills them." Adolphus needed the best person to lead the search. After signing off, he looked around the busy Ankor control center, and his gaze fell on Cristoph de Carre, who was chatting with Lodo. The General called him over.

"Mr. de Carre, I have a new assignment for you."

25

For two days, Bolton had continued driving over the rough terrain, alert for pursuit, moving the Trakmaster mostly after dark, trying to remain hidden from observers. He didn't know how long it would take Sophie Vence to realize that prisoners had escaped—likely they were already being hunted down. He hoped Yimidi's makeshift camouflage system would hide them from searches.

Exhausted, lost, and stressed, Bolton had finally pulled the rig to rest near a set of lumpy rock protrusions. They seemed safe and sheltered for the time being, but still tense. He fell into a restless sleep. . . .

Out in the raw and unwelcoming Hellhole wilderness, Bolton awoke to sounds that were unlike the normal, fitful breathing he'd heard during the night. His three fellow escapees were still asleep inside the Trakmaster; Escobar slumped over in the front seat next to him, while the other two huddled in the back. Bolton rubbed his eyes, guessing by the low yellow illumination coming through the windows that it must be almost dawn. He couldn't see outside.

Something smelled bad, like decaying bodies and sour vegetation.

Now, while his companions slept fitfully in various uncomfortable positions, Bolton blinked groggily in the sickly light that filtered through the Trakmaster's windows. A low, whispering sound filled the cab, and he realized that the daylight had an eerie, unnatural cast—it seemed to be vibrating, squirming. To his horror, he realized that the windows and the vehicle itself were covered with thousands of finger-length larvae. Three of the imagers were dark, but the fourth showed a mass of larvae encrusting the Trakmaster, all of them spinning cocoons like hairy blisters attached to the walls.

Bolton shouted for the others to wake up, while he stared at the control screen, trying to get a view from the external cameras.

In back, Yimidi woke and started shouting, but his words were garbled by a long fit of coughing. Escobar and Vingh also scrambled awake, while Bolton tried to start the vehicle's engine, powering it up from the shutdown.

When the engine thrummed as Bolton tried to activate it, the outside noise of the larvae increased to a buzzing, skittering sound. Escobar pressed his face close to the window, trying to discern the myriad swarming creatures. "They're going into a frenzy."

"They want to keep us from escaping," Vingh said. "We have to move!"

Bolton kept working the controls, but the engine refused to start. Larvae must have infested the mechanical components as well. "We may have to abandon the vehicle."

"And go outside?" Yimidi said in disbelief, then coughed so hard he doubled over.

"Is that worse than staying in here?" Vingh asked.

The four escapees ransacked the Trakmaster for anything they could use to defend themselves, found a repair torch, a flare launcher, and a projectile weapon, but Bolton couldn't guess how any of that would prove effective against so many squirming creatures.

"We can hole up, hope they go away," said Yimidi.

"I don't want to stay trapped here. What if they nest around the Trakmaster?" Escobar asked. "Major Crais, get this vehicle moving!"

Bolton kept trying, but without success. "They may

have ruined the engine, sir." The unnerving scratching, squirming noise became so loud that it drowned out all conversation.

Then he heard a muted popping noise outside, followed by many more in the distance, like small staccato explosions. Maybe Sophie Vence's searchers had found them. In truth, he would much rather be back in the fenced camp—even ashamed and defeated—than eaten alive out here. But the hollow popping sounds were not like weapon fire.

The covering on the windows began to smear away, peeling loose and drifting off to allow the entrance of brighter light. Thousands of small cocoons studded the hull of the Trakmaster as well as the ground surrounding the vehicle. In a remarkably swift transformation, the cocoons were bursting open to unleash swarms of sharp-edged flying insects. Their wings were bright orange, but they looked more dangerous than beautiful. Each cocoon split open with a puff of spore-smoke that wafted around like heavy mist. The husks of the shriveled cocoons dropped away from the Trakmaster.

Bolton worked to start the engine again and finally heard the power levels hum on. Without performing any other checks, he engaged the rugged tracks and rolled forward, crunching across the field of still-hatching cocoons. He could barely see through the clusters that remained on the windshield, but he kept going anyway.

In the back, Vingh was sweating, and Yimidi looked ill. Yimidi coughed, said, "And the Constellation is fighting to get this rotten world back? Let the General damn well have it!"

"We're fighting because General Adolphus is our enemy," the Redcom snapped. "He is a threat to our way of life. I'll have no defeatist attitudes! We *will* survive, men. We will make our way off this planet and get back home. That's our duty."

The flurry of bright insects changed formation, drew together like a swarm of locusts, and then surged upward en masse. As the Trakmaster plowed ahead, Bolton realized that the thrumming, popping noises had gone blessedly quiet. He heard only the growl of the vehicle's heavy engine and the grinding of the treads over the rough rocks. He used built-in sprays of chemical solvent to clean the reinforced glass. He had already used most of the fluid two nights before in a fruitless attempt to get rid of the crawling algae. When he could finally see better, he increased speed.

Ahead, he could make out a line of dark brown hills with a lighter-colored ridgeline beyond, but the sluggish insects followed, settling like a blanket on the moving vehicle.

In back, Yimidi coughed, wiped his mouth, and cleared his throat. "Are they flying, or just drifting like seeds on the wind?"

Again, the insects settled on the Trakmaster, clinging to the windshield and obscuring the view. Through gaps that provided limited visibility, Bolton saw the insects just floating along without twitching their wings or segmented legs, as if they were already dead, their bodies borne on the breezes.

"Zombie bugs," Bolton said, with a shudder.

"Maybe we're all dead, too," Vingh said, "and we just don't know it yet."

Escobar hunched over the nav-system, but the screen remained a blizzard of static. "We've lost our calibration. Onboard guidance systems can't lock onto wherever we are with the terrain database. I think Yimidi's stealth system overloaded some of the satellite maps—

not that they were much good anyway—and Major Crais didn't follow the original route we planned."

"What does that mean?" asked Vingh.

"It means we're driving blind," Escobar said. "We're lost." He seemed to be blaming Bolton for going off a course that had never existed in the first place.

Yimidi was about to say something, but his words vanished in a quick coughing spasm. He forced out, "We don't dare uplink to a satellite, or they can detect us."

"We should have made a better plan before escaping," Vingh said, "just like Major Crais suggested."

"We were better off back in camp," Yimidi added.

"We need to work together to get to safety," Bolton said. "I'm more interested in survival than recriminations."

Stewing with obvious anger, Escobar sat in the front, studying the useless nav-system.

Bolton kept driving, finally managing to pull away from the drifting, lifeless insects. The hum of the Trakmaster's engine shifted slightly as the first of two backup fuel-pellet chambers switched into place.

Everyone would remember that it had been the Redcom's stubbornness that had led to their disastrous defeat in the first place, and the deaths of more than a thousand Constellation soldiers. It was Escobar's fault that they had been forced to surrender to General Adolphus. He was the commanding officer, and Bolton knew that if their misfortunes continued, the simmering resentment would build against Escobar.

The escape from the camp was yet another blunder, and this time Bolton didn't see any way out of it.

26

After launching their assault from Sonjeera, the Army of the Constellation arrived at Tehila without incident. Commodore Hallholme was still alarmed by the dramatic explosion in Council City just before their departure, but he had his own mission and very clear orders. The fate of the Deep Zone was at stake. Timing was critical.

Taken off guard when Diadem Michella unexpectedly insisted on joining the mission, the Commodore did his best to respond appropriately, and as always, he placed his personal feelings aside and did as the Diadem commanded. He needed to devote his full faculties to establishing a forward base on Tehila and then launching the final offensive against Hellhole. And he had to rescue Escobar.

Two gigantic military stringline haulers cruised up to Tehila's terminus ring. Ever since General Adolphus's current rebellion, the route to the distant DZ planet had been off-limits to traffic from Sonjeera, with the substations en route and the terminus ring booby-trapped for emergency destruction in the event of a Constellation advance. Thanks to Administrator Reming's purge, though, the Tehila line was secure. Hallholme could arrive without fear of being cut off.

Arriving at the planet, Percival dispatched an impressive battle group to guarantee there would be no resistance. The first military hauler docked at the terminus ring while the second hauler secured the ring connected to the Hellhole line. Hundreds of Constellation battleships dropped out of their docking clamps and filled Tehila's orbital lanes like a pack of guard dogs.

The Commodore didn't feel much like a conquering

hero, though. The battle here had been over before his ships even left Sonjeera. By seizing the stringlines and arresting all known Adolphus loyalists, Reming had engineered a relatively bloodless coup, and Tehila was now back under Constellation control.

Step one, complete.

This was just a staging point, however—an entry into the Deep Zone network so he could launch his real offensive right down the General's throat. "It's a step in the right direction, Duff," he said to his adjutant while standing on the flagship's bridge. "Have all my officers been briefed on how we'll establish control over the planet?"

"All briefed, Commodore. If the Tehila populace welcomes us and cooperates, as Reming promises, we could be ready to launch our main offensive within days. A week at the outside."

Diadem Michella bustled onto the bridge deck nearly half an hour later. "Commodore, you should have delayed so I could announce our victorious arrival. We missed an opportunity."

He flinched at being scolded in front of his crew. Had she expected him to halt the military haulers outside of orbit and wait for her? "Your pardon, Eminence. Time is of the essence, and I wanted to secure this rebel world with all possible speed." He would have to find some tactful way to remind her that he was in command of the military operation. "Allow me to present the planet Tehila, newly restored to Constellation control."

Looking at all the guardian ships in a bright, powerful stranglehold on Tehila, Michella was unabashed in her delight. "Congratulations, Commodore, on our first major conquest in the Great War of Reunification." She stepped closer to the main bridge screen, as if to get a better view, then glanced back over her shoulder. "Be sure the ships perform appropriately impressive maneuvers. We'll use the footage when we write our history. Make the recapture of Tehila look like a grand battle."

Percival struggled to keep a respectful tone in his voice. "There won't be any battle here, Eminence. Administrator Reming has already eliminated resistance and delivered the world to us."

She waved a gnarled hand in a dismissive gesture. "I don't want to give him too much credit. He was one of the traitors who initially sided with the rebel General, after all."

Michella's aide, Ishop Heer, appeared furtively behind her, as if he didn't belong here. The Diadem had dragged him along on her impulsive decision to accompany the fleet, but the man didn't seem pleased to be part of the operation. Percival had never liked Ishop Heer, had always found something slippery and unpleasant about his demeanor. During the stringline flight to Tehila, Ishop had been edgy, disconcerted. Although the Diadem seemed oblivious to his mood, Percival saw the sharp gazes and quickly hidden expressions of distaste Ishop shot in her direction when she wasn't looking.

That was none of Percival's concern. His only goal was to complete his operation successfully and swiftly. His career would culminate with the final defeat of General Tiber Adolphus, the release of all the Constellation prisoners of war, and an end to the Deep Zone Rebellion. Then he would go back home to his grapevines on Qiorfu, back to his grandchildren and a peaceful life. He had earned that long ago.

Adkins returned with a report. "Commodore, a diplomatic shuttle is on its way up from the capital spaceport. Administrator Reming wishes to present Tehila to us and reaffirm his loyalty to the Constellation."

Diadem Michella interrupted. "By all means, bring

him here. I will accept his surrender and assert a full Constellation crackdown. This unruly planet is now under military jurisdiction."

Ishop Heer said, "I'm not sure that's how Administrator Reming views this situation, Eminence."

She turned to him. "I don't care what he thinks. We are in control here. Commodore Hallholme has seen to that. When I need your political advice, Ishop, I will ask for it." Her sharp tone surprised Percival. During their stringline voyage he had also noticed her belittling the aide at every opportunity. He glanced at Adkins, and they shared a look. Percival had never treated his loyal adjutant that way.

Michella turned her back on Heer, issuing commands as they awaited the arrival of the diplomatic shuttle. "Establish an iron grip here on Tehila, which will become our long-term base of operations, the springboard for reconquering the Deep Zone. First, Commodore, you must totally crush General Adolphus." Her voice grew even harder. "I have given you chances before—I want no mistakes this time."

Percival gave a slight bow, suppressing anger. "No one can guarantee that errors won't occur, Eminence, but I will devote the full extent of my talent and experience to assure the success of this operation."

Michella didn't seem to hear him. She merely repeated, "No mistakes this time."

A sentry force of armed destroyers surrounded each terminus ring, and Percival dispatched an armed squadron to each station to prevent any possible sabotage. As Michella watched the maneuvers, she nodded, obviously impressed. "If we control the stringline path back to Sonjeera, we can send a courier drone back to announce our success, correct? My people must be hurt and frightened after I saved them from the terrible danger of alien contamination. They need good news, and this comes at a perfect time."

Percival cautioned, "Eminence, that would not be wise. We must keep this conquest secret from General Adolphus until we've established our base and launched our strike against him. No announcements."

She was visibly disappointed. "Of course, Commodore. Besides, we should record Administrator Reming's surrender before we send a confidential message back to Sonjeera. I have no doubt Lord Riomini's taken it upon himself to manage the day-to-day affairs of the Constellation for me during my unexpected absence."

Reming's diplomatic shuttle reached orbit, where it dodged among the military ships swarming into position. The administrator had some difficulty determining the flagship among the many ominous warships, so Percival dispatched a cluster of escort flyers to guide the shuttle into the appropriate docking bay.

In the meantime, Diadem Michella tasked Ishop with finding a suitable chamber to serve as her surrogate throne room. Duff Adkins had already suggested a small meeting chamber for the formalities, but the Diadem wanted something much showier.

Ishop seemed flustered by the assignment, which he must consider demeaning. "I am unfamiliar with the layout of these military ships. Perhaps—" He glanced at the Commodore, who obliged.

"The convocation auditorium where we induct new officers," Percival suggested. "It is a place designed for ceremonies."

"That will have to do," Michella said, then frowned at her aide. "I'm sure you could have determined that yourself, Ishop."

Adkins dispatched crew members to assemble a temporary platform and to take a captain's chair from the

Commodore's private quarters to serve as the Diadem's makeshift throne. She had come aboard the flagship in such a rush that she had no formal trappings whatsoever, not even a change of clothes.

Percival's people did not disappoint him in their efficiency. They managed to turn the convocation auditorium into an impressive diplomatic reception chamber even before Administrator Reming had disembarked from his shuttle. Bright pennants of the Constellation, as well as the Duchenet family crest, dangled from the walls, while ribbons and streamers adorned the ceiling.

Percival pulled on his formal uniform jacket and went to stand at the base of the raised platform, shoulders squared, arms straight at his sides. He wished he could be directing the military consolidation of Tehila instead of this ceremonial nonsense.

Adkins led the Tehila administrator to the chamber. Karlo Reming wore a formal business suit and carried a sheaf of documents he had drawn up to commemorate the occasion. He had a formal demeanor, but his façade crumbled as soon as he saw Michella seated on her surrogate throne.

He gasped. "Diadem! Eminence—I had no idea you were here in person. I am deeply honored." He scuttled forward, unsure whether to fall to his knees or shake her hand. From her raised seat, she frowned in displeasure, but she didn't deign to give the man any explanations, or any hint as to how he should respond, or what, if anything, he had done wrong.

"It's fortunate that you've come to your senses," said Michella, "though I wish you hadn't made my response necessary in the first place."

Reming paled, then fumbled to extend the documents. "It is with great pleasure that I deliver Tehila to you. My planet has always been a proud part of the

Constellation, and we are glad to be back under your personal protection. The terminus rings and the stringline routes are yours. The Army of the Constellation now has a straight shot to Hellhole for a complete victory against the General we all hate."

Michella remained stiff. "Be glad you didn't force us to conquer Tehila by military force. I love all my people, even the deluded ones who joined this foolish rebellion. Fortunately, we didn't have to kill you all and incinerate your planet, as Lord Riomini did to Theser."

Administrator Reming swallowed. Percival saw beads of sweat on the man's forehead and could almost smell his fear. "I . . . agree, Eminence. The terms of our bargain were that there would be no punitive measures against Tehila. The General brought us unwillingly into his reckless schemes. We had no part in creating the Deep Zone stringlines, and we did not accept the rebel declaration of independence."

"And yet, you didn't speak out when the crisis occurred." Her wrinkled lips puckered into a frown. "However, I am a loving Diadem, and I will be true to my word. Provided Tehila's citizens cooperate, there will be no reprisals—but I'll not forget those who defied me. Complete forgiveness may come in time . . . but not until the Constellation has recovered from all the damage done by General Adolphus."

27

Ishop Heer hated the fact that he was forced to be here, at the side of the loathsome Diadem Michella. Her impulsive and panicky decision to join the expeditionary fleet had taken him by surprise, and now he was stuck with her. Michella had never intended to come out to Tehila, and although he shared her disgust and fear of the alien contamination, he had never imagined she would act so disastrously. Destroying half of her own capital city! He had been reeling since the vicious bitch told him she'd murdered Laderna.

He'd been swept along, when she fled to the Deep Zone, but now what did she intend to do out here? Did Michella expect the people back in the Crown Jewels to applaud what she'd done? Ishop would be doing the Constellation a favor—not to mention giving himself a great deal of personal satisfaction—if he found a way to kill her. And the sooner the better. He remained alert for his chance to do that.

The Constellation troops maintained a tight cordon around Tehila. In the first days after their arrival, three unsuspecting DZ commercial vessels arrived on schedule along the Hellhole stringline. The enemy ships were immediately captured, taken off the line, and impounded. No word could be allowed to get back to General Adolphus.

According to the best projections, Commodore Hallholme expected to have six full days before anyone back at the Hellhole stringline hub noticed that ships had gone to Tehila but not returned. General Adolphus would send ships to investigate, which would give the Army of the Constellation a little more time.

Hallholme's troops locked down Tehila without incident, establishing a foothold at the spaceport. With Reming's assistance, they arrested and detained General Adolphus's soldiers, locking them in secure brigs. The Commodore wanted no troublemakers loose to cause unrest on the surface.

As far as Ishop could tell, Tehila's populace wasn't thrilled that the Diadem had reasserted her "benevolent" control, despite Administrator Reming's promises to the contrary. Tehila had been a small colony to start with, and now it was a locked-down military garrison.

Seeing that the operation was going so well here, Michella seemed to think she had something to do with the success. She strolled off to the flagship's landing bay. "Ishop, accompany me to the surface. These military vessels leave much to be desired in personal comforts, so we shall find better accommodations down there. I am already tired of ship's quarters. Tehila must have an appropriate mansion or two for our temporary stay."

Ishop said, "I'm sure we can find something, Eminence."

"I want my feet on solid ground again, on the surface of my new planet." She gave him the familiar grandmotherly smile that had never fooled him. "I need you at my side."

"Of course." How he loathed her! "I'll make the arrangements."

—⁂—

As their commandeered shuttle descended to the Tehila landing zone, a hastily reassigned honor guard of Constellation soldiers sat on perimeter passenger benches, looking unhappy with the Diadem's whims. Oblivious, Michella wanted Ishop to sit next to her. She patted the bench.

He had served her well for many years, bloodied his hands countless times, ruthlessly accomplishing anything the Diadem asked. The two of them had an understanding, a viable partnership. She claimed to appreciate him, but she'd laughed at his aspirations to reclaim his family standing.

And now she'd killed Laderna.

He felt exiled out here. All of his connections were back in the Crown Jewels. And after what Michella had done to the Sonjeera spaceport—blowing up part of her own city, vaporizing tens of thousands of her people—did she think she could simply return home as if nothing had happened?

If he found a way to kill her, however, he might return home a hero. . . .

"Why so preoccupied, Ishop? You look deep in thought."

He chose his words carefully. "Sometimes my mind just races with ideas."

Michella chuckled. "Always thinking, and that's one of the things I like about you—your intelligence. I know you well, dear Ishop."

After the shuttle landed, they were met by an escort sent from Administrator Reming's office. Michella let herself be surrounded by the men and women in militia uniforms. "I wish to see the town, and I want the townspeople to see me. Come, Ishop, don't lag behind."

Ishop thought Tehila's capital was a disappointment, more modest than even a small city on the least of the Crown Jewel worlds, less impressive even than Michella Town on Hellhole. Soldiers patrolled the streets, wearing the uniforms of both the Constellation military and the Tehila militia. Michella grumbled as she looked around, expecting much more. "It's a surprise they have electricity and plumbing." She asked why crowds didn't come out in droves to welcome her, but the only bystanders looked at her with curiosity, not joy.

Administrator Reming hurried out of his mansion to greet her. "Eminence, I can't emphasize enough how much I appreciate your coming to save us from General Adolphus. Let me welcome you to my humble headquarters."

He led her and Ishop up the wooden steps into the large house. Michella looked around the halls and said, "Yes, humble indeed, and certainly not worthy of my station, but I suppose it's superior to my cramped quarters aboard the flagship. It will have to do. When the Commodore departs to battle the General, it wouldn't be proper for me to accompany the operation—he is the tactical military genius, after all. So, I will remain here. Thank you, Governor. I accept this as my new residence here on Tehila."

Reming stared at her as if he hadn't heard right. "Your . . . residence? But . . . I can certainly find adequate quarters for you in town."

"No need to bother. This will do. Ishop, I'm sure Administrator Reming will find adequate quarters for you in the mansion, too. I'll need you available to take care of any problems that are sure to arise."

Ishop could barely bite off the words. "Yes, Eminence."

Reming looked from side to side. "But the business of government, all of our work here, the offices, my staff—"

"I'm sure your adequate staff will make do," Michella said.

Ishop understood that she was continuing to needle Reming, making him know his place. The sooner the administrator understood and metaphorically bared his throat, the greater chance he had of surviving.

"I'll be nearby at all times, Eminence," Ishop said, always open for an opportunity, "to watch over you and to attend to your every need."

She gave him a humiliating pat on the shoulder. "Of course you will, dear Ishop."

28

As a former noblewoman and planetary leader, Enva Tazaar was not accustomed to keeping a low profile, but as she went to work in the government mansion in her new routine, she maintained a quiet demeanor—a useful but unremarkable civil servant. Each day, she felt as if she were tiptoeing through a nest of snakes.

The Tehila purge was obviously not what Administrator Reming had expected. The Constellation military crackdown had secured the shocked and dissatisfied populace, but Reming had little power now. After letting the wolves in the door, he'd been a fool to expect a warm embrace from the Diadem. Now, after the military takeover of his planet, Reming was forced to set up temporary offices in a small annex building, but he had no real power and nothing to do. Enva wondered if the man realized how lucky he was that Diadem Michella didn't simply execute him, as she'd done with Territorial Governor Goler. . . .

Enva went to her clerk's job in the mansion, which was swarming with the Diadem's entourage and Commodore Hallholme's military personnel. She dressed conservatively, kept her eyes low, did not speak unless spoken to, and tried to perform her job as if it were any other day. Even with the crackdown on Tehila and the imminent plans to launch a massive assault against Hellhole, the daily mechanics of bureaucracy needed to continue. No matter that historic events were happening, the most important thing to the populace was that the transportation, power, water, and food continued—services functioning as expected, with daily life remaining as normal as possible.

She passed two militia members manning a check-point at the mansion—they did not question her ID badge, which showed the false name Enva Lien. One of the local guards, puffed up in his new costume, recognized her from her work with Administrator Reming. The secondary checkpoint guard, more comfortable in his Constellation uniform, was diligent but uninterested. Enva remained passive, as a clerk should be, and they let her through.

She entered the office she shared with Maruni Li, who was already at her desk. Previously, Maruni had been habitually late to work, receiving repeated reprimands from her immediate supervisor. Now, the woman was scared enough to be punctual (although, as far as Enva could tell, no more efficient). The two of them had little to worry about, as long as they did their tasks and called no attention to themselves.

Maruni looked up. "Oh, Enva! I finished compiling our summary of fuel supplies as well as an inventory of impounded ships at the spaceport." She looked both hopeful and worried.

Enva kept her voice firm. "Did you break down the inventory by ship type? They'll decide what cargo can be confiscated and distributed, and Commodore Hall-holme needs to know which of the captured ships he can incorporate into the Constellation fleet."

Maruni blinked. "I didn't think of that—I just listed them. None of those vessels are military, so why would the Commodore want them?"

Normally Enva wouldn't bother explaining, but she worked through the strategic thoughts herself. "Any captured ship could be useful in a military engagement. For instance, the Hellhole stringline hub will recognize them as registered DZ vessels, so maybe they can infiltrate, with armaments concealed, and strike a first blow.

Or, if nothing else, the Commodore could sacrifice them as cannon fodder, shock troops to take the brunt of the attack." When Maruni's eyes widened, Enva added quickly, "But I'm just guessing. I'm no military expert."

Maruni forwarded the data compilation she had done so far. "Could you help me? It won't take you long."

Enva frowned. It wouldn't take her long . . . but she had no incentive to aid the hateful Diadem. Why should she help the Army of the Constellation achieve a victory? "I have my own projects and deadlines." Maruni looked crestfallen. But Enva's mind kept spinning as she realized that the information might be useful, and she could make a few surreptitious alterations. "All right, I'll trade you jobs. They're both equally dull."

"One project after another." Maruni let out a dry laugh. "It never ends."

Enva got to work, and again noted that one of the impounded ships belonged to the obvious Adolphus loyalists Tanja Hu and Ian Walfor. No one except Enva seemed to have noticed the significance of those two—and the pair of former planetary administrators must still be keeping a low profile on Tehila. Enva examined the records, considered carefully, and then simply deleted the information, erasing all trace that Hu and Walfor were here.

Diadem Michella would be beside herself if she discovered that not only was Enva right here under her nose, but so were two of the General's main coconspirators! If any of them were discovered, they would be executed.

Despite the risk, Enva saw an opportunity to throw a major wrench in the works. Though she had not managed to secure an alliance with General Adolphus before her downfall, Enva Tazaar found the rebel leader to be far preferable to the Diadem. Now, her plan went beyond just a political decision or power play, it was a real chance to thwart the old bitch and bring her down. Now, *that* would be the best day a civil servant could imagine!

Administrator Reming had seized control of the Tehila stringlines and arrested anyone who supported the rebellion; Commodore Hallholme had taken over the planet and was preparing a massive strike against Hellhole. And General Adolphus knew nothing of it. If Enva could somehow send a warning and alert the General, she would change the outcome of history.

But, she had no way to get to Hellhole. The Army of the Constellation controlled the stringline stations and had locked down Tehila. . . .

Michella had requested that a hardcopy of the ship inventory be delivered personally rather than simply transmitted to the office. Apparently, the woman didn't trust Administrator Reming's primitive information systems. The Diadem was always one to prefer formality over efficiency.

Alert and thinking of possibilities, Enva took the document to the main offices usurped by Michella. She walked through the mansion corridors, where she passed guards in Constellation uniforms as well as decorated officers, Sonjeeran nobles who had attended the Diadem at her palace and at various governmental functions—places where they might have seen Lady Enva Tazaar. She could not afford to be recognized here, but her appearance and demeanor were quite different from those days.

Enva came to the anteroom as requested, where she overheard a discussion in the main admin chamber, Michella's familiar voice—syrup mixed with acid—scheming with her advisers. Enva couldn't help but

glance up, saw the withered old woman at Administrator Reming's desk, then turned away to keep from being noticed.

One of the Sonjeeran guards closed the door to give the Diadem privacy, shooting Enva a quick glare for the interruption. Enva delivered her document to a sour-faced receptionist and obtained the signature she needed, then ducked out of the offices, scurrying back toward her desk as a meek civil servant should.

Because she had encountered so many Constellation guards and entourage members in the main corridors, she slipped into a back hallway, taking a more convoluted but less traveled path around the central block of offices.

She tried to think of subtle—or not so subtle—ways she could harm the Diadem's plans. She passed two of her coworkers, who looked harried and nervous; opened a door; slipped through a connecting hallway to avoid them—and nearly bumped into a bald man who was silent, alert, and seemed to belong in shadowy back halls rather than in the main bustle of attention.

Enva froze, recognizing him instantly. She was dismayed at her inability to cover her surprise—and Ishop Heer certainly noticed. She averted her eyes. "Excuse me, sir." She kept her face turned away and tried to shuffle past.

Ishop Heer, the Diadem's hatchet man, had been in the Council Hall when Enva was stripped of her titles and arrested. He had worked for Michella Duchenet for years and had a way of quietly making the Diadem's enemies disappear. If Enva were caught, she had no doubt that Michella would have this man perform a long and painful execution.

Ishop blocked her way. He was a big man with broad shoulders—which always seemed odd to her for one

with such a mastery of stealth. She tried to *will* him not to recognize her, but it was a vain hope.

"One moment—this is very interesting." He grabbed her chin in a firm grip and lifted her head, forcing her to look into his intense, empty eyes. His lips curved in a cruel smile. "Quite a surprise, Enva Tazaar."

"You mistake me for someone else, sir."

"No, I'm certain I do not. I knew you'd fled out to the Deep Zone—to Tehila, in fact. But I thought you would have found a better hiding place than here in the thick of political activity in the administrator's mansion."

Enva clenched her jaw and refused to respond. Denials would be pointless. Then Ishop's smile broadened. "Ah, but of course! You must be planting seeds, making plans for the future. Now, that's what I expected from you, Enva."

"How did you know I escaped to Tehila?" she asked in a hoarse voice. "No one knew."

"Because I sent you here, of course." He drank in her reaction and seemed to be enjoying himself. "I'm the one who arranged for your escape, dear woman. My operatives broke you out of prison, got you on a string-line ship, sent you to the Deep Zone. You're alive because of me."

She narrowed her eyes. "Why would you do that?"

Ishop pondered, as if he had never considered how to verbalize it himself. "Because you and I have a lot in common. Maybe you were too preoccupied with your own concerns to notice? While you were stripped of your noble titles and holdings, I was denied mine in the first place. They scoffed at my claims, tried to sweep me under the rug. After I gave a lifetime of service, the Diadem denied me my due, prevented me from recovering my status. She spurned me as much as she spurned

you." He reached out to touch the side of Enva's face, stroked her blonde hair. She shuddered. "Once, I even thought you and I might make fine partners. That could still be the case." He sniffed. "Now, seeing you here, a wealth of possibilities occurs to me."

She stood firm, alert, wondering if he had installed listening devices to record her answers, to trap her— but to what end? He could already destroy her with a word. "What possibilities?"

The look on Ishop's face became utterly vicious, and his answer shocked her. "I want to destroy Diadem Michella. No, not just destroy her—she is a cancerous tumor that I want to rip out and stomp under my boot heel." He leaned closer. "Does that sound interesting to you?"

Enva's thoughts whirled. She couldn't believe that *Ishop Heer* had betrayed the Diadem, arranged for Enva's escape, and now wanted to kill the woman who had been his benefactor for years. That made no sense! Enva still despised this man, but she also realized that he could be unexpectedly useful—if he was telling the truth. But she didn't trust him for a fraction of a second.

Her other plans now crystallized. "Simply murdering Michella would be satisfying, but there are more effective ways to ruin her—if that's what you truly want to do, Ishop Heer."

"I'm listening." His lips quirked in a smile. "So long as Michella suffers. That detail is rather high on my priority list."

"Oh, she will suffer. But instead of just killing her, we should take her hostage, use her as a bargaining chip."

His smooth brow furrowed. "What would we do with her?"

Enva caught her breath at how the pieces were falling

together. Ishop would turn on her in an instant, but she might use him in the meantime. "Why, we'll deliver her into the hands of General Adolphus, of course."

She could tell by Ishop's bright eyes and crafty smile that she wouldn't need to do any further convincing.

29

Great military heroes never retire," said General Adolphus, "they just become managers."

George Komun, planetary administrator of Umber and one of the original eleven conspirators who had planned the Deep Zone independence movement, arrived at Hellhole for a private meeting. Sitting in the Elba conference room, he commiserated with the General.

The room seemed too large for a private conversation, but it had resonance for the two men. Here, the tight-knit group of planetary leaders had met in secret: Tanja Hu, Ian Walfor, George Komun, Dom Cellan Tier, Sia Frankov, Eldora Fen, and others. In this room they had hatched the scheme for the DZ stringline network that would free the Deep Zone from the Diadem's monopoly. Together, they had plotted the overthrow of the Constellation, and they had succeeded.

"I believe that's why many wars start in the first place," Komun said. "When fighting epic battles, military commanders have a well-defined goal, but during all that bloodshed, in the backs of their minds, they long for peace. Then, afterward, when their lives are dull and normal, they miss the rush of adrenaline and think fondly of the bygone glory days. And so—perhaps unconsciously or perhaps not—they end up starting trouble, so they can go out and fight again."

Adolphus poured himself a second cup of hot, sweet kiafa. "Yes, the old glory days. I certainly don't long for the bloody battles, but it was good to have a clear goal. Conquest is easy—governing is hard."

Komun took a seat. "Rules are more clear-cut under a dictatorship. Now that the Deep Zone is independent, every person has the freedom they thought they wanted, but freedom has a way of providing so many choices that some people are afraid to have no guardrails and no safety net."

Captain Naridar entered the room with his report. Since Naridar's recent decisive crackdown at Hossetea, the General had given him the responsibility of watching over the DZDF forces stationed at the primary Hellhole stringline hub.

Hearing the comment, Captain Naridar frowned. "Now that the Deep Zone has had a taste of freedom, I can't believe anyone would want to go back to the repressive Constellation. The Diadem was bleeding the DZ dry by forcing us to pay for her bloated and out-dated system."

Komun sat back in his chair and regarded him. "I understand your bitterness, Captain. The stupidity on Hossetea was shocking, but in retrospect not unex-pected. The fact that some people would actually pre-fer the old tyranny seems nonsensical to anyone who's been living, breathing, and fantasizing about freedom for year after year. But there are instances—unbelievable as it may sound—where too much freedom, too soon, causes chaos. For the most part, people just want to live their lives and take care of their families, instead of making grand political gestures." He shook his head. "I'm sorry to say that the majority just want to be told what to do and then be left alone."

Adolphus was not happy to hear this, though not

surprised. Komun's planet, Umber, had been a largely self-sufficient world even before the recent rebellion. His people mined a wealth of green sapphires and always managed to hide the true output from the Diadem's inspectors. Umberians complained enough about their allotted tribute to the Crown Jewels that the Diadem never suspected how little pain the tribute payments actually cost.

"The Deep Zone has its independence," Adolphus said, "but as in any transition, the people have to put up with some turmoil. Our honeymoon is over, and this is reality."

Komun gave a snort. "And they're still hung over from the wedding celebrations." He tapped his fingers on the conference room table. "But we shouldn't underestimate the risk of unrest. Hossetea was a warning we cannot ignore. Right now, our single most vulnerable point is the Hellhole stringline hub. It serves as the strategic high ground for the entire Deep Zone. It must be defended at all costs—and that is where the Constellation will try to attack us."

"Soon enough we'll remove that single point of failure," Adolphus said. "Right now, at least five other DZ worlds are establishing their own stringline hubs, which will diversify and strengthen the stringline network. In fact, I'm surprised you haven't started one yourself, George."

"There will come a time for that, General, but I'm in no hurry. My planet is stable, my people are content."

"I wish all DZ planets could say the same," Adolphus said.

Captain Naridar set his display screen on the table between the two men. "Our stringline hub is secure, sirs. The peacekeeper ships I withdrew from Hossetea now provide added defenses. Our direct line to Sonjeera has been cut, so the Constellation cannot make a frontal assault."

"But there are fifty other routes in," Komun pointed out. "If Hossetea had fallen, the Army of the Constellation could have used that to gain access to Hellhole. Thank God Captain Naridar was there and reacted appropriately, but who is to say that another DZ world isn't going to fall? There may be additional restless planets like Hossetea." He arched his eyebrows. "If I might make a suggestion?"

Adolphus met the man's gaze. "I've always valued your advice, George. We're on the same page."

"Defending the hub itself is important, but it's just as important to guarantee the loyalty of the other Deep Zone worlds. Maybe there's a better use for Captain Naridar's extra peacekeeper ships. Representing the DZDF, he could take those fifteen battleships on a security inspection tour from one DZ world to the next. That would be a nice visible reminder that you're here, General, in case the populations start to have doubts."

"But sending those ships away would diminish the security here at the Hellhole hub," the General pointed out.

"It's a reallocation of assets." He shrugged. "But if it lets you sleep better at night, I have fifteen ships for planetary defense at Umber. You gave them to me as a reward because I was one of your original revolutionaries, but I don't need them. Umber is stable. Sure, I could leave one or two ships there as a token security force, but I'll send you the others to guard the Hellhole hub while Captain Naridar goes on his showy patrol."

Naridar said, "It does seem a better use of the ships we have, sir. We don't want another hot spot like Hossetea."

"I wish the Constellation was the only thing I had to

worry about," the General said, frowning. Since launching the new observation satellites from Ankor, Adolphus had been receiving high-resolution images, and his technicians remained vigilant for any unexpected celestial movements, any asteroid attack from the Ro-Xayans.

He rested his elbows on the table and said, "Personally, I believe a bombardment of asteroids is a greater threat than the Diadem's temper tantrum or some discontented rebels who've discovered that real freedom entails hard work and not just bragging and dreaming." He considered, then nodded. "George, if you can eliminate one of my worries, then that in itself strengthens the Deep Zone. I would gladly accept your ships. Thank you."

Komun actually chuckled. "I can see how the threat of Armageddon might lead to some anxiety, General. You send Captain Naridar on his patrol, and I'll dispatch thirteen of my battleships back here from Umber. In turbulent times like these, everything we do makes history, so we have to pay attention to the details."

30

Hurtling in on the Qiorfu line, Lord Riomini's haulers arrived at the main stringline hub over Sonjeera, overwhelming the gigantic transport facility. Thousands of fighter craft, destroyers, and immense battleships from the Black Lord's privately constructed fleet dropped out of docking clamps and fell into orbit, taking up positions around the Constellation's main world. Passenger pods and shuttles sped out and descended toward the capital city. They bypassed the ruins of the

Sonjeera spaceport and headed for Heart Square, using the large parks in front of the government buildings as makeshift landing grounds.

He was coming not as a conquering invader, but as a savior, a rescuer for the Crown Jewels in a time of disastrous upheaval. He wanted to show strength, not intimidation.

Riomini rode in the largest transport, which was itself so heavily armed that it could destroy many frontline Constellation warships; it was also equipped as a mobile command center, where he could meet with his top officers and formulate attacks. He couldn't stop smiling. This was marvelous.

Originally, he had constructed his clandestine military force at Lubis Plain for the protection of his considerable assets. This private fleet was not part of the Army of the Constellation, and not subject to being commandeered by the Diadem for her own purposes. Riomini was well aware that no other noble family had the resources—or the will—to invest in such an undertaking. He had meant for these ships to be his insurance, not an offensive force to overthrow the Diadem.

But circumstances changed.

This was not an overthrow, not a civil war, but the imposition of strength and stability to remedy a dangerous leadership vacuum. At present, the Constellation had no leader, and Michella Duchenet had attacked her own planet, killing her own subjects, as a paranoid overreaction to an imagined alien threat. In obliterating the spaceport, she had destroyed a vital strategic asset for the Constellation—which was, after all, currently at war with General Adolphus. And then she had abandoned her throne.

Rescue and recovery operations continued round the clock on the perimeter of the kilometer-wide glassy crater left by the explosion; countless casualties were still being removed from wreckage on the outer circles. Tebias had also advised Riomini that as one of his first acts, he should endorse the recovery operations and add funding (at least by a marginal amount), to show how he was different from the old Diadem. One of the military ships was loaded with relief supplies; not enough to make much of a difference, but enough to look good.

The citizens were appalled by what Michella had done, and Riomini knew that by now they must hate her, feeling betrayed. In recent years, many of the nobles had already grown disgusted with the old woman's excesses and erratic behavior. Very few would mourn her departure.

No, this was not an overthrow. Selik Riomini saw himself as *the* person to save the Constellation, and fortunately, through his foresight, he had the resources to do so. He had always intended to become the next Diadem, although it was coming about in a different manner than he had anticipated. He would never have a better time, and so now when he saw his chance, he acted. For the good of the Constellation. After what Michella had done, everyone would welcome a strong leader, like him.

Riomini's preparations were not just military, as the rest of the Council was about to discover. Oh, some would complain about his obvious ambitions, as they always did, but the Crown Jewels had no other viable options. Previously, his closest competition in the succession had been Enva Tazaar, but she was disgraced and stripped of her position, vanished into the shadows somewhere. She was nothing.

He had been planning this for a long time, and he expected his assumption of the diademacy would go smoothly. The descending passenger pods and troop transports contained more than soldiers: He'd brought along an army of bureaucrats, diplomats, legal and constitutional scholars—enough functionaries to take over every detail of day-to-day government operations. His people would replace all managers, supervisors, and even some of the rank-and-file workers who had served Michella Duchenet. He even intended to set up his own court system, if necessary, which would process any challenges to his rule.

Yes, he had it all planned.

As his armored transport landed directly in front of Council Hall, people scattered in all directions, frightened. Additional escort flyers and troop carriers landed in the surrounding streets, while the rest of his massive fleet secured the perimeter of the city.

It was late morning, local time, and he'd timed his arrival to coincide with the emergency session of the interim Council. Surrounded by his elite guard force, Riomini marched toward the Hall. The Council was already in an uproar, leaderless and in turmoil after Michella abandoned the government. The interim committee spent more time raising measures and arguing about them than actually establishing law—business as usual, but Riomini would change that.

Now he would arrive as the obvious new leader, a hero to solve all their problems. Selik Riomini was the Diadem's clear successor anyway, so it was just a matter of stepping forward and assuming the throne that was rightfully his. Given the emergency situation, Riomini didn't have time for subtle manipulations, gradual coalition-building, votes and revotes.

The scale of Riomini's unexpected military force, however, astonished the nobles. Previously, they had assumed that all viable warships in the Crown Jewels had been given to Commodore Hallholme to fight the rebels, and they were shocked by the sudden arrival of a huge and unexpected fleet at the main stringline hub.

"This is a crisis," Riomini announced as he strode into the large chamber. "And I am here to ensure order and safety."

Numerous nobles lurched to their feet and shouted protests. His female guards surrounded him protectively, but made no threatening moves. Behind Riomini, more of his black-uniformed soldiers filed into the chamber and took positions around the perimeter, and down the center aisle.

Lord Horatio Dodds, the ruler of Barassa, had been addressing the Council and now looked befuddled by the interruption. The tall, mustachioed man remained at the podium, perturbed and then indignant as Riomini's guards moved him aside so that the Black Lord could take his place.

"It is my turn to speak," Riomini said calmly. "Time to get the Constellation back on track."

Dodds retreated, mumbling in displeasure as he left the central stage. The other nobles scrambled to resume their seats, uneasy but eager to hear what the new arrival had to say. Messengers rushed in and out of the hall, whispering to particular representatives, explaining the extent of the military force Riomini had brought with him from Qiorfu.

As he gazed around the chamber, he paused to study various faces, scowling at some and smiling warmly at others who had previously expressed support for him. After a dramatic moment of silence, he said, "Michella Duchenet committed a devastating, treasonous act against her own people. She showed herself to be an enemy of the Constellation, attacking our capital and fleeing to the Deep Zone—enemy territory! By her actions, she has abdicated her role. In such an emergency, the Constellation needs strong leadership, an immediate replacement. As the presumptive successor to the Star Throne, I offer myself as the next Diadem. I anticipate your immediate and unanimous support in installing me to the role, for the good of the Constellation." He looked out at the faces. "My forces have restored order to the orbital hub and the capital city, and they are prepared to protect us against any attack from General Adolphus."

He let the words sink in, saw the expressions of surprise, shock, and uneasiness, although a few saw the inevitability of the succession.

A silver-haired woman rose to her feet in one of the center rows. "I propose that we accept Lord Riomini as the acting Diadem, until such time as the matter can be fully debated and decided." Elegantly dressed, Lady Arlene Marubi was known as a moderate, sometimes voting in support of positions that Riomini espoused, and sometimes against them. She had come to the obvious conclusion and did not want to waste any further time.

"*Until* such time as the crisis is over," added a middle-aged man, one of those Riomini had consulted, and bribed, ahead of time. Riomini knew that, given proper manipulation of events and reports, the "crisis" would never be deemed over.

Riomini looked at them all sternly. This was his opportunity, and he needed to deal with the situation immediately. "*Acting* Diadem? We must be unified, and General Adolphus is not an 'acting' enemy. I hope this—" He paused for effect. "—this august body formally recognizes my authority with all due speed. That is what the Constellation needs." He squared his shoulders. "*I* am what the Constellation needs."

Lady Marubi rose back to her feet, with more to say. "Point of order: This cannot be a legal decision unless and until Diadem Michella has formally abdicated."

"Or until we formally remove her," said a minor noble, Lord Hikon Rikter, another of Riomini's supporters. "I submit that she formally abandoned her role when she attacked Sonjeera and fled." Angry mutters rippled through the audience. Few people could stomach supporting Michella Duchenet after what she had done.

But a weak-voiced older man, Lord Ilvar Crais—father of Major Bolton Crais—did speak up. "The Diadem transmitted a statement explaining her actions. She announced that she had stopped an insidious alien plot and that she prevented the release of deadly contamination that would have destroyed us."

"Paranoid nonsense," Riomini chuckled.

Crais did not back down. "Nevertheless, the claims of the Diadem deserve to be considered, not dismissed outright. What if she did save us?"

"Ask that of the hundreds of thousands of innocent citizens who were vaporized," said Lord Rikter.

Grumbles, even mocking laughter, filled the hall, and Riomini knew he was winning. "Then let her come back and explain herself—at her trial as a war criminal. If Michella saved us all, why did she flee? If she has evidence to support her actions, I am sure the families of her victims would like to hear it." That was greeted with loud agreement.

Riomini pressed further. "She may very well believe that she sterilized a dangerous threat, but by fleeing out to the Deep Zone, she wants to see if any of us becomes contaminated before she dares to return." He looked around into the deepening, concerned silence. "Is that the sort of leader you want?"

A number of noblemen shouted out support for Riomini, but Lord Crais again broke in. "One slight problem remains. We do not have a quorum, due to transportation disruptions—along with the losses of Lord Klief and Lord Cherby in the spaceport explosion. A Diadem can only be voted into office by the unanimous consent of all twenty ruling families. Unfortunately, the successors to Lord Klief and Lord Cherby have not yet been appointed."

Lord Tanik Hirdan, a loud and stern man who had not previously expressed consistent support for Riomini, now let out an impatient bellow. "Enough of this nonsense. We must not blind ourselves with red tape during an emergency. I propose we install Lord Riomini by acclamation."

Surprised, Riomini gave Hirdan an appreciative nod. Following a moment's hesitation, the chamber erupted into a standing ovation, with boisterous shouts of support for the new Diadem. No, he had not underestimated their antipathy toward Michella Duchenet.

This part, at least, was done.

31

There was little time to implement the abduction of Diadem Michella and escape from Tehila before the Army of the Constellation launched, but Enva knew how to seize an opportunity.

Though she didn't like Ishop Heer, he was also a man of action and flexibility, as Enva was quickly discovering. Both of them happened to be in useful positions, with the resources and official connections they needed to kidnap the old Diadem.

The overall plan blossomed quickly in Enva's mind. Before being caught in the undertow of the sweeping purge here, she had already been pondering how she might restore herself to power. Working discreetly in her civil servant office, she monitored the military preparations, looking for an opening amid all that distraction.

In short order, Percival Hallholme had secured both stringline terminus rings, consolidated Tehila's defenses, and made the planet an armed camp. The Commodore was anxious to launch his assault on unsuspecting Hellhole. If Enva could warn General Adolphus of the imminent attack and deliver the Diadem as a hostage as well, the General would embrace her as an ally. Together they could turn the tables, sweep back to Sonjeera, and bring the Crown Jewels to their knees.

That had been Enva's plan all along. She would rule the Crown Jewels, and Tiber Adolphus would rule the Deep Zone in a commercial alliance to benefit all concerned. Except for old Michella, of course. . . .

And then there was Ishop Heer. Although he claimed to have turned against the Diadem, Enva didn't trust him. She could take care of him later—right now, she needed him. Time was extremely short; they had to pull off their scheme in a day, or their warning would come too late. Ishop also felt the urgency. He told her, "I cannot destroy the Diadem soon enough."

While Enva continued to work in the government offices, Ishop pulled strings of his own, granting her increased access throughout the administrative mansion, including the Diadem's main offices. He also gave her passcodes to the most secure levels of Tehila's admin networks, then sent coded and self-erasing messages to let her know his plans and progress. Once Enva had access, alternatives would spread out before her; she just had to tie the different strands together.

She pretended to be bored as she worked on the inventory of impounded spacecraft, but Enva was actually rearranging the embargo, earmarking certain seized ships for special deployment as part of Commodore Hallholme's assault. Since those orders came directly from the main government offices, marked with the Diadem's personal signature code (forged) for confirmation, she was able to designate Ian Walfor's ship as cleared and ready for immediate departure.

Next, she had to bring them into the plan and make the last piece fall into place.

—⁂—

Militia troops were assigned to the section of the city where the Candela refugees were held in slapdash community housing. The people had gone through a devastating ordeal upon evacuating their planet, losing their homes and worldly possessions.

Tehila had not warmly welcomed the refugees, and now the military takeover had thrown them into a cauldron again. The refugee settlement was not a prison or an armed camp, and the militia guards were there to ensure that the refugees did not stage an uprising of their own, but rather than calming them, the additional security and the repressive atmosphere had the opposite effect.

Enva knew that Ian Walfor and Tanja Hu had to be somewhere in that refugee complex. As an unobtrusive clerk, she obtained an official pass bearing the Diadem's seal and a stamp from Administrator Reming, which granted her permission to speak to a representative of the refugees. Her stated goal was to manage a smooth transition, now that Tehila was restored to good graces in the Constellation.

Outside the refugee complex, the guards were skeptical, even amused at the bureaucratic obliviousness. "Would you like an armed escort inside, ma'am?"

She played up her naïveté, showed the Diadem's pass as if that was all the protection she would ever need. "Oh, that won't be necessary. They're citizens, and I'm just trying to improve their conditions. Uniformed guards would only make the situation seem more awkward."

"They aren't too happy about the new administration," a guard said. "A lot of people in town are grumbling, not that there's anything they can do about it." He smirked. "But the Candela refugees have always been complainers."

"They'll come around soon enough," Enva said as she passed through the gate; then she hesitated, as if another thought had occurred to her. "Diadem Michella wishes to ensure a harmonious consolidation, so we have to try to understand their concerns. Soon—perhaps today or tomorrow—I will be taking refugee representatives over to the Diadem's offices. I hope you won't give me any headaches about that."

"No, ma'am," said the guard. "I'll pass the word to the personnel on duty."

Inside the refugee housing, Enva found open yards where people gathered, families sitting together and talking under large tent awnings. Most of the refugees looked gloomy, still in shock. They looked up when she arrived in her officious bureaucratic outfit, carrying her paperwork. If Walfor and Hu had vanished into the crowds here, they would never be found unless they wanted to be. Enva Tazaar did not have time for games.

She addressed no one in particular, but had their attention. She changed her tone of voice. "I'm looking for

Ian Walfor and Tanja Hu. I wish to speak with them as soon as possible. Please assure them it will be a mutually beneficial conversation."

Seeing the downtrodden people, she did not expect them to react with enthusiasm, nor did they. She could feel a wave of resentment building around her, but Lady Enva Tazaar knew how to address large crowds, knew how to infuse authority into her voice. She discarded her demeanor as a mere governmental clerk and became an entirely different person, commanding and confident.

She crossed her arms over her chest. "I know that Ian Walfor and Tanja Hu are both here. Their ship arrived several days ago, but I have not reported it to the Diadem or to Commodore Hallholme. If I were going to betray the two of them, I would not have come here. The Diadem would reward me well if I revealed that the fugitive Buktu planetary administrator was right here under her nose." Enva narrowed her eyes. "And she would be even more interested to capture the woman who sent the head of Territorial Governor Undine back to Sonjeera."

She regarded them all; she definitely had their attention now. "I promise Hu and Walfor will want to hear what I have to say, and it'll definitely help your situation here on Tehila. It's a matter of some urgency, and if we don't act soon we'll lose our window of opportunity." She glanced at her chronometer, hardened her voice in case anyone here tried to betray her. "If I haven't returned to my offices in one hour, the Diadem's forces will receive an announcement, and they will mercilessly sweep this entire compound."

Enva sat in silence and waited, daring them to call her bluff.

The two refugee governors came to her in a few minutes. Enva appraised them, saw a strength and confidence that was different from the sad, hopeless resignation of many Candela refugees.

She rose to her feet and faced them. "I know you, but you don't know me . . . unless you look closely." Their faces showed no immediate recognition. "We need to go somewhere we can talk in private."

"You're Enva Tazaar," Tanja finally said.

"And I need your help bringing down the Diadem and saving Hellhole."

—∿—

It was dusk, and the shifts changed among the militia guards. The headquarters staff was heading home, more concerned with dinner than politics.

Ishop could barely contain himself.

He had watched the time all day. After receiving the go-ahead from Enva Tazaar, he studied the spaceport records and made sure that Walfor's impounded ship was ready to go. This would be their only chance. Another day, and it would be too late.

Commodore Hallholme considered Tehila sufficiently consolidated that he was ready to launch his Hellhole assault. After he and Enva abducted the Diadem, however, Ishop knew those plans would change.

His mind felt like a mass of snakes, his thoughts twisted and lashing out with all the myriad reasons he had to hate Michella Duchenet. She was cold and vengeful, self-centered, clutching onto power with a clawlike grip. She had used him. She had laughed away his hard-fought and well-earned noble name.

And she had murdered Laderna.

Ishop was not inclined to be a forgiving person.

Simply killing the Diadem would have been so satisfying, but Enva was right: far better to deliver Michella helpless to her mortal enemy, the man she hated most in the entire universe. Eventually, the old woman would learn that Ishop was the one who had betrayed her, so he could take satisfaction from that, too.

As the Diadem finished her day and readied herself to face another dreary evening in these primitive and squalid buildings, Ishop presented himself with the well-oiled smile he had practiced so much it seemed almost natural to him. "I have a special treat for you, Eminence. Something I must show you myself."

She exhibited no interest. "I'm tired, Ishop. What is it?"

"After searching the impounded ships at the spaceport, I found something that will delight you—a whole array of black-market delicacies! So many, and in such assortment, I don't know which of them to bring you. Luxury items fit for a Diadem. They were intended for Administrator Reming, but I intercepted them for you."

She smiled. "Ishop, you're such a dear, always thinking of me. What would I ever do without you?"

"You would have great difficulty without me, Eminence." He gestured for her to follow him. "Come, everything is stored in the reserve pantry. We'll take a side corridor."

She sighed. "Oh, Ishop, just prepare a gourmet dinner for me. You know what I like. And you know I can be very grateful."

With great effort, he kept the edge out of his voice. "Yes, I'm very familiar with your gratitude, Eminence. But you need to see this for yourself—it's on the way to your suite. There are also several cartons of the

special-blend tea you like so much, and a lot more. . . .
I wouldn't presume to choose for you." He took her
arm, encouraging her. "It'll be like a treasure hunt, just
you and me."

She chuckled, let herself be persuaded, as he had
known she would. "Oh, very well."

He led her out a side hallway, knowing she was glad
to bypass the constant guards and pestering officials.
Ishop also knew Enva Tazaar would be waiting for
them. He was unarmed, because he was searched whenever he came into the Diadem's presence. Enva, though,
had managed to acquire a powerful hand stunner, which
she smuggled through security on her own.

When Ishop guided Michella into the large pantry
chamber, Enva Tazaar was waiting for them inside, stunner drawn. Ishop closed the door as Michella looked
aghast. "Ishop, protect me!"

She started to scream for guards, but Enva felled her
with a crackling stun blast. The Diadem collapsed like
a heap of mummified bones.

His eyes sparkled. In preparing for this, the two of
them had cleared out many of the packages in the pantry and left an empty cargo container marked with Constellation insignia. "Help me get her in here," Enva said,
keeping a businesslike edge to her voice, demonstrating
that she was a hard and imperious noblewoman, just
like she had been before her disgrace. "I've already got
the manifest written up and approved, and there's a
ground hauler waiting. We'll take her to Ian Walfor's
ship at the spaceport."

Ishop took great pleasure in unceremoniously dump-
ing the old woman into the cargo container. He was
practically capering with joy, pleased at how well their
plan had gone. Only a few more steps. It should proceed like clockwork.

"One more thing, Ishop," Enva said. He turned to her and found himself staring down at the stunner. "I don't trust you either. And just in case you need plausible deniability later—"

When Enva blasted him, the big man collapsed perfectly into the cargo container, falling on top of Diadem Michella.

32

The unexpected purge and military crackdown on Tehila had created chaos, turmoil, and fear, but it also presented a range of opportunities to Tanja Hu and the Candela refugees. They had known they needed to move quickly or it would be too late to warn the General, but they didn't have a plan.

Even with all the reasons not to trust Enva Tazaar, the disgraced noblewoman gave them their best and perhaps their only realistic chance. The fact that they had to move that night meant that she and Ian Walfor didn't have time to overthink their strategy.

Now, Tanja wiped perspiration from her forehead and glanced at the chronometer. Minutes ticking down—they had to get going. "We're in this up to our necks."

"Maybe so," Walfor said, "but let's try to be optimistic. I'm your knight in shining armor."

"Just be my pilot and get our ship out of here. That'll be good enough."

With the Commodore's massive fleet turning Tehila into a military base practically overnight, Tehila was in a frenzy. Too many people were giving orders, and many of the instructions were contradictory. The low-ranking soldiers were flustered, resigned, and dismayed. Enva Tazaar's bold plan took advantage of that.

Tanja and Walfor easily obtained militia uniforms, which were distributed widely in hopes of increasing the visible numbers of the militia. Tanja didn't like wearing such a uniform, but it was an important element of her disguise. She plucked at the sleeves and tugged at the seams, but couldn't make the blouse hang correctly. "This looks like it was made by a cut-rate costume shop."

"Probably was. The militia had to produce large quantities of them somehow." Walfor brushed his own chest and lifted his chin as if to cut a striking, heroic pose. "Actually, I think it fits you rather well."

She shot him a sharp glance. "Let's get to the spaceport. It's time."

Full night had fallen, and the landing zone lights shimmered a harsh white. Tehila's military-grade ships had already joined the fleet in orbit for scheduled departure the following day. Their window of opportunity was closing.

As they approached the spaceport's main guard gate, Tanja felt a knot in her stomach. Sensing her tension, Walfor reached over to squeeze her arm, but they had to maintain the appearance of two militia officers with a duty to perform. Tanja pulled away and whispered out of the side of her mouth. "You sure we can trust Enva Tazaar?"

"No, but we'll find out for sure soon enough."

Tanja Hu instinctively despised the noble families of the Crown Jewels, including the Tazaars. They were corrupt, ambitious, self-centered, and had run roughshod over the DZ colonists for years. But Tanja also knew that Enva had previously made secret overtures to General Adolphus; even before her disgrace, Enva had been clear in her desire to overthrow Diadem Michella. Tanja didn't like being allied with such a woman, one of the corrupt nobles from the Crown Jewels, but she had to take the chance.

With a cocky and impatient smile, Walfor stepped up to the spaceport guard. He showed his access credentials and paperwork. "Special assignment to prepare one of the civilian ships as a decoy for the military assault tomorrow."

The guard was a squarish, middle-aged woman who looked all muscle and no fat. "Why wasn't I informed of this?"

Walfor pushed the documentation in front of her. "You're being informed now."

Instead of being suspicious, the woman let out a sigh. "Idiots. Approvals can't come through this office. I've told them three times since yesterday."

Tanja stepped forward. "We have all the proper signatures and access prints."

The guard squinted down at the papers, read them twice. "Yes, you have official signatures and access prints." She called to another guard, who sat inside a small shack, "Ched, do you know about this?"

"Not a peep," said Ched. "I try not to, though. My head is still spinning from all the other screw-ups today."

The female guard handed the paperwork back and grudgingly called up a map on a screen. "Yes, here it is. The ship is already cleared for takeoff. It looks like you have a delivery scheduled before departure, one cargo container. They're bringing it in through the west gate."

"That's part of the operation," Tanja said, trying not to show her relief.

The guard, who seemed anxious to have her gate quiet and empty again, waved them inside. "You know which ship it is?"

Walfor scanned the impounded vessels inside the fenced area, locked his gaze on one. He had a special sparkle in his eyes. "Oh, I most certainly do." He looked like a man seeing a lost lover after several years.

"Is it all fueled and ready to go, per orders?" Tanja asked.

The guard frowned, as if to emphasize that this wasn't her business or responsibility. She flipped to another screen and said, "Yes, completely fueled—rationing's been imposed, so most ships don't get this much—but someone got around that for you. You're all set."

Walfor hustled Tanja along. "We're on our way, then."

When they reached the ship, he was grinning, eager to get to the controls, and Tanja was anxious to get away. Before walking up the ramp she scanned the paved area, saw other ships sitting silently under the harsh illumination. Maintenance crews moved about, but most of the preparations had been completed for the imminent launch of the fleet.

She saw no sign of the arriving cargo container, however, nor of Enva Tazaar and her coconspirator. She frowned. If they didn't arrive as planned, she and Walfor would have to escape anyway. It was imperative to warn General Adolphus, with or without the Diadem as a bargaining chip.

Then Tanja spotted a low hauler humming across the landing area, weaving among the ships. The driver was obviously in a hurry, but didn't seem proficient operating the vehicle. The hauler pulled alongside Walfor's ship, towing a medium-size cargo box. Enva Tazaar swung out of the driver's cab, wearing her bureaucrat's uniform, which looked out of place in the loading area.

"Help me get this aboard—it's precious cargo." She chuckled, hard and sharp. "Or maybe it should be marked 'Hazardous Waste.'"

The three moved quickly together to bring the container aboard the ship.

Enva opened the lid of the cargo box. Inside, like two rag dolls, lay the unconscious forms of Ishop Heer and Diadem Michella Duchenet. Upon seeing the old woman, a sour taste rose in Tanja's throat.

"How long will they remain unconscious?" Walfor asked.

"Another hour or two, enough time for us to tie them up."

"Enough time for us to fly out of here." Tanja cast a suspicious glance around the spaceport. "You have the clearances?"

"I've submitted them," Enva said, "but it's all a house of cards. Even so, incompetence and confusion are our friends now. The worst thing that could happen would be for us to blunder into people who know what they're doing."

Patrol flyers cruised low over the spaceport. Enva glanced up at them and compared their flight patterns with her projected launch path. "Let's hope they stay out of our way," she said in a low voice.

Walfor powered up the engines. Warning signals came in across the control deck—but no emergencies yet. The comm activated. "This is Spaceport Operations. We're detecting an unauthorized departure. All ships, stand down and wait for our security staff to investigate."

"How very polite." Tanja looked at the other woman. "Now what do we do?"

Enva switched on the comm. "This is an *authorized*

departure. All flight paths and paperwork have been filed. Double-check your records, but do it quickly. We're on a tight schedule here. The fleet is getting ready to launch."

The three of them sat tense, but Walfor didn't wait. He continued to go through his prelaunch checklist. "This was a half-assed revolution anyway. I knew that if worse came to worst, I might have to break my ship out of here. Security patrols in this city are like a bunch of drunken gnats."

"But they can still cause problems," Tanja said. Walfor was the best pilot she'd ever seen, but she hoped he wouldn't have to demonstrate that now.

Spaceport Operations came back on the comm. "We found a request and authorization, but it's from Tehila Admin HQ. Groundside paperwork shows this ship is part of the military operation, which is under the jurisdiction of the Constellation forces in orbit. Please stand by while we check the irregularities."

Breathing faster, Enva responded in a clipped voice, "If you check my access code, you will find that my authority comes from the highest level, from the *Diadem's* office. That overrides your traditional channels."

The spaceport operator answered in a cool voice, sounding unmoved. "With all due respect, Diadem Michella is not in charge of military operations here. Commodore Hallholme is the supreme authority. I've submitted a priority request to the flagship and dispatched a copy to Diadem Michella's office. Thank you for your patience. Security has been tightened with the imminent departure of the fleet."

"We'll stand by," Enva said, sounding calm. She switched off the comm.

"Now what do we do?" Tanja asked.

Enva looked hard at Walfor. "We launch anyway. Now!"

He grinned. He was already activating systems and increasing power to the takeoff thrusters. "Back to my original scheme, then."

"I don't believe in a single-pronged plan," Enva said. "And I've arranged another surprise at the terminus ring, for insurance."

Tanja called up the copilot's screen, plotted their vector, and expanded the error bars to give them room to move. "If this had gone smoothly, we could have traveled to the terminus ring, slipped onto the Hellhole stringline, and been gone. Now we have to bypass the terminus entirely. Ian, are you sure you can find the iperion trail on your own?"

He studied the controls, caressed a screen with his finger, as if for encouragement, and smiled at her. "Of course I can. I did extensive system mapping already, just like I did at Candela when I found your killer asteroids. The actual terminus ring is for amateurs who need training wheels."

Perspiring, Enva looked at the ship's chronometer display. "Are we going to go?"

"Without further ado." Walfor punched the accelerator, and all the ship's thrusters ignited at once, pushing them off the landing field with a great leap into the sky. Then the turbos kicked in and shot them toward orbit.

Immediately, the alarm boards lit up. Spaceport security started squawking in contradictory shouts over the comm lines. Additional banks of lights flared like novas below. The low-flying airborne patrol ships veered in toward the ascending craft.

"I didn't think they would respond this quickly,"

Walfor remarked, "but don't worry. Everyone, lock down your safety straps. Is the cargo container with the hostages secured?"

"Not really," Tanja said. "They'll be bounced around pretty badly if you make any extreme moves."

"Oh, well." Walfor concentrated on his flying as he shot toward orbit, curving away from the main cluster of Constellation warships and the two stringline terminus rings that were under tight military control. He said with more boyish glee than concern, "Hang on."

33

On the night before launching a major military operation, Commodore Percival Hallholme knew the wisdom of getting a good night's sleep. He needed his mind fresh and thoughts clear, his reflexes and responses sharp.

And yet, unfailingly, he was interrupted by a stream of last-minute details that no underlings could—or wanted to—solve themselves. Even when Percival was alone in his private stateroom with the lights dimmed, lying on his bunk with a strict "do not disturb" indicator on the door, he remained awake, his thoughts buzzing with a cascade of possible consequences, decision tree to decision tree.

He had faced General Adolphus before, numerous times. Once the military haulers launched for Hellhole, they would have a five-day journey along the iperion path, and Percival had no doubt he would experience several more restless nights on the way.

Sometimes, he just gave up on sleep, put his uniform back on, and went to the bridge. Now, as the massive fleet prepared to depart, the Commodore chided himself: He should have known better than to try to sleep.

He put on a fresh uniform and prepared a cup of kiafa from his room dispenser. If he was going to be awake and restless, he might as well do so on the bridge where he could make certain all the preparations were completed to his satisfaction.

Once more into the breach . . .

His previous engagement with General Adolphus at Hellhole should have been a victory. His plans had been impeccable, his surprise approach on the abandoned Buktu stringline executed without a hitch. He did not underestimate his old nemesis, but the destructive alien attack had been a shock.

Assuredly, he would face that invisible telekinetic blast again, and he could only hope that his ships' additional shielding would protect them long enough to seize the stringline hub, defeat the rebel General, and free the Constellation prisoners—including his son. That would more than make up for Percival's previous failure, and Escobar's as well. Afterward, he could let Diadem Michella consolidate her rule throughout the Deep Zone, while he just went home for a well-deserved retirement.

Resigned, Percival had accepted the distorted legend of his career. He had not wanted to reenter this fight, had never wished to face Adolphus again, a foe who had been so dishonorably treated by the Diadem. But he had chosen sides and sworn loyalty to a leader with feet of clay. And that loyalty was his only path to continued honor.

Emerging from his stateroom, he was startled to see Duff Adkins rushing toward him. The faithful adjutant was just as surprised to see him awake. "Commodore, there's a crisis!"

"There's always a crisis, Duff." Percival picked up his pace, and the two walked briskly toward the bridge. "What is it this time?"

"Someone stole a cargo ship from the Tehila spaceport."

"That's a crisis? Send teams to intercept it."

"We're trying, sir. But this pilot is extremely adept, and his engines have been enhanced. We checked—the ship has high-level authorizations, but they're counterfeit. This isn't just some impatient trader trying to get away—I think it's a realistic threat, sir."

"How do we know it has anything to do with us?"

"If not, then why take the risk of flying now? If the pilot just wants to slip away, he could easily wait for our fleet to depart. After tomorrow, he'd have a much easier time of it. But something forced his hand now."

They arrived on the bridge to find the crew scrambling from station to station. Screens showed the path of the escaping craft and the pursuit vectors of air patrols. Many small ships flitted about in space, but all the larger Constellation vessels, including the flagship, were firmly mounted in the huge hauler frameworks, ready to depart.

Percival guessed what the fugitive ship was up to. "I think that pilot intends to warn General Adolphus." He studied the screens, listened to the chatter. "Even if he gets away from the planet, our control of the terminus rings remains firm?"

Adkins glanced at one of the tactical officers, a woman with short-cropped black hair. She answered, "Both stringline rings are under friendly control, Commodore."

Percival's tension eased. "Then the pilot will never find the iperion line. The best he can do is to lose himself in this star system. If our fleet launches on schedule, we will get to the General long before any warning can possibly reach him."

An urgent communiqué broke through from Spaceport Operations. "I have vital information for Commodore Hallholme—an extreme emergency! Diadem Michella Duchenet is missing. We believe she's been abducted from the administrator's mansion."

The flagship's comm officer glanced over his shoulder, watching the Commodore for a response. Percival had not wanted Michella Duchenet along on this operation at all, and any delay could compromise the mission. Trying to think of a reasonable explanation, he recalled the Diadem's capricious moods. What had she gotten herself into now? "Why do you believe she's been kidnapped? Make certain she hasn't just toddled out to go observe a walump village under the stars."

Spaceport Operations reported, "A search is already under way, Commodore, but there is definite cause for concern. All security eyes in the headquarters mansion were conveniently blinded, just before the Diadem entered the area with her assistant Ishop Heer. When we backtracked the access, it appears the Diadem's own assistant Ishop Heer was working with a low-level clerk named Enva Lien. Those names are also associated with the counterfeit documentation that provided launch clearance for the cargo ship that is currently fleeing Tehila. The connection is clear, sir. They have the Diadem."

Percival assembled the pieces in his mind and raised his voice to the bridge personnel. "All forces, pursue and intercept that ship! Apprehend and board only. Do *not* destroy it under any circumstances."

Suddenly the flagship's deck lurched, and a resounding *clunk* echoed through the vessel. Artificial gravity was skewed severely off-norm for a few moments.

"What happened?" Percival demanded.

Adkins kept his balance by gripping the side of a tactical station. "We just dropped free from the docking clamp, sir. We're drifting inside the hauler framework."

Percival looked up at the screen, saw that dozens of other nearby ships—all of them painstakingly mounted aboard the giant framework for transport—had also come loose, and were tumbling free. Proximity alarms blared as the ships drifted. Before he could say anything, two vessels collided, then spread apart in a slow-motion ricochet. The flagship's hull groaned as another warship scraped against it.

He opened a system-wide channel. "All ships, use maneuvering jets! Maintain stability—battle shields on to avoid collisions!"

The flagship drifted and tilted until the navigator managed to stabilize it. "What the hell happened?" Percival demanded. "Why did we disengage from the docking clamp? All the ships were loaded for departure."

"Some sort of control glitch, Commodore. All docking clamps released their ships simultaneously."

The comm officer touched his earadio. "Same thing happened on the other stringline hauler, Commodore. Our entire fleet disengaged from the frameworks. It's complete chaos."

"Not by accident," Percival growled. "There's a saboteur aboard the terminus ring. Find out who it is and detain him or her for questioning. I want to know how many traitors there are!"

He had never been convinced that Tehila would welcome the military crackdown with open arms. There had to be numerous rotten apples in the ranks. His troops hadn't had time to run full security protocols on all of Administrator Reming's technical staff.

A comm signal came from the DZ terminus ring.

Screens showed crewmembers responding to an alarm. One screen flashed with a small explosion, then went to static. Others listed damage reports coming from the ring.

Adkins focused on a different screen, watched the fleeing cargo ship reach orbit, then arc over to the planet's dayside before accelerating out into space, taking advantage of the chaos in the disorganized fleet. The local Tehila patrol ships dropped back, unable to continue the pursuit at such distance, running out of fuel.

Percival dispatched sixteen Constellation ships that were drifting loose from the haulers. "Capture that ship—don't let it get away!" He didn't dare let it slip through his fingers.

The pursuing vessels scrambled, but they were disoriented. Deciding not to let such a vital task fall to just any ship that happened to be drifting in space, Percival ordered the flagship's engines to full power, disregarding safety protocols. If that cargo ship got away with Diadem Michella as a hostage, the whole nature of this operation would change.

Reports came in from the terminus ring. "We captured an Adolphus loyalist, sir. She planted an explosive, damaged some systems, but the stringline is intact. We believe it can be fixed."

"Make immediate repairs—we have to launch the fleet!" Percival shouted.

The man on the screen sounded flustered. "Commodore, the damage is extensive. Minimum, four or five days before we can get out of here—*if* Tehila has the necessary spare components. And that's not likely."

"Bring the saboteur to the screen—I want to talk with her."

"Sorry, Commodore, she was . . . killed during capture."

As the hundreds of displaced ships drifted free, pell-mell and confused after being ejected from the hauler framework, Percival's flagship accelerated away from the stringline, accompanied by a group of scattered but ambitious pursuit ships. Roaring through the system, ignoring the amount of fuel they were burning, they began to close the distance.

But the trader ship was on an erratic course, jogging back and forth along a generally defined course, as if . . . searching? For the stringline? No pilot could find the stringline without the anchor point . . . unless he had extremely accurate prior mappings.

As the flagship closed the distance to the escaping vessel, Percival opened a direct channel to the pilot. "This is Commodore Hallholme. I demand that you stand down. You cannot escape. Your ship will be captured and returned to Tehila."

Surprisingly, the pilot responded. "Commodore, when you pose a challenge like that, you're just *asking* me to prove you wrong. And you've given me absolutely no reason to surrender." The man had a cocky look and showed no fear. His gaze hardened as he continued. "And I've still got a bone to pick with you after what you did to all my people at Buktu."

Percival blinked. "Administrator Ian Walfor, I believe?"

A beautiful woman with a hard expression and long dark hair moved into view, nudging Walfor away. "And I'm Administrator Tanja Hu, formerly of Candela." She signaled to someone off screen, then turned back to the Commodore. "Everyone on Sonjeera knows me. I'm the one who executed the Diadem's crony, Marla Undine, and sent her decapitated head back to Sonjeera. I'm sure it made the news." She raised her eyebrows in a mocking look.

Percival knew about the horrific package, as did everyone aboard. "Why do you feel the need to tell me this?"

Walfor and a second woman wrestled a limp body into view. Diadem Michella Duchenet. Tanja said, "I reminded you about Governor Undine because we have the Diadem as our hostage. Though unconscious, she is unharmed—so far. But if you don't break off pursuit immediately, I will personally execute her . . . and you know I'll do it, Commodore, if you leave me no other choice. I'll dump her severed head out of our disposal chute, and your ships can retrieve it if you like."

Tanja Hu terminated the transmission, and Percival stared at the screen, appalled. "Follow that ship, but maintain a safe distance."

He had to figure out how to capture the vessel and save the Diadem.

Next to him, Adkins spoke in a low voice. He wore an expression of great concern. "What do we do now, Commodore?"

"Duff, if I let the Diadem get killed, that will be the greatest failure in my career." He had no great love for the callous old woman, disagreed with many of her decisions—but she was still his commander in chief.

"They're bluffing," Duff said.

"Maybe, and maybe not. Call up every record we have on Tanja Hu. We know she did execute Governor Undine, and the Diadem is her only bargaining chip now." In his heart, Percival dreaded that they intended to kill Michella Duchenet, regardless. In which case, better that he was seen to be actively trying to save her, rather than procrastinating while the old woman was held hostage.

Then the choice was taken out of his hands as, somehow, the trader located the iperion line, activated stringline engines, and hurtled off in a disappearing wink of light, far faster than even photons could travel.

Percival and Duff Adkins were left staring at the empty space where the ship had vanished.

34

After she regained consciousness, the Diadem's outrage trumped her fear—until she learned where she was being taken. Then cold dread filtered down to her marrow.

As she recovered from the stunner, Michella couldn't understand how this had happened. Her body ached and twitched, nerves misfiring, her head pounding. The roar in her ears was definitely not the roar of cheering crowds. She felt bruised and abused.

Her last moments of consciousness were blurred and uncertain, but she recalled being with Ishop when they were confronted by a woman with a weapon, a stunner. . . .

Michella found herself sealed inside a small harshly lit room with metal decks, bulkheads, and no windows. Ishop couldn't possibly be involved! Vibrations implied this was a moving spaceship. Her clothes were rumpled, and she realized to her horror that she had soiled herself. She had heard that upon suffering a heavy stun blast, some victims lost control of their bodily functions—but certainly not a Diadem! Michella was disgusted with herself, and with her captors that they would do such a barbaric thing to her.

She lurched toward the sealed door, but the controls failed to respond. She pounded and shouted. "I demand to be released!" She yelled until she was hoarse, then looked around to find that her small cell had no water dispenser, no sanitary facilities—it appeared to be just some kind of storage room. This was humiliating!

That increased her anger, and she launched another cycle of pounding and shouting until the door slid open. A woman she recognized—but couldn't place—stood before her. She had long black hair, high cheekbones, and a murderous expression. "You are in no position to make demands. Those days are over for you, Michella Duchenet. Don't you remember me?"

"I can't be expected to recall all my underlings across the Constellation," Michella snapped as she struggled to come up with the name. For some reason, this woman held an unreasonable grudge against her, as did so many of the Deep Zone yokels after they were brainwashed by General Tiber Adolphus, or maybe even possessed by aliens.

The woman said, "Tanja Hu, planetary administrator of Candela?"

Finally, Michella did remember this woman, and when she did, a cold knot formed in her stomach. Tanja Hu . . . yes, the rebel Candela administrator. Ah, the insane woman who decapitated Marla Undine!

Now Michella realized how helpless she was and what might happen to her. "What have you done? And where are you taking me? Where is Ishop?"

"Your lapdog is in another cell similar to this one. He must be less resilient, though, because he's still unconscious." Tanja's smile was like a slash across her face. "Because of your stature, we gave you a slightly larger compartment. I hope you're comfortable here." She wrinkled her nose, as if picking up the odor of Michella's personal problem.

The Diadem lurched toward the open doorway, and Tanja held up a stunner, smiling. "I would love to have an excuse."

Michella froze. Yes, she was sure this woman would do it. "You have no right to hold me here. Your actions will bring down the fury of the Constellation. You've brought about your own annihilation."

Tanja was unimpressed. "More so than you were already planning? I think there's a chance—a small one—that you may actually be worth something. If I'm convinced otherwise, I'd happily throw you out the airlock."

Another hard and angry woman joined Tanja Hu, this one a blonde. How many traitors were there? More memories began to spark out of the fog of unconsciousness. Michella identified her now—Enva Tazaar.

"We're currently en route to Hellhole, where we'll deliver you to General Tiber Adolphus." Enva smiled. "I'm sure he'll figure out what to do with you. Or maybe just declare you a war criminal and command your immediate execution. It'll be up to him."

"He is the General, after all," Tanja said.

That made the words dry up in Michella's mouth. Her defiance withered away, but she managed to say, "Release me at once! Return me to Tehila and I'll see that you get a pardon, even a safe exile on some DZ world. Despite what you've done, I can be merciful."

Tanja just rolled her eyes. "We'd rather make you useful. With you as a hostage, we can stave off Commodore Hallholme's attack and protect the Deep Zone. And I'm sure the General will think of things to do with you as his prisoner. He has even more reason to resent you than we do."

"Let me see Ishop Heer!" Michella said. "I want to

know that he's unharmed." Maybe he could get her out of this. . . .

The other women seemed to find that amusing, but didn't explain why.

"You have enemies everywhere, Diadem," said Tanja Hu. "Be thankful we're taking you to the General. At least he'll have political reasons to keep you alive."

Enva added, "In fact, he's more likely to care about your well-being than we are."

Enraged, Michella again lunged toward the door. Tanja Hu swung up the stunner, but hesitated. Instead, Enva closed and sealed the door, leaving Michella alone and impotent in the tiny cell.

—◦w—

After another day of being treated as an animal, Michella was finally allowed to clean herself up. Her captors provided her with meager rations and lukewarm water, as well as a spare set of baggy ship's clothes to wear while her soiled garments were laundered. She learned later that Enva Tazaar had forced Ishop to operate the laundry apparatus. Her aide was just as much a captive, but treated even more poorly, since he had no political worth whatsoever.

Michella struggled to reassemble her pride and tried to figure out how she could turn the table against these traitors. But she was utterly impotent now. She had sat upon the Star Throne for decades, ruling twenty Crown Jewel planets and another fifty-four Deep Zone worlds. With a single command from Sonjeera, she'd been able to change the fates of millions of people.

She'd fallen so far, had never felt so small.

Although Michella had clashed repeatedly with

General Adolphus, she had been in the same room with the man only once, more than a decade ago, when the defeated rebel leader was brought before her in shackles.

Now, in a humilating turnabout, she would be dragged before him on *his* turf. Still, Michella swore to herself she would stand straight and face that evil man, find a way to defeat him. But with a chill she thought of how she had treated the General's own emissary, Territorial Governor Goler—first seizing him as a political prisoner, then executing him. Just because she could.

General Adolphus had no reason not to do the same. But she was worth more to him alive—she knew it. At her advanced age, Michella did not necessarily fear death, but she could not face the horror of being contaminated by the aliens. What if the General forced her to be possessed by the hideous things, and then turned her loose back in the Constellation? That would be worse than any death! She felt sick at the very thought of it.

Hellhole was infested with those slime-covered creatures who possessed innocent humans and imposed their will. Her own daughter was one of them, gullible and vapid Keana whose mind and soul had been filled with strange memories.

Michella wasn't surprised that her weak-willed daughter had been duped by the bizarre Hellhole religion, the baptism in alien lives. Yes, she had a pretty face but never had a mind of her own . . . nor was it surprising that Ishop had so easily tricked Keana into running off, poorly prepared and naïve, to chase down a fairy tale. And now her daughter was irretrievable, forever contaminated. A total loss.

But what if General Adolphus coerced Michella into one of those disgusting pools? Under the rules of civilized behavior, he wouldn't dare . . . but he had already proved himself to be a barbarian, a monster.

Michella huddled in her small cell, felt the vibration of the ship as it raced along the stringline, and she tried to form a plan.

———※———

When the ship finally arrived at the Deep Zone stringline hub, her captors released her from the cramped chamber and let her come to the bridge. Ishop Heer was also there, his hands bound behind his back, his eyes darting, his expression angry.

Before Michella could speak, Ishop said, "They betrayed me as well, Eminence. We are trapped. Mere pawns."

The ship's pilot—Ian Walfor, former planetary administrator of Buktu—said, "Diadem Michella is a pawn. You, Mr. Heer, aren't much of anything at all."

Ishop glowered at him.

Michella tried to be dignified. "I am the Diadem of the Constellation, and I demand to be treated with proper respect. If I am a political prisoner, then certain conditions must be met. Even General Adolphus, for all his crimes, understands the necessities of politics, and of decorum."

"Proper treatment . . . just like you showed the people on Theser?" Tanja Hu asked. "Lord Riomini leveled the entire colony without warning, killed every single civilian, including Administrator Sia Frankov." She made a bitter sound. "Don't talk to *me* about expectations and respect."

Ishop struggled against his bonds, but Michella could see that he had no real hope of breaking free.

"Before we take you to meet the General, we'll shackle you as well, in keeping with precedent," Enva Tazaar suggested. "Enjoy your relative freedom for now. Don't give us a reason to take it away."

Walfor's ship decelerated toward the large stringline hub above the blasted planet. Numerous ships were there, some at the hub, others riding in space. Michella knew those vessels would not be enough when the Army of the Constellation swooped in to destroy the rebels.

"Commodore Hallholme will come for me," she said, her voice hard. "He won't be far behind."

"I'm afraid the Commodore encountered some unexpected difficulties back at Tehila," said Walfor. "A saboteur damaged the terminus ring. He won't be able to launch his ships until repairs are made."

Tanja interjected, "And he knows we have you as hostage. I told him we'd kill you if he pursued."

"He'll know you're bluffing," Michella said.

Tanja raised her eyebrows. "Are we? I reminded him about what I did to Governor Undine."

Michella's heart felt heavy. Brave Commodore Hallholme, a staid and formal commander who did everything by the book, would never take the chance. With the Diadem in enemy hands, and the stringline to Hellhole damaged so that he couldn't launch his fleet, the Commodore would have to make up his own mind. She trusted him to know what to do; he was loyal to her.

As Walfor's ship approached the stringline hub, he transmitted a message and immediately received clearance to dock his ship at the hub, where a special escort shuttle would take them down to the General's headquarters.

Michella looked through the cockpit windowports, saw the blasted planet below, the enormous impact crater that looked like a bull's-eye hundreds of kilometers wide. This was the hellish place where she had exiled the defeated General, fully intending for him to perish.

Now she was the one trapped here, and she doubted if even Ishop Heer could help her.

Hellhole . . .

35

General Adolphus had never dreamed of such a complete turnabout: a defeated Diadem Michella Duchenet brought before him in chains. He didn't gloat over his victory—that sort of pettiness was dishonorable, and it was beneath him—but having the Diadem as his captive changed the very nature of the war. And he would indeed use that to his advantage.

Waiting for the arrival of the prisoner, he and Sophie Vence met in his Elba offices, completely in control; Sophie stood in support beside his desk, exuding righteous anger. She had always blamed the Diadem for the Deep Zone's misery. She reached over to place a firm hand on his shoulder. "You've waited a long time for this day, Tiber."

He considered. "I waited for Destination Day, when our stringline network was complete and we could declare independence. And I've waited for the day when the Constellation decides to coexist with the Deep Zone. But waiting to gloat over her? No. I will treat the Diadem as a rival leader should, not as a barbarian."

Ian Walfor and Tanja Hu arrived with the Diadem and her aide as prisoners, both of them with wrists and ankles bound with symbolic chains. They were accompanied by a blonde woman he did not at first recognize, then he placed Enva Tazaar. Not long ago, the former ruler of Orsini had reached out to him, proposing a secret alliance against the Diadem. She had been stripped of her rank and possessions, and had disappeared. Now that was a surprise.

But his attention was riveted on Michella Duchenet.

Seeing the old woman before him, broken and helpless, made Adolphus recall when *he* had staggered forward across the floor of the Council Hall, a prisoner after his first failed rebellion. The seats had all been filled with nobles, many of whom hated him. He had been sure he would be sentenced to death, but had hoped to negotiate clemency for his followers.

He'd gotten neither. Instead of execution, the Diadem had sent him to a hellish planet and exiled his followers as well. Now the tables were turned. He met her gaze calmly, not provoking, but supremely confident. She had to see that she had no power here, no leverage.

Adolphus rose from behind his desk, and the old woman lifted her chin. Defiance flashed in her eyes. "What will you do now, General? Drag me through the streets? Make a show of denigrating me before you kill me?"

He was surprised and let disappointment creep into his voice. "If you imagine I would do such a thing, Michella Duchenet, then you know very little about me. You must know that I am a man who respects authority and honor." He glanced at Tanja. "The shackles are not necessary. Please remove her restraints."

Though the others seemed wary about this, Tanja released the manacles. Diadem Michella lifted her age-spotted arms, rubbed her wrists. She offered no thanks for the courtesy.

"What about me?" Ishop Heer lifted his manacled hands. "Unshackle me, too, as a show of good faith?"

Adolphus sat back down behind his desk. "I think not—I know you well enough, Mr. Heer." He didn't trust Michella Duchenet, but he did not fear her. Her lackey, however, was an entirely different sort of enemy, a loose cannon, someone utterly dishonorable who would come up from behind and slip a knife in a back. "This is between me and the Diadem."

He turned to the old woman again. "Some realities, first. We've worked hard for our freedom and independence in the Deep Zone, and I have no desire to continue this conflict. We're caring for thousands of Constellation prisoners that we'd just as soon send home in exchange for the Buktu civilians you still hold. We captured most of your Constellation fleet and chased Commodore Hallholme back to Sonjeera with his tail between his legs. And now he has seized one of my DZ planets, so I'll have to defeat him again—and I will, with or without you as hostage."

His voice grew harder, louder, as anger built within him. "I intend to use you as a bargaining chip if I can. You will not be harmed, nor will you be allowed to create unrest. My first order of business is to deal with Commodore Hallholme and his fleet at Tehila. After I've made certain that he poses no threat, we can negotiate terms for your release." He raised his eyebrows. "Perhaps in exchange for Constellation recognition of Deep Zone independence, and all of our prisoners freed."

"That will never happen," Michella said. "If you send me back right away, I *may* allow some of your followers to live."

Adolphus remained calm. "Please, no ridiculous posturing. It's not worth my time. The war is over, and the Deep Zone is free. Now that I have you as hostage, the rest is all details."

Adolphus summoned his personal security guards to take Diadem Michella and Ishop Heer to secure chambers here at Elba, where they would be kept under constant guard for the time being. After the prisoners were gone, he let Tanja Hu and Ian Walfor go to tend to their ship, but he asked Enva Tazaar to stay. "You've made a surprise appearance in the Deep Zone."

She looked hopeful. "I suffered unexpected setbacks, but I am on your side, General. I already suggested an alliance with you, one that would have brought down Michella Duchenet."

"I remember it well," Adolphus said. "Unfortunately, the timing was not right, and now the situation has changed drastically."

Enva said, "Change is inevitable. We can either implement the change, or be overwhelmed by it. With my family connections, I would still be a powerful ally, General."

He could see she was ambitious, but he wasn't convinced. "My understanding is that you have no power whatsoever."

She shrugged. "Circumstances change. The old noble alliances can be resurrected and new ones formed." She smiled, but with only a hint of humor. "My original offer still stands. If we topple the Diadem, you could give me leadership of the Crown Jewels while you administer all the frontier worlds. As allies, we would bring this mess to an end."

"True leadership positions are not given. They are earned."

Enva looked at the General with barely concealed astonishment, turned toward the door. "I orchestrated the capture of Diadem Michella. I warned you of Commodore Hallholme's surprise attack, and arranged for the sabotage of the stringline hub to delay his launch.

Before that, I endured exile, waiting and hiding and planning just to build something for myself out in the Deep Zone. I delivered your worst enemy to you at the most crucial time. You now have the Constellation over a barrel." She glanced at Sophie, then at the General. "How can you suggest I haven't earned anything?"

"You have earned my respect and my gratitude," Adolphus said. "But the Crown Jewels are not mine to give."

She paused, reassessed. "I have to start somewhere. I'm here and ready to reestablish myself as a leader. Give me a planet to administer. I'll even run Tehila, if you manage to take it back from Commodore Hall-holme."

"Still thinking big?" Sophie said with a wry smile. "I hate to admit it but we could use another strong leader in the DZ. I believe Hossetea is in need of new and loyal leadership."

The General realized she was right. After researching Enva Tazaar when she had first proposed the pact with him, he knew she was both formidable and capable. She was hard, sometimes even ruthless, but her record had been impressive enough. He did owe her some kind of reward, so he would give her a chance to prove her worth.

"The planet Theser is a better option," he said. "Devastated after Lord Riomini's attack, but habitable. Empty and unclaimed. Many Candela refugees are still displaced, not just the ones trapped on Tehila. They'll be willing to work, anxious to establish a new home rather than crowding an already-strained DZ world. It will be a hard place to reestablish a colony—but not much different from when the Diadem sent me here to Hellhole. After you prove yourself there, then perhaps we can talk. If you think you're up to the task."

Enva narrowed her eyes. "I remember what you said back at the end of the first rebellion: Better to rule on Hellhole than to serve on Sonjeera. It's better than being a civil servant. A step in the right direction. I'll take it."

Adolphus leaned forward, folded his hands together on his desktop. "We can send the tools, prefab structures, and supplies they'll need. Many of the remaining Candela refugees will jump at the chance for a fresh start. You'll have Theser to administer as an interim governor. Demonstrate your abilities, and in a year or so, we'll leave it up to the people there to pick their own leader. What happens next depends on whether you've impressed them or not."

Enva Tazaar began to consider the possibilities. "I will impress them, General."

36

It was the third day since the four Constellation officers had escaped from the camp. Bolton continued driving the camouflaged and damaged Trakmaster over rough, rocky ground; his stomach was in knots—he had no sense of where they were, or where they were going, because the onboard nav-system could not recognize the surrounding terrain. Escobar insisted on heading "forward" without having a solid idea of what that was.

In the early morning, Bolton drove through an arroyo, heading for yet another line of hills in the distance. From the high point, they hoped to receive a nav-signal or at least find some distinctive landmark to get their bearings. They had to reorient themselves, so they could head toward Michella Town . . . and escape.

"For all we know, we're heading in the completely

wrong direction," Escobar said with a groan. "We don't dare let searchers find us."

"That might not be a bad thing, at this point," said Yimidi. Bolton had heard him sleeping fitfully, coughing himself awake and then trying to go back to sleep. The junior officer sounded exhausted, and his throat was raw.

"The General has been looking for an excuse to get rid of us," Escobar said. "If we're recaptured, he'll order our execution because we tried to escape."

Bolton tried to sound determined and encouraging. "We have to survive on our own and get off this planet. It's our duty to get back to the Constellation, somehow."

In the rear compartment, Seyn Vingh sat as far from Yimidi as possible. "I hope we don't all catch whatever the hell you've got. Some kind of plague . . . how do we know it's not contagious?"

"You want to just abandon me so you can go on?" Yimidi asked.

Bolton raised his voice just enough to let them hear the unexpected steel there. "That is not what we do." If the disease had been contagious, with the confined vehicle and the recirculated air, all four of them would have been exposed by now. "He needs medical attention."

"Be my guest, Major Crais—find us the nearest hospital facility," Escobar said in a sharp tone.

"I don't think it's contagious," Yimidi said, rasping. "One of those algae things tried to get in my mouth. I'm still tasting it, smelling it. What if it left spores or something inside me? I could be . . . infested." He coughed, doubled over, and hacked in a much more violent spasm, as if his rib cage would crack open and his lungs spill out.

Bolton found a level clearing and pulled the Trak-master over, grinding the treads to a halt. "We need to help him," he said, without knowing how. They had already given Yimidi antibiotics and antivirals from the med-kit, as well as using emergency disinfectants tailored to indigenous Hellhole hazards, but there was no assurance that any such treatment would have an effect.

Vingh reached into the back cargo compartment and brought out the med-kit again. "We can give him a tranquilizer to calm him."

Yimidi let out a ripping howl, and with a horrific coughing scream he ejected an acid yellow projectile that struck the inner windshield next to Bolton's head. The sputum writhed, wriggling away—the same ambulatory algae that had pursued them through the canyon, but denser now; it glowed with an angry phosphorescence.

Yimidi kept screaming as he coughed again and regurgitated more algae. Some of it landed on Vingh's clothing; in a panic, Vingh punched the controls and opened one of the Trakmaster's hatches and dove outside. Escobar sat in horror, paralyzed, while Bolton tried to help the writhing Yimidi, holding him down.

Outside, Vingh was shouting curses and tearing off his smeared clothing before the algae could eat it away and come in contact with his skin.

Yimidi kept ejecting the live vomit, and Escobar pulled Bolton away. "Don't let any of it get on you, Major!"

In the rear passenger area, the pulsing algae began crawling from the puddles, and more spilled down Yimidi's face, eating away at the skin. The man's face was purple-red, his eyes bulging, as he continued to tear himself apart with coughing spasms.

Escobar jumped out of the Trakmaster's cab and

dashed toward Vingh, who used a boot to smash as much of the algae as he could.

The Redcom yelled, "Major, we have to get the rest of our food supplies, water containers, med-kit, survival packs, and weapons out—anything we might need." He turned and locked gazes with Bolton. "We're abandoning the vehicle here, but we have to salvage what we can!"

Bolton didn't want to leave Yimidi, but the man was already as good as dead, even though he still convulsed. He hoped Vingh had not been harmed. He evacuated the main cab with a last glance behind him to see the regurgitated, intensely glowing algae spreading across all surfaces. After gestating inside of its human host, the slime was replicating with amazing speed, engulfing Yimidi's body, digesting him.

With no way to help his comrade, Bolton hurried around to the rear of the Trakmaster to assist Escobar and a staggering, shaken Vingh in salvaging the last items from the storage compartment, including a spare jumpsuit, which he tossed to Vingh.

He stared at the infested vehicle. "How far can we go on foot?"

Facing ahead, Escobar pointed toward the hills. "We should be able to make it that far by nightfall." He took a small projectile gun from the emergency pack, the only weapon in the vehicle, and tucked it into his waistband.

In shock, without speaking of their doomed companion, they loaded everything they could carry in a duffel and two emergency packs they had rescued. Escobar led the way, setting off down the arroyo.

They trudged for an hour, weighed down by dark thoughts. Bolton remembered how they had all nearly starved aboard the stranded stringline ships out in deep space, another bad decision Redcom Hallholme had made. But he didn't accuse Escobar now.

Hot and sweating, Vingh leaned against a rock, shaking. "Can we have a water break, sir?"

Escobar nodded. "A small drink—until we find more."

Vingh opened one of their containers and took an eager sip. Then he grimaced and recoiled in horror. "The water tastes like that algae!"

Escobar took the canteen, peered in through the opening, then scowled. "It's contaminated." He tilted the container, and water trickled out, accompanied by hair-thin strands of the slick algae that swelled as soon as they reached the open air. He cast the container aside in nervous concern. "We don't dare drink it."

Vingh spat violently. "I only had a little." His eyes were open wide in panic. "Do you think I'll be all right?"

"I'm sure you will," Bolton said, but he didn't feel that way at all. With a knotted stomach, he unshouldered his pack, pulled out the food packets. They were still sealed, but when he cracked one open, he saw that the slimy residue of algae had penetrated the rations as well. "Everything is tainted. We don't dare eat any of it."

"We'll starve!" Escobar cried. "We need supplies or we won't survive out here."

"The alternative is to die like Yimidi did," Bolton said. He had a dismal and foreboding feeling, but didn't let himself show it. They had to maintain their hope, keep pushing on. Resigned, the three escapees dumped all the food and water packs they had salvaged from the Trakmaster, then set off with alarmingly lightened loads.

When they reached the end of the arroyo, they

climbed onto a section of scrubby land that stood between them and the hills. Using a pocket high-power
scope, Escobar scanned the terrain. "I think there's a
stream running between those hills." He pointed, but
Bolton didn't see anything. "We'll go that way."

"Glad you're still navigating for us, sir," Vingh said,
in a bitter, fatigued voice. "I'm sure that will save us.
You've done such a great job so far."

"No more of that!" Bolton snapped. Escobar, to his
credit, seemed more focused on keeping their little
group alive than on personalities or moods.

Vingh didn't look well. Abruptly, he coughed and
doubled over, then hacked in increasingly violent
spasms, as Yimidi had done. His eyes widened with horrified realization.

Helpless, Bolton and Escobar could only watch as the
insidious creatures took over Vingh's body as they'd
done with Yimidi, but much more swiftly. Like a man
on fire, Vingh scrambled away, screaming and regurgi-
tating the contents of his stomach. He fell, with wriggling algae covering his face, digesting his skin so
rapidly that his cheekbones showed through.

Looking dizzy and sickened, the Redcom shocked
Bolton by pulling the small projectile pistol and shooting
the man in the head. Vingh's screams stopped abruptly,
and then Escobar bent over and vomited. Bolton hoped
his sickness was not due to algae contamination. "It's all
we could do for him," Escobar sobbed.

Bolton swallowed hard, looked at the motionless
body and the writhing algae. "You put him out of his
misery, sir. We both knew what was going to happen
to him."

Escobar stared for a long bleak moment, then turned
and trudged away, moving on. Bolton hurried after him.
The sun beat down as they crossed a wasteland dotted

with dry succulents that eventually gave way to hardy yellow grasses. Escobar looked through the pocket scope again, but he spoke without enthusiasm, as if he'd resigned himself to the same horrific fate as their two fallen comrades. "Yes, I'm sure I see water next to that hillside, a stream."

Bolton could not forget the awful screams and retching of Yimidi and Vingh as the algae tore them apart, and he knew that any local water might also be contaminated. But with nothing to drink, he and Escobar would perish soon enough, too. They plodded on.

Bolton felt an emptiness inside him. He had come to Hellhole to rescue Keana, but had failed miserably. Another poorly thought-out plan . . . When he'd seen her again at the surrender ceremony, and later in the POW camp, he had understood that she was completely changed, sharing herself with an alien personality.

Now he and Escobar would likely die out here, with no one knowing what had happened to them.

A thunderous rumble seemed to come from all around them, and the ground trembled. The pair looked at each other, expecting a quake or an eruption of some kind, and the noise grew louder, closing in. Bolton saw a line of dust on the other side of the open prairie, watched it come closer.

"It's a herd of animals," he said. "Large ones, I think." They were out in the open, with no shelter, no place to run.

Escobar shaded his eyes, then used the pocket scope. "And they're closing the distance fast—not leaving much behind them." He pointed to the thorny succulents that dotted the landscape. One thicket looked large enough to give them some shelter—barely. "Head for those bushes!"

The two men ran, but the thicket was farther away

than Bolton had estimated. The native animals rumbled closer, a huge herd flowing across the plain, impossible creatures on such a barren world, animals that were at once terrifying and majestic. They looked like alien bison with large horned heads.

Bolton ran as hard as he could. He felt dust in his mouth and throat, and his body seemed incapable of going faster. The herd beasts were almost on top of them. The men reached the thicket at the same time, hurling themselves into the thick vegetation. Spine-covered limbs sliced into them.

Like a single, flowing organism, the thundering animals bypassed the thicket. The ground shook from the trampling of countless hooves, and a huge cloud of dust rose around them. The snorts and groans of the big animals were deafening as they continued toward some destination that only they could understand. Finally, the beasts receded into the distance.

For several minutes the two men remained in the thicket, exhausted and terrified, unable to believe they had survived the bizarre stampede.

As they picked themselves up, Bolton heard a buzzing noise overhead, and he looked up through the spiny limbs to see a silver aircraft cruising above them. He started to scramble out into the open, shouting, but Escobar grabbed his arm. "What are you doing? That's got to be one of the patrol aircraft looking for us!"

"I'm counting on that, sir. We're lost, out of supplies, and two of our companions are already dead. We need rescue."

Escobar's eyes flashed. "We've sacrificed too much to get this far. We will not give up now!"

The flyer cruised past the thicket, following the traveling herd. Bolton swallowed his anger, although this seemed like another bad decision. "Yes, sir."

The aircraft buzzed off into the distance.

Bleeding from their scratches, and coughing in the airborne dust, the pair emerged from the thicket. Bolton breathed a sigh of relief, but his heart was pounding so hard in his chest that it seemed about to break through.

"Come on, Major. We have to get to that stream," Escobar said.

They started out at a rapid walk, which grew into an awkward run as they reached the water. The stream was thick with red weeds, but felt cool and refreshing. Bolton was so parched he pushed aside any worries about impurities in the water. The two of them drank until they were more than satisfied, then lay back on the rocky ground to rest.

Looking up the slope, Bolton saw plenty of vegetation alongside the stream, enough to give them cover when they climbed. They had no idea, however, what lay on the other side of the ridge.

—⁂—

Aboard the scout flyer, Cristoph de Carre and five fellow searchers had seen the vast herd of beasts, another amazing sign that Hellhole was indeed awakening. Centuries after the devastating asteroid impact exterminated virtually all life on the planet, even the larger animals had returned. It had seemed impossible, but now they knew that these species came from embryos seeded by the Ro-Xayans.

Cristoph and Keana had seen such animals before; they had watched them from outside the opening to the deep museum vault, but this herd was much larger.

He flew the aircraft low, but the dust of the animals' passage obscured much of the view. Working the controls, he banked away from the hills and the trampled ground and flew east, still searching for the foolish, escaped prisoners although he didn't hold out much hope for them. Skimming down over an arroyo, he and his team kept their eyes open for any sign of the stolen Trakmaster. Since the escape, they had received occasional pings from their detection satellites, but the large vehicle proved difficult to find—so difficult, in fact, that he wondered if the fleeing prisoners had rigged some way to camouflage it.

One of the searchers, a muscular noncommissioned officer named Eliak Derry, leaned close to the starboard window and called out. "Something strange down there." Tapping the pane, he pointed to the afternoon shadows in the arroyo. All members of the search team were veteran soldiers, handpicked by Cristoph because of the importance of the mission. "Could be the Trakmaster."

"Worth taking a look." Cristoph circled back and put the flyer into hover mode. They saw a large, motionless object on the ground, mostly metal but covered with a black-and-yellow mound that glistened and twitched. The noise of the flyer affected whatever it was, because the organic covering began to withdraw and separate into smaller segments, oozing away from the remnants of a vehicle and crawling away into fissures.

"It *is* the Trakmaster," Cristoph said, "but it's a wreck."

"Let's hope none of the escapees were inside," said Derry. "Or we won't be bringing good news back for the General. Have we seen that type of organism before?"

"Some kind of algae," Cristoph said. "Every time I think I've seen the strangest thing Hellhole can throw at us—"

Theirs was the largest of the four patrol craft sent out to search for the escapees; it had conversion features that enabled it to fly, or traverse land and water. Cristoph dropped a ladder from the main compartment, so that Derry and two other soldiers could scramble down the rungs, with weapons and rescue kits strapped to their shoulders. The other team members remained aboard the hovering flyer.

Below, Derry led the soldiers in a cautious approach. They peered inside the vehicle and took images with cameras on their weapons. Then they beat a hasty retreat, hurrying back to the ladder and ascending one at a time.

Derry was the last to climb aboard, and he pressed forward to the cockpit. "At least one human body inside. Couldn't identify it, not much left but scraps, including half a skull. Everything else has been eaten away. And given that infestation, we didn't want to get close enough to take a DNA sample."

"But four prisoners escaped from the camp," Cristoph said.

"Could be the others were entirely digested. Or they abandoned the vehicle and set off on foot."

Cristoph's heart sank, as he doubted the other three would last long in the Hellhole wilderness. After the team retracted the ladder, he swung the flyer back toward the line of hills, following the direction the Trakmaster had apparently been headed. As the searchers skimmed over the landscape, Derry grumbled, "If they're out here, we should let them die for escaping in the first place. Hellhole tends to punish stupidity."

Flying onward, Cristoph remembered how arrogant Escobar Hallholme had been when he marched in to take over the de Carre family's estate on Vielinger, following the orders of Lord Selik Riomini. Escobar had chased Cristoph away, forced him to seek a new life out in the Deep Zone. Apparently, from what other prisoners were saying in the camp, this commanding officer had rubbed a lot of people the wrong way.

"We've all done stupid things," Cristoph said. "And I don't want to go back to General Adolphus without a real answer. We have to keep looking."

37

Instead of being a pampered "new beginning" like other Deep Zone worlds, Hellhole was a rough-and-tumble colony that had always attracted an unruly, independent, and even lawless breed of settlers. Thus, Michella Town needed a secure detention facility with short-term holding cells where brawl participants could cool off and where the accused could await trial.

It was a good enough place to hold a Diadem, at least temporarily.

Sophie accompanied the General as he led a security escort to take the haughty and defiant Michella, along with Ishop Heer, to secure quarters in the prison. "This place was designed to hold thieves, rapists, murderers, and the occasional terrorist or saboteur." Sophie gave Adolphus a smile, ignoring Michella's glare. "I think it can hold one old woman."

The security escort whisked the prisoners into the sturdy building, just as crowds began to gather in the streets. Adolphus said, "I'm more concerned with ensuring her safety. She's not worth much as a hostage if the people lynch her."

"You're all barbarians," Michella said, her voice acidic. She seemed like a ticking bomb, not yet resigned to her new circumstances.

"Not all of us," Sophie replied, barely able to control

her loathing for the woman who had caused so much pain. "But I will say that you're not very good at making friends."

After Ishop Heer was sealed in his own cell, separate from the Diadem so that they would be unable to communicate, the General addressed Michella coolly, "This will hold you until we determine our next step. Since we weren't anticipating your arrival, Diadem, our plans are still fluid."

"Your plans will end soon enough when Commodore Hallholme arrives."

"I am impressed by your optimism," the General said. "If I have to defeat the Commodore again, I will."

Adolphus turned and led Sophie away from the sealed cell. She hated Michella for what she had done. "I admire your restraint, Tiber. As for myself, I can barely stand to look at her after what she did to the people of the Deep Zone and, more importantly, what she did to you."

The General maintained his composure. "I will accord her the respect due her *office*, even if she doesn't deserve it herself."

Sophie slipped her arm through his as they left the prison. "Well, somebody has to resent her on your behalf." She was able to read many details in his expression: Love for her, concern for the Deep Zone, stress from his many responsibilities, and the intensity of conflicting thoughts as he worked on solving problems. "It's what she did to *you*. That's the part I take personally."

Years ago, Sophie had come to Hellhole voluntarily, bringing her young son Devon to start from scratch, to prove to herself and to the rest of the universe that she was a worthwhile person, and a competent businesswoman. In that, she had succeeded beyond her wildest dreams, and she truly shared Tiber Adolphus's dreams and goals. She wanted a life with him, but she also wanted a strong and independent Deep Zone.

And when Diadem Michella Duchenet did everything in her power to destroy Adolphus, and had been at least partly responsible for the death of Devon, Sophie could not ignore that. She could almost understand what had driven Tanja Hu into such bitter vengeful violence. *Almost*.

Adolphus mused, "I suppose it's naïve to think we'll ever have our independence neatly wrapped up with a pretty bow. We'll always have to worry about the Constellation or internal threats like the unrest on Hossetea and Tehila." He shook his head. "But, with the Diadem as our prisoner, I can use that leverage to break their backs and solve this conflict, finally. They won't have any choice."

"They already had plenty of reasons to hate Michella," Sophie pointed out. "And after she blew up her own city, they won't have any greater love for her." The realization that Michella had almost certainly wiped out Tryn-Clovis, the Urvanciks, and the rest of the shadow-Xayan commando team, weighed heavily on both of them.

"That could certainly cause us problems," Adolphus admitted. "But she's still the Diadem."

When they exited the prison, Sophie was surprised to find an angry crowd gathering, people who had heard that the Diadem was being held there. Their expressions were dark, and their mutters grew louder when they saw the General emerge. She recognized some of her own workers from the materials warehouse, shopkeepers, restaurant owners. They worked hard, sacrificed much, and now, because they had demanded their freedom, they were a target of Constellation reprisals. Sophie could understand their anger.

The General assessed them. "They're looking for a scapegoat, but they can't have Michella. I gave my word."

"I wouldn't call her a scapegoat, since she's genuinely responsible for what they're angry about."

With her standing beside him, the General paused to look out at the crowd, gauging their ugly expressions. He took a moment to gather his words, then spoke loudly. "Yes, the rumors are true. Diadem Michella Duchenet is our prisoner. That changes the entire landscape of the conflict."

"Put her on trial!" someone yelled.

"Who needs a trial?" answered another man. "We all know what she's done."

"Governor Goler never got a trial," muttered a shopkeeper in the crowd. "They just executed him. *That woman* just executed him."

The General looked strong and responded with a firm voice. "There will be no lynch mob. Michella Duchenet has committed heinous crimes, but that is no excuse for me to commit crimes of my own. And she's useful. The Diadem is a political prisoner, and I have personally guaranteed her safety."

Sophie spotted Arlen Carter, the manager of her primary warehouse in Michella Town. He was red-faced and upset. "But this is our chance, General! She deserves to pay for what she did to the Deep Zone—for what she did to all those people on Theser."

"And everyone on Buktu! They're being held prisoner."

Adolphus shook his head. "We can use her. She is valuable, and with her as our prisoner, we can force the Constellation to make concessions. She's more useful to us as a bargaining chip."

"You can't let her go free, General!"

"Even if that's the price for our own freedom? I will force them to leave us alone. For now, the Diadem is under my protection. That is my command." He squared his shoulders and stared the hostile people down. They had enough respect for him that they listened.

Sophie said to him quietly, "A hostage is only valuable if the Constellation actually wants her back."

The crowd outside the detention facility reluctantly dispersed. When the streets had cleared again, Sophie and the General headed to her main warehouse in town, where they could talk. On the way, Sophie suggested, "It might be better if we take the Diadem away from here. Her presence would be a constant provocation."

He considered. "It might be better if she stays under guard at Slickwater Springs. The shadow-Xayans won't be as vengeful. Many of them are my own veterans."

Sophie's lips curled in a smile. "And you know how terrified she is of the aliens. There's a certain satisfaction in keeping her so close to the slickwater pools. She'll be too terrified to be intractible."

He nodded. "Yes, and we have the POW camp in the next valley if she causes too much trouble, and with the whole landscape of Hellhole, where is a pampered old woman going to run?"

"That didn't stop Escobar Hallholme and his group from escaping," Sophie pointed out. They had just received word that Cristoph de Carre's search team had found the wrecked Trakmaster and at least one body. No sign of the others. With a sigh, she added, "But Michella's a pampered old woman, not a trained soldier. I'll keep her safe, Tiber, much as I would like to drown her myself in the slickwater. I give you my word."

Adolphus gave her a grateful nod. "One problem solved."

Sophie said, "Now, what to do about Commodore Hallholme? He'll be on his way soon."

She watched his expression change, knew his thoughts were adjusting as he turned his energies to the next crisis. They reached her private office inside the warehouse, where they could talk without other people listening. She waved off three of her employees who had supposedly urgent questions, and she closed the door to her office. "Use me as a sounding board, and we'll decide what to do."

He moved a clutter of boxes from the spare chair so he could sit. Sophie realized she hadn't been at her desk in the warehouse for more than a month. Arlen Carter took care of the administration and sent reports to her out at Slickwater Springs.

The less formal setting allowed Adolphus to relax and think more clearly. "If we hadn't had the warning, Commodore Hallholme would be attacking us already—and his fleet might have been able to seize our stringline hub. We got lucky, and I don't want to rely on luck next time."

"The Commodore means business," Sophie agreed, "but we can put up a fight. We'll be ready for him."

"We don't know how long Enva Tazaar's sabotage delayed his departure. He might still be arriving any day." He worked through his thought process. "That means we have to act right away."

Sophie said, "The safest solution would be to cut the stringline to Tehila and strand the Constellation ships out there. Then we wouldn't ever have to worry about a threat from that direction again."

Adolphus worked his jaw. "That would mean sacrificing an entire world, and I won't give up one of my planets without a fight. The people of Tehila didn't want

Administrator Reming to overthrow the government they put in place. I have to think bigger than that. We can't just blow the bridge every time we perceive a threat. I worked too hard to connect the Deep Zone, fifty-four trailblazer ships on carefully planned missions to lay down the stringlines. We went to great trouble and expense to connect the DZ."

Sophie considered, agreed. "Especially now that we have no source of iperion to rebuild the lines once we sever them. We only have enough on hand for limited maintenance, on a priority basis. But how do we defend ourselves against the Commodore's fleet?"

Adolphus remained silent for a long moment, then a smile curved his lips. "We can't just huddle here waiting for the enemy to come to us. We do the unexpected, we go on the offensive, take the fight to Tehila." He nodded, and his voice sounded stronger. "I intend to launch the DZDF immediately, before the Commodore can possibly expect us. We'll oust the invaders and return Tehila to its people. This is the future of the Deep Zone. I have to do it."

Sophie couldn't hide her warm smile, despite the worry she felt for him whenever he went into battle. "I enjoy seeing you like this, Tiber. You inspire me, and you inspire all of us."

38

In only a few days, Diadem Selik Riomini slid firmly into his duties as the Constellation's new leader. It did not hurt that the previous Diadem's reprehensible behavior had left her with few supporters in the Crown

Jewels; even her closest allies were at a loss to justify what she had done. Riomini's greatest detractors grudgingly admitted that he could be no worse.

He and his hand-picked staff swooped into the Sonjeera offices and also commandeered the Duchenet palace. All of Michella's key employees were replaced, and her personal articles were confiscated, placed in storage, or discarded. The old woman had a fondness for displaying busts, portraits, and crystal-sculpted images of herself; Riomini had all of them removed, wanting no reminders of his disgraced predecessor.

Meanwhile, recovery and reconstruction operations continued at the devastated Sonjeera spaceport, as secondary landing fields were opened around the perimeter of Council City. Anson Tebias had made sure to do the expected duty dances on Riomini's behalf, expressing grief and determination, vowing to help those who had been harmed by the devastating blow. Such gestures brought cheers, but thanks to the expected tangles of bureaucracy, required little immediate action. Riomini could go about his own business, as planned.

He played a delicate balance of showing how swiftly and efficiently he could restore normal commerce, but not so swiftly as to minimize the extraordinary destruction Michella had caused. He didn't want to repair everything too quickly. So long as the people blamed the old Diadem for their misery, Riomini had no incentive to ease their pain.

More important to him, though—his burgeoning legal and constitutional staff busied themselves building a massive legal case against the deposed Diadem. They labeled her a murderer, traitor, war criminal. The list of charges expanded daily, and Riomini received regular reports. When he thought of how the ruthless woman had forced him to watch his loyal team of personal guards be incinerated alive, Riomini imagined how he would personally carry out the Diadem's inevitable sentence.

Yes, it was all going very well, like clockwork.

He stood inside his new office—Michella's gaudy old office—accompanied by Anson Tebias. To celebrate his new rule, Riomini and his top adviser had been brainstorming a gala banquet and a city-wide feast day. Soon enough, as another feather in the new Diadem's cap, they would also be able to announce Commodore Hallholme's conquest of Hellhole and the defeat of the Constellation's greatest enemy.

The slender Tebias suggested a number of possible themes for the dinner, calling up images on his display pad. "Of course, there should be extensive black decorations to honor the Riomini family, but done in a festive manner with accents of silver, gold, and precious jewels. Your coronation is a happy occasion. It symbolizes a return to normalcy and a new prosperity for the whole Constellation."

"I like that." Riomini glanced around the office, which had been stripped of Michella's trappings. All the bare spots would have to be filled with his own furnishings and favorite things, to be delivered from Aeroc. He gazed at an immense empty picture frame on one wall, where Michella's portrait had been removed. At that very moment, one of the best Sonjeeran artists was completing a painting of Riomini standing as the victor in the burned rubble of Theser. The rushed (and expensive) commission would be finished and installed in a few days. Riomini had already seen a sketch and considered it very dramatic.

Tebias continued to muse, "Because of the landmark

nature of these events, I decided to dig into our momentous, ancient history. That will help put you into perspective, my Lord, as one of the greats of the human race."

Riomini nodded. "We need to emphasize the magnitude of what I have accomplished—and will continue to accomplish."

The other man was grinning. Riomini had never seen Tebias so enthusiastic about planning an event. "That's why I've gone directly to the ancient archives in Council City that contain articles from old Earth, objects brought here aboard the original seed colony ships long ago. Much of that history has been lost in the mists of time, and our citizens have forgotten . . . but what if the feast day has an old Earth theme? We could serve foods made with ancient recipes, and the attendees would be encouraged to wear replicas of old Earth costumes."

Tebias rattled off so many details that Riomini just listened. He liked what he was hearing. "We should come up with something to give away to the masses as well," his adviser continued. "Commemorative trinkets, engraved spoons or plaques, all sorts of collectible memorabilia. An event like that, with an old Earth theme, would show that you are not just a man of force, but you are also a man of culture."

"I like it. Set it up." Riomini waved a hand to dismiss the man. "Don't concern me with more details. A Diadem has numerous other pressing matters to attend to. Oh, and continue to help all those people displaced by the explosion, however much you think is necessary. Just don't make too much of a dent in the treasury— there have always been needy people and there always will be."

After Tebias departed, the Black Lord stood at a large window that overlooked Heart Square and the government buildings surrounding it. Black Riomini banners fluttered on tall poles around the plaza and hung from every public building. In front of the Council Hall, the red and silver of the Duchenet family had been replaced with a new black-and-silver banner emblazoned with Riomini shield insignia and star-studded Constellation crests.

Not only was Selik Riomini the Diadem, he was also the Supreme Commander of the Army of the Constellation. No one had held so much influence in centuries. Before he claimed the Star Throne, Riomini had controlled three valuable Crown Jewel worlds, and now he ruled all twenty. He had wealth beyond his ability to calculate, and so much power that he could do anything he pleased. Once he consolidated the recalcitrant Deep Zone, he would have to consider what other victories he could achieve. He intended to leave behind a legacy that no one could ever surpass.

Yes, as the rightful Diadem, he had to show moderation and tolerance, as well as a firm hand, so that his subjects would see him as a man of justice. If they admired him, that would make them more inclined to obey his orders.

His new court system had a packed calendar, with former aides and functionaries of the previous regime going on trial day after day. After what Michella had done, very few still supported her or defended her actions, but some opposed the manner in which Riomini had taken the throne.

The common people needed little encouragement to despise Michella Duchenet, however. They blamed her for the Deep Zone debacle, for letting General Adolphus humiliate the Constellation, and for causing great economic turmoil to the Crown Jewels. Riomini also suggested that Michella was responsible for the alien attack that had nearly wrecked the Sonjeera stringline hub, causing further chaos in their daily lives . . . and now Michella had blown up most of the spaceport and a portion of the capital city!

Riomini wished the old woman had just retired years ago and handed over the throne to him without such inconvenience. If he had been made Diadem earlier, he would have had so much security throughout the Deep Zone that General Adolphus would never have managed to foment a second rebellion.

—⁂—

Only a fool would suggest that Riomini was not the appropriate leader for the Constellation. Unfortunately, the nobles' council still had a handful of fools.

Later that day, a delegation of three men marched into the nearly empty general audience chamber, where Diadem Selik sat regally, but not comfortably, on the Star Throne. He had already decided he would have the seat modified. The Hall's general audience sections were unoccupied, because he was not yet comfortable with having all his actions and decisions viewed by the public, but he allowed the delegation to address him directly.

The three identified themselves as Kax Dorian, Cole Artemis, and Oneas Bilwar—all unimportant men. He was even less impressed when they announced their indignation at how he had "usurped the sacred role of the Diadem and trampled on the Constellation Charter." He rolled his eyes.

Oneas Bilwar, a paunchy, overdressed man, had the temerity to step forward. "You rammed your approval through by using intimidation. How dare you bring your personal soldiers into the Council Hall? We call for an immediate vote of no confidence and demand the formation of an interim ruling council. The selection of a new Diadem must be a cautious and well-considered process."

Sitting back on the throne, Riomini smiled. "Customs and rules of order are fine for casual decisions in times of peace, but during a crisis—and Michella committed a horrific crime!—the true leader does what he must."

The three men continued to argue, but they seemed very alone in the echoing chamber. His guard commander, Rota Vindahl, moved to stand between Riomini and the delegation, as if to protect him. Bilwar gave her a look of disdain. He tried to step past her. "We formally demand—"

In a flurry of motion, she lashed out with one of the most effective displays of raw violence that Riomini had ever seen, striking all three men in the head with such force that she crushed their skulls. They all collapsed onto the floor, dead.

Observing from the side of the chamber, Anson Tebias scrambled forward, aghast. Riomini rose from the throne, unable to believe what had just happened. He stared at the three bodies. "Your intense loyalty is appreciated, Rota, but I wish you hadn't done that."

Tebias came running to the throne with a despairing look on his face. "Now how are we going to clean up this mess? This goes against the benevolent façade we're trying to place on your rule."

Though he was not, in fact, all *that* displeased to have them dead, Riomini put an edge in his voice as he scolded his commander. "In the future you might allow legal processes to run their course."

Vindahl remained unrepentant. "I dealt with a problem in the necessary way. The men were insulting and disrespectful toward you, my Lord."

"Which is a crime, but it does not warrant a death sentence. At least not immediately." He turned to Tebias. "Well, there's no changing what happened. Complete a report to show that these Michella loyalists tried to assassinate me, but luckily they were stopped by my guard force. One of them tried to evade my guard commander and come at me in a threatening manner, so that fact can be massaged a bit." He sighed. "What happened here is unfortunate, but it does save our legal system the trouble of having to deal with traitors."

"As you wish." Tebias bowed. "Shall I express your dismay at the deaths? That would project the public image of strength and justice."

Riomini smiled. "Yes, of course."

—————

After Tebias and Vindahl worked to clean up and conceal the deaths, Diadem Riomini returned to his offices to study the new reports that had just arrived. He was interrupted when a royal courier in a silver uniform appeared at the door of his office. A nervous young man with cherubic features, he bowed and extended a message scroll, but Riomini waved. "Read it to me."

The man unfurled the parchment with shaking hands. "An urgent communication sent via stringline drone from Commodore Hallholme at Tehila. It's addressed to the Council of Lords, but I was ordered to show it to you first."

"Well, what does he say?" He could feel the smile already growing on his face. By now, the Commodore must have accomplished his mission.

The courier cleared his throat and read aloud. "This is Commodore Percival Hallholme. Please reference my previous reports detailing the consolidation of Tehila and the establishment of a forward base preparatory to our full military assault against General Adolphus at planet Hallholme.

"As you are aware, Diadem Michella Duchenet insisted on accompanying this operation at the last moment, without proper security or escort. I regret to inform you that rebel terrorists have kidnapped the Diadem and fled along the stringline, threatening to kill her if we pursued. We were unable to prevent their escape. Diadem Michella is now a hostage in the hands of our enemy.

"Saboteurs also damaged the Deep Zone terminus ring, preventing the launch of our fleet. We are effecting repairs with all possible speed, but the safety of the Diadem is paramount. The original military plan is now obsolete. If we attack the General, he will use the Diadem as a bargaining chip, or even kill her. Please advise. I await further orders."

Although he would have preferred to learn that General Adolphus was defeated and the entire Deep Zone recaptured, Riomini did not bother to conceal a smile over this delightful surprise. "I will craft an immediate reply." He was pleased at how all of the pieces were falling into place for him so perfectly. He would order Commodore Hallholme to achieve his victory at all costs, without regard to the safety of *former* Diadem Michella Duchenet. In fact, he sincerely hoped the rebels executed the old bitch.

39

shop Heer had already visited Slickwater Springs during his previous inspection work for Diadem Michella. Back then, he had been tricked into thinking that the rumors of resurrected alien memories were merely the ecstatic behavior of a bizarre religious cult. He had thought them all gullible fools. Now he realized how close he had come to being contaminated with an insidious alien presence. The very thought was horrific and repulsive.

And now his captors were taking Michella and him back there! He felt ill and frantic. It was only one more link in this chain of nightmares, defeat after crushing defeat.

He was Ishop Heer, a man trying to reclaim his noble blood, someone who had done everything necessary to succeed. But he had been humiliated by the Diadem, betrayed by Enva Tazaar, and trapped here on this awful planet. Michella had delighted in telling him about Laderna's awful end, and now he didn't even have the satisfaction of seeing the old bitch killed. Enva had stunned him, discarded him—plausible deniability? Ridiculous! She had used him and then destroyed him. No one understood what he was worth. He could no longer stand it!

Under guard, the two of them arrived at the settlement where delusional volunteers immersed themselves in alien-infested pools, voluntarily accepting the contamination. The living conditions at Slickwater Springs were primitive, but not downright squalid. At least he and Michella weren't being thrown into the fenced POW compound in the adjacent valley, a place crowded with thousands of captive soldiers from Escobar Hallholme's fleet. No, they were closer to the insidious alien poison.

Around them at Slickwater Springs, the pools and walkways teemed with people, most of them alien converts who actually reveled in inhuman possession. Beside him, Michella shuddered visibly, repulsed by the bizarre sight. She shot him a sharp, earnest look. "Ishop, promise me you'll kill me before you let them do that to me."

"With pleasure, Eminence." His sincere words only earned him a pained stare from her.

Accompanied by a blond man in an old military uniform, a smug-looking Sophie Vence walked briskly toward them from the complex of pools. Her companion was obviously one of the converts, as his eyes had an eerie, spiraling pearlescence. Sophie said, "Diadem Michella Duchenet, I have every reason in the world to loathe you, both for personal and political reasons. Many good people are dead because of you, including my son."

Michella recoiled from the strange man. "Keep that . . . *creature* . . . away from me! He's obviously possessed."

The convert's alien gaze focused on Michella. He seemed unperturbed by the insult, didn't appear to care what the old woman said. "A great many problems would be solved if you were to immerse yourself in the slickwater and join the greater cause."

Even Ishop's stomach churned at the thought. Michella warred with her own terror, obviously trying to maintain her composure. "You would not dare!"

Sophie smiled at their obvious discomfort. "Oh, I would dare, but it wouldn't be worth the headaches—at least not right now." She indicated the man. "This is Peter Herald, the assistant manager of Slickwater Springs."

He said, "I call myself Peter-Arnex, to reflect the Xayan who lives inside me."

"Yes, Peter is one of our shadow-Xayans. I work very closely with him. We're here to escort you to your living quarters, where you'll be held under guard. I have arranged rooms fit for a Diadem, in a nice bungalow, the best we have to offer." The hatred oozed out of Sophie's voice. "It was good enough for your daughter Keana when she joined us."

"My daughter was a vapid, gullible woman. I am the leader of the Constellation." Michella was clearly angry. "Keep me away from that contamination."

"Then I suggest you don't try to escape. Who knows where you might wander, how you might accidentally be splashed. It would be a pity."

Sophie pointed out converts who swam in the shimmering water and called out in excited tones. Quieter clusters of people who had not yet immersed themselves stood at boardwalk railings to observe the activities. As they watched, one couple made their final decision and jumped into the water together from the edge of a boardwalk.

Standing close to Ishop, Peter Herald said, "You can learn much more if you just immerse yourself." He looked at Michella. "And you, as well."

"I will not!" The old woman's expression was defiant. "I'm not going near those pools! You will not force me to become possessed by an alien."

Herald smiled with his generous mouth. "We force no one."

Sophie said, "I choose not to expose myself either, but most of the converts are perfectly satisfied with taking the plunge."

Two more shadow-Xayans came near, a young couple. The woman said, "It's important for us to get as many converts as possible." She and her companion took a side path toward the large main lodge building.

"Commodore Hallholme will not be bothering us with his warships, and General Adolphus will defeat him soon enough. Everyone is more nervous about another faction of the aliens, who are determined to destroy this planet," Sophie explained. "They recently bombarded Candela, and now the Xayans are convinced they will hurl asteroids here, too." She gave the Diadem a sharp smile, taunting her. "You should hope the Constellation comes to us with acceptable terms soon. You'll want to be away from here before the asteroids come. The Ro-Xayans won't care whom we have as hostages."

"Why should I worry about imaginary enemies when this place is crawling with aliens right here?" Michella asked bitterly. "I hate you all."

Peter Herald seemed agitated. "The Ro-Xayans are not imaginary. And they are much more of a threat than the Constellation will ever be."

Guards led them toward the low, individual buildings where visitors stayed pondering whether or not to immerse themselves. Ishop glanced up at the dusty sky, knowing that Commodore Hallholme had been ready to launch his strike against this planet. Surely a rescue force would be on its way . . . but he and Michella had been trapped here for days. The Commodore couldn't be that far behind.

On the other hand, after Michella knowingly blew up the Sonjeera spaceport and part of Council City, would the Constellation be so eager to rescue her?

Ever since Enva Tazaar had betrayed him, Ishop had tried to decide if he was better off throwing in his lot with the Diadem, or convincing the rebels that he wanted to side with them against her. Indeed, by stunning him and imprisoning him with Michella, Enva made it seem that Ishop was still the old Diadem's lackey. Enva had treated him like garbage—just as the other nobles had when he'd presented his case for his bloodline to be recognized. He had *saved* Enva, secretly rescued her from the Sonjeeran prison and her imminent execution, and she still used him, abused him, betrayed him. So many people did!

His anger turned to anguish as he thought of how Laderna had been his partner, with the same goals, dedicated to helping him achieve success. And what Michella had done to her . . .

Ishop heard shouts of alarm from one of the slick-water pools and turned to see people pulling a limp man out of the water. He didn't respond to any of their rescue efforts, and Sophie let out a groan. "A bad reaction happens every once in a while. Some recover, while others do not." Distressed converts carried the limp man onto the boardwalk and laid him on his back. Sophie looked at the Diadem. "There's still a chance for him. Your own daughter slipped into a coma at first, but she recovered."

"Keana did *not* recover—she is possessed by an alien! Take me away from this horrible place. If you're imprisoning me, at least have the decency to shield me from danger."

Sophie gave her a look that showed how much she despised Michella, but she controlled herself with obvious difficulty, reminding herself of her duty and her promises.

The prisoners were delivered to adjacent bungalows, separate units with guards stationed at the doors. The overhanging leaves of a strange, droopy tree made tinkling sounds when the wind moved them.

Sophie warned, "Don't try to escape. Even if there were no guards, Hellhole itself is enough to crush you if you dare go out into the wilderness. If you doubt me, I can show you images of a growler storm. You don't want to be in one." She raised her eyebrows. "Mr. Heer experienced a growler himself when he was a guest at the General's headquarters. He did not, however, have any firsthand experience with cannibal beetles, quakes, volcanic eruptions, or razor rain. This is not a pleasant place. Best if you accept our hospitality."

As Sophie ran through her litany of warnings, Ishop watched Michella. The pampered Diadem would never make it alone out on rugged Hellhole.

"This is beyond what I can endure." Michella squared her bony shoulders, gestured toward Ishop with a spidery, ringed hand. "Do something to get us out of here, Ishop! If you do, I will reward you handsomely."

She had made promises to him before. Ishop felt bile rise in his throat, hating her, remembering what she had done to Laderna and to him. "I will do my best for you, Eminence. As always."

He thought about the list that he and Laderna had developed together. A Duchenet still needed to die for those old crimes. On this dangerous planet, there were countless ways to kill her. That was something he could look forward to at least.

40

General Adolphus put the Hellhole stringline hub on high alert as he prepared to launch his preemptive strike against the Constellation fleet. Commodore Hallholme could be on his way already, depending on how extensive the sabotage had been at the Tehila terminus ring.

Adolphus summoned the DZDF ships that patrolled Hellhole orbit and launched many other combat-ready battleships from the Ankor spaceport. By now, he had consolidated the Constellation vessels he had captured from Redcom Hallholme's retaliatory fleet. Many of those warships had been damaged in battle, as well as by the destructive computer virus Major Crais had installed in their command systems, but most had been salvaged and repaired, then placed back into service.

Whenever the commandeered warships had come back online, Adolphus had dispersed them as peacekeeping ships throughout the vulnerable Deep Zone worlds. He didn't have time to recall them from all the other frontier planets, so he would have to make do with what he had here . . . even if it meant leaving Hellhole less defended than he would like. It was a gamble. He had to move against the Commodore as soon as possible, and George Komun had promised to bring additional ships from Umber.

Fortunately, Captain Naridar had not yet departed on patrol with his fifteen ships from Hossetea, and so those ships, along with the thirty-five that Adolphus normally kept in place around Hellhole, would comprise a decent surprise attack force against the Commodore's beachhead on Tehila. The combined force would not be quite equivalent to what his old nemesis had gathered, but Adolphus would have the element of surprise, as well as his own sheer boldness.

He'd said his good-byes to Sophie before she took the two political prisoners off to the Slickwater Springs compound, and now he could focus entirely on the military operational plan.

Before launch, Tanja Hu and Ian Walfor joined him aboard the shuttle that was heading for Adolphus's flagship, the *Jacob*, which waited at the stringline hub. "We're going with you to Tehila," Walfor said.

Tanja tossed her long dark hair over one shoulder. "If you're taking that planet back, we want to be there."

"But you just escaped from it."

Tanja's expression hardened. "Many Candela refugees are still on Tehila. Being a refugee is bad enough, but being a prisoner is far worse. My people understand how you tried to save as many people as possible before the asteroids struck Candela—even while your own planet was under attack. I can rally them to our cause. While you worry about the military engagement in orbit, I might be able to assist in fomenting an uprising on the ground."

They sat back as the shuttle accelerated, leaping toward orbit. Over the rumble of the engines, Adolphus said, "That would be fine with me. But what's your role in this, Mr. Walfor?"

The former Buktu governor shrugged. "Military adviser. Consultant. Whatever vague term you prefer. Personally, I'd like to stay with Tanja, unless you have other pressing needs for me."

Adolphus had no objection to that. The two worked well as a team.

Around the stringline hub, commercial ships and passenger transports came in along the iperion lines from other Deep Zone planets. None of the captains were prepared for the sudden high alert, but word spread quickly. Many of the ships rushed off, to be away from Hellhole as swiftly as possible. Other captains offered to stay.

As the shuttle docked with the *Jacob*, Adolphus called for Captain Naridar to be briefed aboard the flagship. The two captured Constellation stringline haulers were brought to the bustling hub so they could be loaded with DZDF military craft as well as another dozen or so private support ships. He couldn't be squeamish or hesitant now. He would throw everything he had into the operation.

Commodore Hallholme was a complex and even—by some definitions—honorable man, now that the General knew more about him. But Hallholme didn't know when to give up. It was time for Adolphus to deliver a mortal blow to the Constellation fleet. It was the only way the Deep Zone could remain independent—and intact.

Once he arrived on the *Jacob*'s bridge, the General felt at home. The flagship was named after his father, patriarch of the Adolphus family, noble ruler of Qiorfu before it had all been taken from them. That planet should have gone to his brother, Stefano, while Tiber Adolphus went off to Aeroc to study in the military, as excess noble sons usually did. He had never intended to lead a rebellion, but when the corrupt Constellation betrayed him—not once, but multiple times—Adolphus had been left with no other choice. Now, the Deep Zone depended on him, as did the Xayans who were striving so hard toward *ala'ru* before their enemies arrived. Surrender was not in his vocabulary.

The deputy officer on duty, Clayton Sendell, relinquished the command seat and displayed a report summarizing the available DZDF ships as well as the civilian captains and crews who had contributed their vessels to the liberation of Tehila. Adolphus scanned down the records, highlighted particular vessels. Even though these ships weren't military, he might need all the assistance he could get.

"I'll leave five DZDF ships here in orbit so Hellhole isn't completely undefended." He summoned a calendar grid. "Mr. Sendell, do we have a projected date when George Komun's reinforcements will arrive from Umber?"

Sendell had the information ready at hand. "Minimum of eight days, sir, given travel time from our stringline hub to Umber and back. Add an extra day or two for him to gather them."

Adolphus said, "That'll have to be good enough. I want to launch our fleet within six hours. At maximum speed it'll still take almost four days to reach Tehila."

"Four days, seven hours, sir," said Sendell. "With all due respect."

Adolphus concealed a satisfied smile. He liked this young man; maybe Sendell would earn more responsibility before the operation was over. "That's allowing for standard deceleration. I think we can tolerate a few aches and bruises if we use extreme braking. Time is of the essence."

Sendell gave a quick snap of a nod. "Yes, sir."

Adolphus called for his DZDF ships to load into the docking clamps. The most impressive-looking military vessels were interspersed with volunteer commercial transports. "The civilian ships don't have any military punch," Adolphus said, "but we can use them to pad out our stringline haulers. Commodore Hallholme will see a huge fleet coming at him—he won't know that many of the ships are just cannon fodder."

Next to him, Tanja frowned, as if doubting the tactic. "Decoys."

Adolphus nodded. "We'll find some use for them."

Captain Naridar arrived on the bridge, and saluted as he presented himself. He seemed energized, proud of his position. "Thank you for including me, General. This is more important than a peacekeeping patrol." He shook his head. "When I think about how Commodore

Hallholme seized Tehila, I can't help but be reminded that Hossetea wanted to do the same thing. If I hadn't acted when I did, that planet would have fallen as well."

"I don't intend to surrender any of my Deep Zone worlds without a fight, Captain," Adolphus said. "The DZ has fought hard and shed blood for freedom. We won't simply give up, I promise."

Meanwhile, a group of five civilian ships, cargo haulers and passenger transports, clustered on another node at the stringline hub, ready to depart along a line that had not been used in two months—the path to devastated Theser.

Enva Tazaar opened the channel to the flagship. "General Adolphus, we are preparing to depart, along with a thousand Candela refugees. Thank you for the good word, Administrator Hu. When I told them I intended to reestablish a settlement on Theser, they couldn't jump to accept fast enough. They just needed someone to point them in the right direction."

"A thousand of them?" Adolphus said. "You don't think small, Lady Tazaar—and I'm impressed by how quickly you moved."

On the screen, Enva smiled. "You did grant me permission, General. What would be the point in waiting? I wanted to demonstrate my dedication along with my leadership abilities."

"You're doing well, so far. I suggest you keep doing so."

Tanja somehow managed to look pleased and troubled at the same time. "My Candela refugees will be scattered, and they'll form their own communities and identities on new planets. I'm not their planetary administrator anymore." She paused. "I suppose I'll just enjoy being footloose for the time being."

Walfor nudged her with his elbow. "Buktu is empty and waiting to be resettled. If we can resolve this mess with the Constellation, maybe we'll free Erik Anderlos and my people. Do you think they'll go for a prisoner exchange, General?"

"It's a possibility," Adolphus said. "Once we recapture Tehila, maybe they'll be a little less intractable."

While the *Jacob* locked into a primary spot on the lead stringline hauler, the General monitored the loading and positioning of the remaining ships. He kept watch on the chronometer, pleased with the progress he was seeing. They might even be able to launch an hour ahead of schedule.

As he watched the last military vessels and civilian ships lining up in the loading pattern, Sophie Vence contacted him from Slickwater Springs. He immediately feared that something had gone wrong, that the Diadem or Ishop Heer had caused trouble—but she was smiling on the screen. "Tiber, I've got great news for you—a hundred and fifty shadow-Xayan volunteers have agreed to help, as you requested. I pressed them, and they're heading to Ankor at this moment."

Adolphus was surprised, but pleased. He needed to take advantage of every weapon, and every surprise, in his arsenal. "I'll take them aboard my flagship. They may prove useful—I have the military force, but telemancy will be my secret weapon. Is Keana among them?"

Sophie shook her head. "No, she's coming here to see her mother. Lodo will lead the group heading with you out to Tehila."

Adolphus felt a warm flush of increased confidence. "Commodore Hallholme won't know what hit him."

Sophie had a sparkle in her eyes that made her look ten years younger and even more beautiful than usual. "That is the idea, Tiber. They're on their way."

Before long, the shuttle from Ankor docked aboard

the *Jacob* just as the last ships locked into place aboard the stringline haulers. Adolphus had already directed Clayton Sendell to find quarters for the shadow-Xayans.

Three converts accompanied Lodo as they arrived on the bridge. Though the rest of the *Jacob*'s crew were familiar with the Xayans, the looming creature drew many strange glances. Lodo's voice vibrated through the membrane across his smooth face. "Shall we begin our military adventure, General?"

Adolphus confirmed with the hauler pilot that both framework vessels were fully loaded, aligned on the iperion path, and ready to speed into space.

"Yes, Lodo, we shall." He made a fleet-wide announcement to rally them, and heard a resounding cheer over the intercom. The haulers launched.

41

Through her connection to Uroa, Keana understood that the real threat to the planet was not a fleet of Constellation ships. The alien presence within her was convinced the Ro-Xayans would try to exterminate the rival Xayan faction.

As the Diadem's daughter, Keana had been brought up in the glitter of Sonjeera, obsessed with her own troubles and minor ambitions. She had resented her mother and court politics, and resented being forced to marry for political reasons. She had dismissed Bolton Crais as not being interesting enough, without bothering to think that she had not made herself worthy of him either. She took Louis de Carre as her lover, and now she wondered if the affair was merely a way of lashing out against her domineering mother. Oh, Keana had loved Louis, she was sure of that; under normal circumstances theirs might have been a romance for the ages. Louis's utter disgrace and suicide was the most devastating thing Keana had endured up until that point in her life. But she had also been blithely cruel to Bolton, and he didn't deserve that.

Now, she realized how utterly trivial her concerns had been. She'd been a spoiled child, self-centered and weak, a creation of her environment. In a sense, she wasn't much different from her mother, although the Diadem wielded much more power.

But Keana had advanced far beyond that, becoming one of the most powerful of the shadow-Xayans. Joined with Uroa, she was helping propel the future of an entire race, guiding them toward their evolutionary destiny—a far more important obligation than any responsibility her mother had.

Keana was an entirely different person from the woman who had naïvely run away from the Crown Jewels. When she faced Michella, she did not expect her mother to understand or forgive what she had done.

As she left the burgeoning shadow-Xayan settlement, she and Uroa used telemancy to levitate her body. They flew across the landscape, heading directly for the compound where the captive Diadem was being held.

The Uroa part of her wanted to remain with the converts, working to increase the race's mental powers to achieve *ala'ru*. If only more volunteers would immerse themselves in the slickwater, they might even be ready to ascend when Lodo and his group of shadow-Xayans returned with the General from Tehila.

But Keana needed to do this, and Uroa allowed her, promising to assist in the conversation—or confrontation—with Michella, as necessary.

Ishop Heer was being held prisoner, too. Back in her

previous shallow life, Ishop had convinced Keana to go haring off to Hellhole looking for the son of her lover Louis de Carre. She realized now that it might have been a trick, a fool's errand to get rid of her. Had her mother put him up to it? She wouldn't have been surprised.

Regardless, it had resulted in her becoming who she was now.

When she arrived, the three slickwater pools were crowded. For weeks now, Encix had been using the threat of the Ro-Xayans as a goad to encourage more converts, and Keana could sense the Original was growing more and more dissatisfied with the promise not to coerce volunteers.

Keana walked to the main lodge house with its reinforced walls and windows that could stand proof against whatever natural threats the planet threw at them. When she met Peter-Arnex, she pushed her human personality to the fore. "You have my mother here. She won't want to see me, but I need to do it."

"She and Ishop Heer are under guard in the outer bungalows," said Herald. "Follow me." Unconcerned, he led her around the main lodge and along the boardwalk toward a cluster of small dwellings.

Most of the small buildings were empty in the bright afternoon. The Spartan interior had only a few articles of furniture, including a chair, a small bed, a table with a light source, and a shelf. Those who came to Slickwater Springs did not stay here for long, and once they became shadow-Xayans, the converts cared little for physical comforts. The Diadem must be miserable without her usual amenities, Keana thought.

She stopped in front of the bungalow door, and the guards recognized her. "I'll talk to my mother first. Bring Ishop Heer to join us in a few minutes."

Herald went to the other bungalow, while the guards opened the door to let Keana enter.

Keana was shocked by her mother's appearance. Michella looked considerably older, her eyes sunken as if constant fury and displeasure had burned the life out of her. She wore drab garments—definitely not the attire her mother normally favored.

Upon seeing her daughter, Michella rose in indignation. The old woman's lips curled downward, but she forced away the expression with a visible effort. "So you survived in this awful place, Daughter. I didn't believe you had it in you. We were so worried we dispatched an entire fleet to recapture this world and rescue you."

Keana stood straight and strong. "No, you didn't, Mother. We know your orders—I've talked with Bolton. Rescuing me was nowhere on the list of priorities that Redcom Hallholme received."

Michella scowled, like a child annoyed that a birthday party hadn't gone as planned. "My priority was to save the Constellation from this dangerous rebellion."

"But you didn't even try to understand the Xayans, Mother." Keana took a step closer. "You murdered the peaceful emissaries who came to Sonjeera to ask for your help. You don't understand the Xayan race, the slickwater, and the memories . . . or all the wonders and powers that I now have, which were denied me before."

The old Diadem recoiled as her daughter approached. "You're brainwashed. Contaminated! Don't touch me."

Keana stopped a few feet away. "How familiar, the warmth and love you've always shown me. This planet has concerns that far outweigh yours. The petty struggles of the Constellation are like the concerns of ants while a civilization tries to build a great city. And there are more terrible threats coming. The Ro-Xayans hammered this planet once, and they will come back again."

"You must release me from this horrid place! You are all barbarians."

Keana smiled. "Barbarians? The Xayan civilization is far superior to the Constellation. Maybe we should take you to the slickwater pools and throw you in, so you can see and know for yourself." She extended a hand toward her mother, but Michella backed away in horror, as expected.

"I am not the daughter you remember. I know who I used to be—weak, preoccupied, and flighty. The way you wanted me to be. You wanted to strip away my ambitions, keep me docile. But I have another life inside me now, a whole universe." She extended her fingers again, trying to touch Michella's face.

But the old woman retreated until she pressed against the wall. "Get away from me!"

Keana made a mental link with Uroa, felt the telemancy build within their shared consciousness. She wanted to demonstrate how much she had changed— not in a vengeful way, but just to convince her mother, to get through the irrational barriers Michella had erected.

Just then the bungalow door opened, and the guards allowed Ishop Heer inside. Though he looked edgy and trapped, he still moved with a prowling grace.

As he saw Michella cowering before Keana, an impish grin crossed his lips. "Ah, a mother-and-daughter reunion. But I advise against hugging her, Eminence. She's not the daughter you remember anymore."

Keana turned to him, feeling more confident than ever. "I believe you tricked me into coming here, Ishop. You hoped that Hellhole would destroy me, didn't you? Just as my mother exiled General Adolphus here, thinking he would not survive. Instead this place made both of us stronger. Sorry to disappoint you."

He chuckled. "Tricked you? I merely told you what you wished to know. The son of your poor dead lover had gone into exile, and you begged for information. Are you angry with me for telling you exactly what you asked?"

"No, Ishop. And you may have been right that I wouldn't have fared well here, but I did survive with the help of the slickwater. Thanks to the Xayans, and Uroa inside me, I'm now more than you ever imagined I would be." She turned her gaze back to Michella. "In fact, I would make a strong ruler, a perfect Diadem with the right breadth of experience, wisdom, and personal power. From what I understand, you've left the Constellation a shambles."

"You should have died on this planet and saved us all the trouble," Michella muttered.

Keana was impatient with the old woman's pettiness. She had always allowed her mother to hurt her before, but those days were long gone. Uroa was inside her as a bastion of strength, but she didn't need his help now. "I came to Hellhole out of love, Mother. I'm sure that's a concept as foreign to you as these alien presences are. I wanted to make amends to Cristoph for what happened to his father. I wanted to share my grief with him, help him to survive. I did love his father very much. Poor Louis . . . I know you caused his disgrace and brought about his downfall. I should have been with him in prison to strengthen him, but you kept us apart. He didn't have me to comfort him, and in despair he killed himself. I blame *you*, Mother—you drove him to suicide."

Ishop made a rude snort. "You can certainly blame her, but you think it was suicide? Comfort yourself with that, girl. Louis de Carre *should* have taken care of matters himself, but I had to make all the arrangements." He shook his shaved head. "That man was a disappointment to the end. He might have salvaged something of his noble house if he had fought for his honor as much as he struggled in the last few moments when I killed him."

Keana looked at Ishop with widening eyes as horror swelled within her. Uroa surged to greater power. She felt a tingling crackle inside her bloodstream.

If Ishop noticed, he didn't seem concerned. He made an oblivious gesture toward Michella. "I was just a tool, though. I acted under your mother's explicit orders. She commanded me to remove that man because she was impatient with your defiance. That's all it was to her, a mother slapping the hand of an unruly child." His chuckle was like broken glass.

Keana directed her fury toward Michella now, whose lips were curled back in disgust and indignation. "You have only yourself to blame, Daughter! If you had paid attention to your own responsibilities, if you hadn't been so damned stupid, none of this would have happened."

Like a geyser ready to erupt, telemancy rose within Keana, a roiling overload of power that demanded to be released. Keana could barely control it. She remembered what Devon Vence had done in his outrage after his girlfriend Antonia had been shot. With a hammer of telemancy, he had crushed Gail Carrington, leaving only a smear of disassociated cells on a bulkhead.

Keana knew she could do that to her mother right now. She could pulverize the old woman's brittle bones, leaving the great Diadem Michella Duchenet nothing more than a heap of squashed, poisonous flesh. She could do that to Ishop, too.

But that wasn't what she wanted. She held on to Uroa inside her, tapped into his stability as well as the power he contained. Keana was wiser now, stronger—mature. Trickle by trickle, she felt the telemancy diminish. Uroa was there; the two of them were firm. When Keana had control over herself once more, she drew a deep breath, opened her eyes. She saw both Ishop and Michella looking worried about what they had almost provoked. They were staring at her eyes, which must have been spiraling wildly.

Keana decided that she wanted nothing more to do with her mother. The Diadem and the Constellation were irrelevant now. Keana had more important things to do. She needed to save Hellhole from the Ro-Xayans . . . and more significantly, she had to guide all of her people to *ala'ru*.

A flustered Sophie Vence appeared at the bungalow door. She ignored Michella and Ishop, focusing entirely on Keana. "Peter Herald told me you were here. Do you need my assistance, or should I just lock the door and leave you alone with them?"

"I had things to resolve, but I'm finished now," Keana said. After the guards escorted Ishop back to his own bungalow, Keana gave the old woman a last glance while speaking to Sophie. "I wash my hands of my mother."

Michella flew into a rage. "I don't want you back. Do you understand? I don't want you back. You're contam—"

Keana and Sophie sealed the door behind them, cutting off the old woman's vitriol.

42

Commodore Hallholme's tension had simmered into numbness. He was hamstrung here at Tehila.

By now, according to plan, the Constellation fleet should have taken over the Hellhole stringline hub and arrested General Adolphus. But plans often went awry. . . .

If Diadem Michella had just stayed on Sonjeera rather than flouncing her way into a complex military operation as if it were some kind of picnic, Percival would have delivered the whole Deep Zone for her to rule—for good or ill. Without doubt, the Diadem would have exacted severe reprisals upon the rebellious colony worlds, which gave Percival cause to reconsider. Was that really the best possible outcome? Who truly would have benefited from that? The Constellation? The Deep Zone? Anyone? Diadem Michella herself?

As he waited at Tehila orbit for repairs to be completed, and for new orders to arrive from the Council on Sonjeera, he killed time in his stateroom. It was hard to be enthusiastic when every possible decision was a bad one.

Though he had spent over an hour crafting it, the letter he had dispatched by emergency courier drone was a weak statement, barely masking his failure, but facts were facts. It did not matter that Michella should never have been part of the Tehila operation in the first place. He had failed to protect the Diadem of the Constellation. Michella Duchenet had been snatched out from under his nose. He could blame no one else for that.

No matter what, the Council would make him a scapegoat. Some noble would remind them all of Percival's recent defeat at the hands of General Adolphus.

They would blame him for Escobar's failings as well, pointing out how his son's blunder had let much of the Constellation fleet fall into enemy hands. Percival had no choice but to accept responsibility for Escobar. The Commodore had trained him, much to his frustration.

After the Diadem had been kidnapped, Percival realized he should have managed the pursuit better, should have had guardian ships ready to intercept any vessel that tried to escape. In preparation for the mission launch, he had installed traditional patrols, increased security down at the Tehila spaceport, but his focus had been on the imminent departure. Under normal circumstances, any military tribunal would have agreed with his command decisions—until something went wrong. And with Michella Duchenet now held hostage by the General, something had indeed gone terribly wrong.

In shock, he had watched the Diadem destroy the Sonjeera spaceport without flinching because of some unverified alien threat, and then she had simply flown away with him to the Deep Zone. It seemed a cowardly, or at the very least a tone-deaf and oblivious act. Now Michella had been abducted and whisked away to the heart of enemy territory.

As a military officer, he knew his choices should be clear-cut. He simply could not allow the Deep Zone rebellion to succeed, but he also found it increasingly difficult to support the Diadem's repeated inflammatory decisions. He also knew the other Council members— especially her heir-apparent Lord Selik Riomini—and Percival wasn't certain that her successor would be any better than Michella Duchenet. Commodore Hallholme was no longer sure what he was fighting for.

He answered the chime at his stateroom door to find Duff Adkins with a report in his hands and a smile on his face. Percival had not seen the man smile much in recent months. "Good news for a change, Commodore."

"You have me at a loss for words, Duff. What is it?"

"Repairs are completed on the sabotaged terminus ring. The integrity of the iperion line is intact, and we've been sending test flights out, ships heading to the edge of the solar system and back. The tests are going perfectly and are almost complete, so the fleet should be able to depart soon. If that is what you wish."

"As soon as we get new orders from Sonjeera."

Percival limped to his wardrobe locker and removed his uniform jacket, which Duff helped him put on. The old Commodore's muscles ached from the degenerative disease that he barely kept under control. Tension was known to accelerate the symptoms of the disease, and he'd had more than enough tension in recent months.

How he longed to be back on Qiorfu, experimenting with different blends of wine, playing with his two grandsons. At his age, after all he'd done, he should be telling war stories and exaggerating his bravery, not trying to make more legends about himself.

Duff carefully straightened the Commodore's collar, adjusted one of his medals. His aide seemed to know his troubled thoughts and provided his advice, as always. "With or without orders from Sonjeera, there really is no other decision, sir. You know it will be worse for you if you vacillate rather than act."

"Yes, Duff. We will proceed with our mission, attempt to rescue Diadem Michella, and defeat our enemy, even though the General now knows we're coming." He brushed down his muttonchop sideburns and emerged from his stateroom. "Just an average day at work for us."

Upon reaching the bridge, the Commodore was pleased to receive successful reports from all the test flights. The damage to the terminus ring had been repaired and checked, and now all the fully armed military ships were reloaded aboard the two stringline haulers. At last, the fleet was ready. He sent an all-ship signal announcing departure in two hours.

Percival had monitored activity at the Tehila spaceport and at the old governmental mansion—with the Diadem gone, Administrator Reming had reassumed the role of interim planetary leadership. Percival didn't care about the local politics. He had established his military base here, but his original orders were to conquer Hellhole. It was not his place to worry about how the Constellation would govern the former rebel worlds once he did his job.

Reming transmitted an exuberant message to the flagship. "Commodore, I wish you the best of success! I pray that you are able to return Diadem Michella to us safe and sound." His expression and tone of voice didn't match the enthusiasm that his words implied.

Then a speedy courier drone raced in along the stringline from Sonjeera, no doubt bearing the long-awaited message from the Council. Percival learned of this with a mixture of relief and disappointment, knowing that the new orders would surely tangle his carefully laid plans. He sighed at the added complication. If only his fleet had left an hour sooner . . .

He ordered the message brought to him immediately. Now, at least, he would know. If they angrily relieved him of command for letting Michella be taken, then so be it.

He carried the code-locked message file to his ready room just off the bridge, intending to review it in private, but then decided that he wanted Duff Adkins there with him. With the door sealed, he played the message. The two men watched Selik Riomini's image shimmer before them.

"Commodore Hallholme, I was alarmed to hear of your recent setback at Tehila, but before I present your revised orders, I must also inform you of changes that have occurred here in the Crown Jewels." He sounded smug.

"After the devastating explosion at the Sonjeera spaceport, the Council of Nobles met in emergency session. By her own admission, Michella Duchenet caused that horrific event, at her direct order. Not only did she destroy a major portion of our spaceport, causing a severe strategic setback in time of war, but she also caused the deaths of hundreds of thousands of people, disrupted our economy, and then turned her back on the Crown Jewels. By unanimous acclamation, the Council removed Michella Duchenet from her position and installed me as the new Diadem.

"Michella Duchenet has been branded an outlaw. You are not to let her situation affect your mission in any way whatsoever. The fact that she is being held hostage by General Adolphus is of no consequence. Michella is no longer of any value to him as a bargaining chip. Our enemy must be made to understand that.

"I, Selik Riomini, am the rightful Diadem of the Constellation. These are my orders: If feasible, the criminal Michella Duchenet is to be brought back to Sonjeera for trial and punishment, but you are not to waste any time or expend any effort on rescue.

"Your original mission stands: Take your fleet, defeat the rebel General, and seize control of his stringline hub. You are ordered to kill Tiber Adolphus. If you had done that the first time, you would have saved us a great deal of trouble." Riomini paused, and even in the recorded image his anger was palpable. "Afterward, as a punitive measure, I want you to raze his entire planet, wipe out the cities and settlements, leave its surface a burning blister, just as I did on Theser." The Black Lord's face darkened, and his eyes seemed to stab directly into Percival's heart as he ended the message.

Hearing this, Adkins recoiled. "He can't possibly mean that."

"I'm afraid he does, Duff. I hope, but do not expect, that his orders stop there. After we finish on planet Hallholme, he may well command us to devastate other Deep Zone worlds." Percival's jaw ached from clenching it so hard.

After the projection faded, Percival was left staring at the vacant space. The Black Lord's disrespect rankled. *If you had done that the first time, you would have saved us a great deal of trouble.* Percival had grown to dislike Diadem Michella's leadership abilities, and now he thought he would like Diadem Riomini's administration even less.

Duff looked at him. "What are we going to do, sir?"

"We're going to planet Hallholme as planned—but cautiously. You can be sure the General will have a trick or two up his sleeve. He's had ample time to prepare for us."

After reviewing Riomini's grim message one more time, the two men left the ready room and returned to the flagship's bridge—just as alarms began to sound.

"Inbound ships, Commodore!" cried the female tactical officer. "Two stringline haulers entering the system at extreme deceleration."

A long-range sensor officer stared at his screen. "The haulers are shedding ships, sir—in full-scale attack mode! Can't determine who it is yet."

Percival stared at the large bridge screen, trying to

make out the tiny bright dots of incoming vessels. "We know who it is."

He sounded battle stations, then prepared to face General Tiber Adolphus one last time.

43

During the stringline journey to Tehila, General Adolphus spent his time planning the operation in the greatest possible detail.

Working with Tanja Hu, Ian Walfor, Captain Naridar, and even Lodo, he mapped out the all-important first few moments of the imminent engagement. Once the stringline haulers dropped off the iperion path and hurtled into the Tehila system, they would have very little time to coordinate. Everything had to be precisely in sync.

Adolphus also met with the captains of the five civilian commercial transports that had volunteered their ships in service of the assault; he watched their expressions fall when he explained what he intended to do—an entirely unexpected maneuver only made possible by the presence of the shadow-Xayans. Telemancy changed the entire tactical landscape of the space battle.

Hearing the plan, the civilian captains were angry or nervous, yet every one of them agreed. Adolphus shook hands with each of them, thanking them for himself and for the Deep Zone. "I wouldn't ask this if it weren't absolutely necessary." During the tense four-day stringline journey, the civilian captains had time to prepare their ships, strip out all possessions and keepsakes, and say good-bye to their craft.

Walfor had left his ship back on Hellhole when he and Tanja joined the fleet. Now he asked for the use of a small DZDF fighter. "I want to be in the middle of the action, General."

"But you're not a military man, Mr. Walfor."

"No, but I'm a damn good pilot—and if Tanja's going down to the surface to rile up the refugees, she'll need somebody to fly her there."

Tanja looked determined as she stood on the *Jacob*'s bridge. "We've already laid the groundwork, General, and I have my contacts down there. I can spark an uprising with a snap of my fingers."

Walfor gave a wry smile. "It may be a *little* harder than that. . . ."

Adolphus found an available ship and let Walfor spend the transit days running simulations. Even though the former Buktu governor claimed he didn't need any more training, he agreed that it was a good diversion to dissipate some of the stress.

Flight engineers had calculated the maximum deceleration that could be tolerated by the material strength of the docking clamps and ship hulls—not to mention the soft biology of the crew members. The General pushed it to the edge. When the haulers finally arrived in the Tehila system, the pilots gave the entire fleet a precise countdown. They were ready.

Fifteen minutes out, Adolphus sounded battle stations. Everyone had been briefed and drilled, and they were all ready to "kick some Constellation butt." He felt a pleasant irony in knowing that most of the ships now attacking Commodore Hallholme were refurbished vessels captured from his own son. Though some ships still looked battered externally from the previous space battle, they all displayed the bright gold-and-silver insignia of the Deep Zone Defense Force on their hulls.

Lodo made his laborious way to the *Jacob*'s bridge, his large caterpillarlike abdomen crowding the tactical and operational stations, but they made room. The Original alien lifted his torso high, and his large black eyes reflected light from the control screens.

"The shadow-Xayans are prepared, General Tiber Adolphus, as am I. Our telemancy is unified. We promised to help defend against outside attacks, even if our awakened race is not yet ready for *ala'ru*. After we remove the distraction of your human enemy, we can devote all our energies against the Ro-Xayans when they show themselves."

"I appreciate that," Adolphus said. "Your telemancy gives me many new options. Now let's show off what we can do."

In perfect coordination, the two loaded stringline haulers dropped off the iperion path just outside of Tehila. With the warning signal, everyone braced themselves as the deceleration slammed its heavy hand down upon them. Adolphus grimaced in the crushing gravity, and Lodo squirmed as well, his soft body distorting, reshaping temporarily, and enduring.

As the haulers braked to normal speed, the clamps holding the five chosen civilian ships slammed open, releasing them like stones hurled from a sling. Though unarmed, the empty craft shot out of the hauler framework like relativistic projectiles.

"Sensors!" Adolphus shouted. "Give us a map and targets. Shadow-Xayans, prepare to reach out with telemancy."

Lodo forced himself to straighten against the continued deceleration. "I am guiding them."

As the tumbling ships streaked toward Tehila, a map projection finally appeared on the screens, showing a large group of Constellation warships already loaded aboard two military stringline haulers.

"Just in time," Adolphus said. "The Commodore was ready to launch."

Crowded in a large mess hall two decks below, the hundred and fifty shadow-Xayans combined their telemancy, reached out with the long-distance invisible force, and guided the hurtling civilian ships toward the Constellation stringline haulers.

The Commodore's fleet scrambled to react. Some of his warships dropped out of the hauler framework, falling into defensive positions. But most of the locked ships could not move fast enough.

Like cannonballs precisely guided by telemancy, the sacrificial civilian ships slammed into their targets one by one at relativistic speeds. The impacts vaporized large battle vessels; no shields could be sufficient against such collisions. The civilian ships obliterated four of the Commodore's best vessels, and the fifth hurtling craft slashed through one of the half-empty military hauler frameworks like a gutting knife, ripping the still-docked vessels into debris.

Adolphus could not have hoped for a better outcome, but the engagement was not over yet. After expending those five surprise projectiles, he still had to manage several other prongs of the plan. The worst deceleration continued for fifteen minutes. When he could finally push himself up to a sitting position in the command chair, he issued another string of orders.

All of his DZDF ships—fully armed, engines powered up, weapons active—dropped free from docking clamps and engaged the reeling Constellation forces. The General was amazed at how much chaos he had provoked in only a few minutes. The rest of his fleet, led by Captain

Naridar's fifteen peacekeeper ships, charged toward Tehila orbit, opening fire with vengeful enthusiasm. On the secure comm, Adolphus reminded them to exercise some restraint. "The iperion path and the two terminus rings must not be damaged."

Following his separate mission, Ian Walfor flew his new ship toward the planet. In the cockpit beside him, Tanja transmitted to the ground and called upon the hundreds of Candela refugees who were crowded in temporary housing and refugee camps. "We told you the time would come. You don't belong in squalid camps. You survived the destruction of a planet. You can overthrow a handful of militia members in silly uniforms."

Walfor's voice joined hers. "You all know you don't want to go back to oppressive Constellation rule. Take back your planet. Be free! General Adolphus is here to help."

The *Jacob* headed toward orbit, leaving the two DZDF stringline haulers empty at the far edge of the battle zone. Captain Naridar guided his assault, while Adolphus directed the second wave. The General knew that he must not give Commodore Hallholme time to rally. As his ships converged on the scrambling enemy fleet, Adolphus transmitted on a known command frequency. "Commodore Percival Hallholme, my fleet is responding to a request for aid from the free people of Tehila. I require your immediate surrender."

A harried-looking Percival Hallholme appeared on the screen. "I don't recognize your authority, General Adolphus. Your rebellion is illegal. Cease your hostilities now, or face immediate reprisals."

The General sighed. "Enough of this nonsense. You know we have Diadem Michella Duchenet hostage. I wouldn't normally stoop to such leverage, but you established those rules long ago at the Battle of Sonjeera. If it saves lives, I'll use whatever I have."

On the screen, the old Commodore looked intently at Adolphus. He appeared to have aged a decade since their last confrontation in Hellhole orbit. His eyes were reddened, his face drawn; his silvery muttonchop sideburns needed a trim. "You should be aware that Michella Duchenet has been stripped of her title as Diadem. The Council removed her authority and installed Lord Riomini in her stead. If I were to return Michella Duchenet to Sonjeera, she would stand trial for treason and crimes against humanity, and would likely be executed." He gave a thin smile. "So, you see, you have no leverage."

Adolphus tried to hide his reaction—he hadn't expected that, but he had never liked the hostage business in the first place. As his ships closed in on the Constellation vessels, preparing to engage, he said, "I'd rather defeat you the old-fashioned way. But with a twist."

The General terminated the transmission, then turned to Lodo. "Use your telemancy to neutralize the Commodore's weapons, as you did the last time. We can end this quickly and without further bloodshed."

The alien bowed his smooth head. "We will do our best, General. Our shadow-Xayans have practiced their skills, and I can sense their eagerness for a real engagement."

A wave of telemancy rippled out to hammer the Commodore's ships, which had their weapons powered up and ready for attack. On the screen, Adolphus watched multiple images, tactical grids, and projected courses. Some of the Constellation battleships reeled under the combined telemancy assault; one grew dark and drifted aimlessly.

Though Lodo remained silent, his entire body

thrummed with the strain. He finally announced, "We deactivated some of his systems, General, but are not able to melt them down as we did before. Their weapons now have powerful enhanced shields. The ships we did neutralize were slow to get their shields in place."

"Concentrate on the lead vessel," Adolphus said. "I want the Commodore's flagship dead in space."

The telemancy pummeling continued. Gathered in the communal chamber, the shadow-Xayans stood shoulder-to-shoulder, some clasping hands. All had their eyes closed, brows furrowed, focusing their energies.

Lodo reported again. "The enemy has a coordinated, fleet-wide firing system, synchronized with our telemancy pulses. They can detect our strongest surge, then adjust their shields to fire weapons in nanosecond bursts while protecting their vulnerable systems." He paused, continuing to strain. "We have, however, shifted the pattern of our telemancy attack. I believe we have managed to neutralize the weapons on the flagship at least. And we have damaged his engines. We might be able to do the same with other enemy warships, but they are already altering their patterns."

"But at least the flagship is neutralized?" Adolphus pressed.

"It is. And their engines are barely functional. The weapons systems are not destroyed, but do not pose an immediate threat. That is the best we can do, General."

Adolphus ordered Captain Naridar to proceed with his frontal assault. Now the Constellation ships scattered, trying to fall back and regroup when they discovered they were unable to fight back.

Tanja Hu transmitted from Walfor's ship as they raced down to the surface. The excitement in her voice was a dramatic contrast to her usual hard demeanor.

"Mobs have appeared at several flashpoints in the streets, General—not just my Candela refugees, but regular Tehila citizens as well. They didn't need much of an excuse to react. They're chasing down any uniformed militia members they can find."

Walfor added, "Our supporters already control the spaceport, General. If Commodore Hallholme decides to stay behind, he won't have any place to go."

The Commodore apparently came to the same conclusion moments later. One of his two military stringline haulers had been gutted by the relativistic civilian ships, but the other was intact, and he called for his surviving Constellation vessels to retreat into the framework.

Defending against constant fire from the DZDF ships, the big hauler maneuvered to the Sonjeera terminus ring and the iperion line that led back to the safety of the Crown Jewels. Captain Naridar's ships pursued the Constellation ships, but Hallholme's forces were well-trained. Adolphus was amazed at how swiftly they loaded aboard the hauler framework in the chaos of battle.

Adolphus had no intention of letting his nemesis get away so easily, though. The *Jacob* raced after the retreating stringline hauler, opening fire. He damaged several vulnerable ships inside the framework.

Adolphus transmitted, "Time to surrender, Commodore."

But the other commander didn't respond. The Constellation hauler accelerated along the iperion path heading out of the system. When the pilot engaged the functional stringline engines, the massive framework quickly achieved a velocity that the DZDF ships could not match. It vanished in a bright flash.

Captain Naridar transmitted to the *Jacob*. "Sorry we couldn't stop him, sir. He chose to retreat rather than surrender."

"He's becoming an expert at that," Adolphus said. "I think he lacks conviction." He straightened in his command chair, letting the adrenaline dwindle to a sensation of triumph. He felt an ache in his joints, a soreness in his bruised muscles after the battering from the extreme deceleration, but he could actually allow himself a moment of satisfaction, even joy.

After so many setbacks, this was an unqualified victory. Nearly half of Commodore Hallholme's ships had been destroyed or disabled, and Adolphus had recaptured a key Deep Zone planet.

He opened the all-fleet channel. "This is a day to celebrate. The invaders are gone, and Tehila is free again! Now we have to put the pieces back together."

44

As both the Diadem and the Supreme Commander of the Army of the Constellation, Selik Riomini should have felt satisfied, but these were not normal times. He recalled an ancient observation, "Once you reach the top, there is nowhere to go but down."

In many respects, he'd felt more powerful *before* becoming Diadem, building his secret fleet on Qiorfu, making his contingency plans. Back then, he'd taken great care to establish the basis of his power, not only militarily, but by cultivating important alliances with certain nobles. Now, with the chaotic and crumbling Deep Zone and unrest among the Crown Jewels nobility, Michella hadn't left him much of a prize to seize.

Still, the Star Throne was his, for better or worse. And he could rebuild it in the way he liked. He already had grand plans, but first, after Michella's steady stream of bad decisions, he had to do a great deal of damage control.

He stood on the safe perimeter of the spaceport blast zone, watching heavy-equipment operators clean up the melted slag and load it into airborne haulers to be dumped in a distant marshland that was ripe for development. Not long ago, this area had been a thriving hub of commerce, with a steady stream of shuttles, landing pods, and cargo vessels landing and taking off.

As the new Diadem, Riomini had ordered the establishment of a temporary spaceport, with a hastily poured polymer landing field and portable support buildings. Orbital craft, passenger pods, and downboxes went in and out of there. It was a mere shadow of the previous substantial facility, but it served the purpose. And it showed his competence as the Constellation's new leader.

In view of the temporary landing zone, Riomini awaited Commodore Percival Hallholme, whose fleet—the remnants of it—had just arrived in disgrace at the Sonjeera hub. Defeated yet again! The new Diadem knew this would not be a happy encounter.

The Black Lord sniffed, caught a peculiar odor in the air—something . . . alien?—but put the thought out of his mind, told himself he'd just imagined it. *I don't want to be like that crazy old woman!*

The edge of the blast zone was an appropriately dramatic place to meet the old warhorse. Riomini wanted to hear the Commodore's explanation of his latest outrageous failure, and he also wanted to show him up close what Michella Duchenet had done—just to ensure the man's loyalty—although Percival Hallholme had also seen firsthand the old Diadem's irrational and destructive decisions. No, this man was not likely to profess ill-considered loyalty to someone like that.

To gauge his own popularity, Riomini had dispatched thousands of government workers to canvas the city, asking probative questions. He actually let people criticize him, without threat of reprisals, but he drew a bright red line at allowing the formation of active opposition groups. Regardless, it was apparent that he was much better liked than Michella had been. He realized that he might even have been able to win the Star Throne without his private military force, but did not regret for a moment how he had claimed his title.

He suspected that the most outspoken people were Adolphus loyalists anyway. With the ouster of Michella Duchenet, they had expected the entire convoluted system to change, which was foolish and unrealistic. They had been aligning themselves with powerful nobles in the Constellation who sensed weakness in his own rule, despite the size of his private military. Thus far, Riomini's spies had produced the names of only three such nobles, but even that small number enraged him. Right now all three were being interrogated.

He had also set up a separate, lower court system to deal with the constant stream of dissenters being picked up by his secret police. Each would be found guilty as a matter of course, but so far he had not imposed executions because he didn't want to be seen as a tyrant. For the time being, they would all be shipped off to incarceration on Ogg or Barassa. He could deal with them later.

Right now, while awaiting Commodore Hallholme's arrival, the excruciatingly slim Anson Tebias spoke with the woman Riomini had appointed to run the interim spaceport, along with a burly contractor who was supervising the cleanup operations.

Riomini heard a smooth engine noise, and looked up to see a Constellation military flyer in a steep descent, landing nearby on the temporary field. Moments later, the grizzled old commander was escorted into the Diadem's presence. Commodore Hallholme moved slowly, hobbling from his chronic, degenerative condition. The medals on the front of his gold-and-black uniform did not shine as usual, and the uniform shirt was soiled and wrinkled.

With a grim expression, the old man gave a crisp salute. "I apologize for my appearance, sir, but I received word that you wanted to see me immediately." He smoothed his bushy sideburns, then stood at attention. His gray eyes seemed more watery and tired than usual. "My congratulations on your new position. Strong leadership is sorely needed in this crisis."

"These are extraordinary times for the Constellation, and I require my best military minds." Riomini did not mention the man's failures, and instead pointed out the wreckage of the spaceport.

Hallholme nodded, said that he had seen the extent of devastation as his shuttle came from the stringline hub, and then he frowned. "I am afraid I must add to your burdens, Eminence. After a major space battle, General Adolphus has recaptured Tehila, and thus removed our only way into the DZ stringline network. I lost many of my ships, and now the Army of the Constellation no longer has access into the Deep Zone."

Riomini scowled, but he had already received the basic report and burned out most of his anger in the past two hours. Commodore Hallholme had to go through this humiliating charade and would no doubt offer his resignation, again. But Riomini wouldn't let him—he had other plans. Fortunately, the summary showed that the new shielding had proved at least partially effective against the alien telekinetic assault. And he had another option that no one suspected.

As the old Commodore reached into his uniform blouse and withdrew a folded document—his letter of resignation, as expected—Riomini harshly told him to put it away. "We have no time for this. You were ordered to defeat General Adolphus and recapture the Deep Zone. I still expect you to do it."

"Eminence, I have lost half of my fleet. The lack of ships does not leave me with a viable battle plan."

Riomini cut him off. "Fortunately, it's not a complete disaster. While you were gone, I made other arrangements of my own. Tehila was not the only weak spot in the General's unraveling web. Hossetea demonstrated that as well, but Adolphus doesn't realize how widespread the discontent is. I, however, *do*." A scheming smile crept across his face. Riomini knew he had to strike now while the Commodore was stinging and angry—and when Adolphus would least expect a new gaping vulnerability. "Yet another world has turned against him, and the General is still unaware of it. We have a window of opportunity that we dare not waste."

Hallholme was clearly surprised. "An interesting development, Eminence, but I don't have a sufficient military force to bring to bear against General Adolphus, even with the element of surprise."

Again, Riomini smiled. "But I have many more ships than you know about—an entire private fleet I constructed on Qiorfu. They are ready to fly."

The Commodore stood stiff and formal, but he was clearly reeling. "On . . . Qiorfu? And I was not aware of this?"

"At the Lubis Plain industrial zone, begun years ago with the assistance of your son. You were retired at the time, tending your vineyards, and I swore him to secrecy."

The old Commodore sighed, clearly wishing he could just go back there.

Riomini kept him focused. "If you depart immediately on this new offensive, I will grant you fifty more top-of-the-line warships, fully shielded and with more firepower than you've ever had. The question is, are you ready to destroy our nemesis, once and for all?"

Commodore Hallholme didn't hesitate. "Yes, Eminence. I appreciate the new chance."

"I've stopped counting the number of chances you've had, but I assure you this is the last one."

In spite of the veiled threat, the Commodore managed a grim smile. "It's beautiful on Qiorfu at this time of year. It'll be nice to finish this so I can retire there. For the second time." He drew a breath. "And I will get my son back. We *can* defeat the rebels, Eminence. We *will* defeat them."

"Yes, Commodore, you will." With the unrest brewing in the Crown Jewels, Riomini had to achieve a golden victory. Afterward, no one would question his legitimacy. "Strike fast, strike hard, Commodore."

Hallholme saluted crisply, then rushed back to his flagship to begin preparations.

45

In the aftermath of the liberation of Tehila, General Adolphus felt energized, pleased, and confident. This had been an uncontested defeat of Commodore Hallholme. How many more were necessary to make up for losing the Battle of Sonjeera?

Some of the Commodore's damaged ships remained helpless in orbit above Tehila. They had been left behind, stranded when they could not get aboard the lone retreating stringline hauler. Lodo and the shadow-Xayans rendered the enemy weapons inert and targeted their engines so they could not escape.

Adolphus's fleet quickly surrounded and captured those vessels; the Constellation crews would be detained in the former refugee camps down on Tehila—Tanja Hu had pointed out that so much security shouldn't be allowed to go to waste. As the DZDF forces shuttled officers and crew down under heavy guard, Adolphus directed mop-up operations from the *Jacob*. He summoned Tanja Hu, Ian Walfor, and Lewis Naridar to his ready room.

"Tehila has already proved to be a vulnerable spot, General," said Naridar. "We don't dare let down our guard. We need to leave a significant defensive force here."

"And we just gave the Constellation a black eye," Walfor said. "Tehila will be seen as a symbol, and Commodore Hallholme will want it back."

"I say cut the stringline," Tanja said. "I've said that all along. Perfect security results from perfect isolation. Cut all the lines into the Crown Jewels, and the enemy forces can't get to us."

Adolphus was troubled. "That seems like giving up. It's much easier to sever an iperion path than to reestablish one—especially until we find a new source of iperion."

Walfor shook his head. "With Candela destroyed, we barely have enough stockpiled iperion to maintain our existing stringlines for a year or two. Unless we find another supply, those routes will dissipate and we'll be isolated—from the Crown Jewels and from one another—whether or not you cut the lines intentionally."

Tanja clenched her fists. "I'm glad to know the old bitch Michella has been ousted on Sonjeera, but Lord Riomini is no better. Ian and I saw firsthand what that monster did to Theser, so we know what he's capable of."

Adolphus reached his decision. "I don't like to keep isolating Deep Zone worlds, but we still have plenty of viable paths to Sonjeera. Cutting off this one, though, will make a statement—a necessary statement." He nodded and spoke to Captain Naridar. "See that the terminus ring to the Crown Jewels is destroyed. It's the only way to be sure."

Naridar smiled. "My pleasure, sir."

The General dispatched Tanja and Walfor to the surface to help manage the ground operations, while he studied assessments and inventories from the *Jacob*. His own losses were more than made up for by the eleven battered Constellation vessels they had seized, as well as hundreds more enemy ships destroyed. Adolphus personally thanked the civilian captains and promised he would make up for their monetary losses threefold.

He thought about Sophie. He depended on her so much, and now she was holding the former Diadem Michella hostage, albeit a now-useless hostage. He felt stronger knowing he could rely on Sophie even though they were solar systems apart.

But he was anxious to bring all these warships back to Hellhole. He felt uneasy leaving the central DZ stringline hub vulnerable since so much of the DZDF had been brought for the liberation of Tehila. Fortunately, George Komun's ships would also be arriving soon for added security.

He knew, though, that he couldn't just withdraw his

fleet and leave Tehila unprotected. After liberating the unruly world, if he left the Tehila settlers and refugees to pick up the pieces—without support or defenses—the resulting turmoil might create a civil war. He needed to leave a significant monitoring force here.

He decided to leave Captain Naridar's fifteen peace-keeping ships—which he had intended to send on a patrol throughout the Deep Zone. They were needed here, at least for the next month or so, as security. He drew up the orders and assigned the veteran captain to monitor the transition on Tehila.

The following day, Ian Walfor transmitted a report to the *Jacob.* "General, we've rounded up the former militia members and imposed a curfew, but the worst part is over. The colonists are still celebrating—I think it would be good if you came down and made an appearance."

"You mean a victory parade," Adolphus said.

Tanja Hu appeared on the screen. "Why not, sir? You deserve it."

Adolphus pondered, then agreed. "It'll be good for reunification, but I do need to return to Hellhole soon. I have more important things to do."

He shuttled down to the spaceport, which had been cleared of Constellation military vessels. Fuel supplies had been released, and the impounded ships were re-turned to their owners. Adolphus had already announced that normal space traffic to the Hellhole stringline hub, and throughout the Deep Zone, would resume within two days.

Tanja and Walfor met him at the spaceport, along with cheering crowds—Candela refugees as well as Tehila supporters who loathed the idea of returning to the repressive Constellation. They smiled and ap-plauded now, but he wasn't naïve enough to think that none of these people had supported the breakaway, at least tacitly.

"What do we do about Administrator Reming? He deserves punishment, but I won't be seen as a tyrant," Adolphus said as they left the spaceport and made their way to the governmental headquarters. He had only met the man once before, when he seemed to be adhering to the rule of law. "The people here should decide his fate."

Walfor and Tanja looked at each other, then away. "About that, General—" They approached the government mansion.

He recognized Reming even with his swollen face and blackened skin. The man had been strung up on a makeshift gibbet outside the headquarters mansion. An ancient but effective form of execution, both a demonstration and a warning. The people here had never wanted his purge, did not support the return of the Constellation; yes, they had made that perfectly evident.

Tanja did not sound overly disturbed. "I'd say the people have already made their own decision."

Adolphus felt a wash of anger and disappointment, then resignation. "And the other militia leaders? The coconspirators who arranged the purge?"

"Executed as well," Walfor said, "but in a less dramatic fashion. It was a swift and complete housecleaning. Now Tehila can be stable again. All of your own loyalists have been freed."

The mysterious walumps had moved into the town and erected mud huts not far from the administrator's mansion. As always, they remained aloof, choosing not to interact with anyone, although they did show a certain curiosity about the hanged man, before continuing about their business.

Adolphus felt uneasy, though. Remembering the

unrest on Hossetea that Captain Naridar had thwarted, he was concerned for the stability of the Deep Zone. One brushfire was occurring after another. If he could remove the Constellation threat and help the Xayans achieve *ala'ru*—which he hoped would also eliminate the concerns about the Ro-Xayans—then he could focus on shoring up normalcy throughout the independent worlds. So many moving parts . . .

He turned to Tanja and Walfor. "Would you two consider remaining here on Tehila as coadministrators? Tehila needs it, and you both seem to be separated from your planets."

They looked at each other. Walfor said, "Buktu is still my home, General, even though all my people were captured. I don't want to give up while there's still a chance I could bring them home."

Tanja said, "After everything that's happened, and everything I've done, I still have too many scars to be a good planetary administrator. I grew up on Candela. I wanted to save it, manage it, and protect my people, but after so much sorrow, so much loss . . ." She shook her head. "No, General, I'm not fit for leadership." She took Walfor's arm and smiled. "Besides, I prefer to stay with Ian, footloose and without red tape restraining me at every turn."

Adolphus understood. "Maybe it's best that we let the people choose their own leaders then, someone from Tehila."

He returned to the *Jacob*, where the officer on duty, Clayton Sendell, had completed preparations for their departure. Ten warships would return to Hellhole, while Captain Naridar's force would remain here until Tehila became stable again.

Lodo joined the General on the bridge. The large Xayan watched all the bustling activity with interest, but had not participated since the heat of the space battle. The other shadow-Xayans kept to themselves.

Now Lodo approached Adolphus. "We must return to Xaya, General Tiber Adolphus. Encix is growing increasingly concerned, and with this group separated from the other converts, we have diminished our strength as our race begins its final push toward *ala'ru*. Time is running out."

"Have the observation satellites picked up any trace of the Ro-Xayans yet?"

"No . . . but they are there. I assure you, General, they are watching us."

Adolphus stood next to the tall, pale alien. "And I am just as anxious to get back home. We have plenty of reasons to worry about Hellhole."

46

When the bungalow door opened to allow the alien monstrosity inside, Michella felt as if she were drowning in a nightmare. All the indignities and torments she'd suffered had already strained her to the breaking point, but this hideous and disgusting thing that squirmed toward her was worse than all the other horrors combined.

She was the ruler of countless planets, and now she felt utterly helpless, frozen in terror. Even the scream withered in her throat. With nowhere else to run, Michella sprang from the bungalow's only chair and retreated to the farthest corner of the room. She yelled for the guards in a cracking voice, but the possessed humans merely stood at the bungalow door and watched her mockingly.

Michella had seen the slimy creatures before, when the passenger pod of emissaries had arrived at Sonjeera. A group of possessed humans and one of the disgusting aliens. Not daring to let them loose, she had sealed that pod in a spaceport hangar, killed everyone aboard, and quarantined the area. She had tried to save the capital world from the contamination, and eventually she'd had no choice but to vaporize the entire area.

Now she was held prisoner in the festering center of the contamination, where her very humanity was threatened every day. Michella had known the things would come for her sooner or later.

"Keep away from me!" Her voice was just a husky gasp.

The monstrous alien paused in the middle of the room to stare at her in a curious, almost perplexed, way. Michella could smell a musky odor, heard the soft wet shuffling of the wormlike lower body. She huddled against the wall, desperate for some way to defend herself, but the guards had made sure she had nothing that could be used as a weapon.

"I have come for you, Diadem Michella Duchenet," said the alien.

Feeling impotent against such a threat and afraid to even touch the creature, she covered her mouth, tried not to breathe any disease or poisonous vapors. She was terrified of becoming one of the possessed humans, half-aliens like Keana, straddling two universes. She shuddered. "I refuse!"

The Xayan loomed in front of her, like a silent serpent contemplating prey. The black, unreadable eyes stared down at her, both hypnotic and terrifying. Michella couldn't help but return the gaze—was the expression inquisitive now? Or did it hold a simmering anger? Who could tell with such an inhuman thing?

She reminded herself that she was the *Diadem of the Constellation*, and tried to keep the quaver out of her voice. "You don't frighten me, monster!" She hoped she sounded strong.

The voice was thrumming and distorted through the mouth membrane. "I am not here to frighten you. I am here to *convince* you."

She wished Ishop were here with her. He'd always been a reassuring presence for her during times of trouble. And he was a deadly killer for her, whenever she needed those particular services. They were both trapped here, prisoners, but they had to find some way to get away.

As if her thoughts had summoned him, the guards opened the bungalow door again and nudged Ishop inside. "Eminence, have they harmed you?" He looked disheveled and red-eyed, probably no worse than she looked. "I heard you cry out." He drew himself to a stumbling halt as he saw the large alien facing her.

With another burst of icy terror, she checked to make sure that Ishop had not been possessed already. His reactions were fluid and normal, and she saw no strange sheen in his eyes. He darted to Michella's side, fidgety, angry, and indignant, but he didn't seem able to offer her much protection. She wondered if he had a plan—he was always scheming, and she knew their goals were aligned, especially now, even if he had seemed irritated with her at times. She had no one else.

The guards closed the bungalow door, sealing them inside with the alien. The thing loomed larger, facing the two of them. "I requested both of you here with me, because you must hear my words. Your cooperation is vital." The black, impenetrable eyes turned toward them. "I am Encix, one of the only remaining Original Xayans. We survived the first asteroid impact in a deeply buried vault, and now we have very little time to resurrect our race before this world is devastated again. I need your help."

The throbbing voice sounded so reasonable. Michella suppressed a shudder. This creature wanted to contaminate them with other aliens. She pressed back against the wall. "Keep away! I know exactly what you're doing."

"No, you do not," Encix said in a much harsher voice. "Your ignorance is plain. That is why I will explain what you must do." The twin antennae on the creature's forehead twitched.

Michella used the chair as a barrier between herself and Encix as she said defiantly, "When one of you came to Sonjeera, making the same pleas, I destroyed him and all of his brainwashed followers—every cell of them has been incinerated. They are annihilated."

"And your violence may have cost our race its best chance of survival. I should despise you for your ignorant fear, Diadem Michella Duchenet, but because my people need you, need *all* humans, more than ever, I will overlook my emotions. And yours."

"We are important hostages, and the Constellation military will soon come to rescue us," Ishop interrupted, sounding brash and defensive. "You don't dare harm us."

"I do not intend to harm you. I require much more than that."

Michella was defiant. "I know what you have done to so many gullible people, but I do not fear death. I'll die before I let an alien presence invade my body."

She wished she had the courage to take her own life rather than let herself fall into this corruption. Her skin crawled at the very thought of it. If she commanded him to do it, Ishop would kill her—she had no doubt of that. But it would be the ultimate disgrace if she let herself die without mounting every resistance, an admission of defeat. And even now Michella Duchenet was not defeated.

The alien facial membrane formed an odd, contorted fold, as if Encix was trying to replicate a human smile. The alien moved closer to them, and Michella had nowhere to retreat. "*Ala'ru* will occur, and none of you unsavory human beings will matter anymore. I wanted to meet you, thinking you might be of use . . . but now I know you are not. Your faction is defective and dangerous. I will not force you into the slickwater pools, for fear that you might contaminate *us*."

Michella blinked in surprise as the alien swung its centaurlike body around and pushed its way toward the door. "There is another ever-growing group of converts out at the Ankor spaceport. You are no longer important, or relevant." The guards moved aside so Encix could pass, then closed the door, leaving an astonished Ishop with Michella, at least for now.

He rubbed beads of perspiration from his bald head. Both of them were trembling, but afraid to admit their terror. He glared at Michella, as if he blamed her!

But Michella knew they might only have a brief moment before he was whisked back to his own bungalow. She leaned closer to him, taking advantage of this brief moment of privacy. "Now tell me you've been working on a way to for us to escape. Commodore Hallholme will be here soon. We have to be ready for him."

"I'll take care of everything the moment I see an opportunity, Eminence," he said, but with an uncharacteristic edge in his voice. "I am your loyal servant, as always."

47

The DZDF fleet returned to the Hellhole stringline hub, loaded aboard a large hauler framework. As the hauler decelerated on approach, General Adolphus was dismayed to see how relatively empty the orbiting complex looked, without a large military force. The majority of his guardian ships had been dispatched to secure other DZ planets, but he was pleased and relieved by the *normal* bustle of commercial traffic, cargo ships coming from frontier worlds loaded with supplies to be distributed throughout the Deep Zone.

How could Diadem Michella have been so naïve to think that the hardy colonists couldn't find a way to become self-sufficient, with over fifty fertile and viable worlds working together to survive?

From his flagship he broadcast the victory at Tehila, knowing the other ships at the hub would widely disseminate the news. He also transmitted the message to Michella Town, Ankor, Slickwater Springs, outlying produce-dome farm complexes, and mining outposts.

"Commodore Hallholme has been defeated once again—maybe badly enough that he's finally learned his lesson," he said. "We destroyed part of the Constellation fleet, captured more ships, and sent the rest running back to Sonjeera. Tehila is now secure. After ousting their traitorous administrator, the people will now establish their own government, as every independent world should do."

The officers of commercial ships parked at the hub congratulated him, and Michella Town celebrated—but Adolphus knew he couldn't let down his guard. His returning ships shored up the defenses around Hellhole, but he wouldn't feel safe until George Komun brought his thirteen additional battleships from Umber. After that, the hub should be able to withstand any military attack.

At the moment, however, Adolphus allowed himself a personal respite inside the ready room just off the *Jacob*'s bridge. He washed his face, combed his hair, and sent a private communication to Sophie at Slickwater Springs. Her eyes sparkled when she saw him on the screen.

He wanted to tell her how beautiful she looked to him, but she understood that and knew how he felt about her. That was one reason why they made such a good team, why he felt so comfortable with her. She was confident enough not to need constant verbal affirmation, but appreciated his love for what it was. She could see it in his eyes and his expression.

"Even though I had complete faith in you, Tiber, I'm always relieved to see you home safe. When can I see you?"

"I have a few administrative details, but then I'm coming straight down to Slickwater Springs. I'll leave Lieutenant Sendell here in temporary command. Is the Diadem still secure?"

"You didn't think I'd let anything happen to dear Michella, did you?"

"Good. I've got news for her that she will find even more distressing than the loss of Tehila and the defeat of Commodore Hallholme."

Sophie smiled. "I can't wait to hear it. I'll be glad to see her taken down another notch."

—∞—

En route to the surface in a troop shuttle, Adolphus reviewed reports from the outlying observation satellites that continued to monitor interplanetary space for any sign of incoming asteroids. Rendo Theris contacted him from the Ankor spaceport, speaking with his usual level of rushed nervousness. "General, the converts seem even more fearful about a threat from the Ro-Xayans, so over two hundred defenders have come here to Ankor, led by Encix. It's quite a large crowd, and I don't know what they expect to accomplish here."

That puzzled him. "Are they interfering with launch or landing ops?"

"So far they're staying outside the paved zones, drawing slickwater from aquifers under the ground, channeling it into small pools. And they're growing more insistent in their . . . proselytizing. Is that the right word? Especially Encix. They keep wanting me and my spaceport workers to immerse ourselves in slickwater. They're frantic to get enough converts for that *ala'ru* of theirs."

Adolphus was disturbed. When he agreed to let people awaken alien memories from the pools, it had been on the strict condition that no one was to be forced. "I'll see what I can do. I'm heading for Slickwater Springs now."

And Sophie . . . Even with all the troubles, he allowed himself a smile at the prospect of being with her again.

He had freshened up and changed, wanting to look his best for her—and unruffled for when he addressed the old Diadem. As soon as he arrived, Sophie embraced him outside the main lodge house, but it was a quick hug, promising more later. She laughed at his awkwardness and discomfort at the public display of affection. "After all this time, Tiber, do you really think we're fooling anyone about our relationship?"

"A military and planetary leader can't look like a giddy schoolboy with a crush on the prettiest girl around."

Her eyebrows shot up in mock displeasure.

He got to business. "Now, I need to see the Diadem. And I think you'll want to hear what I have to say to her—her situation has completely changed."

Sophie led him to the bungalows, where Michella looked haughty, though exhausted and tense. When he faced her, Adolphus tried to measure the defeat in her eyes, but the old Diadem would not be broken easily. The mere sight of him and his rebel uniform caused obvious resentment in her.

He straightened. "It was a complete victory for us. We ousted Commodore Percival Hallholme and his fleet from Tehila. My forces destroyed or captured half of his ships. With only part of his fleet remaining to him, he escaped down the stringline to Sonjeera, and we have now cut the line, so he will be unable to come back."

Michella struggled not to show any alarm, steeling herself with a sneer—her trademark grandmotherly expressions were gone now. "You know Commodore Hallholme as well as I, General—he doesn't understand defeat. He will be back here to rescue me, and he'll leave this planet a smoldering wasteland. The sooner you accept that and make peace with your own future, the better off you'll be. I'll just wait. The Constellation has deep resources, and they won't give up on me."

"Unfortunately for us both, it already has, Michella." He pointedly used only her first name. "The Council of Nobles voted unanimously to strip you of your title. You are no longer the Diadem of the Constellation. You've been replaced by Lord Selik Riomini, and he issued explicit orders to the Commodore that *no* effort is to be made to save you. Should you ever return to Sonjeera, you will face trial for crimes against civilization."

This rocked the old woman. She steadied herself by

holding onto the back of the only chair. "You have no way of knowing that."

Adolphus fixed her with his gaze. "Commodore Hall-holme told me personally."

"You're lying," she said, but sudden fear was in her voice.

"As a bargaining chip, Michella Duchenet, you are of no value to me or to anyone else."

With a solicitous smile, Sophie suggested, "Would you like to request asylum here on Hellhole? I'm sure we can find some menial work for you to do. Something in construction, or perhaps janitorial. If you're willing to put in the effort, you can learn a trade."

The flare behind the old woman's eyes burned away, leaving an expression of defeat.

One of the door guards called for the General. "Sir, the stringline hub reports that Administrator Komun just arrived with his ships, thirteen DZDF war vessels already taking up positions around the stringline hub."

Relieved, Adolphus activated his own portable comm. "Patch me through to him. I want to thank him for helping defend Hellhole."

The guard made a transfer, and the comm officer rerouted the call. Adolphus spoke, giving a sidelong glance to the miserable-looking former Diadem. "George, I'm glad to have you with me. Tehila has been successfully liberated, and now we'll have no further worries from the Crown Jewels."

Komun replied, but without the enthusiastic heartiness with which he should have received the news. "That's not entirely true, General. The political landscape isn't as simple as you think it is."

Adolphus heard something strange in the man's voice and he was instantly on his guard. Sophie looked at him, watched his expression fall. "I don't like the sound of that, George."

Up in orbit, the fully armed DZDF ships from Umber dropped from their hauler framework and took up positions around the main stringline hub. Their weapons were active. Before the *Jacob* could react, Komun's ships took potshots at the flagship, damaging the engines. Then they surrounded and seized the stringline hub.

Adolphus felt an icy dread as he heard the orders over the comm, and tried to shout over them, "What are you doing?"

Of all possible traitors, he had never expected this man to be a weak link. Komun had been one of the original conspirators, the tight group that had plotted how to break free of the Constellation's stranglehold. He had fought valiantly and sacrificed, and now his own world was stable and free. Why would he turn against the DZ now?

Adolphus stepped out of the bungalow, but he could see the expression of malicious glee on the old Diadem's face.

On the comm, Komun said, "Hossetea and Tehila aren't the only planets having second thoughts about a never-ending war with the Constellation. Umber has also turned against you."

Sophie cried, "That's impossible!"

Adolphus knew it must be true, though. In the back of his mind thoughts were spinning, possibilities surfacing as he tried to figure out how to defend against this sneak attack. "But why?"

Komun said, "Lord Riomini destroyed Theser. Asteroids obliterated Candela. The Army of the Constellation took over Tehila. Who knows what else is coming?

We're facing more than we can handle. Your dreams are grand and naïve, General, but the Constellation has existed for more than a thousand years. Did you honestly think a few upstarts could undo all that in a few years? It's not worth the effort. Dreams are for the deluded."

"Then Umber will collapse along with everything else." Adolphus lowered his voice to a growl. "Are you certain you want me as your enemy?"

Komun was dismissive. "Friendship has to take a subordinate role to destiny. Diadem Riomini guaranteed that my planet would be independent of both Hellhole and the Constellation. I will pay no tribute, I'll be able to establish my own stringline hub over Umber, and I can branch out however I like throughout the Deep Zone." His voice hardened. "My forces control the Hellhole stringline hub now, General. Don't test me, or I'll blow the whole thing if necessary. In the meantime, Constellation battleships will be coming directly here via Umber. In fact, I wouldn't be surprised if they're led by Commodore Hallholme himself. Diadem Riomini looks forward to wrapping up this matter in short order."

As Komun's battleships tightened their cordon around the stringline hub, Adolphus heard old Michella sitting in her bungalow, laughing.

48

Although Bolton felt better than Redcom Hallholme, that wasn't saying much. He was actually surprised to discover his own inner strength, and the endurance that let him trudge ahead of his companion on the rugged landscape.

They'd been gone for days, plodding across the endlessly strange and dangerous wilderness; Bolton was in the lead as they descended a steep embankment, struggling to keep his footing on loose rocks and soil. His stomach roiled, no doubt from contaminants in the stream water they'd been forced to drink. Every muscle in his body ached, but at least neither he nor Escobar had suffered from the deadly algae.

Hellhole had plenty of other ways to kill them.

At the bottom of the crumbly slope he looked back to watch Escobar picking his way down. Finally they stood together on the flat area of rust-red scrubgrass. The Redcom looked even more ill. Bolton asked, "Do you need to rest, sir?"

Though his face was gray, Escobar shook his head. "What we both need is a place to settle for the night. And food."

Their supplies had been ruined by the algae and lost with the Trakmaster, and by now both of them were weak and starving. They knew that the native vegetation, based on alien biochemistry, would be indigestible if not poisonous. Despite their terrible hunger, they had not dared to eat any of the strange plants they'd seen growing along the way.

They moved on slowly, painstakingly. Bolton tried to see any hopeful sign in the terrain around them, any smoke or roads, a distant mining settlement or industrial outpost. Escobar plodded along out of habit, but his eyes held little interest or hope.

Bolton led the way across the spiny grass toward a thriving red weed forest that looked like a giant bloodstain spreading across the valley ahead. Though he knew the lush alien oasis was not likely to be any more welcoming than the rest of the landscape, at least it looked vibrant and *alive*. After so many days of bleak terrain, he felt increasingly tired and muscle-sore, fighting to take every step. He just wanted to lie down and go to sleep, and forced himself to keep going, to make his way toward what looked like an island of sanctuary. At least it was a goal, and the lushness seemed tempting.

Escobar followed him as he approached the abrupt edge of the thicket that extended for kilometers in every direction, but the Redcom seemed disinterested. Bolton noted the dense barricade of red weeds, thick scarlet leaves that were like long tongues attached to greenish-yellow stalks that seemed too fragile to support so much weight—but round, lighter-than-air bladders held the plants aloft. The drifting stalks and leaves waved gently in the air, resembling an underwater kelp forest moving in ocean currents.

Suddenly uneasy, Bolton paused to reconsider whether he and the Redcom should enter the strange forest, but the cracked and barren landscape had sapped the energy from them. At least this was different. He knew that nothing useful, and no rescue, lay back the way they had come, and he saw no easy way around the extensive, red weed wilderness.

Escobar looked up, stared at the forest that lay ahead of them, and noted Bolton's hesitation. "We keep going, Major. No choice."

"Yes, sir." No matter what, Bolton acknowledged that the Redcom was still his commander.

But as they picked up their pace toward the abrupt edge of the tall vegetation, the ground began to tremble underfoot, and the surface churned, as if being plowed from underneath. A tiny crater only a handspan wide dropped away nearby. Other pockmarks appeared, as if the soil had started to rot away. The ground bucked, and Escobar lost his balance. Bolton yanked the Redcom to his feet, and they both staggered toward the dubious safety of the alien forest.

In front of them the grass-studded soil also began to roil. Lumps and mounds appeared like ripples on a dirt pond. Escobar's boot caught in a hole and he lurched forward. Bolton helped pull him along toward some rocks, but even there, the ground was not stable. The dirt and grass looked like the churning surface of a cauldron at full boil.

Abruptly, a torrent of small animals emerged from countless burrows. Each creature had spiky dark fur and glistening teeth, and they bounded toward the two men like ferocious wolverines. Hundreds of them.

Escobar and Bolton found a small burst of renewed energy of desperation as they raced toward the alien forest, forgetting their weariness and hunger. They could no longer worry about what might be inside the dense red weeds.

Behind them, a pack of the fierce-looking animals closed in, making high-pitched keening sounds, as if they were communicating with each other. Bolton tried to run faster, but his body was already weak and spent. Escobar staggered along in a jerky, scarecrowish run.

A handful of the ferocious creatures bounded to the forefront of the pack, yelping excitedly at the prospect of fresh blood. Bolton bent to snatch loose rocks on the ground and threw them at the pursuers, bowling over a pair of them—not because he was such a good thrower, but because there were so many of them it would have been impossible to miss. The others rushed after their prey, closing in.

Panting, Bolton pushed toward the red weed oasis, but it was still too far away. With a sinking feeling, he realized that he and his companion would not make it.

Apparently, Escobar came to the same realization, because he stopped and turned to face the vicious animals. He yanked off his pack, tore it open, and withdrew the projectile weapon he'd salvaged from the Trakmaster, as well as a flare launcher. "Run for the forest, Major! I'll give you a chance."

He fired the projectile weapon. His weak hands were shaky, but he managed to hit half a dozen of the wolverine creatures. The injured ones yipped in pain when they fell in bloody heaps, but more kept coming.

Bolton grabbed at Escobar's arm. "Sir, you can't hold them off!"

But the Redcom pushed him toward the red weeds. "Go!" He fired again, killing several more of the animals.

Bolton staggered away, trying to reach the forest. Escobar's sacrifice seemed brave, but foolish and ultimately pointless. Bolton knew that he himself wouldn't make it either.

The first three animals reached Escobar and leaped, tearing into his side. They locked jaws onto his forearm and thigh. He howled, fought back, fired twice more before the weapon ran empty, and let the gun fall out of his hands. More of the attacking creatures fell upon him. Somehow Escobar found the energy to thrash about, knocking the clinging creatures away from him. With his other hand, he launched the flare, which crisped dozens of the beasts in a flame front. That drove most of them back, for a moment. He stood panting, dripping blood from numerous large wounds, as more of the creatures circled him, measuring him, ready to pounce.

Bolton had reached the fringe of the forest, and the red weeds loomed before him. Anguished, he turned, knowing he should head back to Escobar, to help him fight. A futile gesture, he knew, but . . .

Then a strange, pulsing sound screamed through the air, a sonic wind that shoved the pack of wolverine creatures away as if with an invisible hand. The continuing pulse swept the creatures away, and the rest ran off, yelping and keening.

Escobar collapsed into the dirt, his body torn and bleeding.

Before Bolton could run to help him, tall, thick stalks of suspended red weed shifted aside. The wide curling leaves parted to allow a figure to emerge—a large, pale creature that moved on a long caterpillar undercarriage. Energy crackled around the Xayan's gleaming dark eyes, and its feelers twitched.

The defeated pack creatures scuttled back into burrows, while the looming Xayan stood on the edge of the red forest. The unreadable eyes stared at Bolton, then at the motionless and bleeding Redcom Hallholme.

Leaving the alien, Bolton ran back to Escobar and dropped beside him. With a glance, he recognized how severe the injuries were, and how badly he was bleeding. He tore a piece of fabric from his own shirt and tried to staunch the flow of Escobar's blood, but there were far too many deep and severe wounds, ripped flesh, cut muscles.

Moving with a whispering glide, the Xayan came close, looking down at the mangled man in curiosity. Words thrummed out of the strange facial membrane. "You are fortunate to have escaped the burrow foxes. They lie in wait for large prey to come near, then attack in force."

"Thanks for helping us, but my companion needs medical attention. Right away." Bolton had seen Encix several times, as well as the alien named Lodo, but he did not recognize this one. "How many Originals are there? Are you with Encix?"

"I am Jonwi, and I work to restore this planet." The alien appeared to be male, wore a long sash across his torso and a satchel at his waist. "And no, I am not with the other Xayans. I came here to undo the damage."

Bolton could not be concerned with that now. "My friend is going to bleed to death. He needs medical attention."

"I will see what I can do to help him."

Jonwi leaned down and touched Escobar's neck with soft, pliable fingers. The gushing blood slowed, but did not stop. Energy crackled around the alien's head, and the prone form of Escobar rose into the air, lifted by telemancy. Jonwi turned and guided the injured man aloft as he moved toward the thick red weed.

"Follow me," he said, "before the burrow foxes come back."

49

George Komun had obviously made thorough plans ahead of time, and now he worked swiftly and efficiently to secure the Hellhole stringline hub. Belatedly, Adolphus realized that the traitor had learned much of his strategy from the General's own tactics. He tried to react swiftly enough to cut off the debacle, but it was already too late.

Komun's operation went into place with startling efficiency. In rapid order, the incoming thirteen DZDF battleships crippled the already-battered *Jacob* and most of the unsuspecting war-weary vessels that had just returned from Tehila. Now Adolphus regretted leaving Captain Naridar there with so many battleships.

He had focused on the wrong threat! If he lost the Hellhole stringline hub, Adolphus would lose everything.

Sophie knew it, too. "Go! I'll take care of the Diadem—I mean, Michella. Do what you need to do."

He ran to his flyer, contacting Lieutenant Sendell aboard the damaged flagship to get an assessment. He was glad to learn that at least the harm to the engines and weapons wasn't terribly severe, but it would take hours to effect repairs. And in those hours, Komun would waste no time. . . .

The General received reports every twenty minutes as his flyer raced overland—not back to his command headquarters at Elba, but directly to the spaceport at Ankor, which was closer.

He struggled to grasp the betrayal. George Komun was one of his inner circle, a man who had met repeatedly with the other eleven plotters, risking his life and his world in the name of freedom. Adolphus had believed in him for years as they planned their breakaway from the Constellation. But in these perilous, changing times, he should have known better than to trust.

From one of the military ships surrounding the hub, Komun remained in contact with Adolphus. He spoke, not in a taunting way, but simply businesslike. "I know you're planning to retaliate somehow, General. You'll gather your ships, believing you can defeat my vessels in a straight-up face-to-face clash. I may have more ships than you do, but we both know that you're the tactical genius. Nevertheless, many of your vessels are damaged, their weapons depleted after Tehila. I hold the high ground, the stringline hub.

"By the time you rally your ships, I will have every one of the DZ stringline nodes mined. So even if you defeat me, you can't possibly do it before I trigger the detonations—so I suggest you not make a move. If it looks like you're going to win, you know what I'll do. I've gambled everything on this, and I have nothing to lose."

As the General's aircraft roared over the rugged terrain, anger pushed his pulse faster. He considered, then rejected, dozens of ways to wrest control from the traitorous governor.

Komun spoke into the prolonged silence. "I know you're still listening, General. Why don't you respond?"

Adolphus flicked the comm. "It's hard to know what to say to someone who has sunk so low. You know what will happen if you carry out your threat."

"Full well." Komun's rational tone grated on the General. "If I destroy the hub, it cuts off stringline travel throughout the Deep Zone. The planets will no longer be connected, and we both know that many of them are not self-sufficient. They'll starve before anyone manages to reestablish iperion lines—even if sufficient iperion could be found. I know you, and I know you won't risk it. The trap I've laid is like a dead man's switch."

"You *are* dead to me," Adolphus replied. "Now what do you want?"

"Your unconditional surrender. The Constellation insisted that I try to capture you as a requirement for my own independence. I suggest we end this swiftly. If you surrender, I'll guarantee your safety—at least until you get back to Sonjeera for your formal trial. I expect that Constellation warships will arrive within two days—they should already be on their way. I'm sure I can hold out for that long, but I'd prefer to handle this efficiently. That's something you taught me, General."

"Obviously I didn't teach you about honor. I hate to disappoint you, but I won't be offering my surrender at this time." Adolphus switched off the cockpit comm, not wanting to hear more.

He did have one more option. Something he doubted Komun would expect. The wheels continued turning in his mind, as he brought the flyer in toward the Ankor spaceport and found a place to land.

Rendo Theris ran out to meet him from the low spaceport headquarters building. The man would have been a perfectly acceptable person to place in charge during peacetime; he was not, however, the best person to operate under a situation of constant crisis. Despite his harried state, however, Theris usually managed to keep the shuttle launch schedule and maintain an orderly movement of upboxes and downboxes.

He hurried Adolphus inside the bustling control center. "General, we can't launch any vessels right now. With the seizure of the stringline hub, our schedule is on hold, but there are other Deep Zone cargo ships inbound. Isn't there something we can do to regain control? Surely Governor Komun understands what sort of turmoil this is causing."

Adolphus regarded him coolly. "He's aware, Mr. Theris. He graciously offered to return to normal space traffic if I surrender to him." Shifting nervously on his feet, Theris waited for Adolphus to continue. Finally, the General added, "I won't be doing that."

"Of course not, sir. I didn't think you would." Theris scurried to a display screen, as if Adolphus had come for a standard briefing. "At least there's no sign of those mysterious Ro-Xayan scout ships or any inbound asteroids. We've been keeping careful watch with the additional alien satellites. We'll have the best possible warning if there's another threat from space."

Adolphus cut him off. "I came here to speak to the shadow-Xayans. They can help." He could have gone to the primary shadow-Xayan settlement near Slick-water Springs, but he intended to use the spaceport facilities, the shuttles, and personnel transports, and he knew that many of the converts were already here. "I need their telemancy."

"They're preoccupied with their slickwater pools and talking about *ala'ru*." Theris shook his head. "It'll be much calmer once they finally ascend—then we can get back to our daily business. Be my guest, though, sir. Go out and talk with them. Encix is here. She might be able to help you."

Adolphus left the building and headed toward a group of shadow-Xayans tending seeps of slickwater around the spaceport grounds. He had an uneasy relationship with Encix; the leader of the Original aliens was so focused on her own goal of *ala'ru* that he wasn't sure he could convince her to help him more than she and Lodo already had.

He spotted the pale alien surrounded by hundreds of converts who were channeling runnels of quicksilver that welled up from cracks in the ground. The slickwater aquifer was so close to the surface here that it had caused disastrous problems in the expanding spaceport construction. Even so, Encix and these followers were managing to keep it under control, while also manipulating it.

Seeing him, the alien came forward. "General Tiber Adolphus, we have a hundred new converts today, both at Slickwater Springs and here at the spaceport. Your people are beginning to understand the urgency, and our destiny is within reach, but progress remains too slow."

Adolphus interrupted. "There is still no sign of the Ro-Xayans, but a different crisis has occurred in orbit, and it must be dealt with immediately. One of our . . .

factions has turned against me and captured our main stringline hub." He knew the Xayans did not comprehend the depths and tangles of human politics, but they did understand factions. That was what had split apart the alien race and turned the rebellious Ro-Xayans into a destructive, unstoppable force.

"We can no longer participate in your squabbles." Encix sounded callous and aloof. "Our numbers continue to grow, but when you took Lodo and his group of volunteers to fight your battle at Tehila, our power diminished for a time. By using so much directed telemancy, we suffered a disturbing setback. I cannot allow that to occur again."

Adolphus put an edge in his voice. "I have suffered setbacks as well. Unless I solve this problem in a matter of days, an even larger military force will come here—one I cannot defeat. Then this planet will be conquered by the Constellation, and they do not care about your race, or converts, or *ala'ru*. I have reason to believe their standing orders are to devastate this planet and wipe out all inhabitants—including the shadow-Xayans and the slickwater pools."

He watched the translucent skin on the alien's face ripple. Her retractable feelers waved in the air, as if considering.

He continued. "Previously, when the shadow-Xayans operated together, their telemancy was strong enough to drive away Commodore Hallholme's fleet. They destroyed his weapons, and he had to flee. Now I need telemancy again. I want to take a group of converts up to the stringline hub, where I'll need them to isolate and deactivate a set of explosive triggers placed throughout the structure."

"That will be difficult," Encix said.

"But it is necessary."

"Is there no end to the back and forth of your war?" Encix asked.

"I'm hoping for it. With your help, I can achieve exactly that."

Before the Xayan leader could give her answer, Rendo Theris came running out of the admin headquarters, flailing his hands and yelling for the General. "It's what we feared, sir, but we never expected them to move so fast. We don't have enough time!"

Adolphus steeled himself for yet another disaster. "What is it?"

"The Ro-Xayans, sir!"

Encix followed the General back to the spaceport headquarters, where personnel stared at screens, muttering in varying degrees of horror and dismay. Theris led them to the largest display. "The high-resolution Xayan satellites just picked this up in the outer system, but it wasn't there an hour ago, I swear! It wasn't my failure, sir."

"Stop babbling, Mr. Theris. Show me what you know so far."

The screen showed blips, and numerical readings on the bottom gave the estimates of size, density, and velocity. "*Twenty* incoming asteroids, General—and each is larger than the impactor that struck Hellhole five hundred years ago."

Encix's large black eyes were intent on the images. "Exactly as we warned. The Ro-Xayans have come to finish their destruction."

Theris said, "The speed of the asteroids is incredible, sir, obviously not a natural phenomenon. I have no idea how anyone or anything could have accelerated them so fast."

"Telemancy," Encix said. "Powerful telemancy."

Theris called up another projection. Trajectory lines

on the starry field accompanied the closely grouped asteroids. All twenty were heading straight for planet Hellhole. "These asteroids are going to strike in *six days*, sir. All twenty of them."

50

All of Theser was open, uncharted, and ready to be explored, but so far Enva Tazaar wasn't impressed with what she saw. As her patrol craft cruised over the burned-out ruins of the planet, she drew parallels between the devastation below and the wreckage of her own life. Being in charge of a fledgling colony on a damaged world was far from the pinnacle of her success, but it was the best opportunity she'd been given in the Deep Zone. She had ruled Orsini, been one of the most powerful nobles in the Crown Jewels, fancied herself a viable candidate to be the next Diadem. Now she had . . . this.

But she would make do. She surveyed her new domain, the incredible challenge. Yes, she was up to the task. This was a stepping stone.

The first investigative teams that had come here immediately after Riomini's massacre had found underground aquifers that would provide potable water; already, some plants were growing back on the floor of the fertile crater that had been the site of the planet's primary city. The pioneers from Candela—many grim and determined, others enthusiastic to have another chance—scouted the remains of the former settlement, searching for anything they could salvage. They found small animals thriving in the wreckage, burrowing creatures that had saved themselves by digging deep into the ground. Some fish had returned to the streams, while unusual birds circled in the air, feeding on the burrowers.

But there were no people. Lord Riomini had killed them all, eradicating every human being on Theser, as an example.

Enva Tazaar was herself a survivor of circumstances, like the hardy creatures who had come back to this devastation. Now she saw a glimmer of hope, a possible path to success. Done with hiding, she openly called herself Enva Tazaar now, and intended to regain—or avenge—all that she and her family had lost. She vowed to resurrect her life, and this planet.

For starters.

Enva did not delude herself about the magnitude of the task. It would be much rougher to settle here than on Tehila, and vastly different from Orsini, but she would do it anyway; and she would do *more* than merely survive. She and these hardy people would set up a thriving colony here. They would explore this planet, see what it had to offer. The previous planetary administrator, Sia Frankov, had not been driven to extensive curiosity or exploration. But for Enva it was a new world.

Someday she might even have a chance to be creative again, a sculptor or an artist.

Two Candelan refugees accompanied Enva in the patrol craft. More than three hundred people were already on the ground setting up the first encampment. The stringline hauler that had transported all the colonists was still in orbit, unloading more passenger pods and downboxes full of supplies, generators, tools, and components for living quarters, everything General Adolphus could spare.

She saw obvious parallels between Theser and Hellhole—and now she understood how Adolphus must have felt when he was first exiled there.

Enva had mixed feelings about what the General was doing for her. On one level, she appreciated having a new chance—but she had wanted to rule the Crown Jewels, as his equal, his ally . . . not someone who needed to prove herself. Still, she knew her own history, and understood why he didn't entirely trust her. Yet, grandiose dreams died hard. Theser was a proving ground for her. If she succeeded here, and demonstrated her abilities for the General, surely he would let her do more important things.

In the back of the craft, a structural engineer and a terraforming expert spoke in low tones about the blasted landscape, the total devastation caused by the cruel whim of Lord Riomini. *Diadem* Riomini now. That news had come directly from the second-wave follow-up ship of supplies that had joined the group out at Theser as soon as the General returned from Tehila. It was a travesty that such an evil man had risen to that position instead of Enva Tazaar. Riomini's ascendancy reaffirmed the decadence of the entrenched Constellation noble families. Perhaps together, she and General Adolphus could change the Crown Jewels, and set a new course for humankind.

The pilot flew close to the steep crater walls, which had once held towering laboratories and factories where eccentric engineers constructed spacecraft engines. Enva looked out the window, shaking her head. "Not much evidence left that this was once a vibrant city."

Below, she saw charred ground, slag piles, and only a few identifiable remnants of foundations. She stared at a piece of cloth fluttering in the wind.

That, as discovered by her first party of explorers, was the hateful black flag Riomini had mounted in the ruins to flaunt his victory. When Ian Walfor had first discovered the disaster here, he had knocked down the banner, but it still caught the wind from the ground, where it lay with the pole attached. Someday Enva wanted to strangle Riomini with one of his own flags. In fact, she had already decided to create a memorial here, just like the one Governor Goler had built to mark all those who had been slaughtered in the Ridgetop Recovery.

Theser was a planet-size graveyard, with the souls of the dead still present. She intended to do something to avenge them, even if it was only symbolic. And Riomini's flag was a symbol like a knife in the back.

"Set down there," she said to the pilot, pointing to a flat spot by one of the destroyed buildings.

When the patrol craft landed on a stable clearing, Enva emerged to stand before the Riomini flag, which drooped now from a change in the wind. With emotion welling up inside her, she ripped the black banner from the pole and tossed it on the rubble. She asked for the engineer's assistance and poured some siphoned fuel on the fabric, which she lit on fire.

The Riomini banner burned brightly for a full minute, and then the flaming embers were lifted in a gust of wind before vanishing into the sky.

51

Adolphus realized he had bigger problems than a traitor seizing the stringline hub.

When Lodo saw projected images of the inbound asteroids, he quivered. His alien face was unreadable, and he shared a silent communion with Encix in the Ankor conference room. To Adolphus, their mutual dread was palpable.

Lodo had rushed to the spaceport at General Adolphus's urgent summons. He needed the most powerful telemancers to help him develop a swift and decisive defense against the cosmic impact . . . if that was even possible.

The screen display showed fuzzy, very-long-distance images of the twenty clustered asteroids. Orbital projections confirmed that Hellhole was sitting in the middle of the cosmic crosshairs.

"The Ro-Xayans are shoving the asteroids toward us using telemancy," Lodo said, "just as my volunteers turned the empty civilian ships into projectiles at Tehila. The entire Ro-Xayan faction is using the sum of its telemancy to drive those rocks."

Encix added, "With such an outpouring of psychic power, they will drain themselves to nothingness! You see, General, the Ro-Xayans are irrational. They are so intent on preventing us from achieving our destiny that they will destroy themselves to do it."

Tanja Hu and Ian Walfor had joined the General at Ankor. Outside, a dust storm whipped up brown swaths of mist and caused ball lighting to jump from the grounding towers around the launch structures, but the storm was projected to last only an hour. Adolphus had far more to worry about than inclement weather. And he still needed to deal with George Komun's ultimatum.

The storm across Tanja's face mirrored the weather outside. "That bastard's betrayal is bad enough, but those incoming asteroids—it's like Candela, but far worse. Ian and I watched my planet's last hours. We went back to see the aftermath—and that devastation was from only two asteroids. This is *twenty*."

"Initially, the Ro-Xayans thought one would be sufficient to wipe everything out," said Walfor, looking at

Encix and Lodo. "You sure must've made them upset with you."

"That was a long time ago," Lodo said.

Keana had also rushed to Ankor with Lodo, and she was not just representing the shadow-Xayans. Initially, Adolphus had called her to help respond to Komun, thinking that as the former Diadem's daughter, she might have been useful in negotiating with the Constellation. But the asteroid threat was entirely separate from Constellation politics. Nevertheless, of all the shadow-Xayans, Keana-Uroa had demonstrated some of the greatest telemancy skills. Her grasp of alien powers and her communion with her Xayan mental partner set her above most of the other converts. Adolphus hoped she might be able to offer insights—preferably a solution.

Keana shook her head. "Even through Uroa, I still can't understand the Ro-Xayans' venom and hatred." She turned a perplexed expression to the two Originals. Lodo and Encix regarded each other in silence, as if sharing a secret, but they refused to answer.

Tanja was impatient and frustrated. "We went through this already on Candela. We need to begin an evacuation immediately, General! You have more time and resources than I had. Because Hellhole is the main stringline hub, there are ships coming and going all the time. You have the Michella Town spaceport and the Ankor spaceport to get people off-planet. There's every reason to believe you could do a better job than we managed at my planet." She was urgent and desperate, leaning forward. "But you have to start *now*!"

"Komun is in the way. I don't control the stringline hub," Adolphus said. "If he detonates the mines as he threatens, we'll have no way of evacuating anybody *at all*. And if those asteroids hit, everyone dies."

"Komun can't possibly want that," Walfor said.

"Diadem Riomini does," Adolphus said. "He issued explicit orders that this planet is to be sterilized, just like he did on Theser." He clenched his jaw. "If Komun prevents us from evacuating, the Constellation will reward him for it."

Tanja clenched her fists. "Then launch an immediate strike, General. Take back the hub. You don't have any choice."

Actually, Adolphus did have a choice: He could surrender himself to Komun, who would then release the stringline hub. It would be worth the sacrifice if that let him save all of these people, but Adolphus didn't believe for a moment that it would work. He had too much experience with people who issued ultimatums. He would surrender . . . and Diadem Riomini would still order everyone here to be left to die.

"George Komun can't want to see us all dead," Walfor insisted. "He can't! He was my friend, dammit— let me talk with him."

Adolphus gritted his teeth. "*I'll* talk with him. I knew him well, too, Ian . . . or I thought I did." He operated the comm controls on the embedded conference room screen to contact the hostage stringline hub. "Maybe he'll see reason."

But Adolphus doubted it.

Though the traitor's voice had sounded confident, even flippant at times when he last spoke with General Adolphus, George Komun now showed clear signs of stress. On his screen image, the crow's-feet around his eyes had deepened, but he still seemed inflexible. "General, I know about those incoming asteroids. We've detected them, too. Face it, your circumstances have changed. You need to end this now. We both understand the danger your planet faces."

"We appeal to you," Adolphus said. "You know full well what will happen when the asteroids strike. No one will survive. We have to get these people off-planet—and that means we have to go through the stringline hub. We have to start evacuating! We have less than six days."

Komun tapped his fingers together. "General, your decision is clear, and my job is easy. We can end this immediately. Simply come up here in a shuttle, unarmed, and present yourself to me. I'll accept your surrender, we'll take care of the formalities, and then we can start the more important job of evacuating your people."

Adolphus responded in an icy voice, "I had hoped you'd be more reasonable than that, George. I can't believe you'd accept all that blood on your hands."

"Not on my hands. Your stubbornness doesn't make *me* a monster. I'm making a simple enough request, and I have obligations to the Constellation. I'm thinking of my world, too. Which do you hold more precious, General—your population, or your pride?"

Angrily, Tanja Hu pushed her way into the field of view. "George, stop this nonsense! General Adolphus will never surrender, and you know you won't blow the stringline hub because it would mean the death of everyone down here. You also know the Constellation won't keep any promise they made to you. They'll take Umber for themselves after you've given them what they want." Her face was drawn, and her dark eyes flashed. "I already lived through this once at Candela. Thousands of my people died because *I* couldn't get them off-planet in time."

Walfor interrupted at her side. "It doesn't have to be that way. We've got a chance. Don't ruin it."

Komun laughed uneasily. "Yes, I know General Adolphus well. When I came here, I knew that even with the element of surprise I had no more than an even chance of succeeding, but now I've got undeniable leverage—and you have a ticking clock. The sooner General Adolphus surrenders, the sooner you can start evacuating." He gave a thin smile. "I'll even contribute my thirteen ships to help with the effort." He looked back at the General, his expression sincere and sad. "Don't wait too long. Every minute that passes is a minute that could be used to get another load away. You know what you have to do. The asteroids are coming." He ended the transmission.

Adolphus looked toward Keana and the two Original Xayans. "Thousands of your shadow-Xayan converts have been training with telemancy to defend this planet. Can't you push back against the Ro-Xayans, nudge those asteroids and deflect their orbits—or at least slow them down?"

Lodo said, "It would be insufficient. Last time, the entire Xayan race couldn't stop the momentum of a single asteroid."

"But the converts are strong," Keana interrupted. "With our hybrid vigor we're much more powerful than the Originals."

Encix glanced at her as if Keana had insulted her race.

Lodo added, "And there are also many Ro-Xayans. They have been using their powers to push those asteroids toward us, increasing their speed. All the converts combined could perhaps deflect one or two if we poured our concentration into a single telemancy blast. But it still wouldn't save Xaya."

Encix grew more agitated. "The solution is plain! If we had more shadow-Xayans—many more—we would also have more telemancy. You lead the humans on this planet, General Tiber Adolphus. *Command* them to enter the slickwater pools and join us! Once we reach the critical point and achieve *ala'ru*, the Ro-Xayans and the asteroids—not to mention your petty Constellation factions—no longer matter. Force your people to enter the slickwater."

"I will *not*," the General said. "That was not part of our agreement."

"That was before the Ro-Xayans returned," Encix said.

Adolphus frowned. "I will evacuate this planet before I herd thousands of people into the slickwater pools against their will. We have enough time, barely—if I can resolve the problem of the stringline hub first."

"You may save your people," Lodo said, "but we will lose all that Xaya was. In the slickwater pools are a large proportion of our memories, our personalities."

"The Ro-Xayans want to destroy everything. That much is clear," Adolphus said. "They delivered no ultimatum, asked for nothing—neither here nor at Candela. They don't seem to care what sort of collateral damage they inflict."

Keana turned to face him. "I've thought of a possibility," she said.

— ⁂ —

As her thoughts grasped the idea, Keana felt her alien companion respond inside her. Uroa knew the Ro-Xayans, even remembered some of the individuals, and provided her with images of the esoteric factional debates, the friction, and finally the split that tore the race apart . . . Zairic and his visions of *ala'ru*, his dream of the race ascending to a higher plane of existence, while the Ro-Xayans insisted on preventing that at all costs. They wanted to trap the Xayan race to its mortality and physical form.

Through Uroa's thoughts, Keana could remember how the Ro-Xayans had left their planet, abandoned their comrades, and dispatched the killer asteroid to shatter any possibility of *ala'ru*. And the silent, malevolent enemy would ensure that nothing survived this time.

Giving only a glance to the two Originals, she turned to General Adolphus. "The Ro-Xayans are out there right now, guiding the asteroids. I want to go there and face them, talk with them, act as an emissary. If I could have a high-speed ship and a pilot, we'll travel to those asteroids and send out a call. It's been centuries since the original rift—I am both human and Xayan. I can be a liaison, unlike anything the Ro-Xayans have experienced before."

Encix reacted angrily. "That will do no good. We cannot waste our efforts or provoke the enemy. Our only goal now must be to reach *ala'ru* as fast as we possibly can. *That* must be our solution."

Ian Walfor turned to Keana. "I have my ship. Tanja and I can take you out there, but I don't think the Ro-Xayans want to be found."

"A preposterous idea!" Encix said. "You must not communicate with that insane faction."

Keana rounded on her. She thought of her own mother imprisoned in the bungalow at Slickwater Springs. For years, the Diadem had also ordered Keana around, held her back, forced her to become weak and manageable. "You don't command me."

Encix shoved Keana with a wall of telemancy, but Keana dredged up energy from both Uroa and herself. She had been growing stronger and stronger during the joint telemancy exercises, steadily improving her abilities. Many shadow-Xayans were equal to the Originals, but Keana had become more powerful than the others. Now she drove the force away from Encix, summoned her own telemancy, and retaliated. She found a strength that was unfamiliar even to her, and she kept pushing until Encix was forced down.

"You don't order me," Keana repeated. Uroa gave a satisfied whisper inside her mind.

Waves of anger and fear emanated from Encix.

The General's eyes narrowed in concern. "I'm willing to try any possible solution, but the asteroids are already coming. Even if you find the Ro-Xayans, what can you accomplish?"

Keana felt calm and hopeful. "What do we have to lose?"

Walfor smiled. "Why not let us try? If the Ro-Xayans are out there, maybe Keana can make them feel guilty."

After a long pause, Adolphus said, "It may be a fool's errand, but we have no good alternatives. Try it."

"It is not a fool's errand," Lodo said. "I agree with Keana-Uroa's approach, and I volunteer to join the expedition. Perhaps together we can make headway with the Ro-Xayans."

Encix had recovered, straightening her flexible body. "This must not be done!"

"It will be done." Adolphus nodded to Walfor. "Ian, load your ship, take whatever fuel you need, and depart as soon as possible. Meanwhile, I have to recapture that stringline hub so we can start evacuating."

52

After enduring so much adversity already, Bolton Crais had become fatalistic about their chances of survival.

Yet now, as the alien Jonwi guided the two humans into the red weed forest, Bolton felt as if he had received a reprieve. In the back of his mind, he had never expected Escobar's foolish escape idea to succeed; confidence alone wasn't enough of a plan. As proof of that, the Hellhole wilderness had killed Yimidi and Vingh, and seriously injured Escobar.

This strange alien, though, was giving them a second chance.

Once inside the thick oasis of alien foliage, Jonwi placed the comatose Escobar on a thicket of swollen spores and fleshy groundcover that sent sparkling tendrils into the air. Jonwi seemed concerned, but preoccupied, as he moved about his self-contained Eden.

Bolton was numb with dismay and exhaustion, not to mention physically weak and starving. He slumped against the tall, floating stalks of red weed, while Escobar clung to life, still bleeding, still unconscious. Jonwi, who seemed to have an affinity for the lush growth around them, tended to the barely alive man. He pulled the leathery leaves of the red kelp down, separated the fronds, and draped them across the battered and bloody Redcom.

Bolton tried to lift himself up. "What are you doing to him?"

The Xayan turned his smooth head and glassy eyes toward Bolton. His antennae extended and twitched. "I am preserving him, surrendering the energy of some of my plants so that his life functions continue, though it will barely sustain him." Jonwi wrapped the thick red fronds around Escobar, as if preparing a mummy. "Eventually his own survival mechanisms must come into play and do the work."

"Does that mean he has a chance now?"

"A chance."

The thick weed forest was alive with reawakened native species—floating and sparkling spore pods that drifted into the air, insect analogues, small grazing creatures, and even larger predators that avoided Jonwi.

Looking at the cocooned body on the ground as the alien continued to wrap more weed strands, Bolton frowned. "Shouldn't we get him to a medical clinic, one that knows how to treat humans? You could use your telemancy to transport him to the shadow-Xayan colony by Slickwater Springs—or Michella Town has a larger facility. My . . . wife is one of you. Keana Duchenet, and I think her Xayan companion's name is Uroa."

Jonwi froze, then tended to his work again. "I am not part of that faction. My duty is to remain here." He gazed upward, as if looking in the direction of some distant star system. "Those others are not my friends and would not be pleased to see me."

Bolton rose unsteadily to his feet. "But you're Xayan."

"I am *Ro*-Xayan. I came back to awaken this planet, to restore the plants and animals from specimens we preserved before the asteroid impact. We thought our world was ready to receive the gift again. We did not know the others had survived."

Not understanding, Bolton knelt over the Redcom. There, in midday sunlight, Escobar lay on the ground cover, his damaged face visible through the wrapping that covered his body. One eye was swollen shut, and his cheeks showed deep cuts. On his torso, now wrapped in the red weed shroud, the gashes from the burrow foxes were much deeper. Internal organs had been damaged.

But he seemed to be healing under Jonwi's care. Escobar's breathing was shallow. His body needed a great deal of rest, and nourishment, and Bolton could only hope that he could heal himself.

Despite all the strangeness around him, Bolton was not afraid of the strange alien. Jonwi seemed alone, but in charge of this isolated extraterrestrial Eden. Jonwi kept turning his oversized eyes up to the sky, and seemed to have a kindly, if sad, expression—though Bolton was not at all certain he could judge Xayan moods. He found himself intrigued by the creature's calm, almost stoic demeanor.

As night fell, the dense red weeds felt like a comforting shelter rather than a dangerous place. Escobar remained unconscious, and Bolton tried to remain awake as long as possible, feeling obligated to stand guard, but the rushing, humming sounds of insects and the drifting weed spores lulled him, and he finally succumbed. After their ordeal of the past several days, he felt safer than he had since escaping from the POW camp.

The next day, Jonwi returned just as Bolton awoke. The Xayan came up to him, indicated Escobar. "I monitored your companion through the night. His condition has not changed. He is still alive." He parted tall stalks of the weed and gestured with an arm. "Come, let me show you what I have created here."

Bolton followed him. Though constant hunger thrust knives into his belly, the sense of wonder slowly captivated him. Grazing creatures moved over the vegetation, unlike the lumbering herd animals he and Escobar had encountered on the plain. Colorful insects danced among showers of sparkling spores that erupted from bursting, fecund nodules. He found it strangely beautiful. "You . . . created all this?"

Jonwi tended a nest of scuttling crab creatures that retreated from his ministrations. When the alien departed, the crab creatures returned to their activities. "Before the asteroid struck Xaya, my faction was careful to collect specimens of the basic life-forms that were expected to become extinct. We knew that once our planet was ready to reawaken, we would need to rebuild the ecosystem and reseed the planet with all the life-forms we had harmed. In this, we planned quite meticulously."

Jonwi led Bolton through the vegetation, allowing him to drink greedily from a little waterfall—clean, sparkling water that ran down a cluster of rocks into a pool. But Bolton was trembling with hunger, and the native Hellhole species were incompatible with human biochemistry. However, the alien suggested some fleshy plants and fungi that the Ro-Xayans had crossbred with species from other worlds. He suggested they might be digestible by humans.

Despite his gnawing hunger, Bolton asked, "What if it's poison to me?"

"What is the alternative?" Jonwi asked.

So Bolton ate the plants ravenously, realizing he would die soon enough without sustenance. He suffered no violent reaction, so he ate more. He would have to try to feed Escobar as well, perhaps something mashed and liquefied.

Bolton didn't ask how Jonwi knew about human biochemistry. He was just glad to be alive, although he didn't know what to do next. The alien had such a trustworthy, nonthreatening manner that Bolton accepted his suggestions.

When Bolton tolerated the first food, Jonwi showed

him fat, purple berries to eat, a tree with thin strips of edible bark that tasted delicious and chewy, and harmless antlike insects in a tree that could be consumed for protein. After eating from this exotic smorgasbord, Bolton's knotted stomach settled, as did his painfully sore and constricted muscles. Now he just had to worry about the Redcom . . . and about getting back to civilization alive.

But it became apparent that Jonwi did not have any connection with the aliens who were allied with General Adolphus. "A rift occurred in our species," Jonwi explained. "The complex reason for this split is not easy to explain, but it was devastating. My faction departed this planet because we did not wish to take part in *ala'ru*. To stop the dangerous racial ascension, we exterminated our fellow Xayans with an asteroid strike."

Bolton stared. "You were responsible for wrecking this planet?"

"My faction was." He held his head high. "But we saved Xaya's key life-forms. Since the impact, we have been monitoring this world for centuries, waiting until the environment was stable again. When it was ready, we seeded the landscape with embryos, spores, roots, tubers, and cultured seeds in order to re-create the home that we had damaged so severely. But we knew that would be a tremendously long process."

Jonwi seemed to revel in the lushness of the vegetation, animals, and insects he had fostered here. "We understood that Xaya would never be exactly the same as it was, and many of our seeds and embryos did not survive the centuries of waiting. I arrived here only recently to guide the large-scale awakening. Previously, when our scout ships dispersed the basic life-forms, we saw the scattered human settlements, but were unconcerned about them."

As the alien glided through the red weed forest, Bolton followed him, curious. He suddenly understood. "You didn't expect any of the other Xayans to survive, though."

"We did not even know they existed, didn't know about Zairic's slickwater or the preservation chamber used by a handful of Originals. I was sent here to help Xaya reawaken, but now we know that our enemies did survive after all. And, worse, they are rebuilding their telemancy through a powerful symbiosis with humans. They have managed to generate a very strong form of telemancy. They are approaching *ala'ru* once more, and the danger this poses is greater than ever. Their telemancy set off numerous alarms that called my people back from their long interstellar journeys."

Jonwi's strange voice took on an ominous tone. "We had so many ambitious plans for this world, such high hopes. Yet, all of our efforts—all of *my* efforts—have been for naught, our hopes dashed. Sadly, Xaya has only a short time left now. Everything has changed."

He gazed up at the sky again. "The Ro-Xayans have no choice. The threat is too great. My people are coming again to destroy this world—completely this time. The asteroid bombardment is already on its way."

53

Working deep in the Vielinger iperion mines, clad in a decontamination suit with a faceplate, Erik Anderlos climbed the metal stairs to the observation platform. He felt angrier than usual because the seals in his work suit were defective, allowing the ultrafine, toxic dust to sift in. He had coughed up blood from his lungs this morning, and felt raw dryness in his throat. The iperion residue was killing him and all the other colonists seized at Buktu.

They were prisoners of war and should have been kept safe. But Selik Riomini didn't care. He demanded his iperion production and refused to fund adequate safety measures for the workers.

As he held the handrail on the stairs, Anderlos saw the maintenance foreman, Jando Knight, emerge from a side tunnel and stride down a ramp to a lower level. A small, stocky man, Knight seemed preoccupied and rushed; he looked annoyed about something. Above him, the work supervisor Lanny Oberon stood at his high perch, overseeing the delicate excavations.

The Buktu captives were working in one of the largest caverns in the Vielinger mines. Under close monitoring by guards, they operated remote-controlled skimmers to strip iperion from the walls, filling bulbous, refrigerated storage compartments on beelike flying machines. It was cold and damp in the caverns. Anderlos had worked with his fellow prisoners, no matter how dirty or dangerous the job was, and he would continue to demand better treatment.

He had determined that Oberon was a halfway decent man, considering the vile man he worked for, and Anderlos had been hesitant to harangue him too much, but he had to keep advocating for his people. They were prisoners, not slaves, but it seemed as if Riomini wanted them to perish. This place was like a death sentence.

The excavation cavern was large, and the stairway long. Under normal conditions, the observation level could be reached via an elevator, but the machinery had failed. Two thirds of the way up, Anderlos took a deep breath, trying to calm himself for yet another conversation about the same issue. Poor maintenance, dangerous work conditions, the Buktu captives suffering. He felt the stairway vibrating from the machines that droned in his ears.

No stranger to hard labor, in his youth Anderlos had worked at the Lubis Plain shipyards on Qiorfu, on a crew assigned to maintaining mothballed Constellation warships. In those days, Lord Jacob Adolphus had run the facility and the planet. On Qiorfu, Anderlos had seen Lord Adolphus and his son Tiber, but had never met the legendary man who would become known as the General.

When Anderlos subsequently emigrated to the Deep Zone and went to work for Ian Walfor at the remote Buktu operations, Walfor had often spoken of what a fine and inspirational leader General Adolphus was. Now that he was a prisoner of war, Anderlos doubted he would ever have the opportunity to meet the General.

Yet, even far from the Deep Zone, enslaved in the Vielinger iperion mines, he considered himself under the General's command. It gave him something to hold on to, that he was on the right side of the great conflict, even if he was far from the fighting.

Anderlos finally reached the observation deck, felt the unstable platform shift under his feet as he walked across it. Standing at the rail, Lanny Oberon turned to watch him. The mine supervisor was a man in his middle years, his boyish face and thinning hair visible through the faceplate of his protective suit. He looked just as dirty as anyone else in the caverns, and just as unhappy.

Oberon had operated these mines for the de Carre family before the Riominis took over Vielinger. The supervisor knew what he was doing and had made numerous muttered comments about how much he resented the poor safety measures himself. Repeated system failures and numerous mine accidents had led to the overthrow of Louis de Carre, and Lord Riomini had excoriated the nobleman for poorly managing such a strategic asset. And now Riomini was doing even worse.

Anderlos was not impressed with the new Diadem's foresight. Without iperion, the stringlines would eventually weaken and fade; the paths through space would dissipate, and interstellar commerce would fall apart. And yet, when the prisoners could no longer continue, he probably had backup crews ready to go to work.

Anderlos began by saying, "My people appreciate the full-body suits you obtained for us, but they are so old that at least a third of them don't have the proper integrity, and my people are exposed to toxic dust. Almost all of us are sick, to one degree or another."

Oberon said, "I've expressed my displeasure to Lord Riomini. I have requested more suits, along with better safety measures and other improvements, but he is preoccupied with the urgencies of being a Diadem. When he delivered you and your companions to me, I told him I couldn't operate safely with the pitiful budget he allowed. I send letters of complaint to him almost daily." He seemed exasperated. "No one else could keep these mines running with such a box full of setbacks."

Anderlos remained firm. "You have my sympathy, but that won't save my people. You did remove our children from the danger zone and transferred them to other living quarters, but we aren't miners. We are husbands and wives, simple colonists from Buktu. And the suits are getting worse—I'm wearing a leaky one myself."

The other man surprised him. "So am I. Your people

have the only good ones we have left—and there aren't nearly enough to go around."

Despite Oberon's efforts, the suits needed daily emergency repairs with whatever materials the work crews could put their hands on. The protective fabric had a tendency to break down at the seams from caustic dust, and the resealing apparatus worked poorly.

The two men commiserated, but found no solution. This litany of complaints and helpless excuses had become a daily ritual with them.

From the observation platform, Anderlos coughed as he watched an extraction skimmer hover over the blue-veined walls, removing microthin layers. Oberon mentioned the previous lords, especially Christoph de Carre, lamenting the fate of the young nobleman. "He didn't deserve the raw deal his family got. The de Carres treated us with respect, made certain we were paid well and received everything we—"

Oberon's words suddenly cut off as a roaring noise increased in volume like a mounting explosion. Panicked, the supervisor grabbed a voice amplifier so he could shout orders. "Emergency! Leave your stations and get to higher ground! Climb stairs, get onto platforms or ledges, anything!"

Anderlos understood as the roar increased. Water—thunderous water. "It's an underground flood!"

Down on the cavern floor, workers scrambled onto ledges, raced up stairs.

Oberon yelled over the noise, "There's a big aquifer down here. It's been dammed up for years with diversion tunnels and pumps. Jando Knight has been working hard to keep it up, but something's—"

A blast of water hammering into the grotto drowned out his words. Anderlos felt the platform shudder with the strain as workers climbed the ladder, overloading the structure. The flood stampeded into the chamber, slamming against the support structure. He heard screams, saw men and women in work suits washed away and slammed against rock walls.

Oberon descended partway down the ladder, yelling even though his words could not be heard. He gestured the frantic miners toward a smaller tunnel. "This passage goes upward, winds around—eventually it'll lead outside, but you should be able to stay ahead of the rising water."

Anderlos added his own voice. "Now run!"

Not everyone could make it, but many followed the instructions. When the last survivors had made it into the escape tunnel, Anderlos and Oberon charged in after them. Water continued to thunder in the grotto.

Inside the passage, after they had climbed high enough to feel safe, Oberon leaned against a wall, panting. "Lord Riomini is not going to like this. He wants iperion production, and he's not a man to accept excuses. He'll find a way to blame all of us."

Anderlos thought of everyone who had died back there, probably at least a hundred—lost due to some cost-cutting measure that Riomini had ordered. He shook his head. "No, he will have the prisoners as scapegoats. We are expendable, but he still needs you."

54

After he recruited them for his plan, the shadow-Xayans assured General Adolphus they would succeed. The stringline hub had to be recaptured, at all costs. He had already lost half a day setting up the details, and now the asteroids were that much closer.

His only other option would be to surrender as George Komun demanded. And, in order to save his planet and his population, he would do that if necessary, but he didn't believe a traitor's promises.

Before preparing to launch from Ankor, Adolphus had steeled himself and spoke with Sophie over the comm. "However this turns out, we have to begin the evacuation immediately, so start making preparations. I can't lose any more time. Komun will let me call his bluff. And even if Keana and Lodo do find the Ro-Xayans on their expedition, I have very little hope they'll be able to stop the asteroids."

She was alarmed, and obviously wished she could be there with him. "If you surrender to Komun as he demands, he will still let us all die here. He's proved that he's dishonorable."

Adolphus shook his head. "George Komun is not the man I expected him to be, but I think he'd keep his word if I presented myself for surrender. He wants me; he doesn't want everyone on Hellhole to die." Even so, he heard the uncertainty in his own words.

"Then we'd better hope that the shadow-Xayans can do what they say they will."

Since Sophie knew the converts much better than he did, she had helped him pick the best members for his team, even insisting on Peter Herald from Slickwater Springs, whom they both trusted greatly. Herald was racing to Ankor even as a defeated-looking General made his overture to Komun. Herald would wear his old uniform for veracity, and the other fifteen shadow-Xayan volunteers—his escort—would also wear old Rebellion uniforms, brave and loyal veterans standing by their beloved commander. Unless Komun recognized any of them by sight, he wouldn't know they were shadow-Xayans.

The converts would push their human personalities to the fore in order to act as normally as possible, and they would keep their eyes averted so no one noticed the eerie spiraling shimmer that denoted the Xayan presence. He only needed to fool Komun for a short time.

As she said good-bye to him on the screen, Sophie's concern was clear. "They have powerful telemancy—but are you sure fifteen will be enough?"

"Komun won't allow any more than that as an escort," Adolphus said. "We *must* take the chance, now or never. If the shadow-Xayans can perform their task, our fight will be on an even footing again." He looked closely at her. "Don't worry so much, it'll be—"

Sophie held up a hand. "Don't tell me it'll be all right."

"It'll be whatever it has to be, then. Have faith that it will go well."

"All right."

He had already transmitted full instructions to Lieutenant Sendell on the *Jacob*. The flagship had been repaired, its weapons systems restored to full functionality. The other battered ships back from Tehila were also combat-ready, their angry crews itching to do something important. But Komun held them all at a standoff with his rigged explosives on the stringline hub. Time was on his side. The traitor knew that General Adolphus would have to surrender, and soon.

Entirely preoccupied with the threat of the incoming asteroids, Rendo Theris wished him a "swift resolution" to the crisis. Before departing, Adolphus told the spaceport administrator, "Prepare for a complete planetary evacuation, no matter what happens at the stringline hub."

Adolphus marched out toward the shuttle, ready to

go. The fifteen shadow-Xayans who would act as his escort waited for him on the spaceport landing field, resplendent in their uniforms; they would make a fine honor guard.

As they boarded the shuttle, he glanced around and wondered if he'd be coming back to Hellhole. His honor guard took their seats in silence. Adolphus missed the joking and nervous camaraderie of brave soldiers who were about to go on a risky mission.

After the rumbling launch was over, the General opened a channel to the stringline hub, using the wide-field imager so that George Komun could see the fifteen uniformed passengers. "We're on our way, George. Myself and a small escort, as you demanded. We have to start the planetary evacuation immediately. I trust you'll be true to your word."

Komun looked disheartened. "There was a time when you never would have doubted me, General. I give you my assurance that as soon as you surrender, we can start saving Hellhole's people. I'll make all of my ships available to take refugees as well." He frowned. "I know *you* are true to your word."

Adolphus said, "I'm careful when I make my promises—that way I don't have to worry about breaking them. But you've put me in an impossible position. So long as you've got explosives rigged throughout the stringline hub, I will take no action against you. You have the upper hand."

The shadow-Xayans, however, would change all that.

After reviewing all available records of the Candela mass exodus, he had assigned teams to develop and implement evacuation orders for Hellhole. Tanja Hu had done a remarkable job in an exceedingly short period of time, hindered by a lack of ships and resources. Adolphus didn't have that limitation, but he had many other stumbling blocks. Hellhole's evacuation would be frantic, but should be more successful.

First, however, he had to recapture the stringline hub.

On the ride up to orbit, he transmitted to the *Jacob*. "Lieutenant Sendell, I want all your ships ready to commence a full-scale evacuation as soon as I finish my business with Administrator Komun. If all turns out well, he will not restrict your activities."

"Yes, General. Our ships are prepared to go."

"Komun knows that every delay cuts down on the number of people we can save," Adolphus said. Sendell had his orders, but would wait for a signal from the General, which would determine how he was to proceed.

The shuttle reached the commandeered stringline hub without incident. The Umber peacekeeper ships were docked at ten of the hub's major stringline nodes, while five of them remained mobile and prepared for a space battle, weapons powered up and standing by. To maintain parity, Lieutenant Sendell flew the *Jacob* in close while coordinating sixteen battleships that General Adolphus had pulled together. Since George Komun was prepared to detonate his mines and destroy the hub, none of the General's ships dared open fire.

They docked at the orbiting hub complex, which was far smaller than the gigantic Sonjeera facility, but still a large and impressive station.

When the General disembarked in the unloading bay, he was met by uneasy-looking security guards, private hires from Umber who didn't even have formal uniforms. The Umber security team carried projectile sidearms as a formality, although they clearly didn't expect a shootout. He gave them only a dismissive nod and walked past them, followed by his fifteen-member uniformed escort, all of whom appeared to be unarmed.

The leader of the security team hurried to take control. "This way, General. We arranged a room for your surrender. We need a formal record of the event so Administrator Komun can show Diadem Riomini that he fulfilled the terms of their agreement."

Adolphus was impatient. "Just take me to George." He intentionally used the familiar first name to emphasize that they had once been friends and allies.

Following alongside in their rebellion uniforms, his escort remained silent. Adolphus thought Peter Herald and the others looked sleepy, their veiled, human-looking eyes half-lidded, as they went through the motions. But he knew their focus was elsewhere, their minds reaching out with telemancy.

When the group arrived at a reception chamber, the guards frisked Adolphus and his companions before letting them inside. "Sorry about this, sir. We have to make sure you're carrying no weapons."

He sounded indignant. "I gave my word I would bring none." He was just glad they didn't notice the transmitter he had hidden in a button on the cuff of his uniform shirt.

Komun wasn't there yet. The reception chamber was empty, so Adolphus had to wait. The traitor probably viewed his deliberate tardiness as a way of emphasizing control, an amateurish game that Adolphus had not expected. The delay worked to their advantage, though, because it gave his team a few more moments to prepare themselves. The secret shadow-Xayans continued to concentrate.

When Komun finally arrived with his own guards, he looked at the General, then cast his eyes down. He seemed ashamed—as he should be. "General Adolphus, I'm sorry it had to come to this, but I'm glad you finally decided to be reasonable."

"Reasonable? I would define it more as being without options."

Komun frowned. "I don't expect you to understand, but I needed to think of my own people and my world."

"That's the difference between us, George. I'm thinking about *all* the worlds in the Deep Zone, including yours. As well as the Xayan race, who have been marked for genocide. I intend to evacuate my planet, and for that I need the stringline hub that ties our transportation network together. What else could I do? Let everyone on my planet die because of my pride? You forced me to do this." While Komun struggled to find a justification, Adolphus glanced to his side, asking, "Mr. Herald, your report?"

Beads of perspiration covered Herald's forehead. All fifteen members of Adolphus's escort crew were also sweating. At last, the veteran gave a slight nod. "It is done, General. We are safe."

"You are certain of this?"

Komun was growing angry. "What are you talking about?"

Peter Herald said, "Absolutely certain, General."

Adolphus touched the transmitter button at his cuff. "Lieutenant Sendell, this is General Adolphus. You may commence firing."

"What is this? What's going on?" Komun demanded. His guards drew their sidearms.

Sendell's voice was tinny in the miniature speaker, but his excitement was plain. "Yes, sir! Congratulations, General."

Komun pulled out a small handheld transmitter from his pocket, raised it up. "I'm not bluffing, General! I will trigger the mines. One button, and I destroy all the stringline nodes."

"You're welcome to try," Adolphus said calmly, as

small blasts of telemancy flung the weapons from the hands of the guards. "But I think you'll find them inactive."

External explosions rang out, muffled by the station bulkheads—but it was not the booby-trapped bombs Komun had threatened to trigger. Alarms began to sound throughout the stringline hub. The traitor received a chatter of reports. "We're under attack! The DZDF ships have opened fire!" came over the comm system. There were screams, explosions; some of the transmissions cut off in static.

Komun was outraged, and his eyes glistened with tears. He waved the transmitter. "General, you're forcing me to do this. I wasn't kidding—I will blow the stringlines!"

"You no longer have that capability."

Komun's look of despair shifted to furious determination. He pushed the button on the transmitter, but nothing happened. He pushed it again . . . nothing.

The external bombardment against the Umber ships continued, the General's coordinated attack hitting precise targets among the other vessels. He and Lieutenant Sendell had previously identified surgical strikes that would wipe out weapon batteries, but without damaging the vessels themselves unless absolutely necessary. Adolphus knew it wouldn't take his combat-hardened fighters long to defeat these amateur rebels.

Komun looked aghast. "We still have *you*, General. I—"

Peter Herald and the other converts turned toward the Umber security guards, who were attempting to retrieve their sidearms. As the silent shadow-Xayans concentrated, the guards could not move their arms or legs, could not get to their weapons. The alien eyes now shone with an eerie, softly glowing spiraling effect.

Unhindered now, General Adolphus stepped over to George Komun and pulled the useless detonation transmitter out of the man's hands, tossing it aside like a discarded toy.

Adolphus regarded him with an icy gaze. "George, you were with me from the beginning of our rebellion. As the war changed and circumstances changed, so did my tactics. I had to learn new fighting methods to take advantage of whatever was available to me. There are thousands of these shadow-Xayans in our ranks. You were here while we trained them to use their telemancy. You should have planned for that eventuality. I knew it would surprise the Diadem and Commodore Hallholme, but you?" Adolphus shook his head.

Komun's voice quavered. "I didn't understand the extent of what they could do. All right, I . . . I surrender! I'll have my people help you evacuate. You can still use my ships—"

"*My* ships." The General stepped over to one of the still-struggling Umber security men, bent over, and picked up the projectile weapon he had dropped. The converts used their telemancy to gather up the rest of the discarded weapons and fuse them together into a useless pile of metal.

"George Komun, you are a traitor to the Deep Zone and to our independence. You decided to deal with the Constellation after we had already declared our independence. You tried to force my surrender, which would have brought about the downfall of all Deep Zone worlds and would certainly have resulted in my own execution."

He checked the firearm, activated the firing stud. "But worst of all, George, this worthless stunt of yours made us lose *a day* that we don't have to spare, where we could have been evacuating people. That alone may have cost thousands of lives. I have more justification than I need, and I cannot afford any further distractions or betrayals. I have a planet to save. As the duly assigned planetary administrator of Hellhole, as well as the acknowledged leader of the Deep Zone, I pass your sentence."

"Please, General! I can—"

Adolphus fired once in the center of the man's forehead and then turned, not bothering to see Komun fall. His shadow-Xayan escort released the security team from their telemancy hold. The guards were in shock. Two of them ran to the dead administrator on the floor.

Adolphus barked orders. "Now let's move out! We have an evacuation to get under way."

55

Ishop Heer awoke in a foul mood, still a prisoner. This austere, guarded bungalow was so far from what he'd known in the Crown Jewels that he could hardly bear to think about it.

With constant jabs, insults, and humiliations, Michella had provoked his hatred of her. His initial reason for wanting to murder a Duchenet—any Duchenet—had been to avenge an ancient injustice; now, his hatred was personal, a new injustice that was as fresh as a new stab wound. The old bitch had *killed Laderna*! That had been the last straw. Back on Tehila, he had thrown in his lot with Enva Tazaar and her grand plans to destroy the Diadem, but she'd betrayed him at the first opportunity.

Ishop still wanted to kill Michella, more than ever.

Now that everything else had fallen apart—abandoned by the Constellation, stripped of their power and possessions, and now with asteroids hurtling toward Hellhole—he began to realize that murdering Michella must be an end unto itself.

He faced the very real possibility that he might not get away from here, that he might perish on Hellhole—but he had been battered about enough. He had been stepped on, cast aside, but he refused to be defeated. If nothing else, he was determined to see the old crone dead before he died himself.

Through the mesh-glass window in his bungalow, he watched Sophie Vence emerge from the adjacent building with old Michella. The deposed Diadem wore the same dress she'd been captured in, preferring it to the serviceable jumpsuit she'd been given aboard Ian Walfor's ship. Michella looked not only angry, but helpless and pathetic.

In contrast, Sophie stood strong and proud. What a dichotomy between the two women! Sophie had a grace, confidence, and a beauty that did not require makeup or fine gowns. On the other hand, when away from the protective trappings of Sonjeera, old Michella just looked like a hag.

Both women appeared as troubled and dangerous as the low-hanging clouds closing in on the valley. When she noticed him staring through the bungalow window, Michella imperiously motioned for Ishop to come outside, and Sophie told the guards to let him out. The rest of the Slickwater Springs camp seemed in turmoil, people packing, preparing to evacuate, while even the converts seemed more agitated than usual.

Sophie ushered the two of them, under guard, toward the main lodge building. Michella explained to him, as if she were still the leader of the Constellation, "Twenty asteroids will impact this planet in a matter of days. I must be taken to safety immediately."

"*All* of us need to evacuate," Sophie corrected, "but we can't do so, because a traitor seized control of our stringline hub."

"An unexpected loyalist," Michella corrected. "He will let me join him up there."

"If he knows you are no longer Diadem, maybe he won't be so eager to help you," Ishop pointed out.

Michella sniffed. "A temporary situation, easily rectified. I will have the Star Throne back, Ishop. And I will crush all these gadflies who insulted and injured me." She gave Sophie Vence a withering but ineffective glare.

Sophie urged them forward. "It's out of your hands. The General is managing the situation on the stringline hub as we speak."

Alarmed, Ishop insisted, "We are political prisoners. You are obligated to keep me and Diadem Michella safe. I know what General Adolphus told you. You must make arrangements to get us away from this planet before the asteroids get any closer."

Arching her eyebrows, Sophie said, "The General made those promises when you were a valuable bargaining chip. Now you're just an inconvenience. Michella Duchenet is worth no more than anyone else. Never was, if you ask me." As they neared the lodge building, she looked up at the foreboding sky. "We've started preparations for planetary exodus, just in case, but satellites report that a heavy smoke storm is closing in on the valley, so there won't be any outbound flights for a while. We'd better all get inside our primary shelter— and I want Michella close to the comm-center, in case she has to issue orders against deluded individuals who still fight on her behalf."

The old woman sounded petulant. "I will not." She seemed to expect that Ishop would applaud her defiant attitude. He could barely hide his scorn for her.

"If you are so uncooperative, I'll arrange for you to be the last one to evacuate the planet," Sophie said, rolling her eyes. "Or better yet, you can stay outside right now, see how you fare commanding the storm to respect your mightiness." Ignoring the Diadem, Sophie spoke into an earadio, sending orders to resort staff as well as the nearby POW camp for everyone to secure what they could and hunker down for cover.

When they were halfway to the lodge house, the ground shook so hard that Ishop staggered, barely able to stay on his feet. A strong quake. Michella managed to keep her footing, but Ishop could barely keep himself stable as the ground wrenched beneath their feet. The encroaching smoke storm descended into the Slickwater Springs valley like a living thing, with a leading edge of thick mist that curled around the buildings.

Sophie nudged both Ishop and Michella toward the sturdy lodge building. "Inside! These structures are designed to provide shelter against whatever Hellhole throws at us."

People ran for cover, in all directions. As the quake intensified, cracks split the dry ground near the main building, and to Ishop's surprise swarms of burrowing insects poured out from their buried nests beneath the lodge complex. The buzzing sound was even louder than the encroaching storm.

As the shadow-Xayan guards rushed them toward the steps and the main entrance to the lodge, something stung Ishop's arm, and he slapped at it, crushing a dark red insect. More live insects whistled past him, launching themselves like projectiles. Three more struck him like tiny hot bullets, and he slapped them away. He saw that they had no wings.

Sophie swatted at her arms and shoulders as she ran. "Torpedo ants!" She ducked as several more sped past, but the cloud of emerging insects boiled up from the broken nests as if maddened by the quake, the smoke storm, and the moving people. "Get inside."

Michella was shrieking, as if she expected Ishop to take care of the problem for her. Given his preference, he would have broken her legs and left her outside to be devoured by the creatures. Oddly calm and efficient, the shadow-Xayan guards hurried them toward the lodge building, but they didn't seem overly concerned by the insect predators.

Ishop saw that his arm was bleeding enough to soak his shirtsleeve. Around him, the nonconvert workers and visitors to Slickwater Springs bolted for shelter. Clusters of torpedo ants hurtled toward specific targets like a salvo of projectiles, although shadow-Xayan converts used telemancy to deflect the emerging insects. The ground continued to tremble, and the smoke storm rolled in over the valley, whipping up wind and pouring thick dust into the compound.

Despite her age, Michella scrambled ahead of the others up the stairs of the lodge building, where dozens of workers had already taken shelter. After Ishop and Sophie darted through the entrance, the guards slammed the main door shut behind them.

Some torpedo ants were already inside the corridor, buzzing around, launching themselves at the humans. Ishop swatted at the insects, felt a sting on the side of his neck. Ahead in the registration foyer, a dense cluster of the bugs rocketed into the torso of a woman who had taken shelter behind the main desk. Like bullets, they came out through her back. She screamed, stumbled, and dropped to the floor, gushing blood.

The predatory ants focused on that one victim to the exclusion of the others, tunneling repeatedly into her body. Ishop watched in horrified fascination as the woman writhed and finally fell silent. Intermittently, the tunneling insects emerged from her form, then burrowed back into her body.

Sophie Vence yelled to the shadow-Xayan guards, who grabbed the infested corpse and dragged it to the main door. With a nudge of telemancy, they discarded the body outside, where more torpedo ants converged from the emerging swarm.

Through the mesh glass of the lodge windows, Ishop saw thousands more insects buzzing around the building. Sophie was flushed, grim. "We're safe inside this building. Reinforced walls and glass, seals on all the openings." She looked at the bleeding gashes on Ishop, Michella, and herself. "Come, I have a med-kit in my main office."

When she bandaged Michella's minor wounds, she tossed Ishop the supplies so he could tend his own injuries. He was disturbed to see where a torpedo ant had passed completely through the muscle and out the front of his arm, like a tiny bullet. The wound was painful, and he was lucky the insect hadn't hit an artery in its passage.

Inside the lodge building, Sophie's people scoured the corridors and rooms, including the comm-center, to root out any other torpedo ants that had slipped inside.

From her office, Sophie peered through the reinforced glass, where others outside still hunted for shelter, as thickening smoke from the storm whipped around the buildings. She shook her head, looking gray and sickened. "I don't know how many people we lost out there. I hope the shadow-Xayans protected themselves and anyone else nearby. But that storm is getting worse." She glanced at Ishop and Michella. "We're stuck in here now."

Ishop stared at the old Diadem, wishing the insects had devoured her from the inside out, while he watched. Maybe there would still be an opportunity, though. He could always hope.

56

While Ian Walfor piloted his high-speed ship away from Hellhole and toward the asteroids, Tanja operated the sensors and mapped out the vast emptiness. Now that the sensitive Xayan satellites had pinpointed them on the fringe of the solar system, the twenty giant celestial bodies were obvious and ominous.

As the ship flew toward the asteroids, however, Ian and Tanja were looking for something else entirely.

"Ro-Xayan scout ships flew over Ankor and did several overflights on the Hellhole landscape, so we know what their craft look like," she said. "Not detecting any of them on my sensors, though. If they're guiding and accelerating these asteroids with telemancy, I'd have thought the Ro-Xayans would be nearby. Their base or their main ship must be large, but I'm only seeing big rocks. Nothing else."

"Maybe they didn't stick around after they aimed their projectiles and sent them hurtling to Hellhole," Walfor said.

Keana-Uroa came forward from the ship's common area. "We know the Ro-Xayans have been watching the planet. They have been reseeding the landscape with native life-forms, restoring the original environment. All to destroy it again? That makes no sense." She drew a breath. "I hope we can speak with them."

"First we have to find where they are," Walfor pointed out.

"The Ro-Xayans have other priorities." Lodo worked his large caterpillar body toward the piloting deck. "But they *are* near the asteroids. I can sense them."

With sensors alert for any anomaly, Walfor guided his ship toward the cluster of hurtling rocks. The twenty asteroids were oblong and jagged, with enough combined mass and momentum to deal a deathblow to Hellhole.

As the ship approached and Tanja could make out the details of the monstrous cratered projectiles, she felt an involuntary shudder. Walfor had shown her similar images from his flyby of the two incoming asteroids that had destroyed Candela. Her beautiful Candela . . .

Those wounds were raw and painful, but right now Tanja experienced more anger than outright terror. These twenty asteroids would leave nothing but a blasted, sterile planet, just as it was starting to heal and reawaken. The bombardment would wipe out every speck of life on Hellhole, perhaps even break the planet itself into cosmic rubble.

And the damned Ro-Xayans were doing it on purpose!

She left the copilot seat and turned to speak with Lodo and Keana-Uroa, unconvinced that the thousands of shadow-Xayans were as helpless as they claimed. "You have your telemancy. I've seen how powerful you are. Can't you just join forces and push those asteroids away? Deflect their orbits to save Hellhole, or at least grant us more time?"

"That would be like one person using a finger to nudge a spacecraft," Keana-Uroa said.

"Two fingers, if it's you and Lodo together," Tanja pointed out.

"Still impossible," said the alien, waving his stubby feelers.

"Then what if we bring ships filled with shadow-Xayans? Thousands of hybrids. They could all work together."

"Perhaps, with all that effort they could move a couple of the asteroids—but there are twenty of them," Keana said. "The Ro-Xayans are numerous and powerful as well, and they will push back. They have already been applying their telemancy for some time to accelerate the asteroids. Even if all our converts came out here to join the effort, they could not counteract the considerable momentum."

"Encix would never allow the converts to leave, no matter what the stakes," Lodo pointed out. "She would not divert the shadow-Xayans from pushing toward *ala'ru*. That is her challenge, and her priority."

"And just leave us all behind, helpless?" Tanja snapped.

Lodo looked at her with his large, gleaming eyes. "Yes."

"How is *ala'ru* going to save Hellhole? That's the only solution you keep offering!"

"We are offering another possible solution now," Keana said. "That's why we're here. If we can find the Ro-Xayans and convince them not to destroy their sacred planet, then we would at least have more time." Her face carried a distant expression, as she communed with the alien presence inside her. "Like Lodo, I can sense the Ro-Xayans, too. The enemy is here, but I don't know where to find them."

"Maybe they can sense us, too," Walfor said as he

maneuvered the ship around the asteroids. "It might flush them out, or might just make them hide."

Walfor spent hours flitting among the cluster of rocks, mapping them, looking for some small vulnerability. Tanja's scanners detected no sign of the Ro-Xayan scout craft or their main base or ship, though she remained vigilant. She searched for evidence of an outpost on one of the asteroids, but detected no artificial structures. A closer reading, however, indicated that one of the asteroids had an anomalous density. Although the other nineteen seemed normal, the largest one showed a distinct peculiarity.

She frowned. "It's worth investigating."

Walfor was happy to do whatever Tanja suggested. The trailing asteroid in the fusillade, the large stony body that would be the last to impact Hellhole, was the anomalous one. "Let's have a look."

Keana-Uroa and Lodo went to a side windowport so they could observe the asteroid. Walfor spiraled the ship closer, rushing over the uneven, cratered surface. The asteroid was thirty kilometers on its long axis. When this projectile struck Hellhole at seventy kilometers a second, it would vaporize half a continent—and it was only one of twenty impactors.

"The Ro-Xayans are close," Keana said. She turned to Lodo, who seemed more intent than usual.

The alien agreed. "They are strong. I can feel their minds, their collective telemancy. I can hear them in my thoughts . . . many Ro-Xayans!"

Tanja rechecked her scans. "Still no visual on them."

Walfor guided the ship even closer. "Readings are verified. There's definitely insufficient gravity for a rock that size. There must be air pockets or low-density inclusions."

One particularly large crater beneath them reminded Tanja of the bull's-eye scar that the original impact had left on Hellhole.

Then their ship shuddered, and the structural components groaned. Tanja could feel the vibration run through its hull.

Walfor yelped and looked at his controls. "We're caught!" The effect grew stronger, tightening around the hull. "Something has grabbed us." He added more thrust to the engines, and the ship shuddered again. "And I can't break free."

The asteroid spun beneath them, and the view tilted. Tanja's stomach lurched. The ship began to drop toward the asteroid and the yawning crater below them.

When Lodo hummed through his facial membrane, his voice sounded like a disturbed moan. "It is telemancy. More powerful than anything I have ever experienced."

Alarmed, Keana said, "We can't break it. They've got me, too. Uroa is terrified. I can't—"

"It's *hollow*!" Walfor said, and Tanja saw that the crater beneath them was opening to reveal a yawning chamber, and the alien telemancy was pulling them down toward it, like an irresistible tractor beam.

Walfor applied more thrust, and the ship strained, but the grip of the Ro-Xayan force strengthened in response, dragging them downward.

The crater opened into what looked like an enormous hangar. As their ship was hauled inside, Tanja saw numerous starfish-shaped vessels also parked in the giant chamber. She recognized them as the swift and mysterious ships that had flown past the Ankor spaceport and distributed embryos across the Hellhole landscape.

"This is where the Ro-Xayans are," Lodo said. "They have hidden themselves *inside* the asteroid."

The large camouflaged doors that had been the floor of the crater closed above them. Walfor decided not to waste fuel or damage his engines by continuing his attempts to blast away. With the hangar door sealed overhead, even if he did regain control over his engines, he would surely crash into a wall. Held in the grip of telemancy, the ship was forcibly deposited in a large cleared area.

When the vessel came to a rest and remained still for several moments, the four looked at one another. Tanja said, "Keana, it looks as if you'll have your chance to talk to the Ro-Xayans after all."

Lodo seemed hesitant, intimidated. "I fear they will not listen."

"Then *make* them listen!" Tanja said.

Though Keana seemed intimidated, she forced herself to be calm.

"What do we do now?" Walfor asked. "Wait for them to knock?"

"Or we can go out and face them," Keana said. "Is the atmosphere breathable?"

"I'll check, but probably. Xayans breathe the same air as we do on Hellhole." Walfor ran a diagnostic and confirmed that the asteroid chamber had sufficient oxygen for them.

When they all emerged from the ship, the far end of the crater hangar opened, and Tanja saw many more Xayans inside—*thousands* of them—in a hollow grotto that comprised the interior of the large asteroid. Part of their colony.

"This isn't just a temporary base. The Ro-Xayans *live* here," Tanja exclaimed, and then a second realization hit her. "They *inhabit* one of the very asteroids they're going to smash into Hellhole!"

57

Even with the imminent, and unbelievable, destruction of the planet, Bolton had much more personal concerns. Inside the red weed forest, he watched as Jonwi tended Escobar, carefully wrapping fresh leaves around the injured man. The Redcom remained in a coma, not improving, but at least he still lived, if only barely.

The Ro-Xayan had changed the wrappings several times a day, tucking the flexible leaves tightly around him and leaving only Escobar's face uncovered. It was late afternoon now on the second day; the tallest weed trees extended long shadows across the clearing.

"The plant has kept your companion alive," the alien said, "but his injuries are deep and severe. I do not believe he will survive another day." Jonwi turned his head to face Bolton. "Yet that matters little, since none of us will live much longer anyway. The asteroids will destroy this planet very soon."

Oddly, despite the impending disaster, the solitary Ro-Xayan remained devoted to tending his oasis, continuing his work. Bolton compared the alien to Noah . . . but a Noah without hope.

"This is my purpose," Jonwi said. "I can do nothing about the coming asteroids, but I can tend my garden until it happens." His matter-of-fact tone sent a shuddering chill through Bolton's body.

"Surely your own people will come to rescue you," Bolton said. "The Ro-Xayans have got to take you away before the asteroids strike."

"They won't even save themselves. This planet must die. Our entire race must die."

Four white, pantherlike animals entered the clearing

and split up. They prowled, circled, all the while watching Jonwi with bulbous, feral eyes. Bolton crouched and prepared to defend himself, but the alien levitated himself in the air. The white predators gazed upward at him as if hypnotized, then the Xayan drove them away with a strong nudge of telemancy, and the creatures bounded off into the red weeds.

Lowering himself to the ground, Jonwi spoke as if nothing had happened. "I am what my people call a rover. In our wanderings after the Ro-Xayans departed from this planet, I have been stationed on other planets to observe the life-forms there. I even encountered human settlements on one other world, but I kept my presence concealed."

Bolton was surprised to hear this, and the alien continued. "The Ro-Xayans are good at hiding and observing—and assessing threats. I succeeded in all of my duties." He lifted his body up perceptibly, then sagged back down in a sigh. "But in this assignment, here on Xaya—the most important mission I could have imagined—it is no longer possible for me to accomplish anything."

Jonwi's dark-eyed gaze became distant, going inward to his deepest memories. "The factions in my race developed because of deep religious and philosophical differences, a tremendous dispute that centered on *ala'ru*. The others called it their racial destiny, but we believe it is a dangerous idea that could threaten all existence. That is why we Ro-Xayans had no choice but to stop it from happening . . . even if the cost was our beloved and sacred homeworld."

Bolton remembered how urgently Encix was trying to gain more and more converts from the prisoners held in the camp. "What do you mean that *ala'ru* could threaten all existence?"

Instead of answering, Jonwi was caught up in his own recollections. "We waited centuries for this planet to be ready for reseeding. My faction meant to restore Xaya after what we did to it, but we did not imagine that any of our enemies had survived and that they could still pose a threat. As a special precaution before the first impact, however, the Ro-Xayans scattered several small black objects across the surface, detectors that are sensitive to telemancy. If any of the Xayans did survive and begin to build toward *ala'ru* again, the detectors would send a signal. Alas, we received that alarm just as our world was awakening, and my people knew what they had to do . . . even if it undid all that we had accomplished here."

Jonwi glided through the red weeds, and the tall stalks drifted from side to side, buoyed by their spore-filled bladders. "We had hoped for, and expected, a new beginning here, but the persistence of our enemies' delusions forces us to make this an ending—for our entire race."

Bolton was disturbed by the alien's fatalism. With Escobar so severely injured, and while they were lost in the Hellhole wilderness, he doubted they could ever get away in time.

Jonwi mused, "Throughout this discovery and crisis, something has surprised me. Even though I know all my work is to be destroyed, I am actually blessed to be here, part of Xaya in its final days. Before the asteroids strike, I feel a strange sense of spiritual calmness and acceptance of my personal fate. I have no desire whatsoever to leave. If I am going to die, if my planet and my race are going to perish with me, this seems like the proper place for it to happen."

His alarming comments stirred many questions for Bolton, but he didn't get a chance to ask them because

Escobar stirred and mumbled something unintelligible. Putting aside thoughts of the imminent cosmic disaster, Bolton rushed back to his friend and bent over the weed-wrapped form. The Redcom opened his eyes and looked around, appearing confused and upset. His lips moved, but he spoke only gibberish, before slumping back into unconsciousness.

Bolton shook his head. "We have to get him to one of our towns, a medical center." He touched Escobar's exposed forehead. "He feels cold."

Jonwi nodded slowly. "He will die soon. I believe he is beyond the help of even your medical centers. The asteroids are coming. No one can be saved."

58

At dusk, the smoke storm engulfed the Slickwater Springs settlement like a dark blanket. Outside, the torpedo ants continued to batter the main lodge building, which had been built close to their previously undiscovered buried nest complex. The yellow illumination from emergency lights around the compound cast an eerie glow through the haze.

Ishop felt trapped inside the building. Sophie Vence and the others hunkered down, waiting out the storm and the insect infestation, knowing they had to begin the emergency evacuation soon.

Michella demanded to be returned to her bungalow, a uselessly shrewish complaint that made Ishop loathe her even further. Sophie brushed aside the old woman's comment and instead found temporary quarters for them to spend the night. "The lodge will remain sealed against the torpedo ants. No one goes outside. Once the storm passes, the shadow-Xayans can drive the swarm away with combined telemancy, and then we can begin shuttling people from Slickwater Springs to the spaceport. Thanks to General Adolphus, we now control the stringline hub again."

To Ishop's disappointment, Sophie reported the news that George Komun had been defeated and executed and that immediate plans for a planetary evacuation had been initiated, without hindrance. Before having them escorted off to their temporary lodge quarters for the night, Sophie smiled at Ishop and Michella. "Sleep well—and think of ways you can convince us you're worth saving. We might not have the time or resources to get everyone away."

But Ishop did not sleep. The torpedo ants kept up a high, thin chittering and battered their wingless bodies against the mesh-glass windows in his room. Most important to Ishop, though, he was no longer under close guard. With the smoke storm and ravenous insects besieging the lodge, apparently Sophie wasn't concerned about any escape attempt. He and Michella were locked in their rooms.

A simple lock, however, proved to be no challenge for Ishop Heer. He waited, listened, and sat in silence until the quietest, darkest hour of the night. Then he broke out of his room.

He crept through the dim corridor, studying his options, seeing lights and movement in the main section of the lodge, the comm chamber, the offices near the registration foyer. He grimaced at every small noise he made, but no one noticed him. Too much other activity was happening, not just the problems at Slickwater Springs but also the emergency preparations for evacuating the planet. No one cared about the two valueless political prisoners. Back by the rooms holding the two prisoners, everything was quiet.

Yes, this was a perfect opportunity. He slipped along from doorway to doorway, searching, until he found a small maintenance closet. Inside, shelves held a variety of tools in disarray; shelves contained pry bars, chisels, a mallet—any one of which could make a useful and deadly bludgeon. Rummaging, he found a pen-size laser cutter, which he felt was much more appropriate, much more subtle, for his purposes. Yes, he already knew what he wanted to do.

A few minutes later, it was even easier for him to undo the lock outside of Michella's room. He opened the door very slowly, just enough for him to slip through.

The withered old woman slept in an alcove on a window seat that had been converted into a narrow bed with a dimmed lamp next to her bed. Old Michella had fallen asleep, not while reading but no doubt scheming. In the shadows, she looked like a pile of bones bound together with poisonous thoughts—as if a snake had shed its skin and left only the form of this withered crone. The eerie light from outside was more than he needed for his work.

He had killed many people, always through furtive means. He thought of how he had killed old Janine Paternos by slitting her throat in the middle of the night and then vanishing before anyone could find him. This was similar . . . but that sort of quiet and unexciting murder wasn't sufficient for him. And it was certainly not sufficient for a hateful monster like Michella Duchenet.

No, he needed her to feel terror, to understand what she had brought upon herself, how she had created her own nemesis in Ishop Heer. Michella wasn't stupid, and his vengeful hatred couldn't be a complete surprise to her, but Ishop needed her to know. He wasn't the sort who liked to gloat, but he required a certain amount of satisfaction, for his family bloodline, for how Michella had demeaned him and ground him under her heel, but blithely expected him to be just as pleased with her company as before.

He needed to see the look on Michella's face as her whole world crumbled even more than it already had. He had to do it for himself, and for Laderna. Ishop understood that Michella was no longer a bargaining chip worth anything, and he had never been of value himself for a ransom or a trade. Now, with the asteroids coming toward the planet, with the smoke storm outside, the horrific torpedo ants swarming and pattering against the window, and not enough time for a complete evacuation, Ishop had no doubt they would abandon him.

But he intended to see Michella writhe and die first.

Ishop heard her fitful, troubled sleep now, but her face was turned away from him in the dim lamplight. Such a humiliating downfall from her lavish royal apartments back on Sonjeera, where an army of servants attended to her every whim. Here, she had probably been forced to make the bed herself. Poor thing! Ishop felt acid in his throat.

He could not drive away the image in his mind of Laderna in her last hours, sealed in a quarantine chamber, tortured and interrogated, and then exposed to a flesh-eating virus. Laderna had placed herself at risk for him to eliminate the last name on their list. A *Duchenet* name. Now Ishop had to finish that quest, not only for the revenge he craved for himself, but for Laderna, too.

Michella stirred in her uncomfortable sleep. *Soon she'll be out of her misery*, he thought.

Through the room's window, Ishop could see the insects continuing to swarm in the hazy yellow emergency lights, although the smoke storm was dissipating. Next morning, if the shadow-Xayans used telemancy to drive away the voracious insects, he would miss his chance. He had to move quickly.

Ishop brought out the laser cutter, adjusted its range so he didn't need to approach old Michella curled on her bed . . . nor did he want to stand too close to the window. Smiling, he activated the cutting beam and etched a red line around the window frame.

Outside, apparently sensing the hairline incision, the torpedo ants went into a frenzy, slamming their bodies against the reinforced mesh-glass. Their humming and buzzing grew louder, vibrating through the weak spot in the window.

Throughout it all, the Diadem continued to breathe easily, sound asleep. With all the horrors and crimes on her conscience, it seemed impossible that she wasn't haunted by nightmares. Or perhaps Michella Duchenet was herself such an abomination that the nightmares were afraid of her.

Ishop held the laser cutter in his hand, leaned over her, activated the end so that it hummed and glowed, but did not extend the blade. It was close to her sinewy throat, the shriveled wattles of skin, tendons like steel cables. He hoped the cutter would be sufficient to saw through her larynx.

"Eminence," he said, "I've brought you something."

Her eyes flew open, focused on him, saw him leaning over her, but the shadows cast by the light from the lamp must have made him look distorted, like an ogre above her. She squirmed backward, sat up, as if ready to scream, but thought better of it as soon as she recognized him. He remained close, within striking distance. He held the laser cutter.

"I wanted to see your face before I do what I have to do," he said.

She stiffened, looked frail and surprised. "Ishop, what are you doing? Have you found a way for us to break out of here?"

He had given up thinking about a realistic escape, although in the turmoil after her body was discovered, he thought he just might have a chance to slip away, steal a vehicle, race away to a spaceport, hijack a ship. Not likely, but Ishop had survived plenty of unlikely scenarios.

"I don't think you'll like the way I've planned to free you, but it's what you deserve."

She blinked, lifted a scrawny hand, saw the laser cutter. "What is this? Have you found a weapon? Can you fight the guards?"

"I intend to kill you. You've always treated me like nothing more than a dog, someone you need—but when I need something from you, I am nothing more than excrement to be scraped off your shoe. I have noble blood, and you cast me aside. You made the other nobles ridicule me, laugh at me, after all I've done for you!"

"Ishop, stop this nonsense. Put your toy away and then—"

"This toy can decapitate you in an instant." He extended the glowing blade. "I want to see you hopeless. I want you to understand the avalanche of hatred that you yourself triggered."

She seemed baffled more than terrified. "But I've always been good to you, Ishop."

He laughed. "You really don't understand, do you? After humiliating me in front of the Council of Nobles, after destroying my dreams, you think a pat on the back can make up for it? After all your countless poor but ruthless decisions, I was the only friend left in the Constellation—and you spat upon me, too."

Michella now looked angry as well as afraid. "You are out of your place, Ishop!"

"And you are out of time. I planned to kill you before, but after what you did to Laderna, I want you to suffer more than ever. I thought you might even be pleased if she slipped in and killed your hidden sister after all this time. But torturing Laderna to death, letting her rot and scream and die from a flesh-eating bacteria? For that, Eminence, I will take incalculable pleasure in watching you die."

"And you truly think I would have gotten rid of your assistant in such a way?" The old woman's expression was calculating, hard. "I knew you were behind that scheme, Ishop. That wasn't the work of a mere lackey. And I know full well how to control the people I need." She narrowed her eyes, and her gaze seemed as powerful as the laser cutter in his hand. "You know me—do you really think I would waste a resource like that? Do you truly believe I would kill her when she might be useful to me as a way to keep you in line?"

Michella moved slightly, and he tensed, but her weapon was her words. "Laderna is still alive. I kept her preserved on Sandusky. Don't be an idiot."

Ishop was so startled he couldn't stop himself from recoiling with the news. His mouth opened to say something.

But the Diadem was already moving, like a serpent striking. She grabbed the lamp beside her bed and swung it as hard as she could. The old woman was impossibly strong. She smashed the lamp hard against his bald scalp, stunning him, and she was up, using her foot to kick his hand that held the laser cutter, knocking it away. It clattered on the floor, spinning.

She swung the lamp again and pounded his head. Ishop reeled, now trying to defend himself against this unexpected whirlwind. He was a killer, but always a slippery assassin, not a direct fighter.

Michella was shrieking. "Guards! I'm being attacked! Guards!" Even if they were just shadow-Xayan guards from Hellhole, loyal to Sophie Vence or the General, they would still come rushing in response to her shouts. Within moments they arrived at the door and threw it open.

Michella had turned around, and Ishop was backed up with blood pouring from gashes on his head. Now she smashed him in the face with the lamp. Even as the guards rushed forward, the old woman let out a wild cry and shoved him, tripped him backward—and rammed him into the window that he had already cut and loosened with the laser.

The armored glass broke around him, falling in many pieces as he, too, tumbled outside. Ishop scrambled for balance, but fell over the sill and crashed on the ground, dizzy and disoriented, his head roaring with pain, blood streaming down his face. And there were shouts from Michella's room above.

And then a buzzing, pelting sound as the torpedo ants came after him.

Breathing hard, he knew he had to find shelter. He had lost the laser cutter, not that it would serve as a weapon against the swarm. In the pale gray light of approaching dawn, he saw the static of countless insects swirling in the air.

Ishop tried to run, dashing across a dry, stony clearing in the rear of the lodge. He hoped he could make it to some other building, although the people here would hunt him down. Michella would reveal that he had tried to kill her—would they even care?

As he fled, his foot broke through a hardened crust, and the ground collapsed beneath his weight. He tripped and went sprawling into a shallow hole. As he scrambled to get out, the hole widened, collapsing. Beneath him, the grainy dirt was *pulsing* . . . and it reeked with a putrid odor.

The crater walls slumped, widening the hole, and the dirt squirmed and hummed. As he scrambled, trying to climb back out, he realized he was inside a buried nest of torpedo ants. They swarmed over his body, covering him, tearing him apart with thousands of small bites. He flailed, clawed at the crater wall, but the dirt continued to slough away, and he tumbled back down, even deeper into the nest.

Then the writhing, whistling ants parted to reveal a huge insect head and body, a nightmarish, wingless creature that was as large as a man, and glowing with a faint blue phosphorescence. The queen of the nest . . . maybe the queen of multiple nests. A diadem among the voracious creatures.

When Ishop opened his mouth to yell, thousands of smaller torpedo ants streamed down his throat, crawled into his ears and his nose, burrowing into his brain.

Ishop screamed for much longer than he should have, but no one heard him with the exception, perhaps, of the queen and her minions.

59

Duff Adkins stood on the command bridge beside Commodore Hallholme, putting on his best face as the stringline haulers approached the General's stronghold of Hellhole in an attempt to defeat him. Again. "The third time's the charm, Commodore. It's an old cliché, but appropriate under the circumstances." The aide's smile made him look twenty years younger.

Percival could feel his own tension mirrored in his bridge crew as the fleet hurtled toward the target. "There's another oft-repeated phrase, Duff. The definition of insanity is to do the same thing again and again and expect a different result."

Adkins chuckled. "But you're not doing the same thing, sir. This time we have an indisputable advantage."

Knowing that the bridge crew was listening, Percival lowered his voice. "And yet, General Adolphus always finds a way." For the benefit of his people he added more loudly, "But not this time. I'm sure he's run out of luck, and we have a far superior force than we've ever had before. Mr. Adkins, please join me in my ready room. We have last-minute plans to discuss before we arrive at the DZ stringline hub."

Although he had no fondness for the music, the Commodore called for a resounding chorus of "Strike Fast, Strike Hard" to play throughout the fleet. That stirring patriotic refrain had launched his son's abortive assault against the General, but Diadem Riomini had insisted on reinstituting the theme.

The military stringline haulers now carried twenty of the warships he had rescued from Tehila, as well as fifty brand-new frontline vessels Riomini had built at the Lubis Plain industrial complex. Percival had been shocked to learn about the secret fleet. Such an operation did not take place overnight—had he been so oblivious in his retirement on Qiorfu? Had Escobar known what was going on? It struck Percival that the Black Lord must have been intending to overthrow the Diadem all along. Michella's recent actions had made it easy for him.

They were fortunate, Percival supposed, that Riomini had managed to ascend to the Star Throne without all that turmoil; however, those quiet and ambitious schemes only added one more facet to his doubts about Riomini as a worthy leader. Percival understood the law, and his obligations to the Constellation, but he also knew that loyalty and leadership needed to be earned. Diadem Michella had already caused him great consternation with her many unwise decisions. Back when she'd forced him to use dishonorable means to defeat General Adolphus the first time, her orders had broken a fundamental part inside him. He remembered thinking often that honor was like a crystal goblet—even if broken only once, it was still broken.

Though he would not speak ill of his leaders in public, Percival wrestled with his concerns that Lord Riomini was cast from the same mold, and might even be worse than Michella Duchenet. Riomini was not the type of leader who would inspire automatic loyalty. Nevertheless, Percival intended to score a final victory over the rival who had plagued him for most of his career. This would still be his personal triumph, no matter what the Constellation did afterward.

After Umber's administrator, George Komun, had guaranteed safe passage through the DZ stringline node, Percival wasted no time launching his strike. The military haulers departed from Sonjeera as soon as they were loaded with Lord Riomini's battleships, launching with no fanfare, no drills. Time was the most important factor.

By now Komun should have seized the Hellhole hub, but Percival couldn't guess how long the inexperienced man might be able to hold it against the General. The Umber administrator was certainly no match for Tiber Adolphus. Percival had to get there in time.

His fleet had reached the small planet of Umber, which was normally an insignificant stop on a list of unremarkable frontier worlds. Rather than establishing a forward base as he'd done at Tehila, Percival took only the time necessary to move the haulers onto the DZ iperion line. Then his ships were off again, heading straight for Hellhole.

In his ready room, he took a seat and gestured for Adkins to join him. "We have to do it right this time, Duff." He clenched his fist and looked at his adjutant. "We have to do it *right*!"

"You will, Commodore. Even if he suspects we'll be back, the General can't possibly expect us so soon." The adjutant called up models of a scenario. "In our best-case projection, this is what we should see when we arrive." He showed an image of the DZ stringline hub surrounded by thirteen battleships from Umber. "We can anticipate that Administrator Komun will be able to hold the hub for a few days at least."

"If his ruse worked in the first place," Percival said. "Everything is predicated on his being able to commandeer and hold that station."

Adkins populated the simulation with the General's own battleships. "We don't know how many vessels our opponent has. We can extrapolate from what he brought against us at Tehila, but I doubt if he would have withdrawn all of his ships from there."

Percival turned away from the projections. "Duff, we'll just have to plan as soon as we see for ourselves. But this"—he waved his hand through the projection, distorting the images in the air—"is all a pretty fiction. We can plan all we like, but the real scenario never matches what we expected. We have to be swift, adaptable, reactive—and we have to be better at it than the General is."

The bridge signaled that the hauler was starting its deceleration. Duff stood up, ready to march off to the command bridge, but Percival told him to stay. "Not just yet, old friend. As I said, we have to do this right." He unlocked a cabinet beneath his desk and withdrew a bottle of the finest brandy from the Qiorfu vineyards. He recognized the irony of toasting with such a vintage, but saw no disrespect in the fact that this particular brandy had been distilled by Jacob Adolphus, their adversary's father. Percival snagged two small crystal glasses, set them on the desk, and poured two fingers in each. He handed one to Duff, who dutifully accepted the brandy but didn't seem to know what to do.

Percival clinked his glass against his companion's. "Since this seems to be a day for citing old quotes—" He took a sip of brandy, then quaffed the rest in one warm delicious gulp. "Once more into the breach."

As soon as they returned to the bridge and Adkins took the deputy command station, Percival addressed all the ships that were connected to the hauler framework. "This is more than a rematch against our archenemy. This is—this *must be*—an end to the matter. History will view the battle we are about to commence as a watershed in the future of the Constellation. All ships, prepare to disengage from docking clamps the moment we drop off the stringline."

Lord Riomini had equipped all of his new battleships with unorthodox weapons, old projectile guns with high-speed ultra-dense shells, hot scattershot bombardments, and destructive chaff. Percival continued, "I know you all haven't had much time to drill with the new artillery, but General Adolphus will not be expecting them at all. Our enhanced shields should protect us better—they proved their worth at Tehila. Thus, we have the elements of victory in our hands, and you are the major element."

The hauler pilot transmitted from his dome high on the framework, "Arriving now, Commodore."

Percival leaned forward to finish his address. "Now let's find out what's waiting for us."

The haulers fell off the stringline and decelerated toward planet Hallholme. Active scanners sent out probe beams, and signals returned at the speed of light to paint a picture of the scene. The seventy Constellation warships disengaged from their docking clamps, fired up their engines, and raced in toward their target.

As images reassembled from the multiple sensors, Percival recalled the best-case projected scenario that Duff Adkins had just shown him in the ready room. What they saw was nothing like what they'd planned for. Nothing at all.

The stringline hub was a flurry of activity. All thirteen ships from Umber were identified—some severely damaged, others still moving. Additional vessels—cargo ships, civilian transports, large and small military craft—were in disarray. Lines of shuttles rose from both the Michella Town spaceport and another launch complex on the opposite side of the continent. Some of the arriving shuttles were taken aboard the large battleships, while others docked at the stringline hub. Even more shuttles were parked in orbit, holding for a docking node to clear. The activity looked frantic, desperate. No one seemed to be paying any immediate attention to the Army of the Constellation fleet.

Commodore Hallholme's ships swarmed in, easily outnumbering the Deep Zone warships. One of his pilots transmitted, "Commodore, which targets should we choose? There are so many civilian ships."

Percival couldn't understand what was going on. He turned to his weapons officer. "What is the status of the DZDF vessels?"

"They don't seem prepared to defend or attack, sir. They're . . . preoccupied."

Percival expected a scrambled consolidation of defenses in reaction to his arrival, but the General's vessels contniued their own urgent missions.

Piloted by impatient and aggressive captains, two Constellation ships launched rapid explosive projectiles at a pair of outlying DZDF vessels. The weapons struck home, destroying engines in the rebel craft. A flurry of outraged transmissions filled the comm channels, but the General's vessels did not round about and engage in a defensive attack; rather, the unusual activity continued unabated.

"This doesn't feel right to me." Percival sat on the edge of his command chair, wrestling with his decision. "We could turn this into a massacre." He had not forgotten that Diadem Riomini gave explicit orders for him to lay waste to the entire planet, killing not just the General's loyalists, but all civilians. According to his orders, Percival should just mow down every ship in front of him.

But no, that wasn't right—no matter what the Diadem had said.

"Hold your fire," he commanded. "We don't know who's in control there. Every ship, be prepared to launch full volleys at my signal—but not until I give the word."

On the secure military comm, he tried to reach Administrator Komun on the prearranged channel, but got no response. Percival had a bad feeling in the pit of his stomach, but his fleet was committed to the plan, and he had to proceed.

As his ships closed in around the stringline hub, he switched to the common frequency used by commercial traffic. He inhaled a deep breath. "General Adolphus, this is your old friend Commodore Hallholme. As you have no doubt already conceded to George Komun, I now assert control of the stringline hub and all your ships. I have won."

A flurry of chatter ricocheted across the comm channels. General Adolphus took several minutes to respond, but finally he appeared on the screen, standing on the bridge of the *Jacob*. Adolphus looked both harried and annoyed—but he did not look like a defeated political prisoner.

His voice had an impatient edge. "Frankly, Commodore, you are the least of my problems right now. I have to evacuate this planet, with very little time to do so."

Percival was surprised. "Explain yourself."

Adolphus allowed himself to show a slight predatory smile. "George Komun has been defeated and summarily executed." The smile slipped quickly. "And all of us will be dead, if we don't keep to the evacuation schedule. I control Komun's ships and the stringline hub, and all of our resources have been turned to saving my population."

Percival stared at him, momentarily at a loss for words. Damn the man's infernal luck and tactical brilliance! He gave a quick once-over to the vessels clustered at and moving around the hub. He saw little or no damage to either the hub or the DZDF ships.

On-screen, the General turned to acknowledge a

shouted report from one of his bridge crew. Percival's pulse raced, and a too-familiar and unwelcome tendril of uncertainty threaded its way through his confidence. This was far too elaborate to be a ruse. "General, what is your crisis?"

Adolphus gave instructions and sent an officer away, then turned back to face the Commodore, his smile gone. "You're aware of what happened at Candela. At this very moment, twenty killer asteroids are inbound, directed by an enemy race of aliens who intend to destroy this entire planet. Use your long-range scanners and see for yourself. Those asteroids will all strike in a matter of days."

60

Selik Riomini had not intended to commit mass murder today. He didn't wake up that morning in anticipation of slaughtering all of those people. Nevertheless . . .

He was a leader to be respected and even feared— that was the image he wanted to project as the new Diadem—but he didn't consider himself a monster. Firm, yes, and never to be defied—but not a monster.

Even so, there were times when a lot of people had to die to make a point. Theser came to mind. And now Vielinger.

He arrived at the entrance to the iperion mine, responding to the news of the flooding disaster. The trip from Sonjeera by direct stringline had taken only a few hours, and as Diadem he could commandeer any transport he liked. During the flight, his anger had not abated. Iperion was not only one of the key sources of his personal wealth, it was also an extraordinarily vital strategic resource. Without a steady supply of iperion, the Constellation could not hope to maintain the string-line network that connected the Crown Jewels, much less hold the far more extensive Deep Zone network. The fact that such an accident had occurred in one of the few remaining productive mines on Vielinger was a blow he could neither ignore nor forgive.

The Buktu prisoners must have sabotaged the operation. The answer was so obvious, he did not need a costly and time-consuming investigation.

Riomini was accompanied by an entourage of advisers and his ever-present female guards. Lanny Oberon rushed out of the mine office to meet him. His boyish features looked drawn, his eyes reddened. "My Lord, I just received word of your arrival. Thank you for coming to inspect the site of the accident. It is a terrible tragedy."

The stocky maintenance foreman, Jando Knight, was with him. "Sir, we installed safety barricades, and are pumping out the flooded chambers. Bodies are still being recovered. We'll get back to production as soon as possible."

"How much can we salvage?" Riomini asked.

Oberon said, "We managed to save over a hundred of the work crew—"

"I don't care about enemy saboteurs. What about the *equipment*? Iperion extraction requires expensive, specialized machinery, and we need to maintain production or we'll have to start shutting down some of the stringlines."

Knight seemed more nervous than usual. "We are . . . still assessing and taking inventory of the damage, my Lord."

"Now that I am Diadem, the proper form of address is *Eminence*."

"Yes, Eminence." Knight flushed. He wiped his eyes as perspiration dripped from his forehead.

Oberon stepped aside and allowed Knight to lead the way. Both men devoted their full attention to Riomini, barely noticing the entourage that followed.

As they descended by rock stairway and tunnel into the deeper shafts, Riomini heard the roar of running water echoing through the walls. The maintenance foreman explained, "We are trying to divert the underground river, but we don't know if the dams will hold. We're rebuilding and reinforcing them as quickly as possible."

They guided Riomini to a railing-protected opening that showed the flooded main cavern. Crewmen in sealed blue suits hung on slings throughout the chamber, operating remote-controlled machines that dipped in and out of the rushing water. Cranes lowered heavy pieces of construction material from suspended platforms.

Knight's voice cracked as he said, "We almost have a section sealed and holding, Eminence. Pumps will drain the work chambers to expose the active iperion inclusions again."

Scowling, the Black Lord looked at Oberon. "And the saboteurs? Where are they?"

He blinked. "You mean the prisoners, sir?"

"Obviously, they are the ones who caused this disaster."

"Eminence, I witnessed the crisis myself. There was no sabotage—a temporary dam broke, releasing a swollen aquifer." Oberon glanced at Knight, since that was the maintenance man's area of responsibility.

"That dam has exhibited maintenance problems for some time now," Knight said, his face glistening with sweat. "But I thought we had it under control."

Riomini frowned. "I find an accident highly unlikely, and I'm disappointed that both of you were so easily duped. Those captives are militant members of the rebellion intent on destroying the Constellation. An opportunity presented itself, and someone found a way to wreck our operations."

The mine supervisor kept shaking his head. "That's simply not true, Eminence. So many of their own died—"

Riomini scowled. "I'm sure they think they've made martyrs of themselves. I will not let them benefit from their ruthless sabotage. Mine operations have ground to a standstill, and the Buktu captives must be punished." He wondered if perhaps his enemies among the noble families were in collusion with General Adolphus to bring about this catastrophe, or if the prisoners had acted on their own initiative. Either way, this was *no* accident.

He looked at Knight. "The money saved by using a prison work crew—you reported to me that you had devoted those funds to improving maintenance."

"Oh, yes sir, I certainly did everything possible to keep the mines in top order."

"I'm sure you did."

Oberon was still unconvinced about the sabotage. "Eminence, we can't blame the prisoners without evidence. I will organize a team for a full investigation."

Riomini's eyes narrowed dangerously. "I don't like the way you're protecting vicious enemy prisoners."

"With all respect, Eminence, we never should have brought prisoners of war here in the first place. Experienced workers are needed for such a dangerous, challenging job."

"Are you faulting *me* for this, because I assigned the prisoners to do labor?"

Oberon didn't change his expression, but remained calm, irritatingly calm. He'd always been a highly competent man, but he spoke his mind too much. "I didn't say that, Eminence. Mr. Knight already made it plain that the faulty dam had numerous maintenance issues. No doubt he did what he could under the circumstances, but until we have the results of an investigation we won't know what really happened."

Riomini was finished with the conversation. "So long as this mine is not producing iperion, an emergency exists in the Constellation." He looked around. "Where are the prisoners? March them out here. I want to talk with them."

Soon enough, the dozens of men and women captured by Commodore Hallholme at Buktu were marched out in front of the grotto's open deck and ordered to stand against the railing. They faced Diadem Riomini, impertinently angry and grieving at the deaths of their comrades. All along, this group had been more trouble than they were worth, and Riomini wished the old Commodore had never bothered to capture them in the first place. What did he think the Constellation would do with them? They left much to be desired as workers, too, although as saboteurs they seemed to be quite effective.

Riomini told his guards to stand watch. "Keep your weapons trained on them. They have already proved to be dangerous." Oberon frowned as he and Knight stood together on one side, both of them ill at ease. The guards pointed their shoulder weapons in the direction of the enemy prisoners. "Who speaks for them?" Riomini asked.

Oberon identified a blond man, Erik Anderlos. Riomini ordered him forward. "I know you and your fellow prisoners were responsible for the disaster. Whether from direct sabotage or negligence, you played a part."

Anderlos looked defiant. "I wish that were true, but none of my people were anywhere near the dam. These mines are in such bad shape they don't need any help from us to fall apart."

"And maybe you didn't report any flaws you encountered because you wanted these operations to fail."

Anderlos didn't flinch. "I *did* report everything I saw to Mr. Oberon and Mr. Knight, on a daily basis. I admit that my loyalty remains with General Adolphus, but I would never have done anything to endanger my people."

Wearing a troubled expression, Oberon turned to Riomini. "He is correct, Eminence. The prisoner reported numerous issues to me and to the maintenance foreman."

"And my crew worked tirelessly to keep everything operable," Knight interjected. He looked as if he wanted to be anywhere but here. "Now we've brought in outside contractors on an emergency basis, and they're working round the clock to restore operations."

Riomini frowned. "I will reward the contractors when they are finished. And I know you and Oberon have been running these operations for years, so I will assume that both of you did your best." He faced the line of sullen Buktu prisoners. "As for all of you prisoners, I have considered your employment record, and have come to a decision."

Reaching over to one of his female guards, he removed her projectile rifle and shot Anderlos in the face. The momentum pushed him over the railing, and he tumbled into the still-churning water below. The swift current carried the body away.

Then, as if a different kind of dam had burst inside of him, Riomini started firing at the prisoners. At a signal from him, the rest of his guards finished the job with a deafening fusillade. The trapped prisoners were mowed down in a matter of seconds.

As silence returned, his chief guard, Rota Vindahl, said, "Nicely done, Eminence."

Lanny Oberon and Jando Knight stared in horror, unable to speak. The functionaries and entourage members also observed, most of them too terrified or sickened to turn away.

Vindahl walked calmly from body to body, verifying that each one was dead, adding another shot for three who still groaned. When finished, she asked, "What would you like done with the corpses, sir?"

"Just haul them away. If we dump them all down into the mines, they might clog up the operations just as we're trying to recover." He felt hot, flushed. "But first, I want images of all this. Previously, we showed the Constellation what I did to distant Theser as a warning. But this is closer to home."

When he had a file of images, he commanded that they be copied and distributed widely. The most important package had to be sent immediately by courier out into the Deep Zone, via the Umber stringline. "I want Commodore Hallholme to see this. He needs a bit of encouragement to succeed."

61

The largest of the twenty asteroids aimed toward Hellhole contained a microcosm of Xaya—a preserved bubble that replicated life on the once-pristine planet. This habitat was more than a museum—it was real, a true remnant of the ancient paradise that the rebel alien faction had destroyed in the first impact five centuries earlier.

Thanks to Uroa's memories, Keana knew what the original Xaya had been like. She remembered the lush plains of succulent groundcover on which the Xayans fed, the glorious blooms that attracted lazy insects, the fungi that released phosphorescent spores, which could provide a euphoric rush if consumed upon first release . . . and the flourishing oases of red weed that provided arboreal habitats for flying invertebrates, such as bobbing jellyfish that wafted gently on the breezes.

The Ro-Xayans had preserved it all here, rebuilding a semblance of their ruined home over the centuries. The interior of this asteroid was an amazing alien garden. Her human nose did not have the sensory apparatus to appreciate all the nuances of scent patterns that had been part of the music of Xaya just like colors and sounds. Keana found it breathtaking.

Inside her, though, Uroa was shocked at what she saw.

The large asteroid was like a hollowed-out egg, with a camouflaged exterior that made it look like a nondescript celestial rock, but internally the painstakingly preserved environment was a self-sustaining ecosystem.

Keana looked up and saw airborne jellyfish floating along, shifting in pastel shades and patterns of pale blue, pink, and orange. Tendrils of red weed, suspended toward the center of the hollow asteroid, drifted languidly, held up by empty bladders.

She stepped cautiously forward, knowing she had to be a leader, a representative trying to save her world. Internally, Uroa expressed great concern to her. "They are Ro-Xayans—you must not trust them!"

"I haven't even spoken to them yet," she said aloud. Moving on his long undercarriage, Lodo accompanied her into the immense enclosure. She could sense that he was anxious, intimidated. Tanja Hu and Ian Walfor hung back closer to their ship, knowing that Keana and Lodo would be the crux of this encounter.

Inside the gigantic chamber, groups of Ro-Xayans waited for them, looking toward the visitors with curious, unreadable expressions. The powerful rival aliens had used telemancy to capture Walfor's ship, but they made no threatening moves now, did not surge forward to seize the captives. The Ro-Xayans simply waited to face them.

Keana spoke to her companions, as much to reassure herself as the others, "This is what I wanted. This is the gamble I needed to make. We have to speak with them and try to save the planet."

Inside her mind, Uroa cautioned, "You are thinking like a human. You expect them to be reasonable."

"I have to, otherwise we have no chance," Keana said. With Hellhole and the entire Xayan race at stake, she had to try.

As if relenting and deciding to help in her efforts to communicate with them, Uroa fed more details into her mind, giving her new information about the terrible schism, the civil war that had split their race, how Zairic and his fellow visionaries tried to guide all Xayans to their evolutionary destiny. Keana could barely think straight as he continued to flood her with emotions, hammering her with the dismay he'd felt when the splinter faction left, and then the disbelieving horror as the remaining Xayans realized that their own fellows intended to destroy them rather than admit defeat.

Keana forced her own personality back to the fore. "I *will* talk with them," she insisted. "If we fail, Hellhole is going to be devastated in four days."

Tanja ventured forward, looking angry and unsettled.

"But why are they hurling their own habitat asteroid toward the planet, along with the others? Why would they destroy themselves as well?"

Lodo turned to her and said, "Because the Ro-Xayans are insane. Their actions have already established that."

Inside the immense, hollow chamber, thousands of aliens gathered to receive the strangers. All were pale, soft, and abuzz with a murmur of shared conversation, excitement, and concern. Rising from the curved stone walls were buildings, colorful free-form buildings like the ones the shadow-Xayans had erected in their settlement near the slickwater pools. There was even a cloudless blue, artificial sky, with wisps of cloud formations in it. She saw no semblance of a sun, and the light source was concealed.

Finally, the Ro-Xayans came toward them in throngs. These creatures had a different appearance from the four Originals rescued from the deep redoubt; they exhibited more color, splashes of pigmentation and rivers of mottled spots that may have been natural coloration, or possibly artificial body paint.

Since Lodo was the only Xayan there, the aliens focused their dark, spiraling eyes on him, but said nothing. He asked aloud, "Who represents you?"

From the Uroa presence inside her, Keana could understand their language. "We all speak with one voice," said the foremost Ro-Xayan, a tall male with a flair of bright blue that ran up his chest and around to the back of his neck. "You are one of the others."

"I am one of the survivors," Lodo said. Keana realized he was using his telemancy to implement comprehension among their human companions as well.

"I am Zhaday. You are free to address me and address all these others."

Keana stepped forward next to Lodo. "I am Keana,

and I speak for the human race—those whom you would destroy when your asteroids strike Xaya."

"Unfortunate," said Zhaday. "You should not be there. Our goal is to eradicate the Xayan species and prevent *ala'ru*. You are not our enemy." But he looked closer at her eyes.

"You can't smash our planets and expect us to brush it off," said Walfor.

Ignoring this, Zhaday studied Keana and said, "How is it that you have a glimmer in your eyes, a perceptible trace of a Xayan? I find that interesting, and disturbing."

She said, "I am also Uroa, a Xayan leader who remembers your schism, who remembers what you did to the planet the first time. His memories and experiences are preserved within me. I have reawakened them."

Lodo said, "And I remember such events firsthand. I was there in the end days. Several of us were sealed in a vault and preserved, and we have only recently reawakened. I was there when you sent the asteroid crashing into sacred Xaya. I witnessed it with my own eyes."

After pondering, Zhaday said, "I have absorbed countless histories myself. I know the records and memories of many—as well as the justifications for what my faction did. The first asteroid should have been enough to obliterate all of the *ala'ru* fanatics. It should have been enough to save the future. But now, sadly, we know it was not enough. And there is no hope."

"Most Xayans were indeed wiped out," Keana said. "But everything that formed their essence was stored in slickwater. They were preserved to be awakened again. When human colonists came to the planet, they found the slickwater."

The other Ro-Xayans crowded closer, listening, murmuring. "Slickwater is not known to us," Zhaday said.

"It was created by Zairic, our great warrior-philosopher," Lodo said. "He saved most of our race, and we are blossoming again. As we join with human minds, the resulting hybrids are vastly stronger than mere Xayans. You cannot stop *ala'ru*," Lodo insisted. "We are very close."

Zhaday turned in alarm to the other Ro-Xayans. Their background humming language grew louder, like a thunderstorm.

Keana said in a firm voice, "We cannot let you destroy all the progress we've made. Just look at what you've saved here. Let me try to heal the rift between your factions. There is no need for this philosophical war to continue."

"It will not continue," said Zhaday. "It must *end*. We had plans and hopes. We wanted to preserve beautiful Xaya for the future, wanted to restore our pristine world. Before sending the asteroid long ago, we preserved all that Xaya was, intending to rebuild our civilization without the threat of the *ala'ru* fanatics. But we were deluded."

"Yes, Xaya is awakening again," Keana noted. "Vegetation is growing. Species are reproducing and spreading out—thanks to your own efforts, we now know. The Xayan people are awakening from the slickwater. The planet is coming back!"

In a somber, pulsing tone, Zhaday said, "And that is why you give us no choice but to attack Xaya again—this time with even more force. Our determination was insufficient the first time. We hoped a less extreme solution might work, but *ala'ru* is too dangerous for us to ignore, and this time we can allow nothing to remain. There must be no chance whatsoever for resurrection, not the tiniest scrap of life. No memories in your slickwater, no hint of a Xayan mind. No echo of our civilization can remain anywhere on the planet, anywhere in the universe. We must obliterate ourselves along with it, just to be certain." He paused a long moment. "It is that important to stop *ala'ru*."

62

From his fascination with ancient Earth military history, General Tiber Adolphus knew the old colloquialism of a "Mexican standoff." His ships were armed and ready, an impressive defensive force that now included the recaptured warships from Umber. But even the slightest setback in the evacuation would cost many lives, and he was preoccupied with a nonstop effort of filling warships, cargo haulers, and shuttles to get the people away to safety.

He did not intend to take all those people or all those vital ships into battle.

Commodore Hallholme's unexpected fleet had hurtled in along the Umber stringline with orders to seize the Hellhole stringline hub and impose Constellation rule—but that would be an empty conquest, once the planet itself was destroyed within days.

Yes, even though his instruments could detect the cluster of incoming, unnatural asteroids, Hallholme did not budge. "General Adolphus, I have a superior military force. My ships are armed and prepared to fire. I demand your immediate surrender."

Under the hovering threat of the Constellation fleet, evacuation operations ground to a halt, and the Commodore remained implacable. The ships in transit were at risk of capture or destruction. The Ankor and Michella Town spaceports were crowded with panicked people desperate to get off the planet, but all launches were canceled. The shuttles already docked at the stringline hub or loaded aboard the DZDF battleships could not return to the surface to load more evacuees.

Everything remained at a standstill, and General Adolphus resented every lost minute. "Commodore, you can see our urgent situation. Put aside your political obsessions and personal animosity toward me. I have to save my people. You can either assist, or you can get out of the way."

"I'm afraid that's not possible, General. I have my orders."

Adolphus looked at the man, who was quite a bit older than he, hair grayer, face gaunt, eyes more troubled. "We have faced each other for years, and I've taken your measure. If you can sit back and let my entire population die, then you are not an honorable man at all."

Hallholme appeared stung by the comment, but said, "My duty remains unchanged. I have sworn to defend the Constellation."

He had already informed Adolphus that his ships were equipped with enhanced shielding to protect against telemancy blasts, and he promised that his brute-force projectile weapons could cause enormous damage to all the ships crowded around the hub. He doubted if the aliens could defend against all of his weapons.

Adolphus didn't inform him that the shadow-Xayans were unlikely to offer their telemancy defenses, since the groups of converts had withdrawn into a last-minute frantic push to reach their evolutionary ascension before the whole world was destroyed.

"Incoming ship, General," said Lieutenant Sendell. "It's a stringline freighter from Nicles."

Adolphus felt a cold wash of tension, worried that yet another Deep Zone world had folded, just like Umber and Tehila. He asked Sendell to call up shipping records, and was relieved to learn this was a scheduled arrival. The Hellhole stringline hub was still the center of DZ commercial traffic, and word of the crisis had not yet spread to the other planets.

The cargo ship was undoubtedly loaded with grains, processed metals, and crystal data-storage units for which Nicles was known. The Deep Zone was just developing its network of commodities, determining which worlds were the best sources of particular materials, and which other worlds needed those goods. Adolphus felt an inward groan. If only the DZ had a chance to establish a normal existence. . . .

As the Nicles freighter decelerated, its pilot was alarmed to plunge into the middle of the standoff. Commodore Hallholme immediately dispatched three midsize destroyers, which surrounded and captured the freighter before it could reach the stringline hub.

The Commodore transmitted again to the *Jacob*'s bridge. "General, we will hold that ship, its passengers, and crew until you surrender."

Adolphus leaned forward, his voice a low growl. He hadn't wanted to stoop to such measures, but he had little time and no patience for finesse or subtle diplomacy. "Taking hostages and using human shields—once again you show your true colors, Commodore." He had to make the threat clear. "Are you certain you want to play the hostage card again? You said you don't care that we have Diadem Michella Duchenet, but I am also holding thousands of Constellation prisoners of war—including your son."

He cut off the transmission and let the Commodore stew on that, then opened a new channel to Slickwater

Springs. Sophie looked worried when she came on-screen. "We've had an emergency here, Tiber. A smoke storm forced us to buckle down before we could start evacuation prep, and then a quake released a buried torpedo ant nest. Numerous casualties—it's a disaster."

"What about the POWs? Are they safe?"

"The camp is in the next valley over and was not affected. But the Diadem's aide, Ishop Heer . . . he tried to kill Michella, and then he ran out into the storm. He's dead."

Adolphus couldn't say he would grieve overmuch. "What I need to know most of all—have the escaped POWs been found yet?"

She looked tense and disturbed. Everyone knew they had very little time left. She didn't give him the answer he wanted to hear, but the one he expected. "No word yet, but after this much time, the chances of their survival are practically nil. Cristoph is ready to discontinue his search—we'll need to focus on the evacuation. We could be using those search flyers to move people from outlying mining settlements."

"Have them do one more sweep . . . but then send him to Ankor to assist."

He sat back and sighed. Now he had to decide how long he could maintain his bluff with the Commodore.

63

The alien stood in the middle of the clearing, gazing upward into the darkening sky. "It won't be long now. The asteroids will strike in a few days."

"But you are certain they'll come?" Bolton asked. He had no way of getting any sort of technical verification.

Jonwi's words thrummed again. "They will come. There is no doubt."

In the deepening night surrounded by the suspended red weed, Bolton shivered. He knew he should find a place on the soft groundcover to sleep, but what was the point of continuing to look for a way to survive? Of trying to save the Redcom? Despite the red weed that wrapped him, Escobar was obviously dying, and would probably perish even before the asteroid bombardment. Bolton found that tragic.

By now the searchers must have given up looking for them. Perhaps they had found the wrecked Trakmaster and what was left of Yimidi, maybe even the remains of Vingh in the arroyo. But if planet-killing asteroids were indeed hurtling in, why would anyone waste time or effort looking for a couple of escapees? Bolton stood under the whispering, drifting stalks of red weed, which emitted a shower of luminous spores that sparkled like fireflies as they were released into the air.

If only another few days remained, though, he wished he could be with his own people. . . .

As he worked in his pristine oasis, Jonwi seemed like a gentle soul, nurturing, even a dreamer. He had tended Escobar, kept him alive for this long, yet he refused to transport the gravely wounded man to a place where he could receive medical attention. Each time Bolton asked, *begged* for Jonwi's help, the alien rebuffed him, insisting that he would not leave his precious garden.

Bolton stood on the boundary of the red weeds now, peering into the bleak, starlit wasteland, as if daring some alien predator to leap out at him. Though he had enough to eat from the special vegetation that Jonwi told him was edible, his stomach rumbled. After several days, his body was growing less able to draw the nutrients he needed, and the flavors all had a bitter aftertaste. He longed for something familiar on his palate.

Escobar lay in a deep, fading coma. He had not awakened again since his restless mumbling the previous day. The deep gash on his neck was covered with a hardened scab, his skin was clammy and cold, and the pulse Bolton could feel on his neck was barely perceptible.

Bolton needed to take the man away from here! But he could not do so, if Jonwi refused to help. Regardless, he had no idea which direction to go in the wild landscape. . . .

As he watched the night skies, he noticed many tiny lights, an increased number of spacecraft, an apparent flurry of activity in orbit. Surely, General Adolphus would have detected the incoming asteroids—perhaps even now he was evacuating the planet. Bolton hoped at least that the Constellation prisoners in the camp would be taken to safety.

But that wouldn't do him, or Escobar, any good at all.

Sitting alone in the darkness with the humming sounds of native Hellhole life forms all around him, he wondered where Keana was . . . and if she might be worried about him.

When he went back to the glade where Escobar lay, he found that Jonwi had returned from a mysterious inspection of the densest forest. Bolton stood before him, said, "I have a solution, a possible way to save my friend."

Jonwi gazed at him without saying anything, but in the alien's slowly spiraling eyes, Bolton detected what he thought was skepticism. "Your friend is dying. He cannot be saved."

Bolton grasped at any possibility. "Unless we immerse him in slickwater. We were told the pools can heal people. Encix promised miracles when she tried to get us to join the converts. I implore you, help us get back to the settlement and the pools. Please! If the slickwater can save him, then why not give him that chance?"

"The slickwater was created by our enemies. I will not take you there . . . and I will not leave my oasis."

Bolton pressed the issue, sensing that Jonwi wanted to help, if he could. "Look, General Adolphus sent out search parties to find us. It's a very small chance, but what if I were to light a signal fire, a big one? Maybe someone would see it. There seems to be increased air traffic. It would give us a chance! And you could remain here—no one would ever need to know."

To Bolton's surprise, the Ro-Xayan slowly nodded his smooth head. He seemed almost relieved to have the opportunity. "It could be done . . . but to what purpose? All will be destroyed soon anyway."

"For the same purpose that you will keep tending your garden here until the end. We have to at least *try* to save him! There is no time limit on hope."

The big alien stood motionless, pondering for a long moment, as the silhouetted weed fronds drifted in the air. "Very well. We shall take your companion outside of the forest, into the open, where a signal can be seen."

Bolton tensed. "But that's where the burrow foxes attacked us."

"I have moved them away. They will be content with other vast prairies." With an incline of his head and a twitch of the antennae, a faint humming of telemancy rippled out—and Escobar's wrapped body lifted off the ground. "Follow me."

Moving his sluglike body, Jonwi wound through the resurrected Xayan forest, wandering past fungi and drifting jellyfish, until they reached the open terrain. Bolton felt energized, with tears stinging his eyes, but when he looked out at the bleak, rock-studded landscape, he realized it would not be so easy to light a large fire that could be seen by patrol ships.

Jonwi took Escobar's wrapped form over to a flat rock and used telemancy to deposit him gently on top of it. "You will not need to build a primitive fire. I can send the necessary signal—but it will be up to your people to respond. I will remain in the forest, tending my creations until the last days. Your people do not need to see me."

The Ro-Xayan lifted his soft, fleshy hands toward the heavens. Behind him, towering stalks of red weed stirred, as if in anticipation. Psychic energy sparkled and crackled around his head. The intensity increased, the loops and squiggles of manifested energy became stronger, and with a loud *pop* of displaced air, a brilliant pillar of white light flared upward. Soaring high above the rocks and the tallest red weeds, it sprouted into a geyser of light, a spectacular psychic fountain in the night sky. It illuminated the terrain all around like daylight.

Jonwi kept the flare aloft in a brilliant beam of light that he played off the clouds, before finally letting it fade. Bolton stared in awe and hope.

The alien waited beside Bolton for a while, as if to keep him company. Escobar was motionless in his cocoon, but Bolton kept staring up into the skies, waiting for more than an hour. He began to think he had allowed himself to have foolish hopes.

If the General was in the midst of evacuating a world, then every ship, every competent person would already be dedicated to the massive project. Who would be interested in investigating a strange light out in the wilderness?

Then, to his amazement, he did hear engine noises, the thrum and roar of a large patrol craft that cruised low over the landscape, playing the bright spear of a spotlight down on the ground—searching!

"There is no time limit on hope," Jonwi echoed Bolton's words back to him. "I will remember that, and I hope your people can achieve what you need." The alien slipped back into the dense red weed forest as the patrol craft approached.

Bolton stood next to Escobar's form, and he waved his hands to draw the attention of the approaching craft. The light swiveled toward him, swept past, then returned, pinning him in its bright glare. Bolton kept waving, shouting . . . and realized he was weeping.

Armed soldiers leaped out and took Bolton into custody. A uniformed man whom Bolton recognized as Cristoph de Carre stepped out of the craft. "Major Crais? We have been searching for you, but we called off the effort earlier tonight. You're lucky someone spotted your signal. How did you possibly make a flare so bright?"

Instead of answering, Bolton urgently pointed to the weed-wrapped form on the rock. "Redcom Escobar Hallholme will die unless we can get him to the slick-water pools as soon as possible."

Cristoph looked surprised. "He's wrapped up like a mummy."

"The alien weed kept him alive, but he won't last much longer. We have to hurry—my duty is to protect my commanding officer."

"From his own foolishness," Cristoph muttered. He seemed to have other things to say, accusations, questions, but instead he told the soldiers to load them aboard the craft. "Any other survivors?"

Bolton drew a breath. "None."

As the soldiers hustled to load the Redcom into the aft cargo section of the craft, Cristoph stared hard at Bolton. "I've looked at your record, Major Crais. It wasn't your idea to escape, was it?"

"The Redcom made the decision," Bolton said. "And I decided to remain with him, even though I advised him it was a dubious plan. We lost two good men."

The aircraft lifted off, and Cristoph guided them into the night sky for the long flight back to Slickwater Springs. He said, "We will lose a lot more good people. Asteroids are on the way, impact in a few days. There won't be time to evacuate everyone."

Bolton did not let Cristoph know he was already aware of the Ro-Xayans and their asteroids. While the soldiers remained in the rear seats, Cristoph wanted Bolton up front, so he could begin the debriefing.

Yet Bolton was the one who studied the young man and said, "We have an interesting connection, you and I."

"I know. Keana—your wife, my father's lover. She ruined my family . . . and I don't suspect you're grateful for what she's done either."

Bolton drew a deep breath. He had long struggled to identify his feelings for her. "We had very different understandings of who we were and what our relationship was. But she's not the same person now—not the same at all."

Cristoph remained silent for a long moment. "I know. My father died in disgrace and I was exiled here . . . but can I blame Keana Duchenet for all that? My life is different now, and in some ways more important and meaningful than it ever would have been back in the Crown Jewels. I'd certainly be on the other side of the war if I'd remained on Vielinger."

"Have you been able to forgive her?" Bolton asked.

He didn't hesitate before answering. "I have." Then he glanced up. "And right now, she's trying to save this planet."

64

As Tanja listened to the Ro-Xayan's blithe pronouncement of racial suicide, her anger drove away any awe of this wondrous alien habitat.

While Keana-Uroa paused in the face of Zhaday's stubborn mind-set, Tanja pushed her way forward. "What allows you to be such a judge? Why are you a cosmic executioner?" Her voice grew louder as she confronted the creature. "My planet was your last target—hundreds of thousands of innocent people displaced or killed, and now you say we were just collateral damage? That we attracted your attention because a handful of Xayans happened to use telemancy to defend us against an outside attack? Preposterous!"

The bright blue pigmentation on Zhaday's upper body intensified. "We were alarmed and dismayed when the Xayan seed colony there unleashed surprising and tremendous telemancy. We did not understand how any of our people could have survived on that planet, but the danger was clear. We had to eradicate them before they grew stronger. It was an emergency."

More of the Ro-Xayans came closer, and Zhaday continued. "Not until one of our original detection devices on the surface of Xaya was triggered did we understand just how much telemancy had already been restored—causing us to realize that the threat of imminent *ala'ru* was even more dangerous than before. We had to act swiftly and decisively before it was too late."

The crowded aliens were agitated now, and Tanja saw their growing alarm.

Lodo said, "But your asteroids will not arrive soon enough—I know how close our race is to achieving the critical point." His antennae quivered. "In the debate long ago, before your faction left Xaya, I, too, shared some of your concerns . . . but I am now convinced that *ala'ru* is our destiny. Our race has awakened and we are close enough, and desperate enough. You cannot stop *ala'ru* in time."

"We must!" Zhaday said.

A low background of Xayan buzzing increased to a roar, like a storm about to burst.

Keana sounded oh-so-reasonable when she spoke. "But even if your faction doesn't wish to join the ascension, why would you deny that to the rest of your race?"

Zhaday looked at her. "I can sense the presence of Uroa inside you. *He* knows why, and *Lodo* knows as well. *Ala'ru* is not just an evolutionary step for the Xayan race. It would not simply allow the advancement of Xayan minds and powers. *Ala'ru* would change *everything*." He paused, and his thrumming voice deepened. "It would destroy the very universe itself."

Silence fell like a hammer, until Tanja burst out, "What the hell are you talking about?"

"If the Xayan race triggers *ala'ru*, they will create a crack in reality. The ascended Xayans will shift the fundamental physical constants of the cosmos. They will unravel the balance of the universe, rewrite gravity, shift the nuclear forces—the basics of existence will be altered forever."

"Ridiculous," said Ian Walfor. "One race on one

planet in one solar system in a tiny corner of the galaxy? They can't have that much power."

"*Ala'ru* would create a flashpoint," said Zhaday. "And then the ascended Xayans will be able to rewrite the pattern and start again, like gods. But none of the rest of us would survive, no world, no star, no galaxy or remnant of anything that exists now."

Keana wore a look of appalled horror on her face. She turned to Lodo. "Is he speaking the truth?" She reeled as the Original alien just regarded her in cool silence. "It's true and you knew it all along?"

Still receiving no answer from Lodo, she closed her eyes and touched her left temple, delving inward. "Uroa . . . no!" Her eyes flew open again. So, her own alien presence knew as well—and so did Zairic, Encix, all the leaders of this faction. "And yet you went forward, still pushing for this?" She whirled to glare at Lodo. "You convinced the rest of your race that this was their ultimate goal, but you didn't tell them the consequences!"

"It is our racial destiny," Lodo said. "It is our priority. You're just complicating it with facts."

Zhaday drew his large torso up, and his blue pigmentation shifted and pulsed. "They did not consider the rest of the universe. The original Xayan race never looked outward, never sent ships to distant star systems, never communicated with other species, although we did detect signals from afar when we all lived on Xaya, and we had hints of other civilizations. Zairic, Encix, and the other *ala'ru* fanatics did not care about the destruction they would cause. They would change the underpinnings of the universe, become gods—and re-create whatever they wished."

"While the rest of us get caught in the backwash," Walfor said.

"The Ro-Xayans refused to allow that to happen," Zhaday continued. "We pleaded with Zairic's faction to stop. We used violence against them, but they were more powerful. A large number of us finally broke away, hoping that by removing a significant portion of our population the other Xayans would be unable to achieve *ala'ru*, at least not for a very long time. But Zairic's followers worked harder, focused their powers, raised their potential . . . and we knew we had to act. We preserved samples from the ecosystem in order to restore it someday, and then we sent the first asteroid to Xaya. We hoped that would be enough to prevent *ala'ru* forever—but it was a false hope."

A large female Ro-Xayan with a splash of scarlet coloring across her face rose up in front of Lodo, her expression furious, but Lodo did not back down in front of her. "It is our racial destiny," he insisted. "Encix has always been quite vehement about it, saying that it doesn't matter if we leave nothing but cosmic wreckage behind. She can be very persuasive."

"And self-centered," Tanja said. "Either way, the human colonists end up obliterated!"

"By destroying our sacred home planet and our race, we are saving the *universe*," said Zhaday. "Our faction is willing to crush our own racial destiny in order to save the rest of the cosmos, all other star systems, all other races that are out there. The *ala'ru* fanatics care about their own destiny and nothing else.

"We learned our lesson from our first failure, analyzed our mistakes. This time, we will not let compassion soften the necessary blow. We must kill every Xayan, eliminate any possibility of *ala'ru*. Forever. There is no measure of our sadness, but there is no question of the necessity of this action. This time, we will make certain our Xayan brothers cannot hide. With so many planet-killing impacts, not even the slickwater will survive."

In a heavy voice, Keana-Uroa said, "We came out here to convince you to change your minds, to prevent you from destroying Xaya and all the people there, both human and Xayan. I still urge you to negotiate. I am one of the leading shadow-Xayans, and the truth was withheld from my human portion, as well as from the other human converts who were transformed in the pools. I assure you, we did not understand the consequences."

"Encix does," Lodo said. "And she will not stop. She will drive forward, no matter what."

Tanja cleared her throat. "You may prevent *ala'ru* by wiping out the planet, but all your people live inside this habitat, too. If you smash this asteroid into Hellhole, then everything you've preserved will also be obliterated. You'll all die."

"It is extreme," Zhaday said, "but it is the only way. *We* are Xayans as well. Our faction still has the potential for *ala'ru* within us. Our will may be strong now, but generations hence, who can guarantee that some other prophet like Zairic would not arise? What if that prophet claims we were wrong and drives our people toward the ascension again?"

He hung his head. "We know we will all die soon, that we are causing the extinction of an entire civilization, an entire race. Every Ro-Xayan lives in this asteroid habitat, and we will all smash into our world. But it is necessary, the only way to forever destroy the threat of *ala'ru*. And at least humans may remember us after we are gone. Someday they might understand what we did for the universe."

Zhaday's voice rang out with an air of command enhanced by mental powers. "Summon our greatest telemancers. They've been regenerating their powers after such a great expenditure of telemancy. I want them to apply all possible force to accelerate these asteroids, no matter how much harm the extreme effort causes them, no matter how much it drains them. We need to strike our target as fast as possible! There is no time left."

65

Shaken and pale, Percival gripped the command chair and stared at the blank screen, disturbed that General Adolphus would use Escobar as a bargaining chip. Was that unexpected? He understood the man's desperation, understood it very well.

Adkins stood beside him. "What are you going to do, Commodore? Diadem Riomini would not want you to show weakness in front of the General."

Percival growled, "Diadems have a way of issuing orders that cause as much damage to me as to the enemy."

Politically, he had been ordered to discard Michella Duchenet, thus removing her value as an enemy hostage—but he recognized that was as much because of a personal grudge as a tactical move. Yes, the old woman was oblivious to her own fingerprints on all the damage she had done, the thousands of graves. Percival had so many reasons to resent her . . . yet he'd remained loyal to the Constellation Charter, even though he could not have explained why. Selik Riomini was the official Diadem now, not Michella Duchenet, and the Commodore had his new orders. Even if he rescued the former ruler and brought her back to Sonjeera, no doubt Riomini would execute her.

But Escobar . . . Percival had personal priorities of his own.

Now his fleet was in orbit above a hell world, supposedly victorious and yet painted into a corner by a military face-off that fit none of their projected scenarios, nor did it follow any standard rule of military conduct. "Get the General back on the comm. We aren't finished with our conversation yet!"

"General Adolphus seems to believe it's over," Adkins said.

The screen remained blank despite repeated pings by the comm officer.

"He can't wait very long." Percival shook his head. "Every hour of this standoff is costing him the launches of shuttles that could bring evacuees to orbit. He's trying to manipulate me, put me off balance." The Commodore clamped his lips together. He did indeed feel off balance. Under normal circumstances, he would have thrown all of his resources, personnel, and ships into the disaster relief effort. Refusing to do so went against the grain of his personality and smacked of dishonorable conduct. . . .

Finally, after repeated requests for a comm link, the screen activated, and General Adolphus appeared. "I'm busy, Commodore. Unless you've decided to cooperate, I can't waste more time. If you won't assist with the effort, then get out of the way."

"I demand to see my son. Show me Escobar. Prove he's safe and healthy, and then I might consider some flexibility in my position."

Adolphus shook his head. "I have a planet to evacuate, and I won't play favorites or waste personnel rounding up one man so he can have a conversation with his father. Lives are going to be lost due to your harassment and interference—no question about it." He leaned closer to the screen; his dark eyes were hard. "I guarantee you this, Commodore. If we don't have enough ships or time to save my people, then your son will forfeit his position on a rescue vessel. Escobar Hall-holme will be last on the evacuation list."

The General's image vanished from the screen, replaced by archival video, with his voice saying, "We faced a similar threat before, so we know what's in store for Hellhole. Watch—this is only a hint of what's about to happen here." At first, Percival didn't recognize the planet in the images, then he saw two asteroids hurtling in, giant pock-marked rocks that closed on the world. A flurry of ships filled the orbital lanes, being loaded aboard stringline haulers that raced away along the iperion path.

"This was Candela," said the General's voice, "the previous target of the murderous aliens. That world was rendered utterly uninhabitable by only *two* asteroids, Commodore. Now the Ro-Xayans are coming at my planet with *twenty*, and we have less than four days."

On-screen, the General's face replaced the archival images. "My people are going to die, and so is your son, and so are the Constellation POWs, if you don't cooperate. We can't stop asteroids." His expression changed. "You have used dishonorable tactics on the battlefield many times, but you also secretly helped my colony survive when the Diadem wanted us all to die. I think I know your true character, Commodore Percival Hallholme. I appeal to your humanity."

In a voice that wasn't as firm or confident as he wanted, Percival answered, "The moment you surrender, General, we can work together to get those people to safety. Look how many ships I have to help. It'll make all the difference."

He knew the General couldn't just wait it out and

he wouldn't just surrender his leverage. He couldn't see any other way to follow his orders.

Percival stared at the screen, and his nemesis stared back—two battering rams of pride facing off. Adolphus's expression dropped, and Percival could see he had reached a crux point. "All right. I will submit to whatever retaliation you wish, Commodore—*afterward*. First, we have to save as many of my people as possible, or *you* will be responsible for the destruction of this entire colony and the death of your son. Do you want all that blood on your hands?"

Some of the crew members on the flagship's bridge cheered, thinking the impasse had been resolved, but Percival felt an even heavier weight in his chest. "Unfortunately, General, my orders from Diadem Riomini were quite explicit. I am to *ensure* the destruction of your colony. I must see to it that every person on planet Hallholme is eradicated—just like Theser."

His own bridge crew grumbled uneasily—until now, they hadn't been given the full details of their mission, and Percival felt sickened as he repeated it.

"I can't believe you would follow such reprehensible orders," the General said in disgust. "How will you rewrite the history books to disguise *that*?"

Percival said, in a wooden voice as if to justify himself, "I am bound by the Constellation Charter."

Adolphus stared back, then suddenly brightened as an idea occurred to him. "Then allow me to cite the Constellation Charter, Commodore. If you are truly as loyal as you say, then you know the Charter supercedes any orders from a sitting Diadem. My colony world clearly faces an emergency situation, and you yourself have verified the imminent asteroid impact. Therefore I, Tiber Adolphus, planetary administrator of the Deep Zone planet Hallholme, under Code Seventy-three,

Section Twelve of the Constellation Charter, hereby commandeer your vessels for humanitarian purposes to assist in the emergency evacuation of my colony. By law, you cannot refuse such a request."

The Commodore caught his breath and felt a startled smile spread across his face. This was a loophole he could seize, a way to maintain his honor. "I believe you're right, General. By law, that section of the Charter takes precedence over any new orders I might have received." Yes, he could do this, a perfectly defensible decision. He could add his seventy ships to the effort. It was a dramatic shift. "Very well—under tightly controlled circumstances, we can begin. But I insist on rescuing the Constellation military prisoners first."

The General looked pleased. "We have almost four days. With your help, we just might have enough time."

Percival's sensor operator turned from her screen, puzzled. "Commodore, I don't understand this." She looked down at the long-distance projections, reran her results. "The inbound asteroids . . . something's happened."

"They changed course?"

"No, they're still heading directly toward the planet—but they're *accelerating*!"

66

Even trapped in the remote, demeaning conditions at Slickwater Springs, Michella knew the world was about to end. She had survived a smoke storm, quakes, torpedo ants . . . even the treachery of Ishop Heer! But asteroids were hurtling toward the planet—she could not believe it. She had to get away from here.

Her life had been shattered in many ways ever since the vile General reignited his rebellion. The great Michella Duchenet, Diadem of the Constellation and ruler of seventy-four worlds, was broken and humiliated. If she could believe the General's report, she had been deposed on Sonjeera—and she did not underestimate the ambitions of Selik Riomini. Even her most faithful supporters had failed her. The stream of disappointments tasted like bile inside her.

Commodore Hallholme, the once-great military hero, had failed repeatedly; he'd let her be abducted, then lost his beachhead on Tehila, not to mention his previous defeats. What a fool and an ingrate he was. She had resurrected his career, saved the man from retirement, and given him a purpose in life again—to serve her. She had never expected blunder after blunder from the old warhorse.

But now he had brought a fleet to Hellhole, and he had a chance to redeem himself completely. All would be forgiven if he rescued her now! She might even name another planet after him. . . .

Before dawn, now that the weather had eased and the torpedo ants had been driven back by concerted telemancy, Slickwater Springs sent the first group of evacuees to the Ankor spaceport for departure. The possessed humans proved their continued delusions by refusing to depart, claiming they had to remain on their sacred planet until they achieved some sort of magical ascension.

But Michella needed to leave this awful place, no matter what! Sophie Vence insisted that she would be in the last wave of rescued people, to ensure continued cooperation. The woman acted as if she were Michella's equal, when she was just the General's whore!

She was locked once again in her guarded bungalow,

with two shadow-Xayans stationed outside. She was told to sit, wait, and cause no trouble. Desperate, she had watched from a mesh-glass window, still shuddering as she remembered the sight of the monstrous torpedo ant queen that the converts had brought up out of the ground and incinerated in the air. So many horrors here! Only a few scraps and bones of Ishop Heer had been found in the eradicated underground nest.

Ishop's betrayal shocked her the most. For years she had turned to him, depended on him, and he'd never let her down. He cheerfully accepted the most difficult and bloodiest of assignments. But somehow he'd held a grudge against her. Was it because she denied his absurd claims of ancient nobility? As if a modern Diadem would be bound by the decision from some centuries-old council! She was amazed he could be so stupid. And he had tried to *kill* her! She had seen the expression of pure evil as he trapped her in the room with voracious insects.

Well, he was dead at least. Nothing she needed to worry about any longer—she was far more concerned about getting rescued before the asteroids hit.

Fanatical converts continued to gather around the slickwater pools, as if communing with something. Though she was imprisoned here, Michella knew the possessed humans could drag her out at any moment and throw her into the alien pools. Better to have been killed by Ishop than that!

Michella was sickened to be held so close to the simmering alien contamination. Back on Sonjeera, she had been so afraid about a few possessed representatives that she'd ordered them killed and sealed away rather than let them spread their poison. Yet even that hadn't been enough. She had incinerated half of the Sonjeera spaceport and part of the capital city to prevent the corruption from getting loose. Such a sacrifice she had made, such a difficult decision, but it was necessary. And did the people of the Crown Jewels appreciate the terrible choice she had faced? Her skin still crawled at the thought of those disgusting aliens invading her mind.

And now the roiling source of contamination was right there, only a stone's throw from her prison. What if the insidious presence had leaked into the air, into the water? She caught her breath—maybe Ishop had been infected, possessed! Yes, that would explain his incomprehensible hatred toward her.

Worse, maybe *she* was already infected without knowing it. At this very moment, strange, powerful aliens could be seeping into her tissues, into her mind. . . . She wanted to scream.

Michella closed her eyes, tried to compose herself, and huddled down on the hard chair inside the bungalow. She had never felt so alone. The Constellation had deposed her, Keana had confronted and rejected her, Ishop Heer had betrayed her.

But she knew that Commodore Hallholme was up in orbit, fighting the General. . . . What if he didn't know where Michella was being held? If only she could communicate with him, then he could plan how to rescue her. She could promise him promotions, rewards, other planets to rule.

Michella knew there was a comm room inside the main lodge house. If she made her way there, she could send a message to the Constellation ships in orbit. She could give him the information he needed.

With a critical assessment, she looked at the wrinkled skin on her arms, the red and purple cuts and bites from the torpedo ants. She appeared frail, weak, injured— and that was to her advantage.

Michella Duchenet had ruled for the better part of a

century. She might look like a fragile old woman, and for decades many of the nobles on the Council had been impatiently waiting for her to die. But she was more physically fit than Lord Riomini, thanks to her rigorous daily physical training regimen, guided by the most competent and expert assistants.

What she had never allowed others to know—not even Ishop—was that in addition to physical training, she had been privately instructed in deadly defensive techniques. Despite surrounding herself with guards and security measures, Michella knew that the last line of defense stopped with her. For forty years she'd been trained in how to fight. She was a deadly person, and now a desperate one.

She had one possibility, and she had to take the chance. Letting out a loud groan, she pounded on the door. "I am growing ill. Those insect bites are poisonous. I'm having a reaction." She had already seen and assessed the two guards standing outside. She didn't know the extent of their alien powers, but could see that they were physically human. Their bodies had the same vulnerable points that she knew how to strike. She loathed the idea of touching them, but had no choice now.

A Diadem had to be decisive, and ruthless.

As they opened the door, Michella moved in a blur of speed, burning through her fear, using almost every scrap of energy she had. Her nails were long and sharp, trimmed to a razor's edge. Her knuckles were hard and bony.

She slashed across the eyes of the first man, then whirled to the second one, driving a hard punch into his larynx. As he clutched at his throat, she spun back to the first guard with a hard chopping blow to the base of his neck, then followed through with a pummeling fist on the thin bone of his temple.

As the man fell, still clutching at his oozing eye, she used her momentum to slam the second guard onto the floor. She stomped on his neck with her heel, crushing his spine. She delivered another front kick to the fallen first guard, striking him in the head and completing the job there. Both were dead in seconds.

There! She stood over their corpses, heaving great breaths, her heart pounding, but she was confident her body could take the exertion. Several scabs had broken open and were bleeding, but Michella ignored them. She couldn't afford to hesitate. Move faster, get a message to the Commodore, order a rescue.

She hauled both dead guards through the door into the bungalow so neither body would be seen. She searched their uniforms; though she loathed to touch their contaminated bodies, she needed the weapons. She relieved each man of a stun pistol, which she intended to put to good use.

Michella was even more pleased to see that the stunners also had a kill setting. No point in taking half-measures. Every person here had committed treason and deserved to be executed by the law of the Constellation. She was fully aware that under no circumstances would she be allowed to live if she were captured. Well, if she failed now, she would at least take out as many of them as she could.

Michella slipped out of the bungalow, closing the door so that it appeared to be secure, and darted away.

Slickwater Springs was busy with shadow-Xayans frantically immersing themselves in the strange water before the asteroids came, as if that could save them or their planet. Other unconverted humans were preparing to be shipped off to the spaceports. She ducked behind the bungalow and ran toward the main lodge. She knew where the comm room was.

Dressed in drab clothes, Michella moved as if she knew what she was doing and where she was going. For a few minutes at least, the old woman blended in so that others didn't give her a second glance—not at first. She only needed to maintain the illusion until she got inside the main lodge.

Just after she slipped in through a side entrance, two shadow-Xayans walked past her down a hallway, moving with intent expressions before turning into a larger briefing chamber. They paid no attention to Michella at all. When they turned a corner, she sprinted toward the communication chamber.

She had hoped to find it empty, but a man sat inside wearing a typical garment favored by shadow-Xayan converts, made from a fabric of processed red weed. He had a stiff military bearing, and she recognized him as Peter Herald, the first possessed man she and Ishop had met when they were delivered here to Slickwater Springs. He had just returned to join the shadow-Xayans after helping the General recapture the stringline hub from the incompetent George Komun.

Herald looked up when she rushed into the chamber. He saw her—and, unfortunately, he recognized her immediately. When the man rose from his chair, instead of shouting an alarm, his eyes narrowed, and she felt a sudden invisible lurch of telemancy reach out to her.

The psychic touch horrified her, like the slimy tongue of a demon caressing her face. Fighting it, she ripped out one of the stun pistols and fired at him without even aiming. The energy blast struck the man, too fast for him to respond with his alien defenses. He crumpled, falling onto the desk and then sliding to the floor.

Michella stepped up to the man, pointed the energy pistol again, and fired a long barrage on the kill setting, until she smelled burned flesh and singed fabric. She hoped it would be sufficient to neutralize the alien inside him. When the fallen man didn't move, she put the pistol away and rushed to the comm set. She didn't have much time!

Reality began to set in, though. She knew how to broadcast on the general military frequency, but did not recall the specific channel that would let her communicate privately with Commodore Hallholme. Everyone would hear her transmission demanding a rescue. Everyone would know where she was.

So be it.

She activated the comm. "This is Diadem Michella Duchenet calling Commodore Hallholme. Commodore, can you hear me? I've been taken prisoner. I am being held at this location. Send a rescue squad immediately."

After a moment, he appeared on the screen. "I hear you, Eminence, but I am preoccupied at the moment."

"Then assign a portion of your troops to come down and retrieve me! Follow these coordinates. Time is of the essence." She provided details of her location.

"I'm afraid that won't be possible, Eminence. Those are not my orders."

"I'm giving you different orders, Commodore! *I* am your Diadem—I command you to send a squadron to Slickwater Springs, take me to safety, and obliterate this place!"

On the screen, the Commodore seemed weary, and actually looked *annoyed* with her! "You no longer give the orders, Michella Duchenet. You are no longer Diadem. I am currently bound by emergency aid provisions from the Constellation Charter, and outside that I am operating under instructions from the duly-elected Diadem Selik Riomini. He gave explicit instructions that you should be left there to die, and his orders supersede yours."

She seethed. "I know you, Percival Hallholme. You are loyal and moral, you would never leave me to die."

He seemed to consider that, then said, "I do find the orders objectionable. I don't consider Diadem Riomini to be a particularly honorable person, but I could say the same about you. Your previous decisions have left me, the Deep Zone, and the entire Constellation in a precarious position. I have to find the best legal and moral course between two rocky shores."

She was astonished by his insubordinate manner; she had never heard him speak like that. Yet before she could reply, he continued. "First, I have to arrange for the evacuation of all the Constellation soldiers being held prisoner. After I complete that mission, I can consider secondary matters, such as yourself."

Abruptly, he terminated the transmission, and she stared at the blank screen in shock. She was speechless, unable to comprehend what had just happened. And she had no one there to speak to except the dead body of Peter Herald.

Shouts rang out from the corridor of the lodge building. Someone tried to open the locked door of the comm chamber. She heard rising voices outside, closing in.

Michella was trapped.

67

When Sophie discovered the dead guards in Michella's bungalow, she immediately felt anger mixed with sick dread. She couldn't imagine how the disarmingly thin and frail woman could have bested two shadow-Xayan guards, but the old bitch already had so much blood on her hands, what did two more murders matter to her?

She sounded the alarm around Slickwater Springs and called on the shadow-Xayans to help. Only about fifty nonconverts remained, after the first groups had been evacuated to the spaceports, but in the middle of the crisis she couldn't let Michella cause any delays. And the former Diadem needed to be held accountable for the crimes she had just committed.

The shadow-Xayans cast a web with their thoughts, searching the area with swift efficiency. Though they had paid little attention to the old woman at the time, many of the converts had still seen her. A female shadow-Xayan responded to Sophie. "According to our memory records, Michella Duchenet slipped across the compound, masquerading as a potential convert. Someone saw her enter the main lodge house. She is still there."

Another convert stepped up. "Yes, she is inside the building. We can no longer sense Peter-Arnex, though. He was inside the lodge's comm-center."

Sophie called upon the shadow-Xayans to help, and a group responded to her summons. "To the main lodge."

Alarms sounded, primarily to keep the normal humans alert, but now that the shadow-Xayans had focused their attentions, they were better than any alarm system.

Sophie knew that Adolphus would not want his hostage harmed, but what good was the old deposed woman as a bargaining chip anyway? The Commodore's son would have been more useful . . . but Escobar Hallholme was still lost out in the Hellhole wilderness, due to his own stupidity. Cristoph de Carre had spent days searching for him and the other missing prisoners, but with the desperate evacuation under way, the search was being called off. Sophie believed those four fools were dead anyway.

Accompanied by five others, Sophie rushed into the main lodge house and hurried down the corridors to the sealed comm-center. She guessed that Michella would try to call for help, but Commodore Hallholme was already assisting the General in the evacuation; she doubted he would be amenable to mounting a rescue.

Sophie pounded on the locked comm-center door, shouted for the old woman to surrender, but heard no response. She turned to the shadow-Xayans. "Break it down. We need to place her back under control."

Instead of smashing the door with a burst of telemancy, they manipulated the locks and opened the door. Inside, to her dismay, Sophie saw Peter Herald lying dead, his eyes glassy, his garments singed from the kill setting on the stolen energy weapon.

A small window on the far side of the room was open, leading out into the compound.

The shadow-Xayans mentally communicated to their fellows, rallying them to search the crowds for Michella. The converts were a different sort of security—with their combined observation, they easily found Michella and began to box her in, moving her toward the boardwalk and the slickwater pools.

Sophie raced outside the main lodge house, with the shadow-Xayans behind her. Seeing the terrified old woman, Sophie pushed through the shadow-Xayans to reach her. "The General wants us to take her alive!"

"Perhaps she wishes to join us in the slickwater," said one of the converts. "All are welcome. All are needed— now, more than ever."

Her eyes wild, Michella tried to flee, but the shadow-Xayans kept pressing her toward the boardwalks until she had nowhere else to go. Her face was drawn back in an expression of terror, and she was bleeding from dozens of small cuts and bites. Sophie thought Michella Duchenet looked broken and battered, at the end of her rope.

"Stop!" Sophie called to the shadow-Xayans, and they remained where they were. "Take her alive if possible."

Cornered, Michella drew two stun pistols. In unison, the shadow-Xayans flinched, then concentrated—and the weapons began to smolder in Michella's hands. With a yelp of pain, she flung them away, useless.

Sophie stepped forward, knowing she was in control. More converts had climbed out of the pools to stand on the well-traveled boardwalks. The mirrorlike quicksilver ponds shimmered under the cloud-streaked sky.

Michella stood there, isolated and alone.

Sophie said, "You killed three good people today, added to the hundreds of thousands whose lives you cost since the beginning of this rebellion." *Including my own son!*

"Millions," the Diadem admitted with an arrogant smile. "It's the cost of ruling an empire full of cowards and scofflaws."

Sophie stepped closer. "I don't know what sort of pardons or hostage exchanges you think you'll be part of, but if the asteroids don't kill us all, you'll stand trial and pay for the murders you committed today."

The old woman was poised, tense. When the converts pressed closer, she launched herself into Sophie with enough force to propel both of them off the edge of the boardwalk toward the slickwater.

Sophie cried out in midair. She had avoided conversion for so long, refusing to join the shadow-Xayans, and now she would be changed forever. She would lose Tiber Adolphus!

Then she realized that not only had time frozen, but her body hung suspended in the air, cradled in the palm of an invisible hand.

Michella clawed at Sophie's arms, her sleeves, but she couldn't hold on. With a despairing cry that was abruptly cut short, the old Diadem dropped into the slickwater pool and sank with barely a ripple.

Astonished, Sophie found herself still suspended in the air, barely a meter above the quicksilver surface. She felt sure the shadow-Xayans would lose their grip on her, because they longed to have Sophie join them . . . but then she was pulled back through the air and gently deposited on the boardwalk.

The shadow-Xayans came toward her. "Are you unharmed?" asked one man.

"Ruffled . . . embarrassed." Sophie brushed herself off. She was breathing hard, caught her breath. "Thank you. That was unexpected, and very much appreciated." She turned to look at the pool, but saw no sign of Michella.

A shadow-Xayan said, "We don't want you with us by force or by accident."

Then Michella Duchenet rose from the glistening ooze and floated on top, faceup. The alien liquid drained from her matted gray hair. Her skin, which had been covered with cuts and scabs, now looked healed, intact. Even the wrinkles seemed smoother than before.

Sophie had a sudden fearful thought. The old Diadem was evil enough on her own—what would happen if she gained telemancy powers? What if she bonded with a weaker Xayan personality? What if this accident had just created something far worse?

But Michella did not move. Other shadow-Xayans went into the pool to lift her out. Her expression remained blank, but her eyes flickered, just a little. Her arms didn't twitch or offer any assistance as the converts lifted her out and laid her on the boardwalk. The last trails of slickwater dripped off her body and returned to the pool.

Michella lay there like a vegetable, moving just barely enough to show she was still alive, but lost to the world. One of the shadow-Xayans said, "Her memories and personality were erased . . . and replaced by nothing else."

The crowded converts looked with dismay from the old woman to Sophie. "She is not one of us," said a man. "No Xayan personality would accept her."

Sophie tried to understand. "But she is still alive."

The shadow-Xayans remained silent, until an older man said in an emotionless tone, "She is *nothing*."

68

The Ro-Xayan asteroid habitat was marvelous, an alien wonderland filled with mind-boggling sights—but Keana knew it was all doomed.

Overhead, swirls of telemancy-inspired breezes caught droplets of condensed moisture in the center of the hollow asteroid, forming meteorological patterns and sending sparkles of multicolored rain that caught prismatic light. Flying creatures drifted around like predators, hunting the raindrops. Keana saw wafting bladders of the lush red weed break off and float apart to seed other sections of the asteroid interior, while larger animals moved along grassy sections of the curvature to graze.

The poignantly preserved ecosystem was a gluttony of colors, smells, and sensations, all bizarre and wondrous to her. Inside Keana's mind, Uroa identified the sights from memories of his original life. He longed to have a pristine Xaya back, and mourned at how it had been lost in the first place.

"All of Xaya was once like this, before they destroyed it," said his voice inside her head. "We had a beautiful, peaceful world, a superior civilization . . . until these murderers took it all away. And now they mean to do so again."

Keana was strong enough now to maintain control. "You gave me strength and made me a powerful person I never imagined I could be, Uroa—but you also lied to me, concealing the truth so that I would cooperate with you, so that I wouldn't warn the other shadow-Xayans. You *knew* how dangerous *ala'ru* would be!"

"I knew about our destiny," Uroa said. "And you and thousands of other human converts would acompany us as our partners, a select group who will ascend." He seemed to be searching in her mind. "Let me draw from your own references: Does a caterpillar mourn the loss when it sheds its clumsy old husk and emerges from a chrysalis to become a butterfly?"

"A hatching chrysalis doesn't destroy the universe," Keana said. "*Ala'ru* will."

"The Ro-Xayans do not know that for certain," Uroa countered. "They are unnecessarily fearful."

She pressed him, dug into his thoughts, experienced his feelings. Once the old memories opened, he could not prevent her from delving into all aspects of his past. And she was astonished by what she learned.

The old Xayan leaders—Zairic, Encix, Uroa—had told their own people only part of the story: that they would be transformed into gods as part of their destiny. But the inner-circle members knew that the ascension would unravel the tapestry of the cosmos, rewriting physical laws and universal constants. And still they considered the cost worthwhile. As far as they were concerned, the Xayan race would ascend, no matter what harm it did to the universe.

Now, Ian Walfor stepped toward the gathered Ro-Xayans. "You seized our ship with your telemancy, drew us in here—to what purpose? Are we your prisoners, or are we free to leave?"

"We were curious about you," Zhaday said. "We could not understand how the other faction survived, how they were growing powerful again. Now we do." The alien leader swiveled his eerie gaze back and forth, encompassing the visitors. "It all ends within days—for every one of us. If we let you depart this asteroid, where would you go?"

"Back to our own people," Tanja said, "to help evacuate the planet! Just because you wish to annihilate your own race doesn't mean that all humans on the planet have to die in the bombardment, too."

Zhaday said, "The shadow-Xayans must remain behind. They are forfeit."

Lodo had been silent, as if reticent, perhaps even feeling guilty for what he had hidden from everyone. Keana sensed waves of uncertainty emanating from him. "Encix and I are the only two Originals still alive from centuries ago, and I remember the initial debates and leadership decisions. Zhaday, you look at this from a perspective of centuries after the disaster. You Ro-Xayans can feel smug in your accomplishments, but you don't understand what it was like for us."

"You are Lodo," Zhaday said. "My people remember you in the stories from those days. You were an outspoken voice at the time. You raised concerns about *ala'ru*, yet you still joined that faction."

"Zairic could be very persuasive," Lodo said, with what sounded like a trace of resigned amusement. "I had doubts, and I hesitated before choosing one faction or the other. But the Ro-Xayans' merciless demand to eliminate everything pushed me to side with Zairic. By joining them, I hoped that I could guide *ala'ru* to a better destiny than your faction envisioned." He bent his stalk neck, and emotional turmoil boiled off him in waves. "Perhaps I should have made a different decision and let the Ro-Xayans kill us all and wipe out our civilization in the first place."

"You can't mean that!" Keana said, and realized she was being influenced by Uroa, who was offended within her.

Lodo turned to stare at her. "It is true. If I had prevented Zairic from preserving so many of us in slick-water, our faction would have been wiped out, and now the Ro-Xayans could be returning to seed the planet with all the life-forms they saved. They could resettle the world, rebuild Xayan civilization. But because I made the wrong decision, it will all be gone." He turned toward Zhaday, drew himself up, and opened his arms as if to embrace the lost memories of a pristine world. "You all should know and understand the last moments of Xaya. Let me give my substance to you, all my memories, all that I am. You deserve to have that before the end."

The Ro-Xayans had emerged from their oddly shaped dwelling structures, and all were connected by telemancy, participating in the discussion. The nearest ones backed away from Lodo as he stood, his head tilted upward. Thrumming came from his facial membrane. "Take my memories. Understand more deeply. Be a part of *me*, and I will join you."

Zhaday asked, "You wish to become a Ro-Xayan now?"

"No, it is too late for that. But I wish to share with

you. A memory lasts only as long as it is preserved and transmitted from one mind to another. Though you only have a few days left, it is better for you to understand before it all goes."

Keana couldn't comprehend what Lodo intended to do, but Uroa did. He was horrified, and spoke through Keana's voice. "You must stop! Do not give the enemy faction information they can use against us."

Lodo turned to Keana-Uroa. "Use against us? The four of us came here on a mission in hopes that we could make the Ro-Xayans understand. Instead, they made *us* understand. Our faction was wrong."

"You can't change anything by this," Uroa said.

"Change can be, in itself, an accomplishment." Lodo moved forward on his caterpillar body toward the Ro-Xayans. "In those last days, as the asteroid came toward Xaya, I chose not to go into the slickwater, but to remain in my physical body. Now I relinquish my essence, my memories, my life. Take them . . . use them as you will."

Zhaday and dozens of Ro-Xayans crowded forward, their soft bodies undulating, antenna-feelers extended, soft arms reaching out, probing with flexible fingertips, touching Lodo's skin. He squirmed but did not recoil. The Ro-Xayans pressed closer, covering him.

And then Keana saw the Original alien begin to slump, soften . . . and *dissolve*. Lodo didn't struggle or make any outcry, and the Ro-Xayans drained him, pulling away his essence and absorbing it into themselves. He diminished, became shapeless, and more Ro-Xayans came forward to partake, touching what remained of him, gathering his cells, memories, and energy. When they finally drew back, no visible speck remained of Lodo, no mark, stain, or residue. They had taken everything of him, even his husk.

Now Zhaday drew himself up, and his eyes had a different sparkling sheen. Uroa was sickened and angry inside Keana, and she understood what her mental companion feared.

Zhaday said, "Encix and the shadow-Xayans are much closer to ascension than we expected. She intends to force the conversion of thousands more shadow-Xayans in order to attain the numbers she needs. We will not have time to stop it."

Inside her mind, Keana felt Uroa's surge of triumph. She said in a thought, "But the humans who enter the slickwater have to be *volunteers*!" Now, however, she understood that was merely a weak fiction. In desperation, Encix would break the agreement.

Uroa responded, "It is our only chance. We must achieve *ala'ru* before the asteroids strike!"

Keana felt a strange resignation from Uroa's presence, as if he, too, had doubts about the ascension because he now understood something of human civilization. Sharing her mind, he had experienced memories of other planets and people, which was only the barest hint of what the Galaxy had to offer. There were countless other galaxies, clusters, and superclusters of them . . . all of which would be eradicated if *ala'ru* reset the structure of universal physics.

She asserted control of her body. "Listen to me, Zhaday. The shadow-Xayans don't understand what they're trying to do. Encix lied to them. Even I didn't know until just now. Our ship is fast—let us go back there, so I can speak to all the converts and convince them not to proceed. They will listen to me, and maybe I can delay them long enough. The shadow-Xayans deserve a chance. Let me talk with them."

Uroa's voice spoke, in an odd counterpoint out her

own throat. "You aren't strong enough to defeat Encix. You can't drive her back."

"I've fought her before," Keana said. "My telemancy is great, and it's been growing stronger. I can fight Encix—and I can prevent you from intervening. It might just be enough to stop this disaster."

Walfor spoke up. "My ship can fly a lot faster than these asteroids. We will get back to Hellhole in a few hours. It might work."

The Ro-Xayans pondered with a telepathic hum, and Zhaday finally said, "We must grasp at any possibility. We can increase your chances, Keana-Uroa. With the knowledge and power Lodo just gave us, we know ways that you may be able to fight against a powerful Xayan opponent . . . and our faction has knowledge and powers to share. It may be enough for you to defeat Encix and convince the other converts to delay *ala'ru* . . . long enough for the asteroids to strike."

Tanja scowled. "That's an odd way to define victory."

Keana froze. She could no longer move, held in the telemancy grasp. Zhaday came forward, as did other Ro-Xayans, reaching out, touching her face, neck, arms, shoulders . . . it was a flurry of strange alien limbs, contact points that were each like an electrode. She feared they were going to drain her, absorb Uroa, as they had done with Lodo. Inside her mind, she could sense that he was frightened and intimidated.

But the flow went in the opposite direction. She felt a surge like lightning enter through every pore. Her mind filled with other lives and ideas, with a much more comprehensive understanding of telemancy and all of its applications, a grasp of tiny, subatomic nuances. She felt supercharged and in control of the shared body. Her eyes opened wide; she could barely breathe. Zhaday and the others drew back and left her to encompass more telemancy than she ever dreamed possible.

"We transferred what we could," Zhaday said. "Now you must use it."

Keana turned, feeling an urgency as tremendous as the power she now held. But she was deeply troubled. "If I can stop *ala'ru*, will you divert the asteroids so they don't hit the planet?"

"That is not possible, even if we wanted to. With the mass and momentum of the twenty asteroids, even all of our combined telemancy would not be sufficient. The impacts *will* occur. You cannot save the planet. But you can save the universe—if you move quickly enough."

Keana couldn't believe there was no hope, but she didn't argue with Zhaday. But if she could indeed stop Encix and *ala'ru*, she did not intend to stand idly by.

"To the ship," Keana said.

Tanja and Walfor were already running back to the landing grotto in the strange hollow enclosure.

69

Cristoph de Carre's search craft returned from the wilderness in the early morning just as another static storm was building over the line of hills. The sturdy craft had skirted the storm all night. Cristoph had transmitted several urgent messages, announcing that he had a severely wounded passenger, but his transmissions were garbled with static before he could give details. The weather continued to be capricious and uncooperative, as if to further hinder the evacuation efforts.

When the craft landed outside of Slickwater Springs

just after the debacle with Michella Duchenet, Sophie Vence went out in a roller to meet him. The storm sent crackles and pops through the comm line, and Sophie was practically within shouting distance before she could understand what Cristoph was saying. "We found the escaped prisoners—only two survivors. I have Escobar Hallholme, but he's barely alive."

Sophie knew about General Adolphus's standoff and uneasy cooperation with the Commodore. If the man's son died, that shaky alliance might fall apart.

"Bolton Crais is with us, too. He says the Redcom's only hope is the slickwater."

Sophie's heart sank, not sure whether Commodore Hallholme would prefer his son dead or possessed by alien memories. And after what had just happened to Michella . . .

Her roller reached the landed craft as Cristoph and his team were climbing out. Major Crais also emerged, looking drawn and stunned. His clothes were tattered. He watched with deep concern as two of Cristoph's men carried a prone figure wrapped in a cocoon of red weed; it looked like a body. Escobar Hallholme?

Sophie gestured to the roller. "Put him in the cargo bed, and I'll take him to the pools. If you're sure the slickwater is the only way."

Bolton swallowed. "I've had days to think of other possibilities. He'll be dead soon if we don't take extraordinary measures."

Escobar's face remained exposed, and she despised the arrogant and impetuous Constellation commander who had gotten his fleet into so much trouble. He looked older and haggard now, resembling his legendary father more than before. "What happened to him?"

Bolton helped carry the wrapped body. "This planet happened to him."

They placed the dying man on the back of the all-terrain roller; as soon as Bolton joined her in front, she raced the vehicle toward the boardwalks and the slick-water pools. Cristoph and his team secured the aircraft as the static storm dissipated, skirting Slickwater Springs.

As she drove, Bolton reached back and fussed over Escobar in the back of the vehicle. "He's still alive—just barely. The tiniest sign of a pulse. I doubt he'll last long after we remove the red weed. It has only just managed to keep him alive."

Sophie made no comment, racing along. She had no particular incentive to save him. She resented what Escobar was responsible for. Devon . . . Sophie's heart ached for her son. It seemed *wrong* that she was now rushing to save Escobar Hallholme's life. But he was a valuable prisoner, and Adolphus needed him alive.

The shadow-Xayans parted to allow the roller to the edge of the pools, and then they gathered close again. The distant static storm sent strobe flares into the atmosphere, and as the sky darkened, the building lights in Slickwater Springs went on.

Quiet converts used telemancy to carry the body toward the edge of the enticing pools. "The red weed slowed his metabolism," said a young shadow-Xayan woman who had a very old and wise Xayan presence in her mind. "The slickwater will heal him."

Bolton hurried alongside his companion. "This is our best chance. We've lost so much, but maybe we can save him."

"One person." Sophie knew that tens of thousands would surely die, those who couldn't escape the planet swiftly enough, thanks to the evacuation delays.

"One person," he agreed. "My friend."

The converts rushed the weed-wrapped body along the boardwalks and waded into the silvery lake, settling the reddish cocoon into the water and immersing the motionless human form. Holding him up, they peeled away the hardened fronds to let the memory-charged liquid seep through and begin its work. They immersed Escobar's entire body beneath the surface.

Bolton stood next to Sophie, concerned as he scanned the faces of the converts. "Is Keana here?"

"No, she's gone on a liaison mission to find the Ro-Xayans. She hopes she can make them change the asteroids' trajectories."

His eyes widened with fear for her. "Keana! Isn't that dangerous?"

"Everything is dangerous, Major Crais."

He looked up at the crowd of shadow-Xayans gathered on the boardwalk and watching the pool. He gasped when he spotted an old woman sitting silent and motionless nearby—Michella Duchenet, blank-eyed. She paid no attention to the others moving around her. "The Diadem! What happened—"

Sophie told him, "She's been drained of her thoughts and soul."

At the pool, the shadow-Xayans pulled the Redcom's form out of the silvery slickwater, suddenly demanding Bolton's attention. Escobar Hallholme looked intact, refreshed, and alive. His eyes had the peculiar starry sheen of the shadow-Xayans, yet he was alert, drinking in details. Sophie let Bolton go forward as they guided him up onto the boardwalk. The Redcom stood, catching his balance as the last drops fell away and ran back into the pool. He drew a deep breath, extended his arms, flexed them.

Bolton stared. "Escobar, are you all right?"

"I am Escobar," he said, but his voice had a deep, thrumming timbre. "And I am also Tarcov. We are both aware now. We are both strong."

Sophie felt relieved that he was alive at least, although she couldn't guess how the Commodore would react. "Come, we have to let your father know. We don't have much time."

When they entered the main lodge building, Sophie hurried them to the comm chamber. She had much to tell General Adolphus—not just the rescue of the two escaped prisoners, but also how Michella Duchenet had killed three people, including Peter Herald, before losing her mind in the slickwater.

After securing his search craft, Cristoph had already gone into the comm chamber. He looked up at her. "Now we can devote the ships to shuttling people to the spaceports. I'm checking with Ankor. They must be more overwhelmed than ever, and I doubt if Rendo Theris can handle it."

When Cristoph hailed the spaceport, Theris looked even more harried than usual. Inside the Ankor headquarters building, the background noise was a clamor. Hundreds of people were crowded inside. "Mr. Theris, please give us an update."

"Update? Even I don't know what's going on! The General and the Commodore are cooperating now, and we've been given the go-ahead to resume evacuation launches, but I've got thousands of people crowded around the spaceport. I can't launch ships fast enough to make a dent in all these refugees. And when do *I* get to depart?"

Cristoph looked at Sophie, then back to the screen. "That's a question many of us are asking. Launch as many shuttles as you can, and I'll be there within hours to assist."

Theris seemed relieved to know he would have help. "I don't know how to set priorities, can't fit all these people in the vessels here, and we're still waiting for shuttles to come down from orbit, where they've been stalled for half a day. We don't have the fuel supplies we're going to need, and . . . and what about the hundreds of shadow-Xayans? They're gathered by the slickwater seeps, which are now encroaching on our landing areas. We're already crowded past maximum, and the people are ready to riot."

Cristoph looked at Sophie. "I have to go, right away."

On the screen, the spaceport headquarters suddenly became an even louder and more clamorous uproar. People rushed into the control room, scrambling toward the administrator. "The ground is cracking outside. A gantry just collapsed—and there's slickwater everywhere. We're flooding!"

On-screen, the launch headquarters began to shake. Debris fell from the ceiling. Rendo Theris yelled—and then all contact broke off.

Though Cristoph tried to raise them several more times, he got nothing more than a dead signal.

"Go," Sophie said to him. "*Now*. Without Ankor we lose half of our evacuation facilities."

Ignoring remnants of the static storm, Cristoph ran back out to his scout flyer.

70

Though the soldiers aboard the Constellation ships were trained to follow their Commodore's orders without question, they were confused and uneasy to be helping the rebel vessels in the evacuation.

The redcom of a large battleship transmitted over an open channel, angry at Percival. "Sir, our orders are to *level* the colony on planet Hallholme—not rescue them!

Diadem Riomini's instructions were explicit: each spaceport, colony city, and settlement is to be left a smoking ruin. I was with the Black Lord at his victory on Theser, so I know that he intended this to be a punitive strike. Why are you trying to save these criminals?"

Percival was furious at the defiant tone of the officer's voice, but knew this needed to be said. "I was not at Theser, Redcom. If I had been, the results might have been different. Our civilization is built on a foundation of laws that are not to be discarded because of temper tantrums."

"But sir! Diadem Riomini explicitly—"

Percival interrupted. "The Constellation Charter was in place long before Lord Riomini took the Star Throne, and it will be there long after he is gone."

The old Commodore knew how dangerous his words were, but his fleet was far from Sonjeera and in the midst of a crisis. He was in charge of the operations here. "The law is clear, and I am ashamed that General Adolphus had to remind me of it: We *must* provide humanitarian aid in the face of a natural disaster. If you choose to open fire on civilian refugees, or their military leader who has already given me his de facto surrender, then I will relieve you of command and arrest you on charges of war crimes, barratry at the very least, and deal with you appropriately."

Percival made sure his broadcast was heard across the entire fleet. That quieted the objections—for now.

He looked at the estimated arrival time of the accelerated planet-killer asteroids. Only two days. Because the people of Hellhole were even more independent than the colonists on most DZ worlds, they weren't confined in neat cities, nor were they traceable by a census. The evacuation effort would simply have to lift off as many as possible, shuttle load after shuttle load. They would do what they could, focusing on the numbers they rescued rather than the ones they lost.

As the operations continued, he received a surprise message. "Commodore, there's a diplomatic drone coming in on the stringline from Umber. Someone's in a hurry to get a message to you."

"Intercept the drone and bring the message to me. I'll view it privately." He wasn't sure he even wanted Duff Adkins to accompany him. He gave an imperceptible shake of his head as he rose from the command chair. "Mr. Adkins, take the bridge."

In less than fifteen minutes, the drone had been brought aboard the flagship and its message transmitted along a secure channel to the private screen in the Commodore's ready room. Diadem Riomini's face filled the screen. The man looked both angry and immensely pleased, as if the anger itself brought him joy.

"Commodore, by now you will have secured the rebel stringline hub and control access to the entire Deep Zone. Time to consider the next phase. I don't have to tell you this is a tumultuous time for the Constellation. Dissidents are like hyenas, sensing weakness, and they attack everywhere. We have no choice but to react sternly for the stability of the Crown Jewels as well as the Deep Zone. That is the only way we'll stop the turmoil.

"For far too long, the Constellation festered at its core and crumbled on the outer edges. History will remember me as the Diadem who rebuilt our empire and saved us from the brink of disaster." He smiled. "I send you these inspirational images to show justice being meted out against rebel saboteurs, for you may find them useful if you encounter intractable Deezees."

Percival's eyes widened as shocking images filled the screen. The Diadem's voice continued. "You delivered the Buktu prisoners to Vielinger, but they committed sabotage, destroyed part of my iperion mines. Thus, as enemy combatants, they were punished accordingly."

Percival wanted to shield his eyes but couldn't tear his gaze away. He had taken those captives under the accepted rules of war, given his word that they would be treated accordingly and would be released once hostilities ended.

Now he watched the new Diadem and his guards gunning down scores of them. They screamed and tried to flee, but had no chance. After every single one was slaughtered, Riomini and his guards turned to face the imagers with grins on their faces, not noticing the blood spatters on their skin and clothing.

Percival felt sickened. He had promised them safety—and they had trusted him.

"Obviously, killing a few prisoners won't be enough," the new Diadem continued. "Capturing General Adolphus will not be enough. Even eradicating the population of his planet will not be enough—it is just a start.

"The rot goes deeper, Commodore. It has tainted all those colonists who think they can thumb their noses at us. We can't take time to sort out the few innocent ones. Once you've sterilized planet Hallholme, I'm afraid your mission will be long and hard, but I can trust no one but you. In order for the Constellation to flourish again, we need a clean slate. It'll be like the Ridgetop Recovery slaughter, but across the entire Deep Zone. I command you to take your fleet and lead a purge from world to world. I doubt any of the populations will give you much trouble. Afterward, the pristine planets will be ripe for repopulation, and with the crowded conditions in the Crown Jewels, we will be able to find plenty of *loyal* volunteers to repopulate them."

Riomini gave a hard smile as he leaned closer to the

imager. "I know I can count on you, Commodore Hallholme. I look forward to regular progress reports."

The message ended. Percival stared in dismay at the blank screen. Life meant nothing to that man, just as life had meant nothing to Diadem Michella Duchenet. The more Percival thought about it, the more he realized that General Tiber Adolphus, his sworn enemy, was the only man who seemed to think correctly, who mapped out a respectable course and stuck to it, considering his people first, his career and political power second.

Shaking with rage and disgust from the orders, Percival considered simply ignoring Diadem Riomini's hateful commands. Sooner or later, however, someone else would receive duplicate orders and relieve him of command—someone who would not hesitate to do as the Black Lord instructed. He could not stomach this abomination.

Before Percival could decide what to do, the comm officer contacted him. "Commodore, there's a message from the surface! You'll want to hear it."

After what he had just experienced, Percival thought of few messages he actually *wanted* to hear. "Send it to my screen."

Then he stared in amazement, overwhelmed with relief to see a direct call from Major Bolton Crais—and Escobar! "Commodore, the General asked us to communicate with you," Bolton said.

"Escobar! You are alive after all."

His son looked somewhat thin but uninjured—though he seemed to have a wan and distant expression on his face, and he averted his eyes. Strangely, he let Crais do the talking.

"We survived an ordeal on the planet's surface, Commodore, but it was of our own making. Thousands of us were kept in a large holding camp, where conditions are as good as can be expected. But we are stuck on the surface, and we need to be evacuated as soon as possible. The General says that since you are cooperating, he'll let you send your ships to retrieve the POWs. We will give you coordinates for the camp near Slickwater Springs."

Although Major Crais kept speaking, Percival could only stare at his son. "Escobar, are you all right?"

Escobar turned to face the imager. "Yes, Father. I have survived an ordeal, and I am . . . more than I was before."

"What do you mean?"

Bolton Crais seemed uneasy. "Let me explain, Commodore—" He hesitated, cleared his throat.

Escobar looked into the screen, and now Percival could see that his eyes were changed, with a faint spiral around the irises.

"This is for me to tell, Father. I have made mistakes, poor leadership choices that led to many deaths. I got two of my comrades killed who escaped with me and Major Crais from the camp. I was injured, near death . . . but the Xayans saved me. Their slickwater pools prevented me from dying."

Bolton broke in. "We tried to escape, Commodore, but didn't have a workable plan, and soon were lost in a dangerous landscape. When we were attacked by native predators, Escobar fought to save me—and he was mortally wounded in the process. Slickwater brought him back from the brink of death. It was the only way to save him."

Percival tried to absorb the information, remembered how much Diadem Michella had feared something like this. Alien contamination? Possession by another strange personality?

Escobar said, "I have an alien companion inside my mind, Father. I am still your son, but I am also more than that. I am Escobar-Tarcov . . . and I tell you this is not just a planetary evacuation. We have to preserve this precious alien race and not let it be obliterated by the asteroids."

Percival felt a lump in his throat. "I'll send ships down to evacuate you."

"Send as many as possible," Escobar urged. "We have to help the Xayans achieve *ala'ru*. We have almost no time left."

Bolton glanced at Escobar, who appeared perplexed by his comment, but Escobar cut off the transmission.

Percival rose from his desk, his thoughts whirling. This was the last nudge to his own epiphany. He could not do what Diadem Riomini commanded. He could not serve such a ruthless and bloodthirsty leader, could not make another fatally bad decision, another one that would fester within him for the rest of his life. And he believed that most of his own followers had a core of humanity within them. He had to believe that, and now he had to make that gamble.

He strode onto the bridge, feeling fresh determination. Yes, he knew what he had to do.

The crew was in a flurry as the evacuation continued, with Duff Adkins snapping instructions to one station after another. Seeing him, Adkins sprang out of the command chair, relinquishing the role to Percival. "Commodore, we just lost all contact with the Ankor spaceport . . . and there appear to be riots in Michella Town."

Percival wasn't surprised that panic had begun to set in down there. "They're hindering their own evacuation efforts. Proceed with all possible speed." He sank heavily into the command chair.

Adkins stepped up to him. "What was the message, Commodore? Did Diadem Riomini issue new orders?"

"He did, Duff. I do not, however, intend to obey them. I hope you will support me."

The adjutant's eyes widened. "That goes without saying, Commodore."

"Good," Percival said, "because I cannot stomach what the Constellation has become or what the Diadem demands of us. I'm betting that most of my crew will feel the same."

Percival cued up the damning message the Black Lord had transmitted, the unspeakable orders that blithely commanded the absolute massacre of more than fifty planets. Knowing he was about to plunge off a precipice, he broadcast the message for all the vessels in his fleet to hear, along with the DZDF ships.

At the end of Riomini's appalling message, Percival spoke firmly. "We are not going to follow those orders, because if we did, we would be mass murderers and war criminals, not professional soldiers. It *will not happen* under my command, and I do not intend to resign."

He paused for a long moment, then added, "Honor is like a crystal goblet—even if broken only once, it is still broken. Sadly, in following the commands of both Michella Duchenet and Selik Riomini, I deviated from the course on which honor *should* have led me. In my past military career, I shattered that crystal goblet. But it will not happen again. Today we become more than a military force, fighting blindly for a tattered cause. We are a humanitarian force."

Now, even if the goblet was shattered, Percival Hallholme would try to pick up the pieces.

71

Not so long ago, Bolton Crais's wife had considered their marriage to be insubstantial and inconvenient. Back on Sonjeera when he'd received his rank of Silver Major—through noble connections rather than any demonstration of talent—Bolton had earned the nickname "Major Setback" because so many of his initial efforts had been lackluster at best.

As a consequence, his military career had been arranged so that he was placed in figurehead positions where he could cause no harm, yet he was given no chance to demonstrate his abilities. Redcom Hallholme's supposedly glorious retaliation mission had been another setback as they were sucked into the General's trap, and then the ill-fated escape into the wild Hellhole landscape . . . Bolton was tired of being beaten down by circumstances. Now he would do what he could to help organize the evacuation so the POWs could get away. The Commodore was sending down a retrieval mission within the hour.

When his own personality finally came to the fore, Escobar insisted that he be taken back to the POW camp. He explained to Sophie Vence, "My father will do what he can to see that they're saved. Major Crais and I will make preparations on the ground. It is imperative that I be with my soldiers."

Even if the shadow-Xayans had no inclination to leave, Sophie had to consider the evacuation of her remaining personnel at Slickwater Springs. She happily granted Bolton and Escobar one of her Trakmasters so they could roll overland to the large camp in the adjacent valley. She would take care of the rest of the shutdown work at her own settlement.

The POW camp was well maintained, but not equipped for the long-term support of thousands of people. General Adolphus had established it quickly as a holding area for the unexpected influx of captives. They had shelter, water, and regular supplies of food; the reinforced buildings offered sufficient protection from Hellhole's merciless storms, quakes, and other natural hazards. Sophie's people administered the camp, and the General's guard forces maintained security, but everyone concerned would have happily sent all of the unexpected guests back home.

Now, as the Trakmaster rolled up to the fence gates and Bolton and Escobar disembarked, the concerned military prisoners came forward to meet the two haggard-looking officers, surprised and relieved to see them still alive. Exuding an air of confident leadership that Bolton had not seen before, the Redcom moved forward with gliding footsteps. He seemed taller, more powerful now . . . less angry, yet more commanding. After wasting away from his injuries, his muscle tone appeared to be returning.

"Are we going to be stranded here to die when the asteroids come?" said a man in a now-tattered sergeant's uniform. "We haven't even started to evacuate yet, and there are thousands of us!"

"Is rescue coming, sir?"

"We know how close the asteroids are, but we will not need rescue." Escobar's voice had a resonance now, and his words carried easily across the crowd. "Our best, our *only* hope is for the Xayan race to achieve *ala'ru* before it is too late. If they succeed in that—if *we* succeed—then we need not fear mere pebbles from space."

The prisoners murmured. Another POW shouted, "That doesn't help us much here. You expect us to just sit and wait?"

Bolton looked at his companion, surprised by Escobar's words, and lifted a hand for attention. "Commodore Hallholme and the General have reached an accord in orbit. The Army of the Constellation is sending down ships to rescue us. They're on their way."

Now the chatter grew louder, more excited. Bolton's reassurance had dulled the edge of panic.

Escobar stood like a statue beside him. He didn't twitch, didn't move a finger. Bolton had never seen the man so motionless. When the excited chatter died down, Escobar spoke again. "The rescue ships are irrelevant, because we have a far higher calling. Our time is short, and this is your last opportunity. I add my voice to the urgings you have heard before from the Xayans. Believe me, the only way we can truly end this crisis forever is if our Xayan allies achieve *ala'ru*. They need your help. *I* need your help. If you will join us in the slickwater pools and participate in the resurrection of the glorious race, you can help us accomplish what no other human has ever done."

His eyes were intense, shimmering and spiraling. The prisoners seemed confused.

"I am a shadow-Xayan now. I was barely clinging to life, mortally wounded, and now I am stronger than ever before. The slickwater pools and my internal companion Tarcov saved my body as well as my soul." His voice grew louder, insistent. "I want all of you to go to the pools and join the greatest force in the history of the universe. You can be part of something incredible—it's not too late."

The POWs were uneasy at Escobar's comments, as was Bolton. "That wasn't part of our agreement," Bolton muttered, loud enough for the others to hear.

"But we're going to be rescued!" shouted one of the uniformed men.

"We just want to evacuate, sir," said one of the nearby soldiers. The murmur grew louder. "When is Commodore Hallholme sending down the transports?"

Escobar closed his eyes, as if he continued to shout in his mind, then opened them and turned to look across the wasteland, and up into the sky. High above, a tiny dot grew larger, approaching swiftly. To Bolton's surprise, the Original alien Encix drifted in from afar, borne along by her powerful telemancy. She landed gently on her long, sluglike lower body, and raised her torso to face the crowded prisoners.

Although he had come to know Jonwi during their time in the red weed oasis, Bolton could not read the expression on Encix's strange face. She seemed displeased, determined, and her alien eyes took in the crowded, fenced-in humans . . . thousands of displaced people, stirring restlessly.

Her voice rang out like thunder. Bolton had never heard anyone speak so loudly without artificial enhancement. "The Ro-Xayans are coming to destroy us all! This planet is doomed, but I refuse to abandon my race's destiny because of a lack of will. I will do what I must!"

Escobar-Tarcov looked at Encix, then turned to Bolton. "This is our last resort, Major Crais. We can no longer wait."

Bolton felt a quaver of fear. "What are you talking about, sir? The Commodore's ships are coming down. We'll all be rescued."

"Therefore we must act before then," Escobar said. "Don't you understand? If all these potential converts go away, it will be too late."

Flying in from behind Encix like a flock of birds, hundreds of shadow-Xayans used telemancy to swoop in from their nearby settlement.

Seeing them, Bolton's throat went dry. "What is this, sir?"

Escobar joined the arrivals as they alighted gently on the ground. The POWs backed away from them, confused and intimidated.

Bolton hurried after him, continuing to press, "Redcom, tell me what you're doing! We've already solved—"

Encix and all the shadow-Xayans raised their hands in unison. "We do not have enough combined telemancy to accomplish what needs to be done . . . but we are so close that our agreement can no longer be honored. We need all of you to become shadow-Xayans—*right now*!"

The ground began to rumble beneath Bolton's feet, sharp shocks from deep beneath the camp. The tremors intensified. Somehow, Encix and the shadow-Xayans maintained their balance like poised dancers, while the panicked prisoners lost their footing.

A jagged crack split the ground, and the POWs backed away in different directions to keep from falling into the fissure. The fence surrounding the camp prevented them from escaping. The General's guards staggered forward and waved their weapons as the ground lurched, but the shadow-Xayans paid no attention to them.

Bolton stumbled to his knees, fought his way back to his feet. Escobar grabbed him by the arm and held him up, but somehow the grip did not feel supportive or comforting.

"Observe," Escobar-Tarcov said. The tremors began to dissipate, but the ground cracks widened.

With a wave of telemancy, Encix and all the shadow-Xayans pulled at something deep underground. Silvery bubbles appeared, flowing ripples—and shimmering slickwater rose up like a flash flood, filling the cracks and spilling out onto the upper surfaces. The shadow-Xayans added their telemancy, but they stood unaffected. The flow of quicksilver liquid swirled around their feet, then surged like a living thing toward the fence, and all across the camp.

Bolton tried to break free of Escobar's implacable grip, but the Redcom refused to let go. Slickwater bubbled up from crevices inside the camp, surging energetically, frothing and foaming. The prisoners backed away, trying to avoid its touch.

Shimmering waves splashed over the fissures in the ground. Crackles of static electricity bounced from wavelet to wavelet. Colored lights and sparks of psychic energy flickered like a kaleidoscope of reflections—glimmers of memories from an entire population whose lives were stored inside the crystalline liquid.

Encix commanded it, and the shadow-Xayans added their power. The flow of slickwater surged up from the ground. Struggling, Bolton heard shouts of dismay from the thousands of prisoners in the camp. The General's guards couldn't flee either, couldn't open the camp gates in time, although they tried. The soldiers tumbled into the sinister liquid.

Escobar-Tarcov tightened his grip on Bolton's arm. "This is our chance for *ala'ru*, Major! Everyone on this planet must become a shadow-Xayan."

Bolton fought, but Escobar had a mad strength, enhanced by telemancy. The Redcom picked him up, and Bolton was helpless.

Escobar hurled him like a toy into the slickwater.

72

Responding to the alarming transmission from the Ankor spaceport, Cristoph had flown away from Slickwater Springs in the refueled scout craft. While racing across the continent, he tried repeatedly to get any response from the control center, but received only static and silence. No one answered, not the launching operations, nor any of the shuttles.

Ankor was one of two major spaceports on the planet. Right now, Hellhole needed the full launch capability of both—every shuttle, every craft of any kind that could ferry people off the planet in the little time they had left. But riots over interrupted fuel supplies had caused delays in Michella Town, and now Ankor had fallen entirely silent.

Swearing, he nudged his aircraft to greater speed. Even now, he should have been rounding up settlers from scattered mining operations, farm complexes, and other areas. But if they couldn't get the ships launched again, it was all a moot point.

By the time he reached the Ankor complex, it was midmorning beneath a hazy, greenish sky—a color that often foretold bad weather. A severe Hellhole storm could further disrupt spaceport operations—and there was no time for that!

He saw other ships coming in, cargo craft loaded with passengers rounded up from outlying villages, atmospheric craft scouting for more refugees. Chatter over the comm came from many of the inbound ships; everyone sounded agitated because they were receiving no answers from the Ankor headquarters. Some ships circled the spaceport, sending more and more frantic transmissions. Others just landed wherever they could.

Exasperated, Cristoph took his heavy scout craft to one of the landing zones, alert for other ships that might get in his way. He saw many spacecraft, upboxes, passenger pods, even military personnel transports, just waiting in the paved launch zones. None of them were taking off.

Alarmed, he began breathing harder. People needed to be filling those passenger pods and shuttles, heading up to the stringline hub where they could be whisked off to safer planets in the Deep Zone. There was no time to be idle! On the ground he saw people crowded around the landed passenger pods, the launch areas, the gantry complexes. Fuel tankers sat motionless—probably empty.

After landing, Cristoph disembarked and ran to the crowds around the admin building. He heard a rising roar of angry shouts, loud commands from security officers who failed to keep the crowds under control.

"We need to get aboard shuttles or passenger pods!" someone demanded. "Why is this taking so long?"

During his flight, Cristoph had learned things over the broad-channel comm. Now that the Commodore and General Adolphus had joined forces to evacuate as many people as possible, all operations should have resumed by now. He feared that Rendo Theris had suffered a breakdown, unable to cope with the stress—and these people were going to pay with their lives if the launch activity didn't resume.

He made his way through the multitude, heading for the headquarters building. If Administrator Theris had indeed collapsed, Cristoph would have to take over— and he was willing to do it. This would be far more difficult than running the iperion mines on Vielinger . . . and infinitely more important. Every delayed shuttle and passenger pod departure would cost lives.

The people milling about were terrified, with good reason. Given how little time they had before the asteroid impacts—less than two days!—they knew many of them wouldn't make it off-world. But oddly, as he fought his way toward the main building, many of the people seemed calm and unaffected.

Then he realized they were shadow-Xayans—a great many of them mingling with the regular humans, as if to dampen their panic. He could identify the converts by their demeanor, the strange sheen in their eyes. Now, in the background noise of the crowd, he heard many of the converts speaking in thrumming voices that had a distinctive alien tone. It gave him an uneasy feeling, and he sensed that something even more strange was happening here than the incomprehensible spaceport shutdown.

Before he reached the headquarters building, though, Cristoph felt a crackling energy in the air, a skin-crawling intensity of increasing levels of telemancy. Luminous tracings of light appeared in the air above the shadow-Xayans, growing brighter. Scattered throughout the crowd, the converts seemed to be concentrating, doing something together.

The crowd noises shifted to shouts and cries of immediate alarm from the normal humans, and then the pavement quivered under Cristoph's feet. The press of the crowd shifted, people screaming as they scrambled away from a jagged crack that ripped open the wide landing field. Secondary cracks rippled away from the main fissure, and the ground tore open so violently that people tumbled into the openings.

Many of those standing around, though, were not running away at all. Shadow-Xayans stood along the edges of the largest fissure, doing absolutely nothing to help the people who had fallen in and were trying to scramble back out.

A flood of thick sparkling liquid welled up from below and spilled across the pavement. Slickwater! The shadow-Xayans were actively drawing from the aquifers beneath the spaceport, flooding the crowded landing grounds with the liquid. They were doing it on purpose!

Now the converts moved with unexpected speed and determination. They selected regular humans in the crowd, using telemancy to propel them into the slickwater. As the fissures continued to fill with shimmering liquid, the shadow-Xayans began a wholesale, forcible immersion of everyone in the area.

Several hundred meters away, one of the towering gantries collapsed, and the ground gave way beneath its foundation, which was swallowed in a widening sinkhole.

Cristoph finally made it to the headquarters building and pressed his way inside. The lobby was already crowded with masses of people, presumably others trying to escape the insidious flood of slickwater—and then he realized that these were shadow-Xayans. All of them.

As he turned to run, the converts reached out to him, and he felt an unseen force spin him around and propel him back out onto the field. He could not break free of their telemancy.

Helpless, he was flung forward, borne on a psychic wave toward the slickwater. Victims were being hurled into the liquid, the whole crowd converted at once. Hundreds of new shadow-Xayans climbed back out of the fissures as they began to assimilate their new alien lives and powers.

Cristoph could already hear the screams diminishing

as more people were replaced with the strange alien voices, a wave of mass conversions.

And then the telemancy plunged him into the flowing slickwater.

73

The orbiting fleet lost contact with not only the Ankor spaceport, but with Michella Town as well. General Adolphus felt as if he had gone into freefall. Critical evacuation sites were offline.

He had been prepared for the unruly disorganization of people trying to escape a planet before Armageddon. Chaotic crowds would rush to the two spaceports by any means possible, frantic to get to the dubious safety of orbit. Neither spaceport had the capacity to hold so many people. It was a disaster that was no longer waiting to happen.

After battling one setback after another, with the delays caused by the fool George Komun and then the arrival of Commodore Hallholme, Adolphus already faced an impossible challenge. Now, with the compressed timescale as the asteroids accelerated, he realized that it was simply not possible to succeed, even if he had the complete cooperation of everyone, even if every step went precisely according to plan.

He had begun something the number of lives that would be lost—not by his own failures, but because the universe had thrown so many sucker punches at him. Yet he was General Tiber Adolphus, and he refused to admit defeat. He would keep striving and fighting, saving as many people as he could.

On the bridge of the *Jacob*, he sent transmission after

transmission down to the spaceports and to Michella Town. Looking at his comm officer, he asked, "What happened down there? Was there an explosion, some kind of sabotage? At *both* spaceports? Why can't they communicate with us?" He couldn't conceive how every single transmitter in the main colony town and the two spaceports might have been shut off.

Long-range observations began to report quakes and building collapses, as if the planet itself had begun to convulse, as if cringing from the twenty asteroids that were due to impact very soon. But he knew the gravitational pull of the asteroids could not be causing such titanic upheavals.

The comm officer shook her head. "Our outgoing communication signal is strong, sir, but . . . they just don't respond."

Adolphus pursed his lips and felt as if an asteroid were weighing down his chest. "Keep trying. Someone has to answer." He knotted his hands, then changed the comm channel. "Get me Commodore Hallholme."

True to his word, his old nemesis was cooperating, throwing his not-insignificant forces into rescuing people rather than killing them. Adolphus had gambled, hoping that the Commodore's sense of honor would define his actions. The requirements of the Constellation Charter were clear enough to give him a plausible reason to do what he knew was right, but even that hadn't been sufficient to drive the man to outright mutiny against the Diadem. When the old officer revealed the appalling new orders he had received from Diadem Riomini, however, Adolphus saw a sea change. That unconscionable, bloodthirsty demand had finally broken the Commodore. Adolphus was surprised and pleased to discover that he and his former mortal enemy were actually on the same side.

For years, Percival Hallholme had been conflicted by the reprehensible orders he was forced to follow, and had clearly regretted some of his unacceptable compromises. He'd even admitted that, plagued with guilt, *he* was the secret benefactor who had slipped desperately needed supplies to the fledgling Hellhole colony in its first years.

After so long, though, Adolphus couldn't accept the man's sudden conversion without some skepticism. "Commodore, I've lost contact with my main city as well as both spaceports. We're in the midst of the evacuation." He hardened his voice. "I hope you'll be honest with me—do you have another operation under way? Is this some sort of secret attack to keep me from evacuating my people?"

On the screen, the old Commodore's fallen expression gave Adolphus all the answer he needed. Hallholme was clearly surprised by the suggestion, a reaction that was followed by a rippling flush of anger and indignation. "General, I give you my word. I have done nothing to betray you. My fleet is focused on rescuing as many inhabitants of your planet as possible. By now, per our agreement, the bulk of my troop carriers are en route to the POW camp to retrieve all of the Constellation soldiers held there, and then to Slickwater Springs. That is my priority." He paused, then added, "We are closely monitoring the incoming asteroids—your planet doesn't have much more than a day left. I am not so foolish and single-minded as to assume that any political disagreements or orders from Diadem Riomini have relevance here. I just want to get the people to safety. We'll do what we can, working together."

After the Commodore ended the transmission, Adolphus turned to his second in command. "Mr. Sendell, dispatch a fast scout for a recon flight over Michella Town. I need to know what's happening there."

Seconds and minutes ticked away, and still no more evacuees were launched from the surface. No matter how effective he was, no matter how hard he worked, Adolphus knew that for the rest of his life he would keep counting the ones lost, not the ones he saved.

Startled, the comm officer turned to him. "General, the communication line is open again. I have a message from Ankor."

Adolphus felt a wash of relief. "Finally. Let's get back on track again. Is it Theris?"

"No, sir, it's Cristoph de Carre."

"Good enough," Adolphus said. "Put him on."

On the screen behind the young man, the Ankor headquarters appeared damaged, many of the stations abandoned. Portions of walls had fallen in, and ceiling panels hung down. Sparks showered from a smashed control panel. Oddest of all, though, was that Cristoph de Carre looked absolutely calm, at peace. He had a bland smile and a distant expression. Something in the eyes? "General Tiber Adolphus, I am pleased to report good news. There is no longer cause for concern."

With no way of deflecting the fusillade of asteroids hurtling toward the planet, Adolphus knew there damn well *was* cause for concern. He felt a heavy dread in his chest. He knew this brash, ambitious young man, who had chosen self-exile to escape Constellation politics. When he'd come to Hellhole, de Carre had insisted on proving himself to the General, willing to do the worst jobs before Adolphus would give him important responsibilities.

Now, however, Cristoph looked changed. His eyes, voice, and expression—Adolphus was dismayed to recognize the signs of alien conversion.

"The slickwater has risen up at Ankor, General. Many thousands of evacuees were already here, and they have now been successfully immersed. The same thing is happening in Michella Town and at Slickwater Springs." Cristoph's lips curved in a strange smile. "Evacuation of the planet is no longer necessary. We almost have the numbers we require, and we will reach *ala'ru* in time. It is assured."

74

In its final hours, the entire planet seemed to have gone insane, convulsing in death spasms.

Sophie and forty-six nonconverts still needed to be evacuated from Slickwater Springs, but around her, thousands of shadow-Xayans refused to leave their sacred planet. They spoke of *ala'ru*, which she considered an act of desperation . . . or delusion.

Even if the aliens did achieve their ascension, Sophie was not convinced the transformed Xayans would have the power to deflect the asteroids and save Hellhole. By now, having heard nothing for too long, she had given up on the hope that Lodo and Keana-Uroa would meet the enemy faction and somehow convince them to stand down. The Ro-Xayan way of solving disagreements was to smash planets with immense rocks.

There was simply no way to evacuate everybody. Not enough ships or time. Tens of thousands of inhabitants— maybe more than that—would be stranded when the asteroids struck. Commodore Hallholme was supposedly sending ships down to retrieve all of the soldiers at the POW camp. And if so many were going to die, did those Constellation soldiers who'd come here to slaughter every settler deserve to live more than the hardy colonists who had worked so hard just to eke out a living here?

Sophie had never wanted the prisoners there, and they certainly didn't want to be in the camp—but they were human beings and she couldn't abandon them. She was not a judge or an executioner. She would get as many away as possible and not think about who was worthy or not.

Slickwater Springs had enough overland shuttles to get the human inhabitants to Michella Town; two of those ships were even capable of achieving orbit in a worst-case scenario. She knew Adolphus would be worried about her, and he did not need the extra stress or distraction. She wanted to be inside the main lodge house, talking with him, but she decided just to load the forty-six people and get them away, including herself, and leave everything behind.

Deep in her heart, unreasonable as it may seem, she still expected the General to find some miraculous way to save them all.

Arlen Carter entered the lodge house. He managed her warehouse operations in Michella Town while she administered Slickwater Springs, but he'd come out here in the last days, away from the madness in town. He had a look of deep concern on his face now. "The shadow-Xayans are doing something out there, Sophie. They've asked you to join them but . . . I don't know. It gives me the creeps." Carter was a workhorse, loyal and reliable; it wasn't like him to get panicky.

Leaving the lodge house, she saw the shadow-Xayans gathered at the slickwater pools. The handful of remaining humans also emerged from their temporary housing. Sophie sensed that something had changed.

The air smelled of bitter ozone and crackled with

energy, as if the converts were pooling their telemancy. As soon as she emerged from the lodge, the large crowd turned toward her as if choreographed, staring at her with an eerie unified expression.

One of them spoke, "Sophie Vence and all fellow human visitors to Slickwater Springs, we need you now to help save our race."

As if a trigger had been pulled, the placid, mirrorlike pools of slickwater began to churn. The turbulence rose from beneath the surface like an awakening maelstrom. Telemancy crackled from one shadow-Xayan to another, accompanied by occasional sparks of visible electricity. The alien ponds shimmered and glowed, and the liquid rose up, swelling from beneath the ground as if replenished by infinite aquifers. The pools flooded their banks and overflowed the boardwalks, spilling across the ground.

The shadow-Xayans stood there, unaffected.

Carter bellowed, "What the hell?" Sophie backed toward the lodge house, though she doubted it would provide much shelter. The human workers and visitors retreated, some murmuring, others yelling in panic.

The shadow-Xayans began to move toward them in concert. Outnumbering the humans by hundreds to one, they grabbed unwilling people and dragged them toward the swelling slickwater.

Like an uncontrollable flash flood, the alien fluid rushed across the compound. Some people tried to outrun it but were swept up in the flow. Waves reached up like pseudopods to engulf other humans. Crackles of lightning inside the pools showed the sheer energy it contained.

Sophie saw what remained of Michella Duchenet standing among the shadow-Xayans, not moving, her eyes glassy and face blank. Slickwater flowed around her ankles and calves like a churning stream, but she didn't try to avoid it. Silvery blue geysers spewed up from the pools like gushing oil wells.

Sophie darted inside the lodge house, calling for Carter to follow—but as he reached the door, slickwater drenched him, and he froze, then collapsed. He grimaced and writhed as he tried to fight off the substance, then gave up and rolled back into the rising water.

All around the compound, unwilling converts joined the others as they absorbed and incorporated their dominant new alien personalities, the memories and lives—and the obsessive drive toward *ala'ru*. As more of the last humans were swept up and became shadow-Xayans, the number of converts grew, as did their strength and telemancy. They converged on the handful of stragglers.

Sophie locked the main doors of the lodge, but it was a large building with many windows and entrances, certainly not secure if hundreds of shadow-Xayans tried to break in. She reached the comm-center, activated a channel, and shouted, "Tiber, it's the slickwater, the shadow-Xayans—they've gone berserk, swallowing up everyone who isn't already converted! Don't know how much longer I can last."

She looked around, saw the silvery flow burst in through the lodge's door and pour along the main corridor like a living, searching thing.

"Wish I had a better chance to say a proper goodbye. I—"

Before he could answer her, sparks flew from the comm-set, and the screens went dark. Knowing she couldn't wait any longer, Sophie dashed out of the comm-center, racing ahead of the flood, and climbed the stairs. She reached the upper level of the large building, but had nowhere else to go.

The gurgling slickwater was like a living amoeba that quested after her.

With a chair she hammered at one of the upper-story mesh windows until it finally broke out of its frame, and she managed to climb outside. Reaching up, she grabbed an overhang and hauled herself onto the roof, almost slipping in the process.

All around the lodge house, slickwater pooled like a prowling watchdog. Shadow-Xayans massed together, unaffected, as the liquid flowed around them.

Panting and terrified, now completely cut off, Sophie huddled on the edge of the roof, looking down at all those people. In unison, they turned their gazes toward her, focused on her. Collectively *wanting* her to join them. Previously, the converts had been complacent and nonaggressive—but not any longer.

Diadem Michella stood there as well, but off balance. She didn't struggle as the currents knocked her over and swept her away. Nothing more than the husk of an evil old woman, she submerged in the slickwater.

Maybe she was the lucky one.

Around Sophie, the water levels kept rising, and the crackling static of telemancy built up—all directed toward her.

—◦◇◦—

Success.

At the prisoner camp, Encix guided the surging slickwater as it bubbled up from beneath the ground and sought out the last of the POWs. They were trapped inside the fences. All of the General's guards had been immersed, joining the converts. The female Original had targeted them specifically so they would cooperate. With each new convert, the level of telemancy grew. The reservoir of mental potential increased across the planet, by orders of magnitude.

Encix needed *numbers*, a massive number of converts, and she had very little time left. Now, though, the transformation was inevitable, the telemancy power gain exponential. With a collective mind of its own, the slickwater flooded the temporary tents and shelters, hunting anyone who tried to avoid it. Once the unwilling converts had been touched by the slickwater, the newly awakened shadow-Xayans assisted in the conversion of others.

The deep slickwater aquifers were surging through the pools at Slickwater Springs as well as Ankor, but Encix had enough for her purposes here. Thousands were now converted. The pearlescent liquid glided along, questing like insubstantial tendrils. Whenever the slickwater touched a frightened prisoner, they always succumbed. The stored Xayan memories and lives were coming back to life like a hurricane surge of resurrection.

Yes, even though the Ro-Xayan asteroids were coming, Encix would trigger *ala'ru* before it was too late. It would be their greatest achievement as a race, the greatest event—and the last event—in the history of the current universe. Nothing else was more important.

Looking confused and bedraggled, still struggling with the new presence inside him, Major Bolton Crais stood beside Escobar Hallholme. The two men wore their uniforms, as if clinging to original parts of themselves, despite their alien change. Encix sensed that they were wholly dedicated to completing their destiny. It would only be a few more hours.

Encix thrummed through her facial membrane. "So close."

The slickwater began to recede. There could not possibly be anyone left in the POW camp who had not been touched and blessed by their new reality, with very few mistakes or casualties. Those didn't matter.

In the skies above, they saw ships swooping down, descending at steep angles. Troop transports.

Escobar-Tarcov stared up, identifying the configurations. "Those are from my father's fleet. Constellation rescue ships to take us away."

"But we no longer wish to go away," said Bolton.

Yet Encix understood something more when she saw the vessels coming in to land. "No. But they contain many more potential converts."

75

Tanja didn't complain about Ian Walfor's erratic flying. He guided the ship out of the hidden crater in the hollow asteroid, then accelerated away toward Hellhole. Now that the alien faction had released his ship, Walfor could maneuver freely without being hindered by telemancy.

Behind them, the yawning mouth of the crater held all the Ro-Xayan scout ships permanently docked there. Those strange, swift craft would not be flying again; their original mission to distribute resurrected native embryos was no longer relevant or necessary. Nor would the Ro-Xayans be observing the curious human settlers who had established a foothold on their devastated ancestral home.

The last of the rebel aliens were holed up inside their asteroid habitats as they hurtled toward their fateful impact. They would annihilate an entire race and an entire planet—and that was the *preferred* scenario. The choice was between letting a world . . . or a universe . . . be destroyed.

It would happen only if Ian's ship got there before the slickwater converts triggered *ala'ru* and eradicated the foundations of the universe. And only if Keana-Uroa could stop Encix in time. In their fast ship, they could reach Hellhole well ahead of the asteroids, but not necessarily soon enough to prevent *ala'ru*.

Full acceleration pushed them all back against their seats. Walfor soared away from the inbound asteroids and set course toward the planet. The ship seemed oddly empty without the hulking form of Lodo. And in the back compartment, Keana sat silent and preoccupied, possibly trying to contain all the new power within her body. She closed her eyes and clenched her hands in her lap, reaching out with her mind, questing with telemancy to gather information.

Suddenly she opened her eyes in alarm. "Encix has gone out of control! We have to hurry."

"This is what hurrying feels like," Walfor said. "Any more acceleration, and I don't know if the ship will hold together."

Nevertheless, he squeezed more speed out of the engines, ignoring the risk of disaster or fuel cost. Tanja looked at the controls, saw the readings edging into the red zone. She hoped the ship could take it.

When they approached Hellhole, Tanja was astonished to see all the warships surrounding the stringline hub. The planet looked like a hornet's nest of activity. "What's going on here? Those weren't here when we departed."

Walfor ran a second high-resolution scan. "Most of those are Constellation ships. Do you think they're helping with the evacuation? An act of mercy in the midst of war?"

From the back, Keana said, "We can't concern our-selves with who they are and why they're at Hellhole. There's no time. Encix is pulling together all of the converts down there, summoning the slickwater, and engulfing thousands more. She will reach the critical point soon, and there will be no stopping *ala'ru*."

"So where do I go?" Walfor asked. "It's a big planet."

"Slickwater Springs. We'll start there."

Tanja scanned the trajectories of the asteroids. The Ro-Xayans continued to apply the full force of telemancy, pushing the asteroids toward Hellhole.

Walfor was scanning the surface, mapping out the ships crowded in orbit, the stringline haulers departing from the hub, no doubt loaded with refugees. Orbital space was like a shooting gallery, and he had to guide his own craft in without crashing into any evacuation vessels.

Alarmed, he reported, "Ankor seems to be shut down. There should be hundreds of shuttles and passenger pods rising up loaded with people, but there's not a sin-gle one from what I can tell. The gantries and control center are inactive." Walfor switched the channel, listen-ing in on Michella Town. "The other spaceport's in tur-moil, too. Don't they realize time is running out? They need to get those ships loaded and into orbit!"

Keana hunched over, as if struggling against cramps in her chest and a pounding migraine in her head. "The evacuation is a lesser concern. We must get down there—*now*!"

"I'm trying!" Walfor said.

Tanja scanned the ship traffic patterns, shaking her head. So much had happened in the short time they were gone. This had been a chaotic mess when they de-parted, and now it was even worse. She snorted. "You go away for a day or two, get captured by an alien race and held inside a hollow asteroid, and the whole world goes to hell."

Walfor shot in toward tight orbit, cruising along the daylit side of the planet, dodging ships, not bothering to respond to inquiries. He maintained full control, cutting corners so he could shave time off their flight, using the autopilot for suggestions only. They streaked over the gigantic bull's-eye impact scar. It was awe-inspiring, hinting at the power of the asteroid strike . . . and that was only a prelude of what the Ro-Xayans had set in motion this time.

From behind them, Keana said in a hoarse voice, "I feel something extraordinary down there—psychic power building. Encix is unleashing all of the slickwater, triggering the Xayan survival systems. I feel the telemancy surge growing and growing. But now I sense something else—"

She lifted her hand, opened her fingers, and then squeezed them into a fist. "All the energy that Zhaday and the Ro-Xayans gave me and the leftover resonance from Lodo . . . I can barely control it." Her shoulders hunched, and she lowered her head. "Encix grows stronger, too, though. So many more converts! The shadow-Xayans are vastly increasing in numbers."

Walfor's ship began to rattle and shake as he took a steep dive, plowing through the atmosphere. "I'm heading for Slickwater Springs. I'll have to skim the edge of a growler storm, but this ship can take it. Caution isn't a good idea right now."

"An undue moment of caution could bring about the end of everything," Keana said.

"Direct course for Slickwater Springs, then."

Tanja called up the scanners, probing the surface. She found the settlement around the three primary slickwater pools and detected turmoil there. Tanja couldn't guess what the shadow-Xayans might throw against them, but she feared they were facing a huge fight ahead.

76

Clinging to the rooftop of the lodge building, Sophie had little time for regrets. She would fight to the end, but the foundation and walls of the lodge were trembling. The viscous fluid flowed upward from the underground aquifers, as if searching for her.

Feeling helpless but defiant, Sophie shouted from the rooftop, "Am I really that important? I'm not worth all this effort!"

Below, the shadow-Xayans remained eerily silent, communicating by their own means. Sophie didn't suppose hurling curses at them would do any good.

A silver ship streaked through the air, flying low. She heard the sonic boom as it approached. She craned her neck, watching the glint in the air, wondering where it was headed. Not long ago, she'd seen dozens of ships heading toward the POW camp in the next valley, presumably Commodore Hallholme's rescue vessels—but they wouldn't be coming here. She was on her own.

This new ship, however, wasn't part of that group, but rather a small cargo runner, decelerating hard as it approached. She could hear the roar of its engines ripping the sky. Ian Walfor's ship!

With a surge of hope, Sophie leaped to her feet on the rooftop, waving her arms frantically to get the pilot's attention. The ship circled, came in tight. She saw only part of what Walfor must be seeing from up there. Slickwater Springs had been flooded and devastated; most of the bungalows were collapsed, the tents washed away. And as the glistening waters withdrew from other areas, a great crowd of converts stood around, waiting.

Walfor's ship buzzed the besieged lodge building, then arced around and swooped past again to signal that he'd seen Sophie on the roof. His engines roared with the strain, decelerating until he came around and dropped lower, switching to stabilizer power so he could hover above the lodge house. A side hatch opened, and Tanja Hu leaned out, clinging to a support bar, extending her hand. Still much too far away.

The ship edged closer to the roof edge. There was a yawning gulf between Sophie and the hatch, and only roiling slickwater below waiting to claim her, but Sophie didn't hesitate. She sprang across. Tanja caught her and swung her inside. She collapsed on the deck, gasping.

Keana-Uroa stood in the back compartment, grim and determined. "Ian Walfor, you must land. I need to address the shadow-Xayans."

Walfor called from the cockpit. "It doesn't look stable down there."

"I intend to make it stable," Keana said. "With the new infusion of power from the Ro-Xayans, I think I can control the slickwater. And I can protect us if they try to attack us with telemancy."

Sophie's heart was pounding. She wanted to have Walfor fly them up to orbit, where she could board the *Jacob* and watch Hellhole's final day at the side of Tiber Adolphus.

"No need to land," Sophie said. "I must be the only one here who was left unconverted. There's nobody else to rescue. Only shadow-Xayans are down there now, and they don't want to leave."

"We are not rescuing any of *them*," Keana answered. "We are trying to save the universe."

Sophie blinked, thinking the full answer would likely be a long story. "Then it sounds like you have a busy day ahead of you."

Keana went to stand at the open hatch of the hovering ship. She directed her gaze like an invisible battering ram, and beneath them the slickwater swirled, twitched, and began to pull away, draining back into the primary aquifers.

"Land in front of the lodge. The shadow-Xayans need to hear me. There are thousands here . . . and others will hear me through telemancy." She lowered her voice. "I can only hope they will hear me in time."

From the cockpit, Walfor looked at Tanja, who paused a moment, then nodded. "We're in this, no matter what, Ian. We know what's at stake."

But Sophie didn't understand what they meant. "We don't have much time to escape to orbit. There are ships waiting to take us aboard."

"Not our priority right now," Tanja said, then explained—to Sophie's amazement—what they had learned about *ala'ru*.

When Walfor finally landed his vessel in the strangely dry clearing in front of the lodge building, Keana went to the hatch. Looking regal, she stepped out to face the multitude of shadow-Xayans who crowded together, regarding her with puzzlement.

One of the shadow-Xayans called, "We are going to achieve *ala'ru*, Keana-Uroa. Join us."

From where she watched in the ship's back compartment, Sophie was dismayed to spot a transformed Arlen Carter standing among the crowd, as well as other Slickwater Springs workers who, like herself, had previously refused to immerse themselves.

"We have learned that *ala'ru* is a lie!" Keana enhanced her voice through telemancy so that it boomed and echoed across the compound. The shadow-Xayans could also hear, understand, and *believe* her through their own psychic connections. "It is much more than you were told. *Ala'ru* is not just an evolutionary step, an ascension to a greater state of being—it is the end of all existence! Every planet, solar system, and galaxy will disappear. *Ala'ru* will undo the fabric of the universe. In achieving its destiny, the Xayan race will annihilate everything else."

She paused. The shadow-Xayans remained silent, tense—some disbelieving, some angry, others frightened.

"This is the truth," Keana insisted. "We learned from the Ro-Xayans what Zairic didn't want you to know, what the Originals refused to tell you. Even most Xayans were not aware of the consequences—they merely went along because their leaders convinced them. All of you converts, touch the Xayans inside your minds, reach for the truth. Speak to your mental companions. We cannot allow *ala'ru*! We must protect the universe, even if it means the end of the Xayan race. It is a terrible, but necessary price."

Sophie tried to understand what Keana was saying. *Ala'ru* had always been an incomprehensible prospect, but now the idea that it could trigger the end of everything seemed even more impossible.

She heard concerned murmurs growing among the gathered converts, but then a distinct change entered the rising tone. Though Sophie and Tanja were reluctant to venture onto the unprotected ground where the slickwater had surged only moments ago, they could see the open sky and what seemed like a black blur: thousands of tiny flying forms rushing toward them.

It reminded Sophie of one of the large clouds of predatory insects that occasionally gushed forth from nests on Hellhole, like the voracious torpedo ants that had killed Ishop Heer. Sophie tried to discern the forms—they were much larger than insects, and they looked *human*. She'd seen this before, when all the shadow-Xayans had flown across the continent. And she could make out the large alien form in the lead. Encix.

All of the converts at Slickwater Springs stared at the approaching swarm. Keana squared her shoulders. "It is Encix and thousands of new shadow-Xayans." She paused for a long moment, then said in a smaller voice, her own human voice, "They may be too strong."

———

As wave after wave of shadow-Xayans came from the skies toward Slickwater Springs, Keana stepped away from Walfor's landed ship and looked up, preparing to face them. Thousands of possessed humans came in, borne by telemancy, and hundreds more milled around the settlement. Keana was caught between the two groups—and she had to be strong.

Encix looked ungainly as she flew in the lead. Her extended alien body was not sleek or aerodynamic, but she still sped smoothly through the air. With Lodo absorbed by the Ro-Xayans, she was the only remaining Original, the last of those preserved in a vault deep beneath the crust—the last living Xayan who remembered the pristine planet, Zairic's ambitions, the terrible rift that had torn the race into factions. Encix was not aware that Lodo was gone, nor that Keana had a portion of his powers and memories, along with the combined strength of Zhaday and the other alien faction.

Standing by herself, Keana turned back to Sophie Vence, Ian Walfor, and Tanja Hu. "Remain inside the ship, for your safety. If I do not succeed, you may be able to escape." She did not point out that if she failed to prevent *ala'ru*, there would be no place to which they could escape.

Seeing her rival, Encix maneuvered with telemancy. Keana did not flinch as the large Xayan's soft body settled to the ground in front of her. Like human-shaped raindrops, the converted shadow-Xayans gently landed all around her. They filled the grounds of the compound, spreading out around the slickwater pools, swelling into a huge army that covered the landscape.

Keana would have to stand against them, by herself. More important, she would have to stand against *Encix*—who was obsessively driven to achieve *ala'ru*. But Encix did not know what Keana knew.

The only surviving Original lifted her arms, rejoicing. "Can you feel it, Keana-Uroa? The power is in our minds and in the air. At last we have the numbers we need! The Xayan race has fully awakened, our minds and our memories are burning bright. And with the catalyst of our human partners, we are more powerful than our race ever was, even at its pinnacle before the asteroid strike." Encix spread her alien fingers, and the air itself seemed swollen with energy.

A subvocalized humming sound came from all the shadow-Xayans she had brought with her. The converts from Slickwater Springs were more uneasy, having heard Keana's initial warning, but the sound grew louder until the hum became deafening. Encix called on them all, using her pure telemancy to whip them into a frenzy and drive them over the brink.

"*Ala'ru!*" she shouted in her thrumming alien voice.

As storm clouds congealed in the sky—turmoil caused by the energy unleashed by so many shadow-Xayans—Keana could feel all of Hellhole tensing.

Within herself, she summoned her own strength and commanded the Uroa presence to work with her, along with remnants of Lodo. Together, they called upon Keana's innate and grown telemancy, as well as the power and knowledge the Ro-Xayans had given her. Before, she and Uroa had proved that they were as powerful as Encix, and now Keana could draw upon even more alien strength.

But Encix could also summon more from all those gathered with her.

Interrupting the buildup of energy, Keana used telemancy to communicate with the newly arrived shadow-Xayans, as well as the vast numbers of converts across the planet. She had already revealed the dark secret of *ala'ru* to those who could hear her at Slickwater Springs, and now she did the same with the throng around Encix—the ones who had been immersed against their will at the POW camp and the forcibly immersed crews of the Constellation vessels that had landed to rescue them. Their human halves had been forced to join a cause they neither believed in nor understood. Keana sent them the truth, cracked through even the walls of delusions held inside the stored Xayan memories. And she stunned them all with her revelation.

Encix recoiled as she felt the weakness and sudden doubt spread around her and beyond, like unraveling threads in a vast tapestry. The Xayan leader struggled, then pulled the waves of telemancy into herself—and fought back against Keana.

The Original seemed to find an insane strength in the pinnacle of her race's destiny and her personal obsession. Her voice was an angry shout. "You must not weaken us now, Keana-Uroa! You are a shadow-Xayan, so you realize the importance of achieving our destiny. You *know* what we must do!"

Keana scoffed. "No, I know what that destiny *is* now, as do Uroa and the Ro-Xayans. None of Zairic's followers agreed to destroy the universe as a condition of advancing themselves. You tricked them into a destiny none of them really wants."

"The whole reason our race exists is for the ascension!" Encix hammered back at Keana with her combined telemancy powers. Some of the still-deluded shadow-Xayans joined in, recklessly pursuing their false dream.

But inside Keana's mind, connected to the great ocean of telemancy and the stored lives of the Xayans, she was able to commune with others, rational alien minds astonished by the revelations, hesitant to take the risk. If they did not exactly support her, at least they withdrew their energy from Encix, much to the Xayan leader's shock.

But the tapestry of lives that Keana summoned contained more than the original Xayan race—the shadow-Xayans, forcibly converted, had their human halves as well. She could feel the doubts, the resistance, even the horror of all those people who had been swallowed by the inexorable flood of slickwater. They did not all want to help Encix—and now they fought back, pulling against the destructive Xayan destiny.

Keana clung to the unexpected support, called on their strength, and continued to send out waves of her own, taking the new converts away from Encix. She called upon their human partners to question what they were being forced to do. She felt all the shocked and beaten Constellation prisoners who had been shoved into the backs of their own minds, and the numerous refugees who had rushed to the Ankor spaceport.

She found Cristoph de Carre, and he fought back against Encix, against this unwanted abduction. He added a spark to the flames of Keana's own telemancy, and she grew brighter still. Inside her mind, inside *his* mind, she shared how much she had cared for his father, and through her eyes Cristoph could see Louis de Carre—which made him stronger still.

And then she found Bolton. He wanted to help her, wanted to do anything for her, in his complex relationship . . . not just as a husband, but like a brother, a friend. Bolton was there, giving everything to her, making her stronger.

And as doubts weakened the entire group and dampened the surge of eager telemancy, Encix grew increasingly desperate, channeling all her energy into destroying Keana, the focal point of the resistance.

Keana knew what her opponent was trying to do. Encix wanted to wrest control, pull together their telemancy, and force the converts over the critical point before their questions and fears could grow too strong. Keana responded by drawing on the sum total of her own strength while she tried to connect with the overwhelming number of shadow-Xayans on the planet, pulling them to her side.

It was a war of telemancy.

The liquid in the slickwater pools churned and frothed. Geysers blasted upward, and thunderheads congealed overhead. As the struggle raged, Encix fought back. Static electricity in the air caused lightning to leap from hilltops to the clouds. The wind became a deafening roar.

Keana remained immobile, as if her feet were rooted to the core of the planet. Facing her, Encix writhed, her soft body twisting. She raised herself up on the forepart of her body, holding her arms up in the air.

Keana felt a cold rush sweep through her, a weakness inside her gut. Encix was somehow stealing power from her.

But she dug deeper, fought back. Keana had a direct pipeline into a reservoir of strength and lost memories that the aliens could not understand. In all the simmering lives trapped within the surging slickwater, she found young and hopeful Devon Vence, who rose to the forefront, seizing his chance to add strength in this final clash . . . and beside him was his beloved Antonia Anqui, both of them lost in the slickwater, but now reawakened on the cusp of *ala'ru*.

Together, they made Keana stronger.

Deeper still, she found more allies, more lost souls willing to throw in their lot with her desperate last stand: Fernando Neron, the first human to find the slickwater, the man who joined with the Xayan philosopher-leader Zairic . . . and Vincent Jenet, Fernando's hapless friend who had gone to Sonjeera in hopes of peace, but was murdered along with the rest of the entourage by Diadem Michella.

Even the human linerunners Turlo and Sunitha Urvancik, who had been duped into trying to resurrect Zairic back in the quarantined warehouse. They were all connected through the slickwater network . . . and they did not all agree with the Armageddon vision of Encix. They made Keana stronger.

Unable to wait, she pushed back with her telemancy, holding nothing back, pressing harder and harder, pushing the invisible mental wall into Encix . . . causing her large body to bend backward.

Then farther, nearly making her *break*.

The alien finally thrummed a despairing sound and collapsed. Slickwater surged up from the ground, swirling, and as it touched the helpless and defeated Xayan, Encix dissolved, sloughing into a pile of thick gelatinous ooze that spread through the slickwater.

Keana collapsed to her knees, but struggled to remain steady. The mounting telemancy had come close to creating an unstoppable wave of *ala'ru*, just at the very brink. Though Encix had been defeated, all that energy still throbbed inside Keana, desperate to be unleashed somehow.

All these shadow-Xayans had summoned more than enough power that, if used in concert, they would fracture the fabric of the universe. But Keana held the delicate balance, drew the converts together, and did not let the telemancy dissipate. Instead, she used her skills to make her entire being like a net holding the shadow-Xayans in her embrace. She pleaded for them to understand, denying them the release of *ala'ru*.

She succeeded, for the time being—but she could not promise them anything new, could not give them any chance for relief.

Keana had accomplished what she needed to do, but it was a victory without joy, for she knew that even all that desperate energy would not be enough to drive away the fusillade of planet-killers that were going to crash into Hellhole in a matter of hours.

The asteroids were coming.

77

General Adolphus was accustomed to facing hopeless battles and defying the odds, but this was a battle he simply could not fight. Even with all these ships, the competent and loyal people, and the cooperation of the Constellation's greatest military commander, he could do nothing to save Sophie, or his world.

Despite having so many vessels and resources available, his desperate evacuation efforts had collapsed. The Ankor spaceport had been taken over by shadow-Xayans, and all launches were forcibly suspended. Michella Town had rioted, and then slickwater erupted through the streets so that the people there were swept up in alien possession. And all contact with Slickwater Springs had been cut off. Sophie had sent him a desperate last message, her words abruptly silenced. The slickwater must have risen up there, too . . . and he couldn't save her.

Sophie . . .

Adolphus sat on the *Jacob*'s bridge, watching the orbiting ships depart from the stringline hub. Hundreds of thousands had been saved, but not enough. Not nearly enough. The twenty asteroids hurtled in, each the size of a small moon, driven by ruthless alien telemancy; they could not possibly miss.

"Keep trying to reestablish contact down there," he ordered the comm officer—as he had done repeatedly. The young woman paused, as if to comment on the futility of this, but she turned back to her comm station and transmitted again, without receiving an answer.

Percival Hallholme's drawn face appeared on the screen. This mission had broken the foundations of his belief in the government he had served all his life. "We have run models, General—there is simply no time left," the Commodore said. "Even under the best possible circumstances, we cannot dispatch more ships and expect them to retrieve any more evacuees." The old man's eyes were reddened, his face gaunt. "Fate itself was against us. The retrieval ships to the POW camp have not returned, and my son is still down there." He heaved a devastated sigh. "We made our best efforts."

Adolphus's heart felt like a hole in his chest. "We were betrayed, Commodore."

The General still had countless vessels capable of landing, loading, and evacuating, but the asteroids would hammer the planet within hours. His eyes burned, not with tears but with anger at his helplessness. How he wished he could do more to help his people.

Hallholme said, "My own son and all of those other alien converts! I was able to speak with Escobar one last time, but—but it wasn't *him* anymore." The older man's voice cracked.

Adolphus wished he could hold Sophie one more time, speak with her until the last moment. Over the years he had been so stupidly reticent to tell her his feelings, afraid to show adequate warmth because of the persona he had created for himself, the hardened rebel commander. . . .

As they orbited Hellhole, Adolphus saw the large bull's-eye scar on the terminator line. The slanted light of dawn cast deep shadows of concentric circles from the old crater. He understood what the first impact had been like five centuries ago, for this planet and the Xayan race, but the new strike would be immeasurably worse.

Up here in orbit he could do nothing to stop it. In all his life, after so many battles, this was his darkest hour.

78

From the dubious shelter of Walfor's ship, Sophie had watched the slickwater storm as Keana and Encix engaged in their telemancy battle. Even though she was no shadow-Xayan herself, Sophie had still felt the titanic waves of mental energy building, the converts emanating barely controlled forces. It seemed to her that telemancy had turned each one of them into a volatile powder keg.

In the sudden, crackling stillness following the death of Encix, Sophie rushed to the hatch. Tanja called after her, cautioning, "Careful, there's still slickwater!"

"I don't think it matters anymore." Sophie stepped out onto the ground and hurried over to the shaky-looking Keana. The pretty woman seemed to be boiling with static electricity, every cell in her body ready to go supernova. Her face was in a grimace, showing the effort inside of her. Wrestling with the writhing, uncontrollable telemancy she barely contained, Keana seized control of the many thousands of shadow-Xayans who filled the valley. The air thrummed in the last instant of a chain reaction.

In a strained voice Keana said, "I'm holding them back . . . just barely. I won't let them unleash *ala'ru*—I won't!—but they are ready to explode. The Xayan race has never held so much power, and I can only make them suppress it for a short while longer. Too late? I feel the danger approaching!"

The enormous asteroids were already having long-range gravitational effects. Hellhole's unpredictable weather churned; growler storms appeared in a flash, rippling across the greenish skies.

Sweating, Walfor shouted back at Sophie. "The impact is imminent. We've stopped *ala'ru*, and now we have to get out of here. My ship will still be in the atmosphere for some of the turbulence when the asteroids hit, but there's a chance we'll get away. My ship can fly fast enough to beat the asteroids—but we *have to leave*!"

Sophie was distraught. "We can take a few people with us, maybe a dozen. Keana, get aboard!"

Now that *ala'ru* had been prevented, they could flee

after all. She could make it back to Tiber Adolphus—and together, they could watch and mourn the destruction of the world.

Keana refused, forcing her words through the strain. "I cannot leave this planet now. I can barely hold back all this power."

Sophie clung to an idea. "Then use it to deflect the asteroids!"

Keana turned to her, and her strange eyes looked as if they contained small grinding wheels, emitting sparks. "Twenty large asteroids, accelerated for weeks and still driven by the full force of Xayan telemancy . . . it would be an impossible task. The asteroids are too close. Even though I have prevented *ala'ru*, Zhaday and his faction are intent on annihilating themselves and all of us."

Walfor shouted from the cockpit. "Come on, Sophie! We have to *go*!"

She held her ground. "Keana, you stopped *ala'ru* and killed Encix. Communicate with Zhaday! Tell him there's no longer a threat—they don't need to destroy the planet now." Her voice hitched. "At least ask him to give us time to evacuate the innocents here."

But Keana shook her head. "Even if Zhaday listened, the Ro-Xayan telemancy isn't enough to halt the asteroids now. And neither is mine. The mass and energy involved . . . even with all the enormous power of our telemancy—even if I could somehow coordinate my efforts with Zhaday and use all our combined telemancy, it's not physically possible to divert them. And the Ro-Xayans have made up their minds. They won't take the risk." She looked up, glanced at the ship. "But Ian Walfor is right—you can get away. Go! It's the smallest of victories, but it's all I can offer."

The air thrummed as thousands of shadow-Xayans waited. Turbulent clouds masked the sky.

Keana let out a long, disappointed sigh. "So much energy, just waiting to be released . . ." Her shimmering eyes suddenly brightened. "We can't move the asteroids or fight the Ro-Xayan telemancy that drives them—but I have another idea."

—⚬—

With two objects on a collision course, one could be moved, or the other, yielding the same result. It all depended on the frame of reference.

Keana reached out with her expanded mind, and Uroa assisted her, tapping into the Xayan presences all around them. Through her burgeoning mental bond, Keana reminded them of who they were, made them remember how the Xayan people had taken a last desperate chance by dissolving themselves in the slickwater when there was no hope of escape from the first asteroid strike.

With all the power that Keana-Uroa now channeled, she also tapped into the stored and still-unawakened Xayan lives that were pooled in the slickwater, which generated energy beyond even what Encix had summoned when she tried to push them over the brink of *ala'ru*.

But Keana directed that energy not to an evolutionary transformation, but elsewhere.

She connected with and pulled together every one of the shadow-Xayans, including Bolton Crais and Escobar Hallholme at the camp, Cristoph de Carre at faraway Ankor, and thousands more in Michella Town. The pool of available telemancy grew deeper, wider, and more restless. She was strong enough to sense Zhaday and the Ro-Xayans huddling inside their hollowed asteroid colony, grimly prepared to eradicate their race forever.

Keana would not let that happen. Instead, she absorbed all the telemancy from all the shadow-Xayans. It would be so easy to do, so tempting to trigger *ala'ru* and ascend. But she used that power in a different way.

Instead of expending the energy to push toward their evolutionary leap, she called on all Xayans to release their enormous reservoirs of power.

And move the entire planet.

79

Moments before . . .
      From the bridge deck of his flagship, Commodore Hallholme was speechless.

He had always thought the expression was mere hyperbole, but he found himself completely unable to form words as he watched. The awe and inevitability of the cosmic shooting gallery left him unable to do anything but stare.

Huge, cratered rocks hurtled toward the planet like a broadside of cannonballs aimed at a sailing ship. There could be no doubt that these asteroids were driven by a hostile and supremely powerful force.

And Escobar was down there, where he could not be saved.

Frustrated and helpless, Percival had already withdrawn his ships to well beyond the stringline hub. He felt a deep sense of dismay. Not only had they lost the planet but most of its population as well. All so unnecessary, so malicious.

In moments, everything on Hellhole would be smashed to rubble and burned to cinders. *Everything.* The totality of the impending destruction was still incomprehensible to him.

He felt a sick anger to realize that Diadem Riomini would actually be pleased by this result. He would probably even congratulate the Commodore for completing his mission so thoroughly.

But Percival had already burned that bridge. He'd publicly defied orders and broken with the corrupt Constellation, declaring to his crew that he could not in good conscience follow barbaric commands. Most of his crew were appalled by the ruthless punitive measure and they supported him . . . but not everyone. Even after the asteroids struck, he would still have a great fight on his hands, a mutiny.

The biggest blow, though, was that his son remained trapped down there—by choice, apparently. Someday, Percival was going to have to return to Qiorfu and tell his two grandsons about their father, although he would alter the stories somewhat. Percival had always enhanced the reminiscences of his own war exploits. . . .

Feeling fatalistic as the asteroids hurtled in, he opened a comm channel to the *Jacob*. Percival's battles with this man had been legendary. "General Adolphus, I've had too much time to assess how we've come to this juncture. I know what you blame me for and, for what it's worth, I apologize for my actions."

Percival didn't think the apology was worth much, especially now, but the General accepted it with grace. "Thank you, Commodore. If you and I had been on the same side all along, think of how we could have changed human history. But it's too late now."

The General signed off, and the Commodore sat back. Duff Adkins stood at his side, silent and tense. Everyone on the bridge seemed to be holding their breath as the asteroids moved inexorably forward. When Percival swallowed, his throat was dry. He knew he was about to watch the end of a world.

And then the planet below—the entire gigantic sphere that filled much of the viewscreen—simply *vanished*, as if it had winked out of existence.

He lurched to his feet, unable to believe what he had just seen. The bridge was filled with an uproar as technicians and bridge officers called up readings on their stations, trying to find out what had happened.

The flagship suddenly plunged out of control, and the view from the main screen spun wildly. Emergency indicators flashed on all stations, and alarms echoed through the ship. The deck tilted, throwing Percival against his chair.

Adkins shouted, "The planet is *gone*, Commodore!"

Outside their ship, numerous other vessels were thrown into chaos, their courses altered and unstable. The stringline hub was a massive structure in space, the nexus of travel lines just hanging there, but with no planet beneath it.

Percival realized that if Hellhole had indeed disappeared—he didn't even try to explain that!—then it meant that the orbiting ships no longer had gravity to bind them, no center of mass to stabilize them. While their engines continued to apply thrust, they were hurled off in a chaotic scramble. To his dismay, two Consellation vessels crashed into each other, splitting one ship open. Bodies fell out. The other ship remained intact, but badly damaged and tumbling.

"Helm, get control back!" Percival ordered.

"I can't lock on to anything, sir! All of our systems have gone insane!"

"It's open space," Percival said. "Evasive action. Keep clear of other ships."

The asteroids continued to hurtle in, twenty unstoppable projectiles . . . but now without a target. They shot directly through the gap where planet Hallholme had been. There was no impact. They simply kept moving.

Percival shouted on the open channel, and heard General Adolphus issuing similar orders to his DZDF fleet. "Withdraw! Avoid those asteroids—and avoid each other!"

Hundreds of ships spread out, pulling away from what had been the planetary orbit. With amazing, unnatural speed, the cluster of asteroids began to spread out as well, altering their course, but they could not decelerate fast enough. He didn't see any other collisions take place, although there were a few near misses.

His navigator spoke up in a small voice, husky with disbelief, but somehow Percival heard him over the turmoil. "Commodore—this is impossible, but . . . I think I found it."

"What's impossible?" He knew that his very definition of *impossible* would have to change after today. "What did you find?"

"The *planet*, sir—farther along in its orbit." The navigator displayed an image on the main bridge screen. Long-distance sensors showed a blur, then a ripple. The entire planet, complete with its old impact scar, crystallized into focus, as if reappearing out of nowhere, winking back into existence.

"They moved the whole planet out of the way!" Percival exclaimed. "They *moved a planet*!" He couldn't even imagine the power that such an action would require. He hit the comm and shouted, "General, do you see it?"

Adolphus responded, equally astonished. The General turned to his own helmsman. "Adjust course, maximum acceleration. Get us back to Hellhole."

80

Just when she'd given up hope, Sophie felt as if reality had passed through a slingshot.

With the asteroids hurtling toward Hellhole and the shadow-Xayans pooling all their energies, her body and mind felt suddenly twisted, turned inside out, and then folded back to what she'd been moments ago, along with the air around her, the ground beneath her feet . . . existence itself.

Reality snapped back into place with a resounding ricochet that disoriented her. Sophie's vision doubled, vibrated, and sharpened again. She was left with a feeling of dread and uncertainty, convinced that something fundamental had changed—but she didn't know what.

All around her, thousands of shadow-Xayans stood frozen, poised without breathing . . . and then in unison they dropped to the ground like stalks of wheat struck down by a sickle. Their bodies lay on the ground, motionless, like the aftermath of a massacre. Including Keana.

"What the hell just happened?" Tanja cried, scrambling out of the ship.

Walfor blinked. "You're asking me?"

Sophie stared upward, and the sky overhead seemed

different. The fistlike clouds were dissipating. "Why aren't the asteroids coming? We should have been bombarded by now."

The sky remained clear. The three of them, the only conscious people within sight, stood hoping for some kind of an answer. Sophie had an eerie feeling that they might be the only ones left alive on the whole planet.

Then she heard a sound like a stirring wind, a shuddering breath drawn by thousands of people awakening at the same time. When Sophie saw the shadow-Xayans stir, her heart pounded with relief.

Keana was the first to climb back to her feet. She seemed dazed, and her face was full of confusion. She touched the side of her forehead, looked around in bewilderment, and saw the other shadow-Xayans stirring as well, climbing back to their feet and talking.

Keana turned to Sophie and announced with wonder in her voice, "We are no longer in danger. We moved the planet."

Sophie didn't grasp what Keana had just said. Tanja Hu blurted out, "You can't simply move a planet."

Keana's expression was mild. "We just did. We used its own momentum, accelerated it along its orbit. That was easier than fighting against the Ro-Xayans and stopping twenty asteroids."

The rest of the converts struggled back to consciousness, murmuring in excitement. Their voices were more animated and vibrant than before—no longer the perfect unison of minds connected through telemancy. Each one seemed to show a spark of personality again.

Keana said, "We were ready because Encix brought us—*forced* us—to this point—all the combined mental energy of the Xayan race, enhanced with the hybrid vigor from humanity. So much energy built up, simmering, waiting to be released . . . yes, we could have achieved *ala'ru*. Instead, we expended it all to move Xaya. To save it."

Sophie listened, hardly able to believe what she was hearing, or what she had experienced.

"The effort cost much more than I expected. The Xayans within us are—" Her brow furrowed, and she ran her fingertips along her forehead. "Uroa is still there . . . my companion, my friend, but he is just a whisper now. I can access his memories when I try, but they're like distant childhood recollections. Maybe someday he will grow stronger again. Otherwise, I'll just have to remember him."

Walfor asked, "But you're feeling normal again? All the converts, too?"

With a wan smile, Keana shook her head. "Normal again? After what we've just been through? With what we know and have experienced? Each one of the former converts is fundamentally changed—but for the most part, yes, I am human again."

The crowd milled about, speaking with one another, reuniting with friends. Keana looked up, perplexed at first and then smiling as one of the bedraggled former prisoners from the camp came forward. Major Bolton Crais.

An expression of wonder filled his face. "Keana, is it you?"

"It has always been me," she said. "Just a different me."

Bolton had a longing expression on his face. "I'm different, too. I understand now."

Keana chuckled. "We still have a lot to understand."

"I came here to assure your safety," Bolton said, "but I didn't expect it to turn out like this."

Sophie said, "None of what happened here fits into a tidy military scenario." She looked back at the damaged lodge house, turned toward Walfor's ship. "Ian, we'd better use your ship's comm. The General must be wondering what just happened."

Then she saw a contrail overhead, a swift scout vessel tearing down through the atmosphere. Somehow she knew that it was Adolphus coming for her.

Tanja and Walfor helped to clear an area near the slickwater pools. The crowded shadow-Xayans backed away, granting a generous field for the incoming vessel to land. It was a DZDF shuttle from the *Jacob*.

Smiling, Sophie stepped forward, knowing what she would see. She waited to welcome Tiber Adolphus as he emerged from the hatch. He hurried forward as she went to meet him, and swept her up in a fervent embrace.

Laughing, Sophie said, "Aren't you afraid to be passionate in front of all these people?"

"I thought I'd never see you again. I never imagined I'd set foot on this planet again."

She told him what Keana told her.

"I'm glad to have the help of an entire race," Adolphus said. He scanned the crowded converts and shook his head. "The whole planet was moved about a day's journey ahead in its orbit, and the asteroids passed right through where Hellhole had been. Our ships raced over here to investigate—I thought we might even have to continue the evacuation."

Still holding him, Sophie said, "But the evacuation's a moot point now, isn't it?"

A grim flicker crossed the General's expression. "Maybe not. The Ro-Xayan asteroids are slowing, and they appear to be altering course, but it'll take some time. The sheer power to do that is inconceivable to me. And they have launched their scout ships, hundreds of them."

Sophie's eyes went wide. "You mean they're *still* trying to attack Hellhole? All this was for nothing?"

A young DZDF officer hurried out of the landed shuttle, looking as if he had experienced far too much impossibility in the past few days. "General, we've made course projections—the asteroids are no longer going to impact. It looks like they're going into orbit, sir."

Keana stepped up to join them. "The Ro-Xayans will send emissaries down. We have a common ground now, if they know we can no longer achieve *ala'ru*. They'll have a chance to rebuild their world instead of destroying it."

Another ship descended through the atmosphere, also making its way toward Slickwater Springs—not one of the swift, silvery Ro-Xayan craft, but a Constellation shuttle. The General craned his head upward. "It looks like Commodore Hallholme has decided to join us."

When the other vessel landed in Slickwater Springs, the old warrior emerged, looking wrung-out and disoriented. He drew a breath of the dry air, drank in details, then hobbled toward Adolphus. The two rivals had not stood face-to-face for a long time. "General Adolphus, you have an interesting way of prosecuting a war."

"You're right, Commodore."

In a rapprochement that had once seemed impossible, they clasped hands.

—⁓—

Commodore Hallholme set aside all the countless management details warring for attention in his head. This operation was the most massively complex and confusing he had ever undertaken, and now, with the objective changing hourly, most of his crew had conflicting or unclear orders. Finally, after setting foot on the planet that was so embarrassingly named after him, he focused on one paramount goal.

Among all those here, including the thousands of Constellation prisoners, one of them was his son. He searched for Escobar among the crowds of dazed converts who had *flown* here from the POW camp.

He saw Keana Duchenet reunited with Major Crais. The two had been distant and aloof during their years of marriage, living separate lives back in the Crown Jewels. Now, as they stood together, they seemed like different people.

And when Percival found Escobar, the younger man also looked different. His son approached him, still wearing the uniform of a Red Commander in the Army of the Constellation. He remembered how strange and alien Escobar had looked earlier on the comm screen, when he'd revealed that he shared his mind with an alien presence. Now, though, Percival thought he saw much of the old Escobar in those pale blue eyes—the good part that Percival remembered.

The younger man offered a crisp salute. "Presenting myself to you, sir. I have a lot to tell you."

Percival moved closer, stiff and formal out of long habit, although he was overjoyed. "You are healthy? Unharmed?"

Escobar paused as if to consider. "I am changed . . . but, yes, I am *myself* again." His expression softened. "I think you might like this version of me better, however. I've learned a great deal since I departed with my fleet months ago. I was arrogant and unrealistic. I put my crew in danger, took unnecessary risks, lost many good soldiers. I did not listen to the warnings or the advice you gave me—primarily because it came from *you*, and I didn't want to hear it. That was foolish and immature." He averted his eyes for a moment, then turned back.

"I'm ashamed to admit that I spent little time thinking about my wife, my two sons. I looked toward a distant goal, but didn't see much else. I have been humbled, sir—and made much wiser. I hold another life and a new set of memories inside me, even though they're not much more than mere dreams and echoes now. I didn't have enough time to get to know my internal alien companion, but the experience matured me." He bowed his head slightly. "I hope you can accept me as I am now."

Tears welled in Percival's eyes. "Only if you call me 'father' instead of 'sir.' "

"Of course, Father."

The silver-haired old man reached out to embrace his son.

———✶———

Keana realized that the immense administrative problems facing the colony, the two fleets, and all the ready evacuation ships would be nearly insurmountable. Merely keeping track of everyone who had become a shadow-Xayan was a tremendous challenge.

Still, it was far better than the alternative of planetary annihilation.

With the echoes of Uroa inside her, as well as the shadow-Xayans who were drained of psychic energy, Keana had a far greater question to answer. From the ominous Ro-Xayan asteroids that had gradually gone into orbit above the shifted Hellhole, the alien faction had dispatched their swift silver ships. They pinwheeled down through the atmosphere and landed near the primary slickwater pools. All the former converts could sense the Ro-Xayans coming, and Keana—who had already interacted with the rogue aliens—acted as a liaison.

When the alien ships settled onto the ground and Zhaday emerged, his blue torso pigmentation was brighter than ever. Five aliens accompanied him, gliding forward on their caterpillar bodies. When they touched the dusty surface, they thrummed and swayed with genuine awe.

Identifying Keana, Zhaday moved forward. When the faction leader spoke, she heard his words plainly in the air, but not in her mind. The leftover telemancy had become little more than a whisper.

"We are back on our planet again . . . a seeming impossibility not long ago." He paused. "We would have destroyed Xaya to save the universe, would have sacrificed our entire race, and whatever else it took. We were ready."

Keana straightened and stood before him. "And yet, we found a different way. We clung to *hope*, rather than solving a problem through complete annihilation. And now we can make a new beginning."

Zhaday and the Ro-Xayans looked curiously toward the slickwater pools, which now seemed dull and tarnished, empty. "And the Xayan memories inside you? They cannot ever achieve *ala'ru*?"

"The residue is here, but you, your faction, are the last remaining Xayans. *Ala'ru* is no longer a threat, just a memory . . . a lost possibility."

The Ro-Xayans fanned out, exiting their numerous pinwheel ships. All the aliens seemed stunned and amazed to be here, drinking in new life from the sky, feeling the air on their porous skin. "Our race can come back to Xaya now," Zhaday said. "We can reclaim it, replant it."

Keana hardened her expression. "We can *share* it. This world belongs as much to the humans as it does to your faction. My people fought to save it."

Zhaday bowed. "I did not mean to suggest another conflict."

Surprisingly, a new Xayan came to the valley, riding across the sky on his own telemancy—another alien that Keana had never seen before.

Bolton knew him, though. "Jonwi!"

The alien landed and came forward, his arms making jittery motions, the feelers on his forehead twitching. He was excited, frenetic. Bolton hurried toward him. "Looks like you can continue your work after all. It won't be a wasted effort."

"My work never stopped," Jonwi said. "And now that a real future has returned to us, I suggest that all Ro-Xayans—working alongside humans—help us reseed Xaya with its original life-forms. We can bring back the paradise it once was, tame the remaining ecological turmoil. Never in my life have I felt so much energy and enthusiasm. Can you not feel the life stirring from within the soil?"

"We all feel it," Zhaday said.

After what Uroa had shown her in his ancient memories, Keana could imagine large portions of the blasted terrain covered with renewed alien vegetation. The numerous ordeals and changes she had endured since leaving Sonjeera were steps that helped her become the complex person she was now. Keana was vastly different from the brash and foolish woman she'd been back in the Crown Jewels.

Seeing Bolton next to her, she realized how much he had changed, too. They had a common experience they'd never dreamed possible.

Keana Duchenet, who had once been swept along on a Xayan tidal wave, had been transformed, just as the planet had. The future looked bright, but she didn't delude herself. This was, after all, still Hellhole.

81

When Ian Walfor flew his ship, Tanja insisted on copiloting, but then she felt so physically and mentally exhausted that she could barely move.

She thought back on the months of crises that she and Ian had survived. The completion of the Deep Zone stringline network should have been a new dawn for the fifty-four colony worlds, but instead it had merely triggered an avalanche of tragedies—the infighting, the uprisings on various planets, her despair at seeing the murder of Bebe Nax and then the destruction of Candela. Ian had suffered his own losses when the Army of the Constellation overran Buktu, took the population captive, and the ruthless new Diadem slaughtered all of those survivors.

And yet somehow, impossibly, Hellhole had been saved from even greater devastation.

Seeing how drained Tanja appeared, Walfor smiled at her. "You look beautiful when you're utterly wrung out."

She barely opened her eyes to look at him, managed a small smile. "Right."

He chuckled. "Go ahead and rest—it's over now. The world is saved and, if the Ro-Xayans are correct, so is the universe."

"It's never over, Ian. We've just got a different set of problems to solve. Enva Tazaar went off to set up her new colony on Theser. Maybe you and I should go there and see how my Candela refugees are doing."

"There are plenty of possibilities in the Deep Zone now," Walfor said, "unlimited opportunities."

They raced across the Hellhole landscape, finally arriving at the Ankor spaceport, which was up and functioning again. Repairs had been made quickly so that ships could launch and land once more. Downboxes full of emergency supplies were being distributed to the settlements.

Tanja watched the process as Walfor flew in, looking for a spot to land on the crowded paved areas. The slickwater pools around the perimeter had receded, leaving dry and stable ground.

Tanja narrowed her gaze, nodded. "Opportunities," she said. "Plenty of opportunities."

—✵—

When Adolphus paused to think about the meeting, he could hardly believe it was taking place at all. Elba had played host to his grand conspiracy when a group of rebels first envisioned the independent Deep Zone stringline network as a way to achieve independence from the Constellation. Now, in the same room inside the headquarters mansion, Adolphus sat across from Commodore Percival Hallholme—the man who, for much of his life, had been his greatest nemesis. Yet, at the moment, Adolphus knew the Commodore was one of his staunchest allies.

The meeting included Keana Duchenet, a woman who had once been a gadfly, naïve and unpleasant . . . and who had single-handedly wrested the planet away from destruction. She, too, was his ally. And of course, Sophie; the General never had any doubts about her.

Percival Hallholme wore his formal Constellation uniform, a chest full of medals, his cap, his polished boots. The old man seemed to carry a gravitas about him. His aide, Duff Adkins, accompanied him, as well as the Commodore's son, which caused Sophie some consternation. But Escobar Hallholme deferred to his father.

All across the planet, numerous Constellation ships were coming down to pick up the military prisoners who had been released from the camp, although after being exposed to slickwater, all those soldiers had developed an intimate connection to this challenging world. Many of them were reluctant to leave—especially now that they knew the truly bloodthirsty nature of the new Diadem Riomini.

The awkward tension in the meeting chamber reminded Adolphus of the humiliating surrender ceremony he had been forced to endure years ago, but this was different. Facing him across the conference room table, the Commodore said, "General Adolphus, now it's my turn—I need your help. We all need your help."

"I'm listening," Adolphus said.

"I mean the Constellation . . . which, I suppose, is now comprised of just the twenty Crown Jewel planets." He cleared his throat. "Because I refuse to follow the orders of Diadem Riomini, no doubt he will devote all his resources to making a counterstrike against us. He still controls a large military force that he created in secret. He gave me command of some of the warships, but retained many for himself for Crown Jewels security. He'll keep pressing and probing, trying to find ways to destroy us. He hates you, General Adolphus, and I presume that after what I've done he will hate me just as much."

Keana nodded. "My mother was a monster, and Selik Riomini is no better."

Adolphus said, "I doubt if any peace talks will change his mind, no matter how much leverage we wield."

Commodore Hallholme shook his head. "It's not just the Diadem we need to change. It's the Constellation itself. You can't expect a garden to thrive if the soil is poisoned."

Adolphus leaned forward, placing his elbows on the table. "I agree, the Crown Jewels are corrupt to the core—I've known that since I started my first rebellion. Are you suggesting we get rid of Diadem Riomini and put someone more acceptable in his place?" He arched his eyebrows. "Someone like you, perhaps? Or your son?"

The Commodore raised his hands. "Not me, by God! I retired years ago, and was only dragged back into active duty by force."

"And that wouldn't be for me either," Escobar said. "I've never been interested in anything but a military career."

Adolphus felt weary at the prospect of another lengthy rebellion, a clash of Deep Zone worlds against entrenched Crown Jewel planets. "We need to make fundamental changes at the heart of the Constellation, not just prop up another leader who comes from the same political system."

"But so much is different now," Sophie pointed out. "Maybe the time is right, if we work together."

Assessing the resources available to him, Adolphus said, "We have my DZDF, combined with the Commodore's fleet. Together, we should be superior to any military force the Constellation still has. But we need to strike quickly, before they can build their fleet."

The very idea of General Tiber Adolphus and Commodore Percival Hallholme united against a corrupt system, fighting side by side, was inspiring.

"No matter what forces Riomini has, I think we still have the advantage," Percival said.

"The Ro-Xayans are with us, too," Adolphus said. "Unlike the Xayan converts, they still have powers of telemancy."

Commodore Hallholme rose to his feet and took the General's hand in a firm, tight grip.

"We'll set up the task force," General Adolphus said. "We have a lot of damage to undo at Sonjeera."

82

Well past midnight, feeling oddly alone and unsettled on Sonjeera, Diadem Riomini went to the dark and cavernous Council chamber, where he paced back and forth by the Star Throne. He looked at the great chair with its inset constellations of priceless jewels, touched it, sat on it, even kicked the damned thing—just because he could.

That should have given him satisfaction, but no one was here to witness his power. He'd heard no report from Commodore Hallholme long past the time when the old warhorse should have secured his victory against the rebel General. In a dangerous gamble, but for a victory worth winning, the veteran commander had taken a substantial portion of the Black Lord's private military force. It was inconceivable that he had failed again.

Many of the Crown Jewels had disliked Diadem Michella so intensely that their populations, were happy, even relieved, when Riomini showed a strong hand and took over the leadership. But that damned Adolphus had planted the idea of *independence* even here in the Crown Jewels, not just in the frontier worlds. Many nobles were suggesting a fundamental change of government structure, and he couldn't squelch the talk everywhere. He was going to need another powerful fleet just to maintain order here . . . and didn't have enough ships.

Worse, he had just received a grim report from Vielinger, an assessment of the valuable mines there. Although the iperion excavation facilities had been repaired and production restored, the available veins of the rare substance were shockingly low. The situation was far worse than previously thought. Even in a best-case projection, supplies of iperion would last only a few more years.

And without iperion the stringline routes would dissipate and fray, leaving the network connecting the twenty Crown Jewels to unravel, connected only by much slower space travel—which would render them impossible to govern centrally.

And the Deep Zone would be even farther away, effectively out of reach.

Adding to the debacle, the mine supervisor's confidential report had somehow leaked and spread throughout the ranks of nobles, increasing the unrest further. Like wolves, they could smell blood, sensing that the Constellation was falling apart, and no amount of effort—or military action from Riomini—would hold it together.

He stood in the silent, shadowy hall, pondering. The Star Throne had always looked like a glorious fixture in the chamber, but now he saw it as a mere prop. Though he'd wanted the role so badly, he felt trapped by everything that throne represented, held hostage as much as the General held Michella Duchenet hostage. He felt like taking a cudgel and smashing the chair apart, though that would be a useless gesture.

Unable to sleep in his lavish palace apartments—completely refurbished from when Michella had lived there—he'd crept into the Council chamber in his nightclothes and silk slippers, to think. Two black-uniformed guards had made a security sweep of the empty chamber, then allowed him inside. When they were satisfied that no assassins were lurking in the shadows of the posh seats, they stationed themselves at the outer doors, so he could be alone. Riomini envied them their comparatively simple life.

Every day, advisers brought him reports of dissension and fractures in the Crown Jewels. Just yesterday, emboldened nobles from Tanine and Patel had demanded the right to construct their own stringline hubs, calling the Sonjeera monopoly "a dangerous bottleneck." Not so long ago, Riomini had made the same demand of Diadem Michella, but she had rejected it. Now, he had done the same thing, but his spies reported evidence that the nobles might be building the hubs anyway, in secret. Where did they think they would get the iperion to make those new routes feasible?

He suspected many of the complainers were Adolphus loyalists. He imagined seeing rebel supporters everywhere, and had increased efforts to root them out. In just the past week, he'd put out arrest warrants on thousands of people, and the prisons were overcrowded. Before long he would have to announce mass executions, just to cull out the worst offenders and ease the overcrowding of those prisons.

The rest of his ships from the once-secret Qiorfu fleet were stretched thin putting out brushfire uprisings around the Crown Jewels. In the most recent uprisings against him, three leading noblemen—three!—had mounted military forces against the rightful Diadem. Simply keeping such people in line was costing Riomini too much time and treasure. Sonjeera was not as well-protected as he would have liked, nor were his personal planetary holdings of Aeroc, Vielinger, and Qiorfu. . . .

Deeply troubled, he let himself slump into the great, glittering throne, which was not at all comfortable. With the chamber lights low, he stared at the ornate ceiling with its frescoes and gilded highlights, showing the original twenty Crown Jewels, and—more recent additions—sphere-topped pylons with engraved names, marking each of the fifty-four Deep Zone planets annexed into the Constellation. Now, those markers only served to remind him of what he did *not* rule.

Exhausted, Riomini found himself curling up on the throne, placing a pillow on an armrest for his head. He had suffered insomnia for days, but maybe he could sleep here. . . .

He felt an urgent hand on his arm, shaking him, and the strident voice of Anson Tebias. "Eminence!" The slender man was not his normal groomed self; the dark hair was unkempt and the clothes wrinkled, as if he had just thrown them on. Beside him, guard commander Rota Vindahl stood with a sheen of sweat on her forehead and a strange look in her eyes.

Riomini didn't want to hear it. "Go away."

Vindahl stepped forward, implacable. "Sir, you must awaken! We are besieged."

Flashes of explosions blossomed in the darkness outside the Council Hall. Glare washed through the segmented panes of the ceremonial windows.

So, the discontented nobles had made a move on

Sonjeera after all! A surge of anger made his face hot. Whoever it was, he would sterilize their home planets, just as he'd done to Theser!

Tebias seemed sickened and disoriented. "Eminence, Commodore Hallholme has returned with the fleet."

"Good! Have him crush this uprising."

Tebias looked at Rota Vindahl, who did not hesitate to answer. "Sir, Commodore Hallholme is the one attacking us. And he is allied with General Tiber Adolphus. And . . . and there is more."

Riomini felt a sinking sensation. This was not possible! He had to be dreaming, needed to escape from the nightmare. Shocked, he pressed himself back into the uncomfortable throne. "Go away. You take care of it."

The main doors of the Council chamber burst open to reveal a throng in the doorway—soldiers in Constellation uniforms, citizens, nobles. He heard weapon fire outside, the roar of heavy ships landing in Heart Square. Just as it had been when he had taken over here after Michella Duchenet fled. . . .

Tebias sounded apologetic. "I'm sorry to say this, Eminence, but General Adolphus and Commodore Hallholme have demanded your immediate surrender."

Riomini felt a clamor in his head, muffled by the impossibility of it all. "Nonsense. Bring me my robe of state, and I will speak with them. And close those doors so I can have some privacy." He looked in embarrassment at his nightclothes. No . . . this simply couldn't be real.

At the towering doorway, Commodore Percival Hallholme came inside, his proud stride marred by his characteristic limp. The old warhorse wore his gold-and-black Constellation uniform—and behind him marched General Tiber Adolphus in a blue-and-gold rebel uniform. Soldiers wearing both uniforms, side by side, streamed into the chamber.

Adolphus had been shackled the last time he was dragged before the Star Throne. Now, he wore a ceremonial sword and a sidearm.

While Vindahl stood beside the throne, clearly ready to give her life to protect Riomini, Tebias rushed toward the intruders. He was quite agitated. "May I be allowed to retrieve one of Diadem Riomini's royal robes? For propriety?"

"He won't need anything like that," said General Adolphus. "He's not going to be ruling anymore, and we won't require an extravagant surrender ceremony. They're overrated, in my opinion."

Hallholme added, "It would be nothing more than a formality anyway. Lord Selik Riomini, you are hereby removed from the Star Throne, and the Constellation is freed from your tyrannical rule. You will stand trial for war crimes."

Riomini saw black static around his vision, and his head pounded so hard that he feared blood vessels were about to burst. He felt disoriented, as if his mind were shutting down from too many impossibilities. "I am the Diadem of the Constellation! War crimes do not apply."

"Specifically the annihilation of the free world of Theser," said Adolphus.

"And the murder of protected prisoners of war on Vielinger," Hallholme added in a tone of disgust. "As further evidence, we have copies of your orders instructing me to slaughter the populations of every Deep Zone planet."

In the crowd of uniformed soldiers, Riomini was surprised to recognize Redcom Escobar Hallholme, the incompetent commander who had lost his entire fleet in an ineffective attack against General Adolphus. Hallholme's son stood between his father and the General. "You gave me similar orders, Lord Riomini—to kill every innocent civilian on planet Hallholme."

When they came forward to seize him, Vindahl threw herself in the way, protecting him. Riomini was dismayed when the soldiers were forced to shoot her down. Well, at least someone was loyal and reliable. . . .

Constellation and rebel soldiers dragged Riomini off the throne and hauled him out of the chamber. He felt cold and helpless in his nightclothes, but these intruders showed him no consideration. The crowd closed in and swept him along as he was taken outside.

Riomini stared upward at a night sky filled with Constellation and Deep Zone warships hovering low over the city. Soldiers in DZDF uniforms monitored a large display screen that Michella Duchenet had often used when addressing the throngs of people who pretended to adore her. Now, though, they had rigged the screen to show images from orbit.

All the ships Riomini had given Commodore Hallholme from the Qiorfu fleet were there, closing in on the Sonjeera stringline hub, accompanied by many more battle vessels—the General's own Deep Zone Defense Force, as well as the ships once controlled by Redcom Escobar Hallholme.

And there were hundreds of silvery whirling ships of a configuration he had never seen before; they darted about in impossible maneuvers, flitting ominously around the handful of Riomini's overwhelmed ships. The whirling silver vessels looked . . . alien.

He couldn't understand or accept any of this. It was all too impossible to believe. He started laughing. This wasn't real!

"We have three fleets arrayed against you," said General Adolphus.

The whirlwind of distress and confusion closed in on him, and Riomini could not process the information. He saw fires burning on the other side of Heart Square, and heard steady weapon fire and the roar of crowds in the distance. More and more people streamed into the square. Soldiers were tearing down his black Riomini banners and Constellation flags from poles and buildings.

And then he saw two large, hideous aliens—with pale skin, humanoid heads and torsos, long sluglike bodies— moving toward him across the square. Laboriously, they began to climb the wide stairway of the Council Hall, on their stubby caterpillar legs. Riomini could not cringe away.

It was all so outrageous, so impossible, that he folded inward, squeezing his eyes shut and retreating to the only place he could hide. Inside of himself.

83

When General Adolphus arrived at Ankor with his extensive celebratory force, he found himself surrounded by thousands of cheering Deezees who waved blue-and-gold banners.

Adolphus would have preferred to speak to the crowd in a less formal manner, without a podium, but there were too many people for casual conversations. The platform and podium had been hastily erected for him and the Ro-Xayan leader Zhaday.

In the front, Sophie gave him a broad smile and

silent encouragement. He was reminded of the day he gave the speech announcing the new DZ stringline network, declaring the independence of all frontier worlds. This time, he hoped his speech would create stability rather than turmoil.

When Adolphus prepared to address them, he gazed out at the crowd, but thankfully saw no shimmering eyes or strange behavior in the converts. Their telemancy had been drained away, the powers burned out by the incredible effort of moving the planet. He noticed Keana standing in the front stands next to Cristoph de Carre.

The Ro-Xayan asteroids were in safe, stable orbits around the planet. At night, Hellhole had twenty small, bright new moons.

After waiting for quiet, he pointed upward. "The sky is blue today, but we know how quickly that can change on Hellhole—how quickly that can change in life. We secured a great victory, and in the process we not only survived, but we grew much stronger. For that, it took the combined energy, the combined will, and the military assets of two cultures. We've got a lot of work to do, so we must remain vigilant."

He had to wait for the celebratory noise to die down. "In the Crown Jewel worlds, Major Bolton Crais and Commodore Percival Hallholme—men of virtue—will strive to create a just government that addresses the corruption of the past. We cannot allow bloodthirsty tyrants like the past Diadems."

On the stage next to him, Zhaday lifted his torso and amplified his thrumming words with telemancy. "We remaining Xayans must also be vigilant to ensure that the threat of *ala'ru* does not reemerge. Our numbers must remain controlled, our telemancy limited."

Keana called out from the crowd, "But the Xayans inside our memories will always be there. We will never forget the lives that joined ours." Many of the former converts added their voices to hers, though most only experienced occasional whispers in their memories.

Zhaday made one more announcement in his unusual voice. "The Ro-Xayans are no longer a separate faction. We are all *Xayans*. We are the hope of our future."

Jonwi and several others of his faction merged into the crowd at Ankor, ready to listen to the General's words. Jonwi moved forward and invited all the Ro-Xayans and humans to work with him to tame and replant the damaged world. He promised that the planet could once again become the lush, verdant paradise it had once been—a dream for all to share.

Adolphus continued. "As for the Deep Zone, our planets are independent, free of a repressive government, no longer a source for plunder by a wealthy few. We will be part of a larger cooperative network of commerce for as long as the stringlines continue to function."

His statement sidestepped the very real concerns that their iperion supplies were extremely limited, after the destruction of Candela. The only other known source was on Vielinger, and those mines were nearly barren. Prospectors had continued searching more than fifty uncharted DZ planets for another source, but so far they remained unsuccessful.

Adolphus continued. "I have said that I would rather rule on Hellhole than serve on Sonjeera—so I will not accept any Diadem's crown, nor will I rule the Deep Zone. I will focus my energies on but one planet, Hellhole." He laughed as he mused, "I was exiled here once, but somehow I've grown rather fond of the place."

This evoked a new round of cheering from the crowd. He had already suggested that Enva Tazaar might be interested in participating in the new Constellation government, but oddly she seemed to like the challenge of Theser. He decided he was impressed with her.

The sky at the horizon carried a greenish tinge, which often signified a brewing growler storm, but he knew they could ride it out, no matter how bad it was. Hellhole had toughened him. Even with all the future work of Jonwi and the reseeding efforts of the Ro-Xayans, he doubted if this frontier world would ever be completely tamed. When the first asteroid struck five centuries ago, it had set something loose here that was wild and primeval. And that was what he had grown to like; Tiber Adolphus did not shy away from adversity.

As he went down the steps, Sophie greeted him with a hug. "You led a revolution and tamed a world, Tiber," she said with a gentle smile. "Now, perhaps there'll be more time for us?"

―∾∾―

Adolphus and Sophie were together in the reconstructed Ankor headquarters when Cristoph de Carre approached, grinning. Although he looked a bit weary, he was exuberant. "Fantastic news, General! A message drone just came in from Theser. Enva Tazaar's scouts made a remarkable discovery."

Adolphus felt his pulse quicken, but dared not hope. It could be something else, not iperion.

"One of her prospectors found a large deposit of iperion in the wastelands of Theser, far outside the craters and on the other side of the continent—but it's a confirmed strike." His eyes shone. "It looks like my mining expertise may be needed out in the Deep Zone after all."

Adolphus was delighted. "That changes the future of the Deep Zone. Now we can maintain all the string-lines."

Cristoph delivered the geological report that had been inside the message drone. "We'll need a full assessment of course, but from my initial reading, this looks like a major deposit, maybe as big as the one Tanja Hu found on Candela. In fact, General, given my background from Vielinger, I would like to request—"

"Done, Mr. de Carre. I want you on the next string-line hauler out to Theser. But what about your family holdings on Vielinger? With the changes in the Constellation, they are legally yours again."

"Lanny Oberon is perfectly capable of managing the old mines in my absence. But those deposits are nearly played out, and I want to go where the action is."

Sophie added, "If Enva Tazaar is sitting on that large a deposit, she may indeed become the wealthiest, most powerful planetary administrator in the Deep Zone."

"That could well be," Adolphus said.

—⁂—

When he and Sophie returned to Elba, they shared a candlelight dinner, succulent beefsteaks from a local ranch and a bottle of one of her better red wines. It was a fine, calm evening—for a change—only made better when another message arrived that evidence of a second iperion vein had been discovered, this time in the wilderness of Cles. And there were still more than fifty prospectors hunting across the frontier planets.

Sophie touched her wineglass to his. The deep claret looked like a precious gem. "The future looks bright."

"Indeed it does." He took a long sip. It was not a

great wine—none of the Hellhole vintages were—but he had grown used to the taste.

She said, "You know, we may even have to change the name of this planet."

He considered, but shook his head. "I think I prefer it just the way it is."